dusk

---

ashanti luke

kaiju publishing
www.ashantiluke.com

Printed in the United States of America

For information contact :
Ashanti Luke
Kaiju Publishing
P.O. Box 1434
Colonial Heights, VA 23834
http://www.AshantiLuke.com

ISBN: 978-0-578-49032-8

Author photo by E.W. Cline
Cover design by Ashanti Luke
Second Edition: April 2019

10 9 8 7 6 5 4 3 2

To my mother and father
for never letting the sun set.

prologue

They should have shot him where he stood. If he died here, there would still be hope, and hope was what had brought him from very different beginnings to this point. But if he surrendered, every gram of that hope would be lost.

Dr. Cyrus Chamberlain held the pistol in his right hand over his head with his fingers clearly off the trigger. Four elite soldiers settled in a modified phalanx and trained their assault rifles on him.

He should have been disabled by erratic breathing, high blood pressure, and slowed reactions. But he was calm, his breathing in perfect sync with his heart rate. It was remarkable how losing a son could move the mind to places you could never have imagined when life went as planned.

"Drop your weapon and kick it over, or we *will* finish you!" The noise of the battle behind Cyrus muffled the voice of the soldier at the head of the phalanx, but his words could not have been clearer. Cyrus should have been dead or dying by now, and the soldier who was repeating his threat was standing too far from the men in his formation.

Cyrus pressed the magazine release on his automatic pistol but held the gun so the magazine stayed inside the handle. He slowly lowered his right hand and then let the pistol fall to the ground. As it fell, he shifted his weight slightly forward, expecting to get launched backward by a hail of automatic weapon fire. But the men before him were convinced they had the situation under control even as he lifted his right foot to kick the falling pistol toward them.

Cyrus should not have been this fast, this strong, or this agile, and that had been what had kept him from dying the moment he reached the door because these elite soldiers were reacting to him as if he were a regular human being—even though from his reputation they should have known better.

A sharp pain numbed his foot and sent a shock coursing up his shin as his foot launched the gun toward the soldier in front. The magazine and pistol separated in the air, and the soldier fired, but Cyrus was already launching himself forward with his left foot. He prayed his training was enough as he vaulted forward, covering much more distance in a much shorter time than the soldier expected. The gun and magazine sailed on opposite sides of the man's face and missed, but the soldier's dodge gave Cyrus enough time to cover the distance he needed. Cyrus felt the air next to his left ear crackle as a bullet passed through it and the other rounds of the volley missed him. The other soldiers had fired, but their bullets found their marks where Cyrus had stood. By the time they fired, he was under the lead soldier's firing arm, twisting the rifle and tensing the shoulder strap around the soldier's neck. An elbow hit the right side of Cyrus's neck, but Cyrus used the momentum from the strike to shift his own weight and flip the rifle from the soldier's hand. He lifted the soldier's body from the ground slightly as the loop of the strap tightened even more around the soldier's neck. Cyrus did not have a good grip on the rifle, but he fired anyway. He could not aim, but he only needed to fill the space the other three men occupied with rounds. The gun jumped, vibrating the grip against the palm of his left hand as the stock slammed against his chest with each report. The stock aggravated the bruise that was already forming on his neck. One of the men flipped backward, and one went straight down. The third collapsed on one knee but managed to steady himself with his off-hand and keep his rifle up.

Cyrus yanked the rifle strap to flip the soldier over his shoulder, and the man's neck must have snapped, because his body twitched and fell awkwardly, snatching the rifle from Cyrus's hands.

As the last soldier lifted his gun, Cyrus launched himself forward again, pulling his feet in front of him as he made another extraordinary leap.

An explosion rocked the hangar floor as Cyrus landed on his butt and slid. He could not tell if the man had fired or not, which seemed strange because he *could* hear the snap of the tendons in the man's knee as he kicked the man. The soldier collapsed next to Cyrus screaming, clutching his awkwardly twisted leg.

Another soldier moved out from behind a loading lev with a set of nondescript canisters in the loading clamps. The assault on the hangar caught everything in its normal operational state. Technicians and non-military staff scurried about hysterically and took refuge. The pilot of the lev had left it running and floating above the hangar floor, and soldiers were forming up now on the other side. Cyrus saw three sets of feet visible beneath it as he brought his elbow down across the throat of the soldier he had slide-tackled. He smashed his elbow down again and felt something in the man's throat collapse with a sickening gurgle.

As he saw the barrel of the assault rifle peek from behind the canisters, Cyrus realized he had pulled too far ahead of his own van, but the only chance any of them stood was him taking advantage of the chaos his own friends were causing behind him.

Chaos.

That was not the right word. Chaos was what was going to happen in seven minutes if he did not make it to the ominous grey ship that was more than two hundred meters away–chaos and the bloody destruction of everything Cyrus had fought for up to this point.

Cyrus deftly unhooked a grenade from the belt of the man sputtering and clutching his damaged throat beneath him. Cyrus lifted his shoulder, pressed the activation button on the side of the grenade, then rolled to his left. He counted three beats, rolled again, and released the grenade on the fourth beat. The grenade left his hand, hit the ground between him and the loading lev, and spun awkwardly as it slid beneath the floating vehicle. The soldiers on the other side recoiled, but the explosion sent the lev flipping, toppling the canisters in various directions as the vehicle spun and landed on its side.

Cyrus gambled on the soldiers being shaken by the explosion and was already up and running again. The lev smashed against the ground with canisters boggling around it.

Over his shoulder, he heard more gunfire and glanced to see Dr. Marcus Tanner and Commander Azariah Uzziah run from behind the massive ship that was behind him. They provided cover fire as Cyrus continued to sprint.

A soldier grabbed Cyrus from behind and locked his arms around him. Cyrus felt himself being lifted and pulled away from the destination that lay only meters in front of him. His breathing, erratic from the last attack, now failed him. For a moment he felt his eyes glaze, his head lighten, and in the haze, he saw his son. Not as the man he would be now, but as a boy. The promising eight-year-old he had left too many years ago.

He bit down against the pain, ignored the complaints of his oxygen-deprived brain, and gripped his captor's thumb with his left hand. Cyrus pulled, and as the man resisted, he twisted his own body and dug the back of his arm into his captor's throat. The man tried to shift Cyrus's weight, but Cyrus had gained enough leverage to thrust his left hand over his own shoulder. His thumb, held rigid in a martial claw, struck cheekbone then slid into the man's eye socket, and then Cyrus's feet were on the ground again.

Cyrus kicked the man backward, and a nearby explosion tumbled the man to the ground. Three more men rounded the edge of the ship. The one on point fired as he cleared the edge, but Cyrus was already diving at a rifle on the ground. Bullets tore into the ground where he had leaped from, and he heard someone on his side fire a cover volley at the three men. The first fell as Cyrus scooped up the rifle, rolled, and fired back at the two now taking cover behind the nose of the ship.

Before he had left Earth, life had been so different. It wasn't so long ago that he been just a pudgy scientist, trying to rebuild his body and condition his mind to survive long enough to stake a claim on a barren wasteland.

Cyrus angled toward the entrance to the ship, pulling the electronic key Dr. Taewook Jang programmed to defeat the security system. All that mattered was getting onto the ship. The men who had come with him covered the front of the ship with suppression fire. The hull would hold under the assault of the small munitions, but if one lucky shot from any of those soldiers found his flesh, their entire plan could be for naught.

Cyrus fired a volley of his own with his left hand as the key, now magnetically attached to the door, decrypted the security code. Someone squeezed off a burst at Cyrus, and bullets sparked as they hit the ship just in front of him. Then, something caught him low on his left shoulder. He reeled back and to his right, but he continued with the momentum and pressed himself against the rounded edge of the ship. He steadied the rifle with the side of the ship and fired again, one-handed. The rifle jumped violently, but it was enough to make his attackers use their cover. Cyrus's right arm began to throb with pain. Something might have been broken, but the shear Comptex suit had stopped the shell from penetrating his flesh. It was not the first time he had been shot. It was not the first time Comptex had protected him, but Cyrus prayed once he got this ship out of this god-forsaken hangar, it would be the last time for both.

Then, there was a gush of air as the seal broke on the giant cargo door, and Cyrus ducked inside with Commander Uzziah behind him, still firing as he cleared the threshold.

"Five minutes and this whole place turns into a chimp rodeo!" Uzziah yelled, already moving toward the bridge.

That meant they had a little more than two minutes to get the ship started, with only a rushed training and a little bit of luck to help them.

But that was what had to be done. The sun was setting them all, and that ship was the only way he, or anyone else he had grown to love in this forsaken place, would ever see the sun again.

part one

Soft on the sunset sky
Bright daylight closes,
Leaving, when light doth die,
Pale hues that mingling lie,
Ashes of roses.

ELAINE GOODALE EASTMAN

one

—*Tell me a story before I go to bed, Dada.*

—*What story do you want to hear?*

—*The story about Aryal and the Unicorn.*

—*You always want to hear that story. This will be the 50th time.*

—*No, just the 47th time.*

—*You counted? I can't believe you want to hear it again.*

—*Come on Dada. I like hearing you tell the story.*

—*Okay, Okay, for the 47th time. Here goes...a long, long time ago, before the world was as complicated as it is now, in a time when people appreciated their lives and the world around them, there was a growing village bordered by a raging river on one side and a dense forest on all the others.*

—*How dense was the forest, Dada?*

—*It was so dense that, even during the day, the forest was as dark as the darkest midnight, and whenever anyone ventured too far outside the village, they became hopelessly lost. They not so creatively named this no-man's land 'Where Angels Fear to Tread.' Well just on the edge of 'Where Angels Fear to Tread' there lived a beautiful black unicorn with a golden horn. For as long as anyone in the village could remember, the unicorn had always lived there, and whenever anyone became lost in the wilderness, the unicorn would always show up and lead them back to the village. There was a myth in the village—or it was a long passed rumor anyway—that if anyone could speak the name of the unicorn, he would stay with them forever and lead them to a magnificent treasure. Many people ventured into the forest just to see the unicorn and all marveled over his beauty and his power. Everyone except Cellius Wormheart.*

—*Tell me about Cellius. I like the way you talk about Cellius.*

—*Cellius Wormheart was a blacksmith who owned the largest and toughest safe in the village. Everyone loved him because he kept their gold safe even though he wasn't a very nice person.*

—*Why wasn't Cellius very nice?*

—*Well, no one was sure, but some of the elders said it was because his parents spent so much time building the village that they didn't pay very much attention* to him, so he took his anger out on the village. But I think he was bitter because no matter how much he built, or how much money he made, it didn't make him happy.

—Maybe it was a little of both things, huh, Dada?

—You may have a point there. Either way, Cellius was determined to find the unicorn's treasure, so he built an elaborate trap and captured the unicorn. He then prepared a large pen and kept the unicorn in the center of the village where he charged people to look at him. He made a good deal of money, but it wasn't enough, so he began to starve the unicorn and treat him poorly to try get him to reveal the location of the treasure. Meanwhile, the people of the village would accost the unicorn every day, screaming any name they could imagine at him in hopes one of them would be his real name.

—What happened to the unicorn, Dada? What happened?

—The bitterness and spite around him, coming from people he had shown nothing but kindness, changed him. Slowly, he became more beastlike, more hideous, until he was completely unrecognizable as the unicorn. He began to snarl and snap at people, and he tugged at his reigns each day until his legs bled and he collapsed into a bellowing, exhausted heap. People began to question what they should do with the beast that had once been the unicorn. No one paid to see him anymore, and Cellius had grown weary of him and wanted to kill him.

—He wanted to put him to sleep?

—No, Darius, kill him. People who can't own up to their own actions 'put animals to sleep.' Cellius was many terrible things, but he was no coward. He could not get what he wanted, so he wanted the beast dead. The village folk would not have it though, until one day, a young boy paid to see the beast and threw a tomato at him, and while he had turned to his friends to taunt and jeer, the beast bit down on the boy's arm and dragged him through the bars where he devoured him.

—Ouch.

—Ouch indeed. Well, the town was outraged, so they barred anyone from entering the tent where the Beast was kept, and the Commissary of the town ordered the beast summarily destroyed.

—Summarily means in public right in front of everybody, right?

—Well, it means without delay, but is usually for all to see. The people were so angry they made preparations to make a fancy ceremony of the whole event. Someone even painted 'Where Even Fools Fear to Tread' on the outside of the tent, thinking it was a clever thing to write.

—But it was their fault, Dada. Why couldn't they see that? Why didn't they just leave the poor unicorn alone?

—*I don't know, Dari. I've been trying to figure that one for years. It must take a wiser man than me. So, one day, this little girl wanders near the cage.*
—*Aryal.*
—*Yes, Aryal. Aryal wasn't the most beautiful girl in the village, and she didn't score in the highest percentiles in her school, but she had a kind heart, and she always looked at things for what they were not what she wanted them to be.*
—*Why did she think that way when the others didn't?*
—*Maybe it was because she wasn't beautiful. Because she wasn't smart. Maybe she needed to see things differently just to survive—to know she was more than people saw her as. Well, Aryal wandered to the cage for the first time ever because she was poor, and before the execution, her parents could not afford to take her to see the unicorn. Not that they would have anyway, for they were angry and spiteful people, and they resented having such an unspectacular daughter they couldn't brag about to their friends. So she went to see the beast before the execution, and instead of a snarling, angry beast, she saw a sad, wounded creature that was wounded to his very soul by treachery and ingratitude.*
—*Maybe she saw a little bit of herself in the unicorn beast.*
—*Quite possibly. Either way, the next day, the day of the execution, Cellius found the cage unlocked and empty. Both Aryal and the unicorn had disappeared, never to be heard from again.*
—*What happened? Where did they go?*
—*Most think Aryal spoke the creature's name, and he took her away to the treasure, and they lived there until the end of time.*
—*And how did she guess the unicorn's name?*
—*She didn't guess. She just did what no one else could be bothered to do.*
—*She just asked.*
—*Exactly.*
—*So Dada, what do you think the treasure was?*
—*You tell me, Dari.*
—*I don't know. Before I guessed gold, money, or candy, but I'm pretty sure now it wasn't any of that stuff. I'm beginning to think there was no treasure. Maybe it was anyone who actually could do what they needed to find it actually had it already.*
—*You know, I never thought of it like that. Maybe you're a wiser man than me.*
—*No, Dada, not me. You know everything.*
—*Not everything, Dari. The wisest man knows what he knows and what he doesn't, and he is comfortable with those things he can't know. Sometimes, it seems like I don't know what I should, and I think I know what I can't. Hopefully, when you're my age, what you do know will be clear, and what you can't know will be even clearer, so that what you don't know can exist in an attainable spot somewhere in between.*

—*I'm not sure what that means, Dada.*
—*Me neither, but I think, by the time you're my age, you will understand much better than I do.*

• • • • •

To Dr. Cyrus Chamberlain, everything seemed smaller. He couldn't tell if the launch station being so close to home was good or bad—if he had had to travel to Houston or Florida, at least the entire process would have mirrored the weight he now felt on his shoulders. The other scientists milled around the inside of the large craft that levitated above the track leading to the launch pad. The tension inside the massive cargo barge, which had been converted into a mobile ballroom, was almost tangible. The faces of everyone there, whether somber or excited, were full of emotion. The hazy morning light that filtered in through clear plastic windows surrounding them gave everyone's face a morbid, orange glow. The pain of not seeing loved ones and friends for another ten years, if ever, was visible–as clear as the craft set on the horizon to take those loved ones away. There were twenty scientists in all, each surrounded by several family members and colleagues that had come to see them off. They moved slowly over the metal-laced track toward the looming Unified Nations Rosamond Land Dock in the distance, and the closer they got, the more the ballroom felt like a mortuary. Some cried, mourning those that still walked among them, at least for the next hour or so. Cyrus stood with his wife Feralynn, his son Darius, and his best friend, Dr. Alexander Kalem and watched the dust of Antelope Valley float in lazy swirls as he felt the sting of his choice—he was leaving this overpopulated rock forever.

Cyrus, premier astrophysicists in the Unified Nations, was notified the moment they had discovered Asha. Ten years later, he was formally asked to join the team of scientist-pioneers who would make up the first expedition to this planet they hoped would become the sister-world to Earth. Only a few months later, the Unified Nations Census revealed the Earth now held more than ten billion people—and that was discounting the Fringe States that had held out in the Unification. And now, Cyrus was about to leave his life behind for a new one, and it floored him.

To Cyrus, Kalem had always looked older than he actually was. And it seemed he had purposefully promoted that image. The grey flecks in his hair made his skin look lighter. The pale light that streamed in through the large windowed side of the conveyance vehicle gave his light skin an odd glow, and it accented the lines of his face that made him look serious even when he smiled.

Cyrus imagined Dr. Kalem would have made an excellent poker player if he had believed in gambling. But the man, who had been his closest friend since his matriculation to the physical sciences tract of the Arcology, was too interested in a concrete sense of security to gamble on anything except his own mental ability, which he had in droves.

The lines in Kalem's face seemed an odd contrast to Feralynn's. It was hard to read her expression, but Cyrus had grown accustomed to seeing the lines that formed around her jawline whenever she was quietly upset with something he had said, or audibly upset by something he had done or something he had not done that he should have. But today the lines were gone. She seemed torn, but she was not combative. She was not usually quiet about her emotions, whether she understood clearly what she was feeling or not, but today, her mixed feelings were solemn and unmanifest. Standing there in the pale orange light of the smog-tinted sun, Cyrus could see the fire in her eyes that he had recognized the moment he met her—the fire he had not seen in the eight years since his son had been born.

Cyrus looked up at the browning film that limited visibility even out this far from the growing sprawl of Los Angeles. Most of the desert had been consumed by urban renewal and the need to accommodate more and more people. "People just don't die like they used to," David Chamberlain, his father, had once said. It wasn't until now, looking at the dinge-filled sky, Cyrus really understood what he meant. The Silverlake Terraforming Processor had been cleaning the noxious city air now for more than half a century. Ironically, this technology, made obsolete by the discovery of a planet that could sustain humanity without terraforming, now served to make Earth itself more inhabitable—all the while, forcing the filth out here to the desert.

People weren't even born right anymore. Podcenters robbed the mothers who could afford it of the last trimester of motherhood to eliminate birth defects and disease. Human beings were surviving better than ever, and that survival was killing them. No one had officially stated that this mission was to 'save humanity,' but the shoulder pads in their month-long briefing definitely acted as though this mission had more riding on it than just human curiosity. Something was about to break, and he and the nineteen other eggheads on this barge were being lined up to put their fingers in the dam. No one said it. The words probably didn't exist to call out the problem by name, but Cyrus could feel it. The thought alone was so ominous it seemed like a promise. He could tell his son felt it too.

Cyrus ran his fingers through the curly strands of hair that always seemed to collect on the front of the boy's head. The curls made his head look too big for his body, which was smaller than it should have been. Cyrus took his wife's hand in his other. Her hand was warmer than he expected given the chill he felt in his own. Her long black hair concealed her face, but he caught a glimpse of her eye as she turned her head toward him, and he saw a glimmer there. She squeezed his hand and held her grip, then turned slowly to meet his eyes. The glimmer had been a tear forming on her tear duct, yet refusing to run down her face. Her porcelain skin was a strong contrast to his own, but he had always liked that. She didn't bother to wipe at her eyes, but the tear moved down her cheek slightly as she turned. She opened her mouth to speak, but then turned back to the window, squeezing his hand even tighter.

Darius had been looking through the window of the conveyance lev. "Dada," he asked, continuing to look toward their destination—it was endearing that his son, as eloquent as he could be for an eight-year-old, had never grown out of that particular moniker.

"Yes, Dari?" Cyrus continued to look out of the window as well as the Land Dock grew in the distance. The Mercury Six was moored to the massive platform. It would take them to the Eros Slingshot where they would rendezvous with the larger Paracelsus that would take them to Asha.

A tumbleweed rolled away from the lev as it sped down the track. "Miss Hasabe says a long, long time ago they used to land the first space ships here."

"That's right, Dari. Five hundred years ago, they would land a space ship they called the space shuttle here. It was a military base then too, but not for the Uni."

Darius looked up at his father, his eyes wide. He began to say something, stopped, looked outside at the sky for a moment, then finally turned back again. "Will they have the Damocles next to the Paracelsus at the Eros station, Dada?"

"They haven't built the Damocles yet," Cyrus said as Darius turned to face him. Something moved over the boy's face, and it was as if those words alone carried the pain of how long it would be before he would see his father again. He didn't cry, but the look of horror on his face was worse than tears. Cyrus wanted to comfort him, but he could only manage a weak, "I'm sorry, Darius."

Dr. Kalem saw Cyrus and Darius and moved closer to them. Cyrus shook his hand and pulled him in, hugging him brusquely. "Take care of my family, old friend." The lines on Kalem's face deepened, and his lips parted as if to say something, but he only smiled and gripped Cyrus's shoulders tightly. When Kalem released him, Feralynn stepped between them, agape with tears. Cyrus pulled her close as she sobbed and suddenly felt the heaviness between them lifted. At that moment, it was just the two of them, as they had been during their years at the Arcology. Someone more inclined to melodrama would have described the feeling as warmth, but even in that moment where the entire universe was a small space that included only them, Cyrus knew that warmth was no longer a part of their equation. The raw emotion between them had no name, and it was too humble to be overwhelming, but it filled the expanse that had grown between them for the last eight years. And for a moment that seemed longer than the trip Cyrus would soon embark on, he coveted the feeling of every sensation of every gram of flesh where their bodies touched.

As they embraced, the conveyance lev reached the Land Dock. Feralynn pulled away from Cyrus, punched him rather abruptly on his shoulder, then turned away, lowering her head. Cyrus backed away slowly. He understood more of her mixed emotions than maybe she did herself—enough to know nothing he could say in the time they had left would change them. But he paused anyway, almost apologized, then saved his words, turning to hug Darius one more time. Cyrus almost convulsed as he felt the warm moisture between their cheeks. Then, he set his son down, turned as quickly as he could, and walked down the jetway with some other scientists. It felt as if he were walking through a swamp as he trudged toward the airlock. He wanted to turn to get one more glance at his family, but he pressed himself to keep moving toward the ship.

Suddenly, there was a commotion behind him. He heard a shout and a shuffling, and Cyrus turned to see a soldier trying to restrain Darius. Darius flailed his elbows to squirm out of the soldier's grasp. The soldier moved his hand to get a better grip, and Darius twisted and spun, leaving the soldier holding nothing but the collar of his jacket. The soldier cursed under his breath, but Kalem placed his hand on him, spoke some words, and the soldier relaxed and did not give chase. Darius barreled up the jetway, and if he had been six or seven kilos heavier, would have tackled Cyrus. As Darius looked up, he was gasping for air and his cheek was wet, but he did not appear to be crying. Cyrus could not tell if the boy was gasping from crying earlier,

19

from his struggle with the soldier, or from trying to get his words out too fast.

"Dada! Dada! Remember the other day when I said I felt selfish?"

"Yes, Dari."

"I don't feel so selfish anymore. I feel like it's gonna be impossible without you, but I don't feel so sad anymore."

"I'm glad, Dari, but what changed?"

"I figured out what the treasure in the Aryal story was!" He paused to wipe something from his nose, sighed a little, and then continued, "The treasure isn't a thing, at least not a grabby kinda thing. It's a feeling–a feeling that someone loves you enough to give up a part of themselves because you need it." His words came in between sniffles, but he managed to hold back his tears.

"That's pretty deep, Dari, but I'm not sure I see what I'm giving up."

"That's because you aren't. I think you need something, Dada. I'm too young to know what it is, but I'm Big Man enough to let you go look for it, at least for a little while. But you better find it before mommy and me get to Asha because you leaving is *almost* too much once. I know I couldn't do it two times."

Then, he couldn't hold back the tears anymore. His body began to shake with sobs, and he turned, buried his face in his hands, and stumbled back toward the soldier that still held his jacket. Feralynn moved to the soldier and sidled past him, pulling her son to her side with one arm. She looked up, tears in her own eyes, and Kalem put his arm around her and Darius. Kalem nodded to Cyrus before uttering some quiet consolation to his wife and son. With her free hand, Feralynn blew Cyrus a kiss, her tears adding a melodramatic twinkle to her eyes. She had never looked as beautiful as she did at that moment. It was as if the pall that had hung over her for the last eight years was lifting, slowly, but lifting nonetheless. And that was how Cyrus knew he would never see her again. Darius would make it to the Damocles, but she never would.

two

—Dada, why are you leaving me and mama?

—I'm not leaving you. You will be meeting me on Asha with your mother once the Damocles is built.

—That's gonna take five years for them to build it though.

—But it will land a year after the Paracelsus because it will be a bigger and faster ship with a much more efficient drive.

—But I'll be a grown-up man like you before I see you again.

—I know Darius, but this trip may help us understand things we couldn't understand before. Things we would never be able to see and study here on Earth.

—What's Asha like Dada? At school, they say it's like a really big desert.

—Well, there's a huge ocean that runs under the surface. But the surface is barren and dry as far as we can tell.

—Why is it like that?

—Because it spins on its side like Uranus. We think a large comet hit it when it was a young planet. The impact created a giant crater we call the Bereshit Scar and knocked Asha on its side. Because the comet was made mostly of ice, the ice melted and filled the gaps under the surface. The comet created the conditions that will allow humans to live on the planet. But because the planet turns on its side like that, a day on Asha is half a year, and it's night for half a year. A year on Asha is twenty-five Earth years, so it's good the ocean is underground because the water would evaporate, and Asha would be covered in clouds like Venus.

—But I don't get it. Why is Asha so important?

—Because it's like a young Earth. Studying the planet up close might help us learn how life on Earth started. Plus, pretty soon there will be too many people on Earth, we will need a place to go, and that place will need to be prepared.

—Can't you wait until I'm older to leave?

—I wish I could, but we have to leave now because it takes so long to get there. At the speed the Paracelsus goes, it will take one hundred ninety-six years to get there. A machine called the Hyposoma Apparatus will keep my body from aging until the ship begins to slow down. It takes the ship five years to slow down *because it is going so fast, so we use the five years to make our bodies healthy again because the Hyposoma makes our bodies and brains weak.*

—*The Paracelsus will travel at ninety-Five point oh five percent of the speed of light, two hundred, eighty-five thousand, one hundred fifty kilometers per second, right Dada? Miss Hasabe taught us about it.*

—*That's right. But because the ship goes so fast, it takes one hundred ninety-six years on the ship, but it will be six hundred thirty-one years for everyone else because traveling close to the speed of light bends time.*

—*So while you're in bent time, me and mama and everyone else will be in straight time, and we'll get older. Then, me and mama will go on the Damocles, and we will go into even more bent time, and everyone else will get old and die, but we'll be okay because of the Hyposoma At-her-at-us.*

—*App-er-atus. And yes, your Uncle Xander already made the arrangements for you and your mother to go on the Damocles when they are done building it. If it didn't have to slow down, it would catch up to us before we got to Asha.*

—*That's because the Damocles travels at ninety-eight point one three percent of the speed of light, two hundred ninety-four thousand, three hundred ninety kilometers per second.*

—*Since when do you pay so much attention in class?*

—*Well, it's not all the time the teacher talks about my Dada in class. Are you sure I'm going on the Damocles? No one at school believes me, and Terry Gallager says only important people get to go.*

—*You're important to me, so the next time Terry Gallager runs his mouth about something he knows nothing about, tell him to stuff it in his undersuit.*

—*Okay, Dada. Is it gonna be fun on Asha?*

—*There will be a lot of work for me to do. But the settlement should be prepared by the time you and your mother get there. So there will be some fun.*

—*I don't want you to go, Dada. I think I'll miss you too much.*

—*I will miss you too. Terribly. But this is work I have to do. It's a chance to do something that could change everything we know and everything we thought we knew. You will be fine, Dari. Before long, you won't even notice I'm gone.*

—*I don't think so, Dada. The launch is forty-seven and a half days away, but I feel like I'm never gonna see you again, and it hurts so much already. It feels like it's never gonna stop hurting.*

—*Well, one way or the other, it will stop eventually.*

—*You're real smart, Dada, and you always seem to know all the right answers, but I don't think you got it right this time.*

—*For both our sakes, I hope you're wrong.*

—*Me too, Dada. Me too.*

• • • • •

A gasp of stale air escaped as Cyrus Chamberlain exhaled the first breath of the day cycle. He rolled sluggishly out of the sleep chamber and onto the warm, slightly curved floor of the claustrophobic sleeping quarters. *At least the floor isn't cold*, Cyrus thought to himself as he slowly inched one barefoot in front of the other. The earthy green walls of the room were as calming as the designer had intended, but the last two mornings had been met with frustration. The first day had been easier because emerging from the Hyposoma, Cyrus could barely remember his own name, let alone move. The second day, he had awakened in this sleep chamber that looked like a medical monitoring station for intensive care patients.

But that was what they were. They would be packed inside these tubes that looked like detached fighter cockpits for another four day cycles. The sleep chambers ensured the microscopic robots that helped to stimulate their bodies back to health were working properly. The sleep units also served to alert the automated Shipmate android if there was a complication. Most of them still lay closed, their occupants opting for rest over attempts at roaming the ship, but Cyrus could not stay in his sleep chamber any longer this day cycle.

Cyrus was not proud of his own progress in becoming more alert and mobile, but he could tell, at least, he was making progress. It was less difficult to walk now than it had been yesterday, and it was definitely easier than the day before, but he still had trouble walking more than three meters without steadying himself on something. *No wonder the sleep chambers are so close together*, he thought as he braced himself on another open chamber. A violent series of twitches in his bracing arm almost sent him stumbling to the floor, but he caught himself with his elbow as the twitching slowed into an erratic flutter. Cyrus broke a sweat pulling himself back to his feet. As he steadied himself again, the flutters began to slide down his thighs and to his ankles. He was only able to take another three steps before a cramp almost sent him face-first into an occupied sleep chamber. "Damnation," Cyrus muttered to himself as he slowly made his way to the lav.

After relieving himself for what seemed too long, Cyrus stared into the mirror giving his eyes time to adjust. He was sure his pupils dilated faster before he had entered the Hyposoma Apparatus 192 years ago. The lines of his face were much more evident now. Apparently, the Hyposoma caused hair to grow much more slowly, so he only had stubble on his face even after spending most of the last two day cycles in the sleep chamber. They had all had the option of having military cuts before entering the Hyposoma, and most of the scientists had gotten them. What little of Cyrus's hair had grown back seemed less curly than before his haircut. Even though the lines alongside his nose were more pronounced now, and the ones around his mouth seemed more pronounced as well, the new thinness in his face made him look wiser and oddly younger at the same time. *Not bad for 225 years old*, he thought, straining weakened muscles to smile.

"You'll catch a cramp if you keep that up," a familiar voice said from the entrance to the lav. It took longer than it should have to register the voice with the face, and the name still eluded him. Cyrus hadn't spoken to anyone other than Dr. Fordham in the last 192 relative years—almost six hundred *real* years shrunk by a constant rate of speed approximately 95% of the speed of light. Although he had been released from the infirmary in what Dr. Fordham assured him was excellent health, his brain was still slow to react. He struggled to chuckle, but he could only muster the strength for a staccato wheeze.

"I'm serious. My first time out of the Apparatus, I laughed at a joke, and my whole face was sore for two days." Cyrus still could not remember his colleague's name as he spoke.

"When does the twitching stop?"

Finally, he remembered. The man speaking to him was Dr. Marcus Tanner, archaeologist, anthropologist, certified personal trainer, and all-around geek. He had been selected for this mission because he had been one of the first to test the Hyposoma on a space-faring ship, and he had extensively studied human social behavior patterns in space colonies as a lead researcher at the Arcology of Cincinnati. His skills as a personal trainer were also well-received in the circles that had made selections for the mission. Cyrus remembered Dr. Tanner had been thin but much more muscular before the trip. At every briefing and meeting, he had worn a suit that was not too flashy, but not too conservative either. His hair had always been groomed and close-cut, and he had always looked freshly shaven, even after hours of meetings. He was clean-shaven even here, but his hair seemed thicker and a little bushier than on Earth. He had what looked like a small scar across the left side of his cheek. At most angles, before they had boarded the Paracelsus, the scar looked like a worry line, but here, after too many years in stasis, the pallid hue of Tanner's skin and his more gaunt face made the scar very clear—memories came back slow, and in waves, but once they came back, they stayed.

"The nanocytes that rebuilt your muscles are still working to reacclimatize your body to movement. Once you reach static equilibrium again, you'll hit the sleep chamber, they'll dissolve in your sleep, and you'll wake up feeling like a million Uni creds," Dr. Tanner reassured.

Another twitching attack sent Cyrus's face into a violent contortion that made it look like he was about to vomit out of the left corner of his mouth. "They never said it would be like this in the briefing. I feel like the last leper in hell."

"You look like you've lost about thirty pounds in the Hyposoma. Plus, your brain has been frozen in place for almost two hundred years. I'd say you're doing well considering most people can't even remember how to talk until the fourth day out of the Apparatus. Then, they have to learn to walk all over again."

Cyrus felt around his abdomen, admiring the absence of the gut he had been forming since his fourth year of marriage. His belly was soft but flat. As he rubbed his fingers across, he could feel the minute vibrations caused by the nanocytes exercising his stomach muscles. "Is all this really necessary?"

"Come on, you should know better than that," Dr. Tanner chided.

"I'm an astrophysicist, not a physician, Dr. Tanner."

"Touché. Hyposoma is as close to death as a human body can come without actually being dead. After more than 190 years of it, you'd come out looking like Stephen Hawking without the nanocytes."

"Who the heck is Stephen Hawking?"

A smile spread across Dr. Tanner's face but quickly turned into a wince. "Either you're trying to get me to catch a cramp, or the Hyposoma had your brain stem in a serious choke hold."

"Well, I'm not exactly the fastest ship in the fleet right now. It took me two full minutes to remember my own son's name when I first got out of the Apparatus."

"That is pretty bad. You couldn't stop talking about him before we left Eros. Darius is his name, right? He's following us on the Damocles with your wife, is he not?"

Cyrus's body lurched feebly over the sink. He looked like he was about to vomit, but nothing came out. After his attack, he turned back to Dr. Tanner. "You seem sharp as a laser bit and stable too. How'd you fare so well through this whole wretched ordeal?"

"I had a two-day head start out of stasis with Dr. Fordham because I was a veteran Hyposomatic. In the downtime before the rest of you guys hatched, I made a point of brushing up on everyone else's dossier. But as far as stability goes, you should have seen me on the first day. I looked like a lab monkey on Galvacet I had the twitches so bad. The Shipmate had to tie me to the gurney."

"Now you're trying to get me to catch a cramp." What looked like a weak attempt at laughter proved to be another involuntary lurch. "But yes, Darius is due on the Damocles, but I don't know if Feralynn is going to make it. Hopefully, my best friend Earth-side will still get Dari on the ship if she doesn't."

"I don't understand. Maybe I missed something in the dossier. Why wouldn't she make it?"

The effort required for Cyrus to stand and hold his head up to face Dr. Tanner forced out rivulets of sweat around the contours of his eyes. They could have been mistaken for tears if not for his poise. "You know, your dossier doesn't say everything—not enough about the man. You see, she and I weren't exactly copasetic when I left. I doubt I could have left if we had been."

Cyrus stood there, perspiring. It seemed like he wanted to speak, but the effort to stand without assistance drew all his strength. Dr. Tanner paused uncomfortably, looking past Cyrus at his own reflection. "We're having dinner in the Common Hall at the twentieth hour for all those who can physically make it. Dr. Fordham and Dr. Villichez want this to be the first of a regular week cycle gathering. I don't know what the Shipmate is serving, but it will probably be liquid, per Fordham's orders."

There was more awkward silence, and Cyrus turned back to look at himself in the mirror. Another less violent wretch broke his composure, but his own thoughts, cavernous and secluded, did nothing to arrest the stillness.

"I'll see you at the gathering." Dr. Tanner said as he took his leave, steadying himself on the wall as he went.

• • • • •

Dr. Tanner sat at the table, his left hand cupped over his right fist, and his face bowed over his tray. He mouthed thankful, reverent words, twisting the lines of his face into an expression of solemn meditation. The others sat quietly at the table, either in observation of or in deference to Dr. Tanner's personal rite. This was the third meal Cyrus had shared with this man whose tactful intuition and inoffensive manner were glaring opposites of his own sometimes abrasive demeanor. It was the first, however, where anyone other than Dr. Tanner, Dr. Fordham, and Cyrus had been present. Dr. Villichez had shown up on the first day, but he had respectfully retreated to his own sleep chamber when he saw that most of the scientists had not made it. The last occasion was an informal meeting where Tanner, Fordham, and Cyrus discussed when the physical training could begin on the ship and how the gravity waves would affect their bodies. At that time, Dr. Tanner had also spent the moments before drinking his pint of blended essential nutrients, which tasted remarkably like smoked turkey, in genuflection. Cyrus had then wondered if the man was truly pious, or if he reserved this quiet devotion for more trusted company. Now, with eighteen other members of academia looking on, Cyrus realized that although two-hundred years of hurtling through the universe suspended by a thin thread over the gaping maw of death had sapped their bodies of physical strength, this man possessed something that not even the stench of the reaper's breath could overwhelm. Even as Dr. Tanner bowed his head, he seemed like a kneeling giant as his gaunt and gangly spectators afforded him his pause. To Cyrus, it seemed whatever Dr. Tanner revered, whatever his vigil stood for, these others had lost long before the Hyposoma nanocytes began depleting their fat cells for the energy to sustain their long catatonic stasis. He could see that even he had begun to lose it before he had set foot on this vessel.

Dr. Fileas Winberg, the least gaunt of the lot, spoke first as Tanner raised his head. Dr. Winberg's cheeks jiggled awkwardly as he talked, and his hair, dusted with as many gray hairs as black, seemed to shake in the same rhythm as his cheeks as he reached for his pint and spoke, "So it seems some antiquated conventions have stowed away with us on our grand exodus." Cyrus noticed that Dr. Winberg had positioned himself at the only seat that could be considered the head of the table.

Dr. Tanner finished a long sip from his pint. At first, he seemed either unconcerned with or unaware of, Dr. Winberg's comment. He set his cup delicately on the table as his eyes moved to Dr. Winberg. "I feel a certain amount of piety and reverence helps keep us balanced. Move too far, too fast and, eventually, you will lose your footing. It would seem in our reaching out to another world, searching for truths about our past and our future, we would want to maintain our balance—or at least I would."

"Understandable, but I as an educated man and an educator, I feel if we are on this trip in search of some sort of greater truth, religious convictions would be more dangerous enemies of that truth than blatant lies," Dr. Winberg answered.

Cyrus had seen this coming before they had even selected him as the astrophysics specialist on this team of eminent scientists and researchers. A crock pot of twenty scientists, all reputed and dominant in their own fields, holed-up and concentrated under the pressures of trailblazing a virgin frontier; it was only a matter of time before teeth bared, horns locked, and intellectual blood was drawn. There was no doubt that Dr. Winberg also saw something in Dr. Tanner, but unlike Cyrus, it was dark and threatening to him. Cyrus had guessed Dr. Winberg would be the first to pound his chest. He was a fellow professor at the Los Angeles Arcology of Science and had as great a reputation for groundbreaking arrogance as he did for groundbreaking lectures. Cyrus had only met him directly once briefly at a conference on the long-term effect of gravity waves on the brain. The brevity of the meeting had kept the situation sociable, but students and teachers alike had known Dr. Winberg to brandish his prominence and knowledge like a standard, and often at the expense of those less prominent or knowledgeable. Even here, it seemed he had a refinement of insult that would make those who responded in a manner Cyrus felt was necessary appear brazen and uncouth. Although Cyrus had expected the first press for the hill to come from Dr. Winberg, he had expected it later in the trip, and he had expected it to be directed at him.

As Dr. Tanner drank, Dr. Fordham added, "Dr. Tanner here is merely exercising his own right to worship as he pleases. He has not sought to offend or accost any of us with his beliefs."

"To Dr. Tanner's credit, I agree. But, personally, in the company of such educated men, I find the very idea of a belief or a religion prostrating any of us as offensive. In my experience, religion itself is a bandage masking the abscess of a frail intellect." Dr. Winberg lifted his pint to eclipse what Cyrus thought must have been a smirk. Any thoughts that his quick assessment of Dr. Winberg had been unfounded drained away as quickly as the thick liquid that passed from Dr. Winberg's cup into his still-pudgy belly.

"Are you suggesting that education is somehow more valuable than imagination?" Cyrus knew this was not exactly what Dr. Winberg had meant, but he figured if he attacked his statement directly, he would be walking into a timeworn, prefabricated response. Cyrus did not want to start an argument this early in the trip, but he could not watch this man posturing himself by pushing others around with his academic ale-belly.

"I don't feel archaic traditions have anything to do with imagination. I think they anchor us to our lower selves, and I feel that knowledge is the only way to free ourselves of those shackles. It seems it should be obvious to anyone who has matriculated through Laureateship as we all have." He spread his arms to indicate everyone at the table. It was a welcoming gesture, but to Cyrus, it seemed histrionic and overblown.

"Only those who are born into the Meritocracy are guaranteed Laureateship, and the Freeschool transfer process is as cutthroat and bloody as an uberhound pit. And, even if you're selected for Laureateship, the Meritocracy taps people to go to the Arcologies virtually at random."

"But they have to pick selective members from the top tier. Surely, you are not suggesting the mass populous is worthy of Laureateship."

"Well, they should call it what it is, a sanctioned *aristocracy*. It's nothing more than an academic cotillion designed to keep the upper echelon free of undesirables."

Dr. Winberg lifted his cup again, this time allowing the smirk to remain as he lowered the pint from his face. "How then do you explain *your* tapping?"

Cyrus raised his brow slowly as he met Dr. Winberg's gaze. Dr. Tanner lowered his pint and pursed his lips to speak, but Cyrus had already released his volley, "As eloquent as that sounded, it's still a cheap shot. As much as you wear your credentials on your sleeve, and as feverishly as you wave the banner of sociological evolution, the notion of Manifest Destiny seems to have escaped your distaste for the archaic. No matter how much you *misquote* Nietzsche, you will always stand as the foremost example of why society made it much easier for me to leave Earth behind."

There was an audible shuffling at the table as if the tension had taken a physical form and was shambling beneath it. Dr. Villichez lowered his empty pint like a gavel. He was short, and he slouched over the table, but the white of his hair and the hard, experienced features of his face lent him authority his posture did not. "Gentlemen, let's try to keep this diplomatic. We have to live together for the next five years on this bucket of bolts. Let us try to keep the dinner conversation kosher."

"Well, as Dr. Winberg here so deftly eluded, diplomacy does not run so thick in my blood as piss and vinegar. I only stood in for Dr. Tanner because I know he is too dignified to respond to such a lowbrow attack. But, if you do not want to smell the beast, don't fan his clothes. If we are to live on this alloyed crucible in a kosher manner, as you put it, Dr. Villichez, Dr. Winberg here will do best to understand that."

"I apologize." Dr. Winberg conceded with a somewhat smug lilt as he passed a deliberate gaze at Dr. Villichez.

Cyrus continued, "Affront or not, my point, Dr. Winberg, is this: God is not dead. He is merely bound and gagged in the morbid cave of our arrogance. Perhaps, when the swelling of our heads has subsided enough, we will hear his muffled pleas and be humble enough to answer them."

There was mild chatter all around the table as Cyrus finished off his drink, but Winberg was still not finished, "So you're a zealot now as well?"

Cyrus chuckled legitimately at the notion, "Not even close. But I still have a certain amount of wonder in my heart. That's why I became a scientist in the first place. And every time there is a new obstacle to tackle, a new theory to test, I am comfortable, even pleased, knowing there are forces in this universe bigger and stronger than me, regardless of the names we give them."

There were more nods and chatter as Cyrus weakly lifted himself from the table. Dr. Winberg's retort seemed less slow and deliberate than his other statements as if he was trying to stick them to Cyrus before he left, "See that is where I must disagree. I believe the human intellect is the greatest thing in the universe. Man eventually conquered flight. He went from stubborn geocentricity to the development of space travel. Gravity remained a mystery for thousands of years and we conquered that as well. The light-speed barrier has long been a stopping block of the universe, and yet, as you should well know, we could conquer even that in our lifetimes—our *original* lifetimes."

There were more nods and murmurs. Expectant eyes fell on Cyrus as he slid in his chair. Cyrus steadied himself against the wall and then moved toward the entrance to the room, "I hate to excuse myself from this challenge of intellects, but I have dire business to attend to. We will have to conclude this discussion at a later date."

Dr. Villichez wiped his mouth with his napkin and clasped his hands together, "As our time on this vessel is far from brief, I'm sure there will be ample opportunity to add to this discussion."

Dr. Tanner looked at everyone else in the room as individual conversations sprouted like a Hydroponic Table Garden. He watched Dr. Winberg turn and engage in another rather weighty discussion with Dr. Gerhard Torvald, preeminent microbiologist who was much more open to Dr. Winberg's distaste for religion. Tanner could see why those who spread religion like imperialists spread culture could create distaste among the less pious. For better or worse, for the purposes of this journey, Dr. Tanner's devotion was his and his alone unless someone else actively chose to join him.

When Cyrus emerged from the lav, Dr. Villichez was there to meet him. He smiled and clasped his hands together, but the smile soon dwindled to concern. "As I am in charge of both the physical and psychological health of all on this vessel, I feel it is my duty to help keep the peace. So please forgive me if I am somewhat out of place in being a little unnerved at what happened at dinner tonight. These meetings are designed for us to commingle and fraternize so that we can exist as a cohesive unit on the planet while we await our families and colleagues."

Cyrus himself was a bit annoyed on being approached immediately after exiting the lav, but he could see the corners of Villichez's eyes quivering, and he could tell the concern, and in turn, the urgency, in his voice was sincere. Cyrus adjusted his jumpsuit slightly. "I am sorry if I had a part in making the dinner unnerving, but I must say, as your family includes more than one eminent primate zoologist, you had to have seen what was going on in there."

Dr. Villichez nodded, then he focused on Cyrus's eyes again, resting a hand kindly on his left shoulder. "I could see, yes, but what I couldn't see was why you felt the need to engage him on his terms."

This split through Cyrus's head as if he had expected him to say something else, anything else. It wasn't so much that Cyrus and Dr. Winberg had butt heads because Cyrus slapped Dr. Winberg's hand away from the prize, but rather they locked horns because Cyrus had also been reaching for it. "Dr. Villichez, I will make an effort to keep my end of our dinner table conversations copasetic, but we're all equals here. We all have our roles. And from now until we settle Asha and leave it to our descendants, whenever Dr. Winberg flexes his academic muscle to berate someone, he and I will have a disagreement."

"Well, son," Dr. Villichez said, smiling slightly and lightly rubbing Cyrus's arm, "I'm sorry you feel that way. Perhaps Dr. Winberg's hubris is not so...ominous."

Dr. Villichez turned and left in the direction of the infirmary, using the wall to walk. Cyrus steadied himself and tried to walk back to his own room with greater difficulty than on his way to dinner, but without using the wall.

• • • • •

At almost two meters tall and only eighty-five kilograms, Dr. Torvald was lanky even before entering the Hyposoma. His flaxen hair, alabaster skin, and angular features had done nothing to make him look less gangly. Despite a stature that should have been awkward, Dr. Torvald possessed a walking grace and a quiet, inviting demeanor that gave him a presence his initial impression did not always indicate.

But now, to Dr. Tanner, as he attempted to complete a push-up, Dr. Torvald's emaciated limbs and arched back made him look like a frightened stray cat. Then finally, halfway through only his third push-up, Dr. Torvald lurched impossibly backward, and a vile mixture of dietary supplements, liquefied nutrients, and stomach acid erupted from his open mouth. The vomit splattered in a fan on the floor and settled in thick globs where he had previously been kneeling. Instantly, the stench of barely processed foodstuffs and hydrochloric acid fumes spread across the fitness chamber like a fog.

Almost on cue, the other scientists moved out of their callisthenic positions and began to reel, wretch, or recoil from Dr. Torvald's general vicinity. Dr. Tanner had turned to face Dr. Torvald as soon as the gagging had begun. "I believe that is a good indication that we are done here," Dr. Tanner said clapping his hands together once.

Someone giggled lightly as Dr. Torvald collected himself, apologized, then shuffled out with the other scientists. Only Cyrus remained, arms locked, elbows wobbling erratically as he struggled through another push-up, his face distended with effort and exaggerated breathing. He lowered himself with alarming focus and determination given his proximity to the vomit. As Cyrus forcefully exhaled, Dr. Tanner moved around the repugnant Rorschach diagram on the floor. As Cyrus pushed himself to the apex of his push-up, Dr. Tanner knelt and put his hand on Cyrus's shoulder.

"The fitness chamber will still be on the ship tomorrow morning; and by then, the Shipmate will have cleaned it," Dr. Tanner smiled.

Cyrus only grumbled and moved to lower himself yet another excruciating time. As he lowered, his right elbow twitched violently and gave. Cyrus's body shimmied in a pathetic effort to maintain balance, and he rolled, sending his overworked legs flailing as he flopped to the floor. Cyrus came to a rest on his back, left arm outstretched, right arm limp on his chest. Exertion, concentration, or the fall had blurred his vision, but his senses returned as he felt oily warmth beneath his shoulder blade. The pungent odor inspired awareness like smelling salts. As his pupils dilated, his vision returned, revealing Dr. Tanner's outstretched hand. "You're going to hurt yourself if you keep this up."

Even with the leverage afforded by Dr. Tanner's helping hand, it took a Sisyphean effort to rise to his rubbery legs. "I know," Cyrus let escape with an exhalation. "I know." Cyrus tried to ignore the reek from the muck that was now settling into the mesh of his jumpsuit, but his breaths were too deliberate. The fetor of his own sweat and of Dr. Torvald's bodily fluids and breakfast assaulted his nose like a siege engine. As another gasp filled his lungs, Cyrus stumbled against Dr. Tanner, spreading some of the filth. Dr. Tanner stood stalwart and unflagging, helping to support Cyrus's weight.

"You know, our brains need exercise too. I have just the thing. Meet me in my quarters after you get washed up."

"Okay," Cyrus coughed, moving away from Dr. Tanner to seek support from the wall, "As soon as my body stops revolting against me."

Tanner smiled. "You know, I read somewhere that the best way to avoid revolutions is to take care of those subject to your control."

"You know, I read that too. I also believe the guy after the guy who said that said something like, 'No man, no problem.'"

Cyrus began to shift along the wall, too tired and out of breath to smile at his own joke. It was hard to tell if Dr. Tanner had perceived it as such. "Well, we're going to need that man on this journey, or we're all going to have problems." It sounded like the beginnings of a lecture until Dr. Tanner smiled it off. "So just make sure you can extend that focus beyond unauthorized push-ups."

"Okay, mother," Cyrus huffed as he shimmied toward his room. Dr. Tanner laughed and retreated. He should have been concerned about Cyrus's mental state. He should have reported the incident to Dr. Fordham and Dr. Villichez. But even collapsed in a pool of someone else's vomit, his eyes rolled back in his head from exhaustion, something about Cyrus gave Dr. Tanner a sense that he had everything under control.

• • • • •

"I haven't seen one of these since I was a Novitiate." Cyrus looked at the corporeal chessboard as if he were a life-weary archaeologist looking on some elusive piece of arcana. "Isn't this an antique?"

"Oddly enough, most people see owning these as a sign of lower status. Even some of the most basic broadcast decks and ephemera have pretty fancy chess holoprograms. Most of the people who own corporeal chessboards can't wait to get rid of them, but wouldn't be seen selling them," Dr. Tanner said, returning to his chair.

"So why do you have one?"

"Maybe as an anthropologist I have a particular affinity for the rustic. I brought it hoping we could leave some of the prejudices of our past behind."

"Well, I think it's plenty stellar." Cyrus admired the workmanship and detail on the king. Minor nuances, beautiful in their subtle imprecision, made it clear that these pieces had not been carved by machine. Few short of ulti-classicist sculptors or artisans on the Fringe of the Unified Territories, who still took pride in working with their own hands, would have focused so much effort on such a small thing.

Tanner picked up his ephemeris from his bed and began scrawling on it with his stylus. Cyrus set the chessboard on his desk and turned to him. "What do you write so diligently into that thing?"

"Just my thoughts and observations." Dr. Tanner didn't look up from the digital pad. "Helps keep me focused. It gives me perspective when I look back at the entries."

Cyrus set the pawn back on the board. "I can't see myself writing my thoughts down on the daily. I spend so much time stuck in my own head instead of the real world. I find my thoughts have often escaped my lips and become real just as soon as they are complete. And people like my wife and Villichez are constantly reminding me of that when they don't like the form the words have taken. Being reminded again, and by myself no less, seems like a unique blend of self-hate and masochism. The world and my mind would have to be on equal terms for that to change, and I don't think any of us want to see that." Cyrus laughed a little, but either Dr. Tanner missed the joke or didn't see the humor in it. "Sometimes I find myself drawn to problems that look like they have solutions. Maybe that's what drew me to the call for participants in this mission. All we have to do is set up camp and prepare the way for other settlers and scientists—hard, but not complicated. Sometimes everyday life is easier than we think, but it's always more complicated than we want it to be. Like that first day at the dinner gathering. I just couldn't sit there and watch Winberg throw his weight around at your expense, but I feel like everyone faulted me for the tension at the table."

Dr. Tanner set his stylus on his ephemeris then looked up smiling a bit, "I don't think people feel too much about it one way or the other—well, no one other than Dr. Villichez—but you were a little impetuous."

Cyrus smiled, but the smile ebbed away slowly. "I dunno. I just don't like 'screwed up' when I see it."

"Understandable, but you do," Tanner formed a hint of a smile at one corner of his mouth, "seem like the type to walk against the wind just because everyone else is getting blown over."

"Sometimes, even though I don't feel ashamed or guilty, I do feel like *I* might be the problem. I always convince myself otherwise, but you know, sometimes, like the other day, the question is still there. But

I do feel like Winberg was out of line, and I hate seeing people step across the line like consequences don't exist."

"Well, that's noble." There didn't seem to be sarcasm in Tanner's voice, but Cyrus wasn't sure.

"Not really. I mean, I'd rather spend my nervous energy going head-up with a problem than being mad at it. It's what makes me, or anyone else on this ship for that matter, a good scientist."

For a moment, Dr. Tanner's eyes seemed to be looking somewhere other than the room. He inhaled softly then sighed, "You know, it's funny, throughout the whole history of man, we remember the rabble-rousers and the revolutionaries, but as time passes, people tend to forget how uncomfortable it is sitting in the room with someone who is just a bit too intense about something everyone else is willing to let pass." Dr. Tanner paused to take a breath, but continued, his eyes clearly focused on Cyrus's now, "Moses was a fugitive for murder. He had a temper so bad he needed Aaron as a *nabi* to keep him in check. Gandhi didn't believe in violence, but he damn sure believed in irritating the folk who were ruining India. Buddha renounced his princedom for his beliefs—if that's not anti-establishment, nothing is. Jesus put every governing Judaic council he came across in a Fringe-fit because his ideas were so avant-garde."

Tanner took another breath and began tapping his stylus lightly against the ephemeris, "Einstein, Faraday, Bohr. Hell, look at Villichez's work on human behavior and Davidson's work on botany and hydroponic mixtures—Milliken damn near lost his Arcology commission before he proved his theories on rock dating, which then turned geology, paleontology, and archaeology on their necks in one big ground sweep. Even Winberg's work on Penrosian brain function horrified the old hat neurologists." Dr. Tanner laughed to himself a bit. Cyrus was not sure where he was going, but his insights were interesting nonetheless. Dr. Tanner's smile remained as he continued, "You know what everyone I just mentioned, and everyone like them, has in common?"

"They were all innovators?" it sounded like less like a question than Cyrus had meant it to be.

Dr. Tanner, laughed to himself, smiling fully now, "Maybe. But that's not the most important thing about them."

"Enlighten me."

"Everyone in that long list, before anyone paid attention to who they were or lauded their ideas for their brilliance—every last one of them, at some point, sat at a table with people who wished they would just shut the *hell* up and eat."

Cyrus did not know how to respond at first, but the joke seemed to lift the weight that had been building in his lungs, and he laughed.

"Not a single one of them needed approval for what they believed the world was and what they believed it should be. A man finds solace on his own terms," Dr. Tanner added, turning his attention back to his ephemeris.

"If he finds it at all," levity was still in Cyrus's voice, but his smile faded. "I guess I found the most focus—and solace—in my conversations with my son. He questioned everything. He kept me on my toes. And when I didn't have the answers, I felt like I needed to find them, if not for me, for him."

"That sounds like as good a focus as any." Dr. Tanner set the stylus back in its sheath on the ephemeris, set the ephemeris on the bed, and moved over to the chessboard on his desk. "So, shall we play?"

"I thought you were never going to ask."

three

—*How was school today, Dari?*
—*I dunno. It was okay.*
—*You sure?*
—*Well, not really...*
—*What happened?*
—*Scott Seal and Terry Gallagher...*
—*What'd those two lab monkeys do this time?*
—*They kept calling me Scariest and Derrière, and they said my name was stupid.*
—*They did, did they? What do you think about that?*
—*Kinda bothers me...I kinda dunno if they're wrong or not this time.*
—*Did I ever tell you where your name comes from?*
—*No, Dada. I thought you and mama made it up.*
—*Well, King Darius the Great helped build one of the strongest empires in the history of the world, the Persian Empire. He didn't gain the throne because of who his father was, or because of politicking. He gained the throne because he was good at what he did and because the people of Persia believed in him. Not only was he a great military leader even before he was king, he was a good leader during peacetime too because he allowed even the people the Persians conquered to do what they wanted, and he didn't try to change them.*
—*What did he do to be such a good leader?*
—*Some say it was because he had the blessing of Ahura Mazda.*
—*Don't they make mag-levs, Dada?*
—*No, that's a different Mazda. Ahura Mazda was what the Persians believed was the supreme god and the creator of the world. Ahura Mazda had two children; Ormazd, who represented good and life, and Ahriman, who represented evil and death.*
—*How could God have both good and evil children Dada?*
—*Well, I think the Persians believed balance was more important than comfort.*
—*I don't know what that means Dada.*

37

—*Hopefully, one day you will. The important thing is that your name represents a strong idea.*
—*Yeah, I like that. But it's still not like the other kids' names. Proxy Instructors still mispronounce my name all the time.*
—*People who don't know you will always have problems with your name. It's the people that do know you that will help add meaning to your name, but most importantly, it's up to you.*
—*What do you mean?*
—*I mean if you live your life well, like Darius the Great, even if your name was Scariest or Derrière, when people will say it, they will smile.*
—*I hope it's not cuz they're laughing at me Dada.*
—*Well, I guarantee, if you grow up anything like your Dada, the ones who do laugh at you won't do it for long.*

• • • • •

Cyrus's chest heaved, but it felt like only hot, noxious air had entered his lungs. He coughed a long, dry cough and pushed feebly against the floor as a stream of drool escaped the corner of his mouth. The string of saliva, thick and elastic, danced its way to the floor in sync with the wobbling of his elbows as he struggled to his knees.

"Again!" Tanner bellowed, his voice barely audible over the throbbing in Cyrus's ears. Cyrus rose to his feet, head spinning from the effort, and snapped his body to attention. "Ready position!" Tanner commanded. Cyrus bent his arms at the elbow, balled his fists, and lifted them to his hips as the other men in the room attempted to do the same. "Fighting stance!" Cyrus thrust his back leg behind him. He could feel the weakness in his arms as he raised them into a defensive position. His knee wobbled from fatigue, and his thigh burned, threatening to cramp. Then, as Cyrus exhaled as deeply as he could, sweat dribbled away from his nostrils and he caught a telltale whiff of hydrochloric acid on someone else's breath.

Trying to hold it in only caused his esophagus to spasm more violently, as Dr. Kristoph Davidson, the ship's botanist, charged with instituting an agricultural program on Asha, ejected his breakfast and lunch all over the fitness chamber floor. The stench washed over Cyrus like a fog, and the cramp took over, sending him to the ground in the puddle of half-digested vitamins and amino acids. As Cyrus flopped gracelessly through the puddle, covering his upper body with the filth, Davidson's deep green eyes looked apologetic, his tawny skin now pale, and his hard features now slack from exertion. He reached for Cyrus in a feeble attempt to help him up, but Cyrus stood on his own, kindly waving Davidson's hand away. Cyrus coughed again, trying to eject as much of the stench from Davidson's insides as he could. "Will these sessions always be characterized with pain and vomit?" Cyrus heaved more than asked, sweat spraying from his nostrils with his words.

Still in his authoritative voice, Tanner answered, "Vomit, no; pain, yes, but the pain you will learn to love."

Struggling to stay in his stance, Dr. Milliken's unkempt, reddish-brown hair fluttered, and sweat dripped from the ends. His normally rosy complexion was now so sanguine he looked as if he were developing a rash. His typical worried-looking facial expression had been replaced with an expression of exhausted determination as he fought gravity and atrophic muscles to hold his current body position. He turned to face Tanner, who paced before him, Cyrus, Davidson, and Torvald as his voice quivered in time with his unconditioned thighs, "Exactly what kind of sadist are you, Dr. Tanner? Why are you torturing us?"

"First, in this dojo, makeshift as it may be, you will all refer to me as *Sifu* Tanner," the consternation in his voice pressed against the padded metal walls that began to close in again as Cyrus struggled to his feet. "And in answer to your final question, I am torturing you so this brutal environment that we will land on in five years cannot." Tanner moved over to Cyrus and adjusted the position of his ankle rather brusquely. "And as far as the question of my particular brand of sadism, it is the only brand you need fear."

"So you're saying we should fear you?" Dr. Torvald asked, almost stumbling out of his own stance as he craned his neck to face Tanner. "That doesn't strike me as very monk-like."

"You need not fear *me*. I," he paused for theatrical emphasis, "am your friend, your colleague. What I meant Dr. Torvald, is that in *this* room, the only paradigm you need understand is that when I hit you, you *will* fall—which means, when you bow at that door, Dr. Villichez and Dr. Fordham no longer exist. I and only I write policy in *this* place."

"So you..." Dr. Torvald began, but a stark bellow drowned out whatever came afterward.

"Enough talk! Horse stances!" Tanner moved to the side of the three men, closer to Dr. Torvald.

As Sifu Tanner passed outside of earshot, Cyrus mumbled to Dr. Milliken, "This man is a lunatic."

Cyrus turned to face forward and square his shoulders, and, suddenly, Dr. Tanner was in his face, eye-to-eye, close enough for

Cyrus to smell his breath. He stood there for a moment, and Cyrus felt something icy at the nape of his neck. It felt as if even his pores had stopped expelling sweat. Then, Tanner turned. It seemed as if he had smiled as he moved to his spot in front of the line and dropped into his own horse stance, deeper and infinitely more solid than those of his students. He demonstrated a punch, crisp and firm, punctuated by a forceful *ki'a* erupting from his diaphragm. "This is a corkscrew strike," he added after the echo subsided. "This is the first attack you will learn."

• • • • •

The dinner table was busy with conversation as Cyrus sat at the seat Tanner had saved for him. For the last few week cycles, the mysterious unction that had served as the staple of their diet in the first month had been replaced with real food, or rather the most reasonable facsimile the Shipmate could produce. The limited supply of nutrients reduced the Shipmate's palate to that of soybeans, wheat grass, and a breed of grape genetically altered to minimize vine length, but that palate, in addition to creative programming, resulted in meals that were a welcome departure from the warm pints of viscous fluid.

As Cyrus took his first bite, he marveled over the taste of the sizzling soy-steak that the Shipmate had placed before him. "How does the Shipmate make this taste like this?" Cyrus asked.

Dr. Davidson swallowed his bite of pseudo-steak and chimed in before it had completely gone down. "The meat is made from a mixture of soybeans and wheatgrass, but the meat taste is a byproduct of the iron and fat supplements added to the food for balanced nutrition." He smiled and basked proudly for a moment before returning to his steak with his shoulders a little higher than before.

"I assume you had a hand in designing the nutritional program for the ship?" Cyrus asked as he put another bite in his mouth.

"Actually, I only designed the hydroponic bed and the aeroponic nutrient delivery system, but I had to work closely with the nutritionists to maximize the quality and longevity of the rations. Also, I helped create a system that can easily be converted for use in the settlement."

"Excellent job indeed," Dr. Villichez added. "I seem to have left most memories of steak behind in the whole Hyposoma process, but this is surely an excellent reminder."

Dr. Winberg finished churning a bite that had been almost too large for his mouth. "You wouldn't happen to have a program for lobster bisque would you?" He laughed at his joke, but the lines in his forehead bespoke a vein of seriousness in the comment. A few of the scientists laughed as others continued their conversations.

"So," Villichez began, dragging the two-letter word longer than necessary, "who would like to open the table for discussion?"

"I have a question," Dr. Taewook Jang, the ship's computer specialist, raised his hand beside his head. "Is there any reason why the committee who chose the delegates for this expedition didn't choose any women?" Dr. Jang brushed his hair over his shoulder as he lowered his hand.

Dr. Winberg laughed openly at the comment. Bewildered by both the audacity and the intent of Dr. Winberg, Dr. Jang smiled unenthusiastically. Winberg noticed the mixture of uncertainty and irritation that seemed to flutter the lapel of Dr. Jang's lab coat momentarily. "I am not laughing at your comment, Dr. Jang. I am merely amused by the notion of men and women corralled in a giant stylus away from their families for five years."

"Well, what would be so bad about that?" Dr. Torvald questioned. "It'd be nice to have some estrogen on this craft to help break up the constant masculinity in this place. We've only been awake for a month and a half and the ship already feels like a locker room."

Dr. Koresh cleared his throat and let his fork clang against the table as he set it next to his plate, "Let me add, first of all, when backed into a corner or 'crammed into a giant stylus,' as Dr. Winberg put it, humans exhibit more monkey-like qualities than we would like to admit."

"What does that mean?" Dr. Milliken asked through his napkin.

Dr. Winberg leaned on his forearm. "What he means is arguments are not the only things caused by the volatile mixture of testosterone and estrogen. Under the pressures of sitting in this oversized bullet-casing for five years, plus the stresses of a year of pioneering, it would not be long before this entire expedition turned into an extended holovision melodrama."

Cyrus chuckled and Winberg zeroed in on him almost instantly. "Something amusing on your plate, Dr. Chamberlain?"

"Well, I would argue holonovella drama is unavoidable under this type of stress, regardless of the number of vulvae present. I agree with your assessment, but I wonder, with the collection of Nobel Laureates and general braniacs we have assembled here, exactly long it would take this *bullet-casing* to turn into a full-blown Bacchanalia. Hell, you don't need to know much Greco-Roman history to know it doesn't take fallopian tubes to have a Bacchanalia. Maybe we should synchronize our watches and start the countdown now."

"Dr. Cyrus Tiberius Chamberlain, must you *always* be so crass?" Dr. Villichez's plate rattled briefly under the weight of a fist clenched around a fork.

"I apologize," Cyrus nodded his sincerity toward Dr. Villichez, "I just wanted Dr. Winberg to know I was laughing *with* him, not at him. Not exactly dinner table fare though, admittedly."

Amidst a volley of mumbles and grunts erupted a barely audible, "Unless it *is* a Bacchanalia!" A wave of laughter spread across the table like a nova. Even Villichez, however reluctant, loosened his fist and allowed a smile to creep across his face. Cyrus could not tell where the comment had come from, but he noticed the bangs of Dr. Jang now hanging over his face, shifting as laughter escaped from rapidly contracting lungs.

four

—*How did the Math Finals go today, Dari?*
—*I don't want to talk about it, Dada.*
—*That bad?*
—*It was plenty fine at first. I had all the other Laureate candidates beat by like five hundred points. I had the highest score by one hundred points.*
—*Well, what happened?*
—*Genivere happened...again. Somehow she managed to make up over two hundred points in the last round. It was a slaughter, Dada. I felt like I was standing still. I don't know why I can't beat her, Dada. No matter how far I get ahead, she always seems to find a way. Always. What am I doing wrong?*
—*Hmm...You know, once, a while ago now, I came to pick you up from Entrance School. You were no more than maybe four. You were a little small, even for your age, but you always played with the big kids. Even then, you said the kids your age were dumb as lab rodents. Not sure how you knew what a lab rodent was, but you said it and meant it. But this particular day, I showed up early to talk to your room steward. She seemed distraught because you had been playing with the older boys all day. They were already tapped as Novitiates; they were just waiting to matriculate. She took me to the playroom, but we stayed in the observation lounge. As soon as I got there, I knew why she was disturbed. You looked like a chipmunk next to the other boys. They were just a little older than you are now. You were playing 'Police and Thieves,' and for fun, they had pegged all the younger kids as thieves. One of the more heavyset boys was sitting on the two of your fellow thieves, and you were hiding in a Styroprene box. They surrounded you with their hands in gun shapes and ordered you to come out. The box shook a little, and they all got ready to give you the same treatment they gave the others. They fired off a round of warning shots, saying 'pow-pows, pop-pops, and bang-bangs,' but just as they seemed confident in their victory, you burst from the box. Styroprene flew everywhere. You vaulted off something that had been in the box, and with both hands shaped like guns, bellowed out 'Doosh! Doosh! Doosh!' carrying more bass than I think I have ever heard in your voice. The older boys were so startled and impressed that they played along.*

43

The chunky kid even got off the other two and clutched his chest as you fired two shots his way. They all collapsed to the ground in undeniable defeat because they didn't know what else to do. If someone comes out of the box with bass in his voice like that, there isn't much else you can do.

—Wow, I did that?

—The room steward said she had never seen the thieves win against those boys because they were too stubborn a set of bullies to ever admit defeat. I told her she didn't have to worry about my *son. Darius Chamberlain would always be all right—one way or the other.*

—I don't feel all right right now, Dada.

—Well, the sting of defeat will do that—especially when victory has been snatched from its jaws by someone else.

—What do I do, Dada? How do I get all right again?

—Maybe the next time, winning or losing, ahead or outnumbered, maybe you need to come out of the box with your Doosh Doosh guns, just to be sure.

—Well, Dada, I wish it really was so easy as that.

—Dari, I don't think easy has anything to do with it.

• • • • •

Cyrus sat on his bed with his ephemeris in his lap. He scrolled through data on the Van Allen system on Asha. Once they arrived, they would have to scan the atmosphere and magnetosphere and gather topographical information before making the final decision of where to set up camp. The Uni had collected years of data from Earth, but Cyrus wanted to have a good idea of where to look before they even turned on the scanners.

Just as he pulled up an image of the projected magnetosphere, the offensively pleasant door chime rang through his room. The intercom clicked on automatically. "Come in," Cyrus called, pressing a button on his ephemeris to save his work.

The door unlocked, and Dr. Tanner entered.

"Hey," Tanner began then paused, noticing Cyrus was sitting too close to the floor, "What happened to your bed?"

"Oh, I took the shock-absorbing frame and set it up against the wall. Supports my neck better. I also think the vibrations of the ship through the floor help me sleep." Cyrus logged off his ephemeris and set it aside on his bed. "What brings you to my humble abode?"

"I just finished the calisthenics class with the other scientists. I'm thinking of inviting Dr. Toutopolus to our kung fu sessions. He seems more motivated than the others." Tanner pulled the chair from the desk and sat facing Cyrus.

"By motivated you mean insane, I assume."

"Well, it takes all kinds."

Cyrus sat back on his bed but slipped on something as he rested his weight on his elbow. "Stupid card," he uttered to himself as he picked up something flat from beneath his elbow and turned it around in his hand. It was similar to the cards that maintenance crews would leave in hotels when they still used humans to service rooms. It informed him that his room had been cleaned, and it wished him a nice day.

"What's the deal with these cards? I don't remember them from the briefing." Cyrus continued to flip it around in his hand.

"Dr. Fordham told us about them at the second dinner."

"What the heck was I doing? I remember being at that dinner."

"I think you were somewhere cleaning bodily fluids off yourself. You adjusted better than anyone else to the Hyposoma, but that doesn't mean you adjusted well."

"Yeah, I think I selectively chose to forget that. Thanks for reminding me." Cyrus tossed the card back on the bed.

Tanner gave a histrionic bow. "At your service." He leaned over to pick up the card. "You're supposed to put it face down on your desk if you want your room cleaned. The Shipmate will come in and clean your room automatically every three week cycles even if you don't, but if the pseudo-meat doesn't sit well one day or something, you can have him clean in here sooner."

"I thought we weren't supposed to have paper on this old tanker anyway."

"There are stores of paper in the cargo hold that we can use if the Shipmate system fails when we're planet-side, but we should avoid the potential for litter at all costs. As far as the room service goes, the Shipmate also scans for anything out of the ordinary and picks up hair, skin, and nail shedding to reclaim for the hydroponic beds. We waste no part of the animal here."

Cyrus had learned about the greatly truncated food chain on this ship in the year-long briefing that preceded their departure, but the idea that there were much fewer degrees of separation between their waste products and their food on this vessel created a slightly more visceral response now. He was reminded of Dr. Villichez's admonishment when Winberg had grumbled about the lack of variety, "You knew what you were getting into when you signed up, and if it was going to kill you,

you would no longer be here to whine about it." That sounded more like something he would say than Villichez.

"I have something I've had on my mind recently," Cyrus shifted his weight forward on the bed, allowing his lungs to expand.

"Go on."

"You talk to Villichez quite a bit, right?"

"Yeah, I like him."

"I kinda like him too, but I don't think he likes *me* very much."

"According to him, he likes you just fine. You probably stand out in his mind more than anyone else though." Tanner clasped his hands together and rested the weight of his upper body on his knees with his elbows. "He likes the fact that you have heart, and that you are honest, and the fact you don't seem like a quitter."

"You're just saying that to make me believe he likes me."

"Why would I do that? I personally think you're an angry clown." Cyrus looked as if he took the comment seriously, but Tanner smiled, and Cyrus relaxed. "I think Villichez is just straight keel. He likes the fact that you are too, but he doesn't necessarily openly approve of all the flotsam you bring to the dinner table. That's what fatherly types are *supposed* to do. I appreciate it because I never really got much of that growing up."

"Your father wasn't around much?"

"My father wasn't around at all." Tanner looked down at his knees and lifted his hands to the sides of his face.

"I'm sorry," Cyrus said. "You don't have to talk about it."

"It's okay. I'm not ashamed."

"It's not that, I..."

Tanner simply continued, as if he hadn't heard the beginning of the qualification, "My mother said she loved my father very much, and he her, but even though they were hard workers, they didn't have much money in the economy before the Unification." Tanner sat up a little and looked at Cyrus, who was riveted and still. "They didn't have money for contraceptive treatment, and eventually, she became pregnant. They needed more soldiers for the Unification War, and they took draftees from the lower classes before anywhere else. My mother said my father was one of the first to go. He didn't regret it, but because health care was not easy to come by in those times, she didn't realize she was pregnant until after he had gone. My father died in the war, somewhere in the occupied Middle East. I was born in an old abandoned schoolhouse, in a place where church volunteers helped administer freebirths. My mother was a cheerful woman, even after all that, but she never met another man. She said that I was enough. When I got older, I felt sorry for her."

Tanner sat up straight. "She said I shouldn't waste any pity on her. She said she had made her choice, and she was content to have a son that could take care of himself and would not let the world bring him down. After that, I was tapped for the Spencefield Laureate, and I began taking martial arts." Tanner realized he had been looking at his shoes. He looked up to meet Cyrus's eyes. "I was determined to turn the sorrow I was sure she felt inside into my strength—mentally, physically, and spiritually. Her health had been failing since I was a Novitiate. She always kept it to herself though, spending every penny she made to keep me in matriculation but never on medication for herself, and she made damn sure I never knew about it. For a while, I resented it, and without a male example to snatch my houndwash out of orbit, I ran wild for a while—even did some things I'm far from proud of. Eventually, when it began to look like I wasn't going to be tapped, I got my butt back on kilter, and I began to care that my mother's life work was going to be lost to my own monkeyshine. Finally, a month after I was accepted into the Arcology of Ontario, she passed, but not before making sure I could matriculate completely. There is nothing on Earth, this ship, or Asha I wouldn't give just to thank her."

Tanner rubbed his hands together and sat up again, "So, Villichez sort of gives me a way to honor my parents in a way I was never really afforded. If that makes any sense."

Cyrus stood and set his hand on Tanner's shoulder. "Makes plenty sense." He didn't know if he felt more sympathy for Tanner, for himself, or for Darius. He felt selfish for just being on this ship to hear the story. Here he was, supposedly on some selfless, noble mission to help solve the growing overpopulation on Earth, but he was hundreds of light-years from his own son, who was either matriculating or not, but Cyrus no longer had any say in it. He trusted his best friend to look out for his family as if it were his own, and yet, Cyrus couldn't help feel like a deserter, a coward to be shot summarily on the common grounds at daybreak. As the full weight of his choice hung pitilessly on his heart, it took everything Cyrus could muster to pat Dr. Tanner on the back, excuse himself to the lav, and exit the room before the tears came.

• • • • •

Cyrus walked into the dining hall, ephemeris in hand, expecting it to be empty. As the door slid open, Dr. Jang looked up from his ephemeris then went back to work at the table. Dr. Jang was sitting three seats away from Cyrus's usual dinner seat, but Cyrus moved to the opposite side of the table to lend him some space. Cyrus sat down and began working on some figures for gravity drive recalibration to the specs on Asha. They were already programmed into the Shipmate, but Cyrus felt data collected from six hundred light years away was inherently dubious.

Dr. Jang worked for another few minutes then spoke, startling Cyrus who was mulling over figures deep in his head. "You don't have to sit so far away," he said, twirling his stylus between his index and middle finger, "I mean, it's okay if you want to sit in your regular seat."

Cyrus entered one last figure then looked up from his work, "It's okay. Dinner's not for another thirty minutes. I just got tired of sitting in my room."

"I know what you mean. I usually work out here or in the codex. The rooms here are a little too...sterile."

"Well, the whole ship is sterile. Makes me wonder what Asha will smell like when we open the doors. I wonder if our sterilized renal cavities will be able to take it."

"Can't imagine it would smell like anything except dust and open air. Maybe salt from the ocean or other mineral deposits or perhaps some sulfur in some places."

"All of which have been systematically removed from the air on this ship." Cyrus smirked a little. "I have to say, I actually miss the smell of air that has to be reclaimed or it will kill you. There's something homey about recycled L.A. smog."

"Yeah, I always thought the air in Busan tasted like warm bread crust. Nothing on this boat tastes like that." Dr. Jang rolled his eyes back a little, remembering something from the past. "You know what smell I miss the most?" Cyrus shook his head. "The smell of a woman who wants you to notice her. It's more like a class of smells, I guess; the smell perfume makes when it rests on a particular neck, the scent of herbal shampoo on hair," he shivered. "Just thinking about it gives me the chills, but then the chills go away just as fast as they came when I realize I'll probably never smell anything like that again."

"There's no one coming to meet you on the Damocles?"

"I never really managed to stay in one place long enough—well one place mentally—for anyone to give up life in Busan or Seoul, or any other place for that matter, for me."

"You seem pretty young. What about your parents—I mean, if you don't find the question too imposing."

"Imposing? Not at all. I don't know. I guess my relationship with my parents was nominal. They squeezed me through matriculation, throwing every extramatricular activity they could at me whether I enjoyed it or not, and they rolled out credits like time code for it. Most of the time, it seemed like all I was to them was bragging rights. There's no one to rightfully brag to on a giant, deserted gumball. They're still in Seoul living out their lives; probably telling anyone they can that their son is saving the human race while they collect the pay for this expedition. I guess they are getting what they paid for all those years now their income has gone up a quintile or two."

"That's a kind of morose position to be in."

"It is what it is. Strangely, I still miss them, and I don't miss the lady friends nearly as much as I expected."

"Lady friends?"

"What, I don't seem like a ladies' man to you?"

"Honestly, no. But then again, I wouldn't know what a ladies' man was if I had a shop manual and a holodeck tutorial."

"You do seem a bit of the man's man type," Dr. Jang saw Cyrus's brow began to furrow. "I mean, like action hero man's man, not boy's boy man's man—not that there's anything wrong with either of those if you *are* one."

"It's okay. I know what you mean, even though I don't see it."

"You don't?"

"Nah, I'm usually just as scared, nervous, and distraught as everyone else, I just tend to be belligerent about it. Besides, most of the bite in me came from my mother."

Dr. Jang looked past Cyrus, twirling the stylus faster in search of some elusive thought. "A little hard for me to see I guess. My mother never said much until I either defied or embarrassed her, the latter of which wasn't very hard to do. Then, it was like you turned on a nag faucet and broke the knob. Only thing I learned from her was how to whine, gossip, and throw tantrums."

Dr. Jang's tone was more matter-of-fact than disrespectful, but it was unnerving to Cyrus nonetheless. "I learned whatever patience I do have from my father," Cyrus said. "My mother was a juggernaut. She was the one who got in enough people's faces to make sure I was tapped when they sent me to Freeschool, and even though Laureateship was unheard of in my district, my father made sure I stayed on top of my game so no one could find an excuse to kick me out. My parents didn't really push me, but my father taught me how to keep people from pushing me back, and my mother taught by example how to push people out of the way of what I deserved."

"She sounds like a good person to have in your corner."

"Well, it wasn't always apples and sweetbars. Once, when I was about eight or nine, I was playing in the lev-run—back when people still had lev-runs in front of their houses. I was playing with some other Novitiates with those Planetwars robots that turned into spaceships. I had just bought a Tiberius Vauxhall. It had working lasers on its arms, and it had little action figures that were supposed to be pilots and engineers. Plus, it was always my favorite because of my middle name. I was so proud because I had saved creds from my allowance and doing odd jobs for relatives to buy it. It was the first thing I ever bought with my own creds."

"I remember that toy. It had the little button on the side that shot missiles out of its chest." Dr. Jang seemed excited by the memory as he lost control of the spinning stylus but quickly regained it.

"That's it exactly. Well, a kid named Fenton Thorougood was playing with us. He was maybe three years older than the rest of us and still a Novitiate. He was long overdue for Freeschool, and evidently, he was self-conscious about it because he was an absolute son of an uberhound. Anyway, he said that my Tiberius wasn't nearly as cool as his Dreadnaught. And I said if he had Dreadnaught, he should bring it so we could have a battle, knowing full-well they hadn't released Dreadnaught and probably never would because the cel-shade had already been canceled. He said he couldn't bring it out because his mom wouldn't let him. I said he couldn't bring it out because it didn't exist."

Dr. Jang laughed. "You were a little snap-monkey even when you were a Novitiate."

"My sharp tongue seems to have developed when I learned to speak." Cyrus tapped his stylus on the side of his ephemeris and continued, "So he got riled up, and he started stomping around the lev-run with my Tiberius. At the height of his tantrum, he held it over his head, screamed some obscenity at me, and slammed it into the ground. It shattered into about seven or eight pieces. I remember it like it was in slow motion. One of the lasers came on and stuck, and a green dot danced across the lev-run as half of the arm flipped onto the house. Tears welled up, and I ran into the house bawling. My mother, who was as omniscient as she was fear-inducing, had seen the whole thing, but she went through the motions anyway. She asked me what was wrong, and I told her through a hail of tears that Fenton broke my Tiberius."

"What did she do?" Dr. Jang stopped spinning the stylus and was literally sitting on the edge of his seat.

"She told me to go back out there and beat his ass."

"So did you?"

"Did I? I was scared out of my mind. I was small for my age, and he was big for his, so the three years difference was just a bonus. I told my mom that he was bigger than me and that I was scared of him."

"And..."

"She looked me in the eye—I can still remember her face clearly—and said calmly, 'Then get a stick.'"

"Wow, how do you respond to that?"

"I stopped crying mid-bawl, I went to my room, and I came back with a vid runner from a broken gram my dad had thrown away. Y'know, back when they used to project the gram from the three plastic bars? I would pretend I was the Laser Knight with the blue light staff from Planetwars. So I grab this thing, and it's almost as long as I was tall, and I take it outside. Can you believe this freebirth was still outside in the lev-run?"

"So what happened?"

"I walked up to him, dragging the vid runner behind me. This kennel waste just stood there looking at me, like the idea of me standing up to him was preposterous. That's what finally set me off. I grabbed the runner with both hands, and I swung it like I was trying to knock his head from his shoulders. The thing caught him right in his temple so hard he spun on his heels. And it must have knocked some sense into him because he broke into a run like that's why he had turned in the first place."

Dr. Jang was holding his chest laughing. "What did you do?" he spat out between laughs.

"I chased him all the way home; I mean like more than half a K, wailing his back with the runner the whole way. That test dummy never bothered me again." Dr. Jang's laughter was infectious, and Cyrus chuckled at the memory himself.

"What happened to the Tiberius?" Dr. Jang breathed out at the end of a guffaw.

"It was finished. I tried to put it back together, but it was never the same again, and my mother wouldn't let me throw it away for a long time. Every time I saw it, it upset me, but I never cried about it again."

"Wow, I wish I had stories like that from my childhood. I didn't get much excitement until I grew up—even then, it wasn't like that. I did flip my lev in a race once."

"You wreck it?"

"No, I had an Interceptor drive in it. You know, like the cops have?"

"The one that gives you z-axis acceleration? Aren't those illegal?"

"Yeah, but that wasn't the problem. The problem was it was an illegal lev race, and the people I was racing with didn't know about the Interceptor. Thanks to the Interceptor, they couldn't beat me over the speed humps in the ave we were doing the laps on. I had hustled them out of a keel-load of creds. I hit a refuse bin that someone had moved into a blind corner on one of the laps and lost my y-axis. Only when I flipped over, my lev just floated there upside down."

Cyrus's mouth was open, his face frozen in a look of confusion.

"What?" Dr. Jang was not sure what to make of the face.

"I'm trying to figure out how that's less interesting than beating a Novitiate with a vid runner."

"Actually, it gets better. These guys were about to flip their lids—and these were some pretty serious *ggangpe*. I mean cut off your hand and send it to your next-of-kin type guys. They speed over to me, and I'm just floating there like something out of an old-time two-D sci-fi vid. So I hit the throttle and flew out of there upside down. Well, someone had called the sniffers on the comm, and I fly past the speed trap upside-down with four tweaked-out mag-levs behind me. Evidently, the sniffers thought *it* was the race, so they rounded everyone up and hauled them in."

Cyrus holding his chest laughing now. "So you got gaffled?"

"You see, that's the thing, I had disabled the sat-link in the lev so they couldn't track me, and I flew into the hovel district—still upside-down mind you—and hid inside a burnt out factory. I was so freaked out, I didn't turn the lev right-side up until I got back into my own district."

Cyrus inhaled deeply then exhaled to settle his lungs as Dr. Jang finished his story. "You sure are a wonder. How many times have you had run-ins with the magistrate?"

"None. They never catch me. My lev was too fast and had too many dirty tricks on it—shifting license code, a speedcam jammer, and I had a deck that would automatically make my lev-rec look clean if they tried to access it within a kilometer of my lev."

"Never expected any of this from you. No offense."

"The sniffers never did either. That was the beauty of the whole deal. I still contend, with the right set up, a Matriculant could get away with murder in the Uni."

"Or, at the very least, vehicular manslaughter." They both had a long laugh until Dr. Cohn and Dr. Hassan entered, engaged in their own heated conversation.

Cyrus collected his ephemeris and moved to his regular seat. "You okay?" Cyrus asked, noting a change in Dr. Jang's expression.

"Yeah, I was just thinking, the smell I'm probably going to miss most of all is the smell of peppermint air freshener under a lev seat and ozone from a tweaked lev drive."

Cyrus leaned back in his chair and grinned. "I bet, but I'm sure you won't miss the smell of coffee and sweetbars on some angry magistrate's breath."

• • • • •

"Shouldn't you be flying the ship or something?" Cyrus scoffed, trying to catch his breath.

"The ship flies on its own, beta monkey, at least until we get planet-side, which is more than I can say for all the flotsam you've been talking." It sounded like Commander Azariah Uzziah didn't realize Cyrus was joking.

"Well, since I can't let my game speak for me, I guess I'll just have to keep up the pro se flotsam." Cyrus lifted the Kantistyka puck into the air and prepared to serve. It began to hum as it left his hand and it hovered on its own. He swung his arm, trying his best to snap his wrist and not use his shoulder as Uzziah had just instructed him, but he leaned in too much and connected with the puck in an awkward swipe.

Cyrus and Tanner were losing two to four to a solo Uzziah, and one of their two points was because Cyrus had botched a volley so badly that the Commander stopped to see if Cyrus had injured himself.

The puck moved forward at an undesirable speed and in a direction even less desirable. Uzziah ran up to the puck and hit it back. It still moved as if it were underwater but moved too fast for either Cyrus or Tanner to get his paddle in front of it. Cyrus dove, extended his paddle, and connected with the puck. It wasn't a graceful dive, and Cyrus hurt something in his leg when he landed, but the puck bounced up slightly then hovered and settled back to chest height. Even though Tanner was not fully acclimatized to the sport of Kantistyka, he moved with all the agility of a race-bred uberhound. Without hesitation, he sent the puck back toward Uzziah before it came back to full hover. Agile as he was, his abilities were still sophomoric, and his volley, albeit faster than Cyrus's serve, missed its mark completely.

Commander Uzziah almost overran the puck, which was losing

momentum as it reached him, but he spun around completely and backhanded it. The electronic puck absorbed some of the force and countered it, but the motion of the swing carried it across the centerline at a constant, and rather swift, speed. It was so swift that it sped past Cyrus and Tanner and came to an abrupt stop just outside the boundary line of the court.

Tanner retrieved the puck and reared his arm back to serve, but stopped before he swung his paddle. "You are pretty sharp. Especially considering you came out of the Hyposoma only a little while before the rest of us."

"I hated coming out of there. It was like someone transplanted my brain into the body of a sick and awkward thirteen-year-old boy. I've been working out every day cycle since I got out of that jetwashed machine." Uzziah looked like he wanted to spit, but he held it in. "Took the whole six months since to gain back half of what I lost."

"You should come to train with us in my martial arts class," Tanner invited, relaxing his paddle. Cyrus saw Tanner slightly raise his eyebrows and wrinkle his forehead like when he was hatching some plan in chess. Cyrus was bewildered at what Tanner was playing at.

"Thank you for the invite, but I prefer training in solitude." Uzziah smiled the forced smile of a man who had not been afforded many smiles in his life.

"You train in *Mao do Justo*?" Tanner asked.

Uzziah's eyes widened, and he lowered his paddle. He seemed more excited than surprised, but he was hesitant nonetheless. "What makes you ask that?"

"For starters, the way you stand and carry yourself says you're not standard military. Also, the idea that you will have to spend the rest of your life with shipload of eggheads seems to be enough to unsettle you but not enough to unnerve you. That gives me the impression you've been in situations like this before—situations where you have to spend a lot of time blending in with people you don't find so stellar." Tanner folded his arms and focused his eyes on Uzziah's. "Also, this expedition is too important to the Uni itself, and the stat counters Earth-side would not have sent us off without a chaperone."

Uzziah rubbed his chin. The pause was entirely too charged to be called ordinary, but it was filled with something far more pleasant than tension. Tanner and the Commander maintained their eye contact until Cyrus broke the silence. "Am I missing something here?"

"The Unified Nations' Reconnaissance and Infiltration Force trains its members in a specialized technique that takes the more vicious elements of Jujitsu, Muay Thai, and Krav Maga, all under the veil of Vale Tudo, and distills them into a highly efficient and deadly martial art called Mao do Justo. Apart from an obvious, and somewhat understandable, distaste for the matriculated, I am sure Commander Uzziah's apprehension to training with us is due to the fact that he does not want to alarm anyone with his hitherto social position on Earth by exposing his highly characteristic martial training. Is that about right?"

"You seem to have taken offense," the Commander said, a little more stern now, but disarmed.

"Maybe to the subterfuge," Tanner relaxed more himself, "but a man has a right to keep his past to himself until it becomes important. Besides, there is no way you could send a message to or receive a message from Earth as far as I am aware, which takes spying on us off the table; and that's assuming I actually did buy into the false image of privacy on a craft of this importance to humanity's future."

Uzziah laughed. It was a short-lived, but it was honest. "I knew there was something about you Tanner—it was definitely not your Kantistyka game—but if there is anything I did learn in the RIF, it's to know when someone has you on their gram, and above all else, to respect it." The Commander raised his paddle impatiently, "Now can we lay this game to rest because Villichez wants me to go to more of his little egghead dinners, and I don't want him giving me the stink-eye for coming in late."

five

—Dada, do you ever think we'll cross the light speed barrier thingy?

—I think one day we might, but I'm not sure how.

—Why not? What is so hard about it?

—Well, the amount of energy needed is a problem. You remember what mass is, right?

—It's the amount of something in something—like how many molecules something has.

—Exactly. The closer something gets to light speed, the more mass it has, and the amount of energy needed to push that thing is increased. Nothing in this universe the size of an atom or larger can move at that speed because it would have an infinite mass.

—And that would mean you would need an unlimited amount of energy to keep pushing it.

—Exactly. Out of curiosity, why do you ask?

—Well, in class today, Miss Hasabe taught us about electrons and protons and neutrons and stuff. And she sent us a page on our decks that talked about how electrons can be in two places at once if they are run through a slit. It also said that if you tried to look at either side, the electron would kind of choose that side because you looked at it. I was thinking that if electrons could be in two places at once, why couldn't a spaceship?

—Well, unfortunately, the bigger things get, the less they follow those rules, and a spaceship is a lot bigger than an electron.

—Yeah, that's the same thing Miss Hasabe said, but then, on the ride home, I was thinking, what if we could make the big thing forget it was big for long enough to send it through a special kind of slit? If we could look at it once it went through the slit, it would remember the way it was supposed to be, and also it would have to pick that side.

—You know, you may be on to something, Dari. We have known for some time now that energy and matter are really just the same thing at different vibration levels.

—Strings, right Dada?

—*Good, so I see you do pay attention.*
—*Well, honestly you're more interesting than Miss Hasabe, but I like it when she talks about the things you talk about.*
—*We may not be able to make the matter forget that it is matter, but really large objects exert a kind of pressure on the universe around them, generating gravity. Near gravity, matter acts a little differently.*
—*So do you think, somehow if we could create pressure like that on the space around the ship, we might be able to make it do stuff it normally couldn't do?*
—*Yeah, maybe, but we would somehow have to create an immense amount of gravity around the ship. We can create gravity waves, but nothing of that magnitude.*
—*Well, people find new ways to do stuff all the time.*
—*True, but it never seems to be when you want it. I guess if people didn't get tired of wanting it, it would never get invented.*
—*Yeah, well, I think if you and I can think of it, that someone somewhere else can too, and maybe they can build it.*
—*I'd like to think that, Dari, but sometimes I think it takes a simpler mind, not less intelligent, but less...bogged down I guess, to get it right sometimes. Between the two of us, I think we might be able to figure out anything, given enough time.*
—*Yeah, me too...I like that idea. Dari and Dada can figure out anything, given enough time.*
—*That does have a nice ring to it, doesn't it?*

• • • • •

For the past few day cycles, the ship seemed colder than ever. Cyrus found himself on many day cycles venturing to the activity room just to feel the warmth of the suncasters. This odd chill had kept him tossing and frustrated in his bunk until the notion of sleep seemed like an idle promise. He had made his way to the codex to occupy his mind and settle the thoughts that now shambled through his brain like refugees from some cold war.

Cyrus looked for something to read on the holographic monitor. He moved through the philosophy section, perusing works in various languages and their Commonspeak translations, and he settled on John Locke's Essay Concerning Human Understanding. Suddenly, a biting caterwaul severed the quiet of the codex. "*Miching gesheki!*" Hairs stood at attention as gooseflesh spread across Cyrus's body. He had no idea what those words meant, but they were far from exultation. Cyrus moved toward the disturbance as the person pounded on the cubicle.

Whoever the scientist was, he now held his head in almost cartoonish distress as he mumbled some other guttural curse at his datadeck.

Cyrus rounded the chest-high divider and saw holographic images writhing wildly on the table top in front of the distressed scientist. His shoulder-length hair and onyx-set pinky ring identified him as Dr. Jang. "Are you okay?" Cyrus asked, keeping his distance.

Dr. Jang reeled around, both startled and embarrassed, and pressed a holographic button, freezing the writhing figures in place. Cyrus's could now see the figures were armored men with spears riding horses in a combat formation. There was fatigue and anxiety in Dr. Jang's eyes as he tried to form words, "I...I..."

Cyrus smiled. "My son plays that game a lot. Conquest of the Ages, right?" The anxiety in Dr. Jang's eyes subsided and gave way to yet more fatigue. He relaxed a bit, laughed, and revealed the frozen battlefield on the table.

"I smuggled a copy of the software onboard and circumvented the lock-out codes. I've been playing while everyone was asleep, but it appears my secret is out now."

"Your secret is safe with me." Cyrus stepped forward to get a better view of the battle. "My son was fond of the spaceship battles in the later levels, but I prefer the Warring States period of China levels."

"Me too," Dr. Jang's eyes widened a little as he faced Cyrus, "but I can't seem to beat this particular level. I'm outnumbered, and the other army's cavalry keeps cutting me to shreds."

"Let me see what you have." Cyrus surveyed the landscape and resources. "So what is your goal?"

"If I can make it to the bases that are further up the gram and kill the general there I win, but the cavalry always runs me down."

"Any idea what kind of garrison is in the base?"

Dr. Jang moved his hand over the battlefield, and it scrolled north. In the north, there was a large wooden fort barring passage between two hills with archers along the battlements, and infantry inside numbering at least that of the force Dr. Jang had at his disposal. There were at least three mounted captains. There was also one mounted officer with a gold lion head on his breastplate and an ostentatious plume with two large streamers erupting from his helm. "Let me guess, the guy with the big stupid hat is the general you need to beat."

"Yeah, and he's no push-over either. Honestly, I don't know what general in his right mind would attack under these circumstances." Dr. Jang scrolled back to where the cavalry was riding toward his men.

"Well, these circumstances give us the perfect opportunity for attack because the enemy would not expect it, and they would be overconfident in their numbers. We should use those things to our advantage."

"How?"

"You have all your men lined up like British Redcoats. Can you move the archers to the top of the hill along the pass between you and the fort?"

"It will take them a while, but yeah, they can make it there. It will weaken our ability to stop the cavalry though."

"You couldn't stop the cavalry anyway, right?" Cyrus smiled. "You have fire attacks on this level, right?"

"Yeah."

"Then that's the plan. Send the archers to cover the pass. Divide the infantry, leaving only those necessary for the fire attack. Send the rest around the opposite side of the pass and have them double-time it to the other entrance. When the cavalry rushes in, set the fire attack on the ground in front of them and keep feeding the flames. By then, your archers should be in place. Have them wait at the top of the pass until your infantry arrives here." Cyrus pointed to the spot the cavalry was charging from. "Then, have them charge from here to here." Cyrus pointed to a spot about three hundred scale meters from the previous one. "Then stop when the cavalry rushes back to engage your infantry. Have the archers unload on them. Then, the only way out will be to charge through a hail of arrows for another three hundred meters and face fresh infantry or to charge back three hundred meters and brave the flames. Any man that makes it out of that will earn a plume for his helm."

"It all *sounds* good, but I don't know."

"What do you have to lose?"

Dr. Jang entered the commands over the frozen battlefield. "Let's see what happens."

He gestured, and the battle exploded to life. The cavalry rushed in, stopped at the fire, and was lured into a hail of arrows. The computer, struggling with three distinct targets, emulated panic remarkably. The cavalry spun and twisted as arrows tore through armor and horses in a well-orchestrated ballet of terror and slaughter. Men fell from their mounts, horses trampled the living and dead alike, and only the commander managed to scurry for cover behind a rock.

"Wow," Dr. Jang exhaled, "it looks like a totally different battle. These guys just rode into the wrong door at a slaughterhouse."

"Pause it. We still have to take over the base."

"Yeah, and we're still outnumbered."

"Scroll over to the side again. What was that structure I saw earlier?"

Dr. Jang scrolled to the right of the main base. "You mean the supply depot? If you take it over, they get confused for a few seconds, but it doesn't help much."

"Will the men come out of the main fortress if assistance is needed at the supply base?"

"Yeah, if you are taking too long to beat the supply captains, or if you set the place on fire, but you have to do that from the inside."

"Hmm," Cyrus thought for a moment, "can your archers help with the fire attack?"

"If you combine them with the fire attack unit, they can launch flaming arrows from a distance."

"Okay, send your archers to this hill here." Cyrus let a feeble yawn escape as he pointed out the hill in front of the supply depot. "Rush your foot soldiers to the front then stop. When the gates to the depot open, fire your arrows inside. If the men here are as clumsy as the cavalry, they will stumble over themselves trying to figure out whether the fire or your foot soldiers are more important. Have the foot soldiers run to the back of the supply depot, and when the reinforcements come, set another fire behind them and rain arrows down on them from the hill."

Dr. Jang chuckled as he entered commands into the game. "We sure are setting a lot of things on fire."

"Even people fascinated with fire are afraid of it. I'd say it's one of the most fearsome things in the human imagination because, one way or the other, everything burns. The trick is getting something warmed up enough to reach its flash point, but once it does burn, it ain't coming back. Fire is decisive, unforgiving, and permanent."

Dr. Jang's eyes focused on Cyrus's rather intently for a brief moment then relaxed as he let out a hybrid sigh-chuckle. He started to say something, reconsidered, then said it anyway, "You ever say anything like that to anyone who *didn't* think you were a twisted freebirth after you said it?"

"I said something like that to my wife once, but she was already convinced I was a twisted freebirth."

"If this scheme of yours works, twisted freebirth or not, you have my respect." Dr. Jang turned back to finish the commands but stopped. "Just do me a favor. Don't tell anyone about me hacking this game into the system."

"If anyone hears it, it won't be from me, but you're gonna have trouble keeping it from anyone else who ventures in here to burn the midnight oil."

"Honestly, I don't mind if anyone else knows or even plays. That would be stellar if they did. I just don't want Dr. Villichez to find out. That guy reminds me too much of my *halabagi*." Dr. Jang exhaled loudly and set the battle in motion, awaiting the conflagration that would push his streamer-sporting adversary to his flash point.

six

—*Darius, how did you score in the seventy-fourth percentile?*
—*I don't know.*
—*You don't know? What does that mean, 'you don't know?' I would think between the two of us you would have the clearest idea. Don't tell me you don't know.*
—*Why are you so serious? It's just seventy-four. It's still above average.*
—*Above average? Where is this coming from? How would you feel if I took your HoloStation and gave you a Viewdeck instead?*
—*I don't know.*
—*You don't know again, huh? Darius, 'I don't know' is the stupid man's mantra when he's backed into a corner. You know full-well what you would feel like if you had to play vids on a Viewdeck. You wouldn't like it, would you?*
—*I don...*
—*Don't you say it, boy. You own up. You answer me like a man and stop dodging. Would you like it if someone took your HoloStation and gave you a Viewdeck?*
—*I guess a Viewdeck is okay if all you got is a Viewdeck. But if I had a HoloStation, especially a HoloStation Prime, and it got traded for a Viewdeck, I guess I wouldn't like it much.*
—*Why?*
—*Because a Viewdeck is bunkus compared to a HoloStation.*
—*Exactly. And here you are, a nominee for the Rothschild Laureate, and you're handing me scores like a Freeschooler.*
—*You said there's nothing wrong with Freeschool.*
—*I did. Just like you said there's nothing wrong with a Viewdeck, but backtracking is...what's the word? Bunkus.*
—*I don't get it. Why do I have to be the best all the time? Why don't I get a break?*
—*You get a break when the job's done, son. It's that simple. And you have to be the best because you* are *the best—at least better than most when it comes to understanding and reasoning.*

—But the job's hard, and it goes on forever. As soon as one thing's done, there's some other boring thing to do. It's not fair.

—Fair? What's not fair is being given the gift of aptitude and not using it. There's some kid right now wishing he were half as capable as you. Why does that Genivere Lim girl always beat you, huh? Do you even know?

—Please Dada, not again.

—Yes, again. Again and again and again until you get it. It's because you don't have the killer instinct—because you don't know how to get the job done under tough circumstances—not because she's smarter than you but because she wants it more. She needs it just to get through the day. She needs it because she isn't smarter, and that's all she has to cling to.

—Then she can have it.

—And she will. And you, you will always be second seed.

—Maybe second seed is enough.

—You ever wonder why I never bought you the HoloStation Prime you're always asking for? It's because you don't deserve it because you don't get the job done.

—I don't see what that has to do with what you're talking about.

—And that's precisely why you still have a HoloStation Beta. The day you realize that sometimes you have to do things you don't want to get the things you do want, that will be the day I get you anything you ask for within my power.

—And when will that be?

—Ask yourself.

• • • • •

As Cyrus hit the ground, pain struck out from his shoulder blade, through his wrist and hand, and out his fingers, letting him know immediately that something had gone wrong. He rolled over the opposite shoulder to his feet and turned to face Dr. Tanner, exhaling starkly and extending his left arm in front of him in a defensive stance as his right arm hung limply against his side.

"That doesn't look good," Dr. Tanner relaxed his stance.

"I can still fight." Cyrus lunged forward with a kick, then, as Tanner blocked, Cyrus ducked around to the left and fired a left hook beneath Tanner's elbow. Tanner dodged to the side as the punch nicked his shirttail.

"Wasn't expecting…" his sentence was cut short as he dodged back to his right under another kick. As Tanner stepped forward to counter, Cyrus launched himself into the air, using his momentum to bring his left foot completely around. Already moving forward, Tanner had to let his front leg collapse under his weight to get under the kick. Cyrus's foot grazed Tanner's lip as he landed. The momentum whipped Cyrus's dislocated arm around, smashing his wrist into Tanner's temple.

The collision snapped Tanner's head to the side, and his body, already off balance, crumpled to the ground. Cold, sharp nettles of pain shot from Cyrus's rotator cuff in an arc, slicing through his elbow and into his fingers, leaving a glacial numbness in its wake. Then, the glacier shattered, and pain washed over his entire body in a deluge. As Cyrus's body collapsed, he imagined he could feel his consciousness, along with the pain, spilling out onto the body of his fallen adversary.

• • • • •

"I hate it when you move your queen out in the opening."

"The only reason I move my queen out in the opening is because I know you hate it."

Tanner rubbed his jaw lightly as he studied the chessboard. "My jaw still hurts," he said, stretching his mouth as he advanced his king-side knight.

"My shoulder's not doing too well either." Cyrus lightly massaged his right shoulder as he considered his next move.

"Are you always this mean, or do I just bring the best out of you?" Tanner adjusted his jaw again.

"You force me to raise the bar because you know what you're doing. Honestly, I have to step outside of myself to even think about beating you, kung fu, chess, or otherwise. At least when sparring, I can pretty much forget about winning unless you slack off."

"But it's not all about winning or losing."

"It isn't, but I try to avoid making a habit of losing." Cyrus advanced his king-side bishop.

"Sounds like pride to me." Tanner had seen this unorthodox opening before and had lost to it, yet he still felt unprepared.

"Maybe, but it's the only thing that gets me through some days."

"You know they say, 'Pride comes before a fall.'" Tanner advanced his queen's pawn one space ahead. He took a different approach than the last game in hopes it would open room for his attack.

"That's funny. I don't plan on falling *without* mine." Cyrus moved his queen-side knight's pawn a space ahead, defending his bishop.

Tanner shook his head. "Always something new with you. You have to be the most unorthodox chess player I have ever lost to."

"I never claimed to be a chess player."

"That doesn't make any sense." Tanner was in a choke hold. All the moves he would have wanted to make had been taken away from him. He moved his queen-side bishop ahead one space. It was safe, but it felt like a waste. Again his opening gamut was shot from the second move.

Cyrus could see the lines stretching across Tanner's forehead. Frustration manifested itself on his brow the same way it did on Darius's face.

"I'm glad you brought a corporeal chessboard. The holographic chessboards are so...alienating." Cyrus looked at the board as if the key to his next move lay somehow beneath it.

"What do you mean?"

"Holographic pieces are so fleeting. They get captured, and they disappear. You speak a command, and they come back." Cyrus lifted his queen off the board and held it by the head. "Here, you lose a piece, you feel it. When it's over, the king hits the board, and the sound resonates through the air and makes you painfully aware of what you just lost." His last words barely escaped the air in front of his lips. The queen teetered then settled between two squares as he set it back on the board. "Let's finish later." Cyrus stood and walked to the door, his head hung lower than when he walked in.

● ● ● ● ●

"Here, put this on." Dr. Davidson removed two gas masks from his backpack and handed one to Cyrus.

Cyrus looked at him as if he had just handed him a birth control calendar. "What the heck am I supposed to do with this?"

"Put it on your face. Unless you want to pass out from methane inhalation." The snap of the filtered mask to Dr. Davidson's face punctuated his sentence.

"I don't smell anything," Cyrus added as he fastened his mask to his face; he wasn't the type to have to get hit with the hammer to believe it hurt.

"That's because pure methane is odorless. The smell comes from additives that make leak detection easier." Dr. Davidson adjusted his hip waders and put his hand near the button to open the door.

"So this...poo gas...helps make our food?" Cyrus asked, the mask amplifying his muffled voice.

"No, the methane is used for ambient heat and cooking, which creates CO2 and water that are used in the hydroponic mist. The room we are about to go into stores our waste products until they are broken down and recycled. Once we land, this room will help make compost we can use to start agriculture on the planet."

When the door opened, Cyrus was sure he could smell the funk of the room through the filtered mask. A mesh catwalk rimmed the circular room and separated the two scientists from the slowly churning unction of a little more than three years of accumulated muck. As Cyrus looked apprehensively at the swirling lake of filth, he asked, "I'm curious. What about me made me the best candidate to muck about with you in this god-forsaken lavpool?"

"Honestly, because for some reason, I like you more than anyone else on the ship. You're honest, almost to a fault, but I can respect that. And you don't seem to believe in ulterior agendas."

"So, do you ask everyone to root through a steaming vat of whipped piss and shit on the first date, or is that reserved only for true love?"

Dr. Davidson's visor clouded as laughter erupted through the mask. He leaned against his sifting pole and waited for the involuntary convulsions to subside. "See, that's what I mean. You can make a man belly-ache even standing in the expelled bowels of nineteen other men. That, and you seem like the type to get the job done no matter how abhorrent."

"Fair enough," Cyrus said, laughing a bit himself. "So exactly why are we here?"

"The Shipmate's systems keep everything pretty much in order, but we still have to make routine checks to make sure the Shipmate isn't malfunctioning. Also, this particular part of the ship will be vitally important on the planet as far as terraforming goes, so I want to train someone I can trust to share that responsibility with me. As an added bonus, it would be nice if that person had enough fortitude to hold his lunch if we found an undigested watermelon seed or two."

"Well, I can promise you I can hold my lunch. However, if we find a watermelon seed in the sewer of a ship that has seen neither vine nor fruit of a watermelon plant in 195 years, I'm grabbing Dr. Tanner's Bible, and I'm leaving, and you can root in piss and shit all by yourself."

Dr. Davidson shook his head, his visor fogging up again, "You see, never a dull moment around you Chamberlain. Not one second."

• • • • •

Dr. Tanner sat reading a corporeal Bible as Cyrus entered the room.

Cyrus stopped for a moment, looked a little lost, and then spoke, "I wanted to thank you for not being offended earlier."

"Offended at what?"

"The distance."

"I figured you would come around eventually."

"If I do, it will be a first. You can mark the date in that ephemeris of yours."

"I'll keep my stylus handy."

• • • • •

The codex looked like the Unified Interplanetary Launch Platform on Eros where the Paracelsus had embarked, only the scientists that had then been confined to the mechanized wombs slowing their bodily functions to the cusp of death now filled the cubicles and holostations instead of the engineers and technicians that had catapulted their inert bodies into the virgin depths of space.

They busily hovered over their respective holograms, each showing different parts of the same battlefield.

"We need to do something about this guy!" Dr. Milliken yelled to Dr. Koresh in the cubicle next to him.

"He can't hold us back forever," Dr. Koresh replied in a slightly calmer, yet still agitated, voice.

Another cry came from across the room, "What the heck? Why are my peasants dying?" Dr. Jang was frantically scanning the battlefield for the source of his problems. He noticed the water source leading into his castle was a mere trickle. "How the..." he shifted down the hologram, following the creek that should have been a river. A kilometer upriver, four dams were built in succession with cavalry and archers protecting them—Dr. Chamberlain's cavalry and archers. "You underdeveloped pod spawn!" Jang exclaimed. He scrolled along the battlefield and found Cyrus's troops engaged with Dr. Koresh's men at the conflagration that had been Koresh's main supply depot.

Jang scrolled back to his castle, selected his vanguard, and ordered them to destroy the dams and the force surrounding them. His castle gates flew open, and his three van leaders charged out into a maelstrom of arrows from behind either hill across from the castle. Unprepared, Jang's men collapsed in a heap of carnage just beyond the portcullis, and the two archer units, plus a unit of infantry that had been hiding, rushed in and took the castle.

A charged cry of, "Damn you, Chamberlain!" reverberated above the clamor. Dr. Jang had not realized how ludicrous his outburst was until the others began snickering. He was sure Cyrus had heard him, but he did not respond. Jang set his head on his cubicle as the death cries of his last bastion subsided. He heard a beep from the cubicle as a private message swept across the hologram. Evidently, Dr. Jang's demise had been so fast the system had not registered it before the message was sent. The message read, "Let's pool our forces and attack him at all at once." It was too late for Jang's army, but he scrolled through the hologram to watch the battle as an observer. Dr. Koresh lowered his drawbridge and sent out the bulk of his forces, leaving only a few foot soldiers to defend the fort. Across the hologram, Davidson's portcullis opened, and his force rushed out as well.

One by one, the others' forces surrounded Cyrus's original keep that only housed a small group of men because he had extended himself across the battlefield. Cyrus was producing new troops with Jang's old fort and the forts of two other players that had been routed, but these new troops were too far away. Jang smiled through his own frustration. The end was near for Cyrus, and his other troops would not be able to save him in time.

Jang scrolled over to another fort, and he caught a glimmer of something odd as the doors closed. "Wait a second," he said to himself and zoomed into the corner of the fort where he saw a hint of ruddy brown in the corner—the same ruddy brown on the capes of Cyrus's elite foot soldiers.

Frantically, Jang's hand moved over the laser keyboard to send a message of warning, but he was in observer mode and was locked out.

He looked around the battlefield. The troops formed a ring around Cyrus's main castle and began their advance, but each of the other players had at least three of Cyrus's elite soldiers inside their own gates. Only, Cyrus's soldiers weren't attacking.

The onslaught on Cyrus's main base commenced, and it was clear that his forces would not be able to hold out for long, but no one seemed to notice the men lurking in their bases.

Jang couldn't hold it in any longer. "Hey, he's already..."

But it was too late. By the time the warnings that their main bases were under attack flashed across their holograms, it was already over. Cyrus's men stood in the center of each of the bases waving the other teams' standards over their heads. A furor of grumbles, sighs, and curse words in various languages filled the room. Dr. Jang was already next to Cyrus as he rose calmly from his chair. "You are a sneaky bastard," Jang said as he extended his hand.

"Thank you," Cyrus said as he shook firmly then yawned. "Now I think I can sleep soundly."

"Sleep? I'm gonna have stupid gram cursors and foot soldiers dancing around in my head all night until I figure out a way to beat you."

Cyrus laughed as he moved toward the entrance as some left, and some moved to shake his hand. "Well, I feel sorry for you."

"Why's that?" Jang asked as Cyrus received a handshake and pat on the back from Davidson.

Cyrus turned his attention back to Jang and smiled, "Because you're going to have to miss more than one night of sleep before you can beat me at being a sneaky bastard." Cyrus winked and then made his way through the mix of admiring and dejected scientists that moved to congratulate him on his victory.

seven

—Dada, I got something to ask you.

—What is it, Dari?

—Something Scott Seal said in class today kinda bothered me.

—Okay.

—He said I was arrogant and that I had a big head, but I don't feel arrogant, and I don't really think my head is that much bigger than anyone else's. What do you think? Tell the truth, Dada.

—I think Scott Seal needs to watch what he says about other people's heads. I've seen his head. I'd be surprised if he can wear anything except button-up shirts.

—Come on, Dada, I'm serious.

—Okay, Dari. Well, I think is that simple people like to use the word arrogant when they feel like they are out of their depth.

—I don't get it.

—Big-headed is just a figure of speech to describe someone who thinks they are better than someone else, but I say, if you are better at whatever it is, not only should you not have to act ashamed, but you should get credit for it.

—Okay, I get that, but how can that help me deal with other people?

—You know that Conquest game you love to play so much? On the Chinese Warring States period levels, the officers all have big hats. Why?

—So you can see the generals on the battlefield, I would guess.

—Exactly. But unlike our society, there, you were awarded higher rank by how well you did what you said you could do—which, in their case, was how much butt you kicked. So if you were on a raging battlefield, and you looked across the horizon and saw a giant hat with feathers and all other manners of gaudy extensions, you checked the size of your own hat, and if it wasn't big enough, you didn't go over there.

—Unless you wanted your butt kicked.

—And who wants that, right?

—So I think what you're saying is, it doesn't matter how big your head is as long as it still fits your hat.

—Precisely. But at the same time, remember anyone can have his hat knocked off

70

his head, and if you piss enough people off, they'll show up at your house with
pitchforks and torches like in those old two-D monster vids.
—What if your hat is big enough to take them all?
—Son, note my words and note them well, there are men who have stood
against the world in the past, and men that will in the future, but no man's hat
is so big that he can stand there forever. No one.
—Not even yours, Dada?
—Not even close.

• • • • •

Cyrus shuffled through the datadeck looking for a book by
Richard Feynman he remembered from the Arcology. It was a rather
antiquated book, but it contained the equation he needed for his
computations.

As it was not after lights-out, the lab was not swarming with scientists
engaging in interstellar warfare, ambushing one another with old-era
tanks, or filling the moats of each others' keeps while archers buffeted
the inhabitants with hails of flaming arrows. Only a couple scientists
were working on projects on the opposite side of the codex.

Suddenly, Dr. Jang appeared behind Cyrus. "You playing CotA
tonight?" he asked as he brushing his bangs to the left side of his head.

Cyrus didn't know if he had overlooked Dr. Jang working, or if he
had been so engrossed in his work that he hadn't noticed him come
through the entrance, but he was decidedly unnerved by his own lack
of awareness. "Where in blistering hell did you come from?"

"Ha," Jang laughed to himself, "unsettled are we? No worries, I was
here when you got here, but I have a reputation for being practically
invisible when I don't want to be bothered. My last girlfriend wondered
if I even breathed when I was working. Honestly, I couldn't tell you."

"Well, if you are that eager to get trounced tonight, I suppose I
could oblige you."

"Your winning streak can't last forever."

"Maybe, but I assure you, it won't end tonight, and definitely not
by your sneaky, 'I-don't-breathe-when-I-don't-want-to-be-bothered'
hand."

"We'll see, Chamberlain. We'll see." Jang brushed his bangs from
his face again and stooped a little to look at the holographic monitor
that floated in the air in front of Cyrus. "What are you working on?"
Jang gave him a pat on the shoulder. "Hope you're sharpening up your

game. Wouldn't want to make the champion look like unfledged pod-spawn."

Cyrus turned a sharp look at Jang's hand as it still rested on his shoulder, grabbed Jang's index finger as if his hand was covered in grime, and gingerly removed it. "You know I liked you more when you were mousy and kept all that lab waste to yourself." Cyrus looked him in the eye and returned the smile. "I was trying to find an equation in an old Feynman book, but it's eluding me."

"Why don't you ask Feynman himself?"

"You got any more of whatever you've been inhaling over there invisi-boy? Unless you're planning on holding some sort of séance, Feynman's as inaccessible as all this newfound skill you plan on using tonight."

"Well, for once, you might be right. Feynman, much like your military doom, is closer than you think." Dr. Jang ushered Cyrus aside. "Watch and learn, young Novitiate."

Dr. Jang exited out of the normal interface into the datadeck backbone. A prompt appeared before them, and he entered the words 'avatar folder' on the laser keyboard on the desk. "You can find this folder in the hierarchical menu, but this is much faster."

"What is an avatar?"

A color wheel with colors that alternated in a pattern as the information loaded appeared in the lower right-hand corner of the image. "An avatar is an interactive personality emulator that uses fuzzy logic to convey information in a more direct manner than any previous datadeck interface."

"You know, I haven't been keeping up with my tech braniac lessons, so I'd prefer you translate that into High Common, at the very least."

The datadeck hologram went blank as the speakers in the cubicle asked in a warm, grandfatherly voice that sounded remarkably like Dr. Villichez, "Whom would you like to meet?"

"Perhaps, it is better to show than tell." Dr. Jang smiled somewhat smugly then turned back to the cubicle. "Richard Feynman."

The system loaded for a moment and then revealed the face of a bushy-haired man in his fifties. Cyrus recognized him instantly. "Good evening Dr. Chamberlain. How may I assist you today?"

For a moment, Cyrus was stunned. "Ask your question," Jang said, opening his palm toward the bust on the hologram in front of them.

Cyrus turned back to the image of the physicist. "I'm looking to configure the comm-sat and the scanning satellite we're going to deploy before we land," Cyrus paused for a moment and turned to Dr. Jang, "Will he know what a comm-sat is?"

"He's linked into the other systems on the ship, so he should be able to reference them."

Cyrus turned back to the image of Feynman. "I need to check my computations against some of your equations for nanotechnology—particularly your work on density functional theory and testing of reaction sequences. I couldn't find them in any of your papers, but I know I've read them before."

Feynman's disembodied head tilted back as he sounded an amused chuckle. "I helped start the push into nanotechnology, but I cannot take credit for those equations. They were developed ten years after I left this world. They were the works of two gentlemen, a Stephen Walch and Ralph Merkle. They were awarded the Feynman Prize for experimental work in 1998 for those equations. I do not believe they have avatars on this system, but I do remember the equations myself. Here, I will write them down for you." Feynman's head recessed into the depths of the cubicle, and a blank white page appeared between Cyrus and Feynman and began to fill with numbers, symbols, and figures.

"I took the liberty of saving the equations in your personal menu so you can reference them at your leisure," Feynman added from behind the formula. "Is there anything else I can help you with?"

Cyrus looked at Dr. Jang. "Wow, he even makes facial expressions."

Before Jang could comment, Feynman himself chimed in, "It is truly amazing the progress that has been made in the last five hundred years in quantum computing and nanotechnology. I personally am very impressed."

Cyrus laughed. "This is absolutely ingenious—light-years ahead of anything I've ever seen."

"Thank you." Jang said, smiling.

"You created this?"

"Well, not by myself." the color that filled his cheeks made him look even ten years younger. It was no wonder to Cyrus why the ladies would have liked him. Jang looked away momentarily then shook his hair to the side as he turned back again. "Dr. Villichez is the real genius. His questions and psychological profiling system are the very backbone of the software. The specs for the neural mapping came from Dr. Winberg. It took us two years to get the right algorithms down and to create a development interface to link with Villichez's profiling system. Once we finally got ahold of the Agamemnon Drei

Quantum processor, we had the power to actually put it all together. Then, it was just the scanning and compilation of material. We would never have been able to get the backing if they hadn't been trying to get everything together for this expedition."

"I thought the Agamemnon processor was just barely in the Zwei generation."

"It was, but they made a special prototype for integration into the Shipmate system here. It's a little bigger than they would ever release on Earth, but it's about twenty times more stable."

"So you worked with Villichez and Winberg before the expedition?"

"I worked with Villichez directly for about five years, but Winberg only sent us diagrams and specifications for mimicking the human brain. I only talked to him maybe twice during the whole process."

"So who else do we have stored in this thing?" Cyrus asked turning back toward the cubicle. He thanked the Feynman image and closed the program.

"Honestly, I don't remember, but the datadeck has the entire Unified Council Library stored in it, and I know Villichez and his lab mapped over five hundred profiles, both living and deceased. I'm pretty sure just about anyone of major importance to academia, past or contemporary should be accessible. If not, someone related should be able to cross-reference the information into the datastream. There are also entries for each of us, but our journals and papers are communicated by other scientists. Villichez thought it was a little too creepy to have our likenesses when we are present on the ship, and if one of us doesn't make it, he thought it even creepier."

"You guys really went balls-out for us eggheads, didn't you?"

"Well, that's what I do. I keep my balls out just for you." Jang laughed. "Besides, I know we stand a chance of finding out more about young Earth by studying Asha, but the environment there sounds more like the *end* of the world to me. So if I'm going to hurtle through space on a one-way ticket to probable damnation, I want to take as much information with me as I can."

"One-way ticket to probable damnation? Well-said."

"Thank you." Jang nodded and brushed the side of his nose with his thumb.

"You're welcome. Sounds a lot like what's gonna happen to you tonight if you show up at that grungy cubicle of yours and log into Conquest."

"Sounds like someone's getting a little big for his britches."

Cyrus looked down and melodramatically surveyed the waistband of his jumpsuit. "Nah, my britches fit me plenty fine."

• • • • •

"Your reign of terror is coming to an end!" Dr. Jang reported across the lab to Cyrus, who ignored his threats as usual. For the fourth time in as many months, all the scientists who had gathered at night to play Conquest of the Ages assembled to compete for the Paracelsine Cup—a cracked flagon that Dr. Milliken stole from the dinner table one day and etched on the words 'Conquest of the Paracelsus.' The last Saturday of each month cycle, they would all assemble and continue to play until only one player remained. But the cup had spent the entire four months sitting on Cyrus's desk, holding down the cleaning card the Shipmate left each week. So far, this night was no different than the others—each of the players tried to gain their foothold in their territory before lashing out at others, and Cyrus had consistently moved in with some surprise attack to slow down one scientist or another. Today, he had set the forests Milliken used for building resources ablaze, and he had dug a moat around Davidson's farms while he was attacking Jang so Davidson's peasants could not harvest food for his soldiers. Dr. Cohn's foot soldiers were preoccupied with an annoying keep that Cyrus had erected in front of his mineral mine specifically to impede his construction.

Cyrus sat in his corner cubicle, quiet and focused. He was a little concerned because Jang, who normally came at him like a Manifest-Destined crusader sacking the last pagan fortress on the planet, was particularly conservative for someone so confident earlier in the day cycle. Cyrus kept his vanguard in his main stronghold and sequestered his champions to a cave opening he had hidden with an observation tower.

Cyrus played his normal, unpredictable game with fresh new tricks. Then, as Cyrus's cavalry engaged Dr. Milliken's and Dr. Koresh's combined infantries in a heated skirmish, an attack was launched from either side of his main stronghold. Jang's infantry had amassed in front of the castle, quickly filled the moat, and was now bashing relentlessly at the gate. From the rear, a battery of ballistae and catapults buffeted the back wall—an excellent attack, but not unstoppable.

Cyrus had kept his siege engines inside his stronghold as a precaution, and they returned fire on the engines in the rear. Luckily, Jang's engines, because of their angle of attack, could only hit the rear wall of the castle. Comfortable in his defenses and preoccupied with smoking Koresh out of his main fortress, Cyrus sent a small but strong group of foot soldiers and cavalry to eliminate the annoying engines at his rear flank.

Koresh's men ran for the hills, fleeing desperately with their standard to keep from being eliminated from the match. Cyrus saw *where* they were running to and realized it was a trap. And when the soldiers Cyrus had sent to stop Jang's siege engines were ambushed by the men that should have been *operating* the siege engines, Cyrus realized exactly how much effort was put into the setup. On closer inspection, the siege engines were out of place—two time-periods out of place. They were fully automatic and only needed two peasants to operate each, rather than the complement of four field captains and four foot that they should have required. No wonder Jang was so eager. Cyrus was spread thin from the monkey chase at Koresh's fortress, and now, a good portion of Cyrus's vanguard was being slaughtered right in front of him.

But it was far from over. Cyrus issued commands to the peasants that were harvesting wood in the forest around his base. The men that ambushed his defenses came out of the hills and made their way to the front of his fortress. They had already constructed a battering ram and had made short order of the door, but as they rushed in and dispatched the defenders of the base, they discovered Cyrus's standard was not there. By the time Jang realized Cyrus's lumberjacks were hacking to pieces the unarmed peasants that operated his bootleg siege engines, Jang's own engines were already being used against the fortress he now occupied. The engines quickly finished what Jang had started, destroying Cyrus's former keep and taking Jang's best men with it. After the destruction was over, Cyrus left the engines where they were because they were well out of the fray.

Cyrus had routed Dr. Cohn and Davidson's forces earlier, and Torvald was fighting a losing battle against the forces Cyrus had sent just before Jang's anachronistic siege engines had appeared. And while Cyrus attempted to recover from the assault on his main fortress, Jang and Koresh's combined forces turned on Milliken.

Jang's men scoured the battlefield in search of Cyrus's standard bearers while Koresh replenished his ranks. Then, suddenly, a message went through to the three remaining scientists' cubicles reading, 'C. Chamberlain:'s forces have been eliminated.'

Jang belted a stream of curses in Korean. He was so incensed that he didn't notice the message was in the wrong color. He didn't wait until his anger subsided to turn on Koresh while uttering something in mixed Korean and English to the effect of, "The cup is still mine!"

But Jang had let Dr. Koresh build up for too long. His forces were formidable, and since they were sharing fortresses, the battle quickly became miserable. Jang had created more of his bootleg siege engines and was now using peasants to bombard Koresh's vanguard in a fortress Jang had lent him, which Koresh was now trapped inside because Jang had locked the gate. At the same time, Jang sent a search party to finish off Torvald. As soon as Jang's soldiers routed Torvald and hoisted his standard above their heads, Cyrus's assassins appeared from the shadows inside Torvald's fortress and killed the unsuspecting soldiers with alarming speed.

"What the hell!" Jang yelled from his cubicle. "Assassins?" It was the first time assassins had been used in a public match because they were considered too weak under normal circumstances. Because assassins did not wear team colors, Jang did not realize Cyrus was still active until Cyrus's peasants were using the imported siege engines to take out Jang's catapults and ballistae that were attacking Koresh's men.

Jang, having no idea how Cyrus was even still alive, gave up looking for Cyrus's standard. He regrouped all his troops in front of his main fortress as the siege engines Cyrus had commandeered positioned themselves for attack.

Jang was entering the commands to launch a fire attack against the ill-equipped peasants operating the siege engines when, from the shadows of the mineral mine that Cyrus had blocked with a previously useless, but annoying, keep, a horde of infantry flooded the battlefield. They completely swarmed Jang's better equipped, but less numerous, army. The battle was fierce and bloody on both sides, but Jang's unprepared forces could not hold back the onslaught. Plus, preoccupied with what seemed like a myriad of foot soldiers, Jang could not stop the siege engines that crumbled the walls of his last fortress. When it was all over, Cyrus's peasants cakewalked into the remains of the keep and hoisted Jang's standard high.

There was a light thump as Jang let his head fall to the cubicle top in defeat. He didn't notice the words, 'T. Jang's forces have been eliminated,' scrolling across his cubicle in bright red—the color they were supposed to be.

Cyrus sat back in his chair relieved. He didn't realize how nervous he had been until a chill moved slowly through his body, tracing the path of the subsiding adrenalin in his blood. He let the wave of standing hairs relax him as he closed his eyes. He didn't realize how much winning meant to him until it looked like it might not happen. He accepted the back-pats and kudos that came his way as the other players shuffled out of the codex. He didn't open his eyes until one hand lingered on his shoulder. He turned and Jang was standing over him, offering him the Paracelsine Cup. "Don't know exactly how you managed to win again, but I'm somewhat glad. I don't think it would have set well winning this way."

Cyrus nodded, accepted the cup, and shook Jang's hand. "You gave me a run for my credits this time."

As they released hands, Jang sat on the cubicle. "Porting those catapults over seemed like a good idea at the time, but how did you know you could use them against me?"

"I didn't, but in the level they came from, there are no peasants. You need specialized jobbers to operate the siege engines. That's why we never play that level in the public matches—takes too long to build up the specialty classes. Whatever port you used had to have had controls that were somewhat ubiquitous. I gambled that you hadn't put a restriction on them so that only your peasants could use them, and my gamble paid off."

"I feel bad because I cheated."

"Well, for better or worse, half of the Unification War was won by breaking the rules." Cyrus held the cup. "A true champion handles whatever is thrown at him in stride."

"That makes sense," Jang said as Cyrus set the cup back on the cubicle, "But I still don't know how you faked your elimination."

"Well, that was easy. You were so intent on finding my standard and beating me that you didn't notice the colon after my name and the color of the public message that I sent. All I did was type apostrophe 's' and 'forces have been eliminated,' hoping you would take the bait and turn on Koresh because even with the infantry I was rush-building in the mine, there was no way I could stop both of you."

"I'm impressed." Jang brushed his hair behind his ear. "I don't feel so bad about losing now."

Cyrus stood with the cup and patted Jang on his back. "Well, the day you *do* take the cup, you'll know it won't be because I fell for some hound-washed scheme. It'll be because you beat me and you deserve it." He tipped the cup to Jang. "Until then, if you want to have a good image of it for your dreams, it will be in my room, on *my* desk." Cyrus smiled and left. His smile was genuine, not smug or snide, and Jang sighed, knowing that as diplomatic as Cyrus had been about the cheating, he meant every word he had just said, and if he had disapproved, he would have said much more.

• • • • •

"What do you miss the most from Earth?" Tanner asked as he hovered over his ephemeris.

"It's hard to say. I don't really miss Earth all that much. Even with Dr. Windbag on the ship, I've had fewer arguments in the past year than I would have had in a week back there. I know today being the anniversary and all has made a lot of us homesick, but apart from my son, I say good riddance to that festering ball of misery and woe."

Tanner set his stylus on the tablet in his lap. "You don't miss your wife?" He looked concerned.

"There are some days where I remember the good times, but then I remember I know better." Cyrus opened his hands, stretched his fingers, and then looked down at his palms. "I don't regret the time I spent, I just..." Cyrus brushed his hand across his face.

"You're not gonna get distant on me again are you?"

"No, it's not just that. I just can't help feeling like I ran away."

"Well, maybe you did, and maybe you didn't, but you're here now, and there's no way we can turn this monkey cage around, so just remember to look forward."

Cyrus let his hand slowly slide from his face. "You know what I miss the most, other than Darius? My conversations with my friend from Laureateship—Dr. Alexander Kalem."

"I'm sure I've heard that name before."

"Most likely. He's a professor of Near Eastern philosophy at the Arcology of Los Angeles. He was in Chicago for a long while after we matriculated, but he moved to Los Angeles because his lungs could not take the mix of cold and smog, and the newly terra-formed Los Angeles was a perfect place for a convalescing asthmatic. There were other Arcologies he could have gone to, but I think he really moved to be closer to someone he could talk to and not have to pick his words."

"Yeah, I could see people who are picky about words being a little unnerved around you. I see it at least once or twice a week here." Tanner smiled.

"It *was* nice to just be able to say whatever was on my mind and not have to qualify it—to just be...I dunno...understood—whether I was agreed with or not. I never got that with anyone else—not even Feralynn. Actually, the first conversation Feralynn and I ever had was an argument. She was studying with Xander for a class that had something to do with Aryans, I believe. I had come to meet him at the cafeteria where they were studying to get some money from him that he owed me. He and Feralynn were talking about the cost of running prototype atmospheric processors to clean the air in Los Angeles and Pittsburg. I said something to the effect of, 'If only poor people were dying from the deteriorating air quality, they would just increase production in the factories and cut their losses, and that only when the rich people started dying would they even bother.' Well, it turned out her uncle was one of the first publicized victims of the pneumatic consumption that came from the smog, and her father's involvement was why they had been talking about it in the first place. After I removed my foot from my mouth, I joined the conversation, but it wasn't for another month or so that we started to talk to each other when Xander wasn't there. Xander would always joke that the first thing my wife ever said about me was that I was an arrogant hound's ass."

"Wait a second," Tanner interrupted, "Xander is what you call him? With an 'X'? He's X. Kalem, the author of the book on the links between Zoroastrianism and the Rig Vedas?"

"The very same."

"That's where I've heard the name. Wait, is his name Alexander or Xander?"

"Well, Uncle Xander is what Darius called him since he learned to talk. Guess it's hard to say 'Alex' with no front teeth." Cyrus paused for a moment. "Funny, Xander and I hated each other when we first met, but I think it was because we could see our own shortcomings in the other, and that mirror was not kind. Over time, we found that even though we were very different people, we shared something pretty deep. I could honestly say, I would not have made it out of the Arcology if it wasn't for him."

"Surprised he wasn't picked to be on this journey."

"Well, he's one of those people that Winberg says gets paid to talk. Besides, he is coming on the Damocles and bringing Darius and Feralynn with him."

"That will be an interesting family reunion. One I don't want to miss."

"Yeah, I..." Cyrus looked as if the words he had intended to say had fallen back down his throat. "I just hope the distance gives Feralynn and me time to miss each other. It just bothers me that even after this long, she's the one I miss the least."

"I guess if you miss her at all, there is some hope."

"You know, my time on this ship has reminded me of a lot of things I had forgotten on Earth, and it's taught me some I don't think I ever really knew, but one thing that has unfortunately eluded the grand, enlightening lesson plan is hope."

"For your sake, I pray that rubric surfaces before all your piss and vinegar runs out." Tanner smiled, but there was worry in his eyes.

"Well then, I believe I have some time because my reservoir of piss and vinegar ain't drying up by damn sight."

eight

—*Dari, what's wrong?*
—*Nothing.*
—*Come on, Dari. If you don't want to talk about it, say, 'I don't want to talk about it.' Don't tell me 'nothing' when I can clearly see* something *has you upset.*
—*Sorry, Dada.*
—*No need for apologies. Did something happen at school today?*
—*Yeah, kind of. Well, not really—not yet anyways. I'm just...a little worried.*
—*Worried about what?*
—*Terry Gallager.*
—*What did he do now?*
—*He says if I don't bring him ten creds tomorrow, he's gonna beat me up and make me lick the lav seat.*
—*Hmm. He sounds pretty creative for a lab monkey.*
—*I guess.*
—*Tell me, what is so scary about this Terry kid anyways? I've seen him. He's no juggernaut.*
—*Maybe not to you cuz you're so big, but to me, he's so mean and strong.*
—*You look here. I don't care how big he is or how strong he's supposed to be. He can't make you do anything you don't want to do. And if he tries to force your hand, you warn him. If he doesn't pay your warning any mind, and he puts his hands on you, you hit him in his throat. I guarantee he won't bother you again.*
—*But Miss Hasabe will get upset. She'll send me to the Disciplinarian.*
—*If this thing does go down tomorrow, and you get sent to the Disciplinarian, you have them comm-sat me immediately. I'll come down there and ask Miss Hasabe why you have to do her job for her.*
—*But Dada, I'm scared.*
—*Fear is what bullies like that Gallager kid feed off of. It's all they have to go on. It's okay to be afraid, but don't let him see it.*
—*But what if he makes me lick the nasty lav seat?*
—*Like I said Dari, no man can make you do anything you don't choose to do.*
—*What if he has a stick or a blade or something?*

—Dari, even if a man puts a gun *to your head, you remember, you can always choose the bullet.*

• • • • •

"So what are we doing today that's so special?" Cyrus asked, too exhausted to manage a full smile. Torvald and Milliken mumbled and nodded in support of both the question and the fatigue, while Davidson looked dejectedly at his shoes. Toutopolus let his stringy, earth-toned brown bangs hang over his boyish, but now fatigued features, his balding patch of scalp glinting in the light of the training room as nervous perspiration formed there.

"Your all-night Conquest of the Ages tryst doesn't seem like such a good idea right now, does it?" Tanner chided as he puffed up his chest, sensing the thin fog of misery visible on the eyelids of the friends and colleagues who, in this room, became his loyal students.

Tanner forced a shrill whistle through his teeth. The Shipmate marched in on command, carrying a large footlocker in his arms and an elongated golf bag slung over his back. After the android set down the chest and golf bag, Tanner thanked him and excused him to his usual duties. The stances of Tanner's five charges faltered under the weight of curiosity, apprehension, and a long night of siege battles.

Tanner flipped open the clasps on the chest and unzipped the bag with deliberate melodrama, milking the tension in the makeshift dojo. His students' adolescent nighttime exploit had created an excellent opportunity for martial insight.

Tanner left the bag and chest unopened and turned to face his five students. Tanner clasped his hands behind his back and addressed them with as much pomp and authority as he could muster.

"Today, you will each make a choice, and you will stick to that choice." His voice resonated off the walls as each of the students' stances stiffened.

Cyrus could take the anxiety no longer. "Sifu, what are we choosing?"

Dr. Tanner turned and knelt. He flipped open the bag and lifted the lid of the chest. Still kneeling, he turned to his students and revealed a sinister grin as he spoke, "Weapons."

• • • • •

Cyrus shambled to the dinner table, favoring his left leg with an exaggerated limp, trying with difficulty not to drag the quarterstaff he carried. He shuffled over to his usual seat, and before he sat, he paused, surveying the area. The seven who were already seated at the table looked on in silent bewilderment—except Dr. Tanner who seemed not to notice. Cyrus leaned the staff against the wall behind his chair, carefully positioning it out of the sweep of Tanner's chair. Cyrus eased himself into his chair slowly, wincing a little as a tender spot in his right leg brushed against the table. Just as Dr. Murphy opened his mouth to question Cyrus, Torvald entered the room, using the wall as support. Something wooden and black was attached impossibly to his shoulder as he pushed away from the wall and steadied himself with a chair. He shifted his weight and revealed an impressive swell developing over his left eye.

"What is that on your shoulder, and what happened to your face?" Dr. Murphy asked, bewildered.

"These," Dr. Torvald set two wooden bars linked with a silver chain on the table, "are nunchakus." After setting the curious implement on the table, he paused to nurse his seemingly useless right hand and pointed to the inflammation over his right eye with the better hand. "This," he paused as he heaved out an exhausted breath, "is what happens when you don't know how to use them."

"So you're saying you did all this to yourself?" Dr. Tsuchiya marveled.

"No, I'm saying I hit myself in the eye with my own nunchakus. Sifu Tanner whacked my hand with a stick I can't remember the name of, and my gimp-like stature can be attributed to the Dr. Chamberlain here, who in a gesture of good will, assisted my decision to retire by introducing the end of his staff to my testicles."

"I don't know if I approve of..." before the sentence could fully escape Dr. Fordham's lips, the door again slid open, and a sound resembling the death knell of some diseased farm animal ushered in from the hall. As everyone turned to the source of the moan, Dr. Milliken collapsed into the room in a sprawl of flailing limbs with some unidentifiable wooden object. Another bovine moan escaped his mouth, as did most of the air in his lungs. Dr. Villichez and Dr. Fordham hurried to help the man into a chair. His body heaved as he gasped and coughed, and even though he weighed less than either of the two older men, the assistance proved difficult. He sat in the chair and leaned what could now be seen as a wooden Chinese broadsword against the back of his chair.

"I was wrong," Dr. Fordham continued, moving back to his chair, "I *definitely* do not approve of this."

"They will be just fine," Dr. Tanner said, sipping from his cup as if nothing were out of the ordinary.

"Yeah, we'll be fine," Dr. Milliken wheezed out then coughed again, momentarily stiffening from a twinge of pain that shot from his malformed lower lip as he attempted to cover his mouth.

"Mother of all things great and small! What has happened here? And why are these barbaric implements of mayhem at the dinner table?" Dr. Villichez, practically shivering with dismay, pointed at the nunchakus and Cyrus's staff.

"Sifu Tanner says that these are extensions of our bodies and that they are more important, on this ship, than our own penises," Cyrus explained.

"I find it hard to believe that Dr. Tanner would utter such a thing and condone this... this...debacle," Dr. Villichez huffed.

"Well, believe it. He demonstrated exactly what he meant by parrying one of my attacks and extending his kali stick..."

"Yeah, that's what it's called!" Torvald interrupted then returned his drinking glass to his eye.

"...into the side of my knee," Cyrus continued, unfazed by the outburst. "Honestly, I would rather the weapon had been his penis— would have hurt much less. And it's a good thing all these weapons are made of *wood*, or they would have implemented more mayhem. Make no mistake, despite all his pious reverence and understated demeanor, Sifu Tanner here is a world-class butcher."

"Yeah, but he knows what he's doing," coughed out Dr. Milliken, finally regaining his composure. "We would have been a lot better off if we hadn't been up all night playing hologames."

Suddenly, icy looks shot from Cyrus, Torvald, and Dr. Qin and focused on Milliken.

"Oops," he muttered and exaggerated another cough. Cyrus shook his head in legitimate disbelief.

Dr. Villichez looked to the ceiling of the dining hall in an overstated appeal to a higher power. "Children! I have been put in charge of past-due children!" He turned his attention back to the grown men still staring at Dr. Milliken in accusation and disdain. Villichez let his gaze settle a little longer on the battered and bruised scientists, especially Dr. Milliken who now stared shamefully into his glass. "And beating each other with sticks! This errant vessel has fast become an asylum!"

Cyrus relaxed his stare and allowed a laugh to escape despite the pain it afforded his battered sternum. "What, pray-tell, do you find so amusing about this circus?" Dr. Villichez bellowed, incensed.

"We are on a hollow metal tube with no windows, traveling faster than any humanmade device has ever traveled, speeding toward a place that we think is a planet-wide wasteland. We left our families, our friends, our countries, and our world behind, and you seem surprised by the fact that we exhibit tell-tale signs of insanity." Cyrus wiped a strand of spittle from his mouth as, with the cut that was now throbbing on the inside of his lower lip, it was hard to talk so long and keep saliva in his mouth. "No disrespect intended, but you must forgive me if I find this whole scene amusing."

Dr. Villichez threw his hands in the air, sending a fork that had rested near the edge of the table toward Dr. Tsuchiya. As the fork came clattering to a rest in the center of the table, Dr. Villichez stood up abruptly. "I cannot take any more of this fiasco. I am retiring to my room to read. And perhaps I can regain my *own* sanity. Good night!" He stormed out the door almost before it could open.

"He didn't have to throw his fork at me," Dr. Tsuchiya said after he was gone, "What did I do?" Coughs and laughter echoed through the bulkhead, and as Dr. Villichez moved to the living quarters, he himself could not help smile, if only for a moment.

• • • • •

"I have something that's been bugging me recently, but I don't want you to get offended."

"Well, Tanner, a statement like that is almost always a prelude to something offensive..." Cyrus looked up from the floor of the fitness chamber, his knees tucked to his chest, Kantistyka paddle at his feet.

"I'm not so much worried about the offense; that would just mean I'd have to pole-whip you the next time we sparred. That, you'd get over. I'm just worried about you retreating until you catch the beating that brings you back to your senses. It's like questions about what's going on inside that thick skull of yours is the *only* thing you ever retreat from." Dr. Tanner stretched his legs out in front of him. "Let me see if I can get ahold of what I'm trying to say. Around the eighth and ninth century, a set of Scandinavian societies believed that their god Odin could bestow great strength on warriors through the spirit of the bear, which was the strongest, most vicious animal they could think of. Being a warlike society, this belief both colored, and was colored by, their everyday lives. There were even warriors that donned trappings of bear hide as armor or dressings over their torso. These warriors, when possessed by the spirit of the bear, were fierce adversaries—

biting their shields, frothing at the mouth, and amassing unheard body counts because their own lives were insignificant next to their thirst for victory. They were called the 'Wearers of the Bear Shirt' or, in their language, *behr sarkr*. That's where we get the term 'berserk' from..." Dr. Tanner paused and looked at the floor as if the remaining words in his treatise had slipped from his fingers and spilled across the treated clay at his feet.

There was a short, yet still uncomfortable, pause. The air between the two men had the substance and texture of a pall. "I follow, I think, but I'm not sure where you are taking me." Cyrus lifted himself and extended his legs. He turned toward Tanner, moving the ethereal veil between them. Dr. Tanner looked up from the floor and met Cyrus's gaze with an unsteady smile until he found the words he had been looking for.

"You see, that was not the only culture of the ancient world that believed in the spirit of the bear. Various indigenous tribes of the Americas believed the bear bestowed power to the warrior and that spirit sent him headlong and vehement into battle, denying him the luxury of retreat."

"I see that you are likening me to your *behr sarkrs*, but I fail to see what's wrong with that."

"Every one of those cultures I just mentioned was also obsessed with death. And they experienced it often."

"So you're afraid I'm going to do something stupid and jeopardize the safety of the colony?" Cyrus's voice had raised an octave, and his words came out with force. It was more an accusation than a question.

"No, I'm not saying that at all. I don't think 'stupid' is a part of your repertoire, especially not if it jeopardizes others," Tanner paused then turned to meet Cyrus's eyes. "I guess what I'm saying is that one of these days, if death does creep up behind you, I'll be there somewhere behind *him*."

Cyrus nodded smiled. "I can't help feeling like I should have been born in another time. Like maybe the only way I'd be happy is if I had a war to fight—but a *real* war, not some houndshit Unification War over commerce and eyewash—something that can either be won or lost. I need a place where the measure of your day is whether or not you are alive at the end of it. It's like we've used all the ingenuity and technology we could muster to siphon every ounce of urgency from our lives until we're all worthless—just a festering pile of ill-used lab waste. I'm tired of feeling like lab waste."

Tanner pushed himself to his feet then extended a hand to Cyrus to help him up."I think you should be careful. In my experience, when life gives you what you ask for, it doesn't stop when you say, 'When.'"

nine

—*Dada, I have a question.*
—*Yes, Dari?*
—*Do you love mommy?*
—*Of course, I love your mother. Why do you ask?*
—*I heard you and mommy arguing last night. You said a lot of mean things to each other.*
—*I'm sorry you heard that, Dari.*
—*Why do you guys argue so much?*
—*I dunno, Dari. I guess sometimes even two people who love each other can get annoyed to the point where they don't act like it anymore.*
—*Adults are pretty strange, Dada. If I don't like someone, I tell them. If I love someone, like you and mommy, I remember that you love me too, and that makes it better.*
—*Yeah, I think adults' lives are a bit more complicated though.*
—*You know, sometimes I think complicated might be the problem. But what do I know? I'm just a kid.*
—*Dari, maybe you know more than we complicated adults give you credit for.*
—*If that's the case, why don't they listen more often?*
—*Maybe sometimes we don't have the ears to hear.*
—*Kinda like what you said before, 'Many will listen. Few will hear.'*
—*Yeah, it's exactly like that. Your mom will be the first to tell you I am guilty of that more times than I would enjoy admitting.*
—*I wonder, Dada, how do you get people to not just wait until you're done talking?*
—*The answer to that is beyond me, but I'm sure one day you will have plenty to say. You just promise me you won't stop talking until they hear.*
—*You got a deal, Dada. I promise.*

• • • • •

Even before the door opened fully, Dr. Torvald was in Cyrus's room wearing nothing but underwear and white socks. He had his nunchakus in hand, panting heavily.

"What's going on?" Cyrus wondered what on a closed ship traveling through virgin space at nigh unto the speed of light could possibly have this man armed and in such a huff.

"Your buddy Tanner has lost his mind! Shut the door, quick!" he gasped. Cyrus couldn't tell if Torvald was trying to whisper or could not speak through his wheezing. Cyrus pressed the button to close the door, and as it slid to the floor, Torvald looked anxiously over his shoulder. "That pod-waste lab monkey jumped out of my closet and tried to keelhaul me with those stupid sticks of his. Luckily, I've been keeping my nunchakus under my pillow. I whacked him pretty good in the knee, and I ran out of the room."

"His knee? You could have wrecked him for good."

"I don't think so. It sounded awful plastic when I hit him. Besides, I just reacted. If he's worried about his knees, he shouldn't jump out of the closet of a jittery, half-trained man with nunchakus under his pillow!" Torvald's breaths were calmer now, but his voice was still a whisper.

"Why are you whispering?"

"Because when I was on my way here, I think I heard him ransack Milliken."

"He's testing us," Cyrus said calmly, returning to his bed. Torvald looked across the dimly lit room and saw the shock-dampening bed frame against the wall and noticed the mattresses on the floor. Cyrus leaned over the mattresses and pulled his staff from the hidden side of the bed. "Wait a second. Did you say you keep your nunchakus under your pillow?"

Torvald's eyelids fluttered slightly and his cheeks vibrated almost imperceptibly. "Yeah well, call me superstitious, but I figure if I keep them close to my head, they will be less eager to meet it during training."

"Fair enough." Cyrus turned off the light. Torvald stuck his ear next to the sliding door to try to hear what was going on in the hallway. "Won't work. Soundproof," Cyrus said matter-of-factly, "which means you can stop whispering."

"How can you be so calm? I'm sure he's gonna bring his little rampage to your doorstep any minute now."

"And we will be ready for him. When he told us to keep our weapons with us at all times, I was sure he was planning something like this. I just didn't think it would take this long. I think he was waiting for us to forget." Even in the dark, Cyrus could see the bewilderment in

Torvald's eyes. "You stay here with your back flush to the wall. I'll be the bait. When he comes through the door, you put the keelhaul down on him, and we'll take him together."

Torvald nodded, not quite convinced of the wall's sound dampening. Cyrus curled up in his bed with his staff, pulled the sheet over himself, and sat for a moment before he kicked twice violently. As Torvald's pupils widened in adjustment, he saw the sheet, now loosened from the weight of the mattresses, flutter back to the bed over Cyrus.

"Lock the door," Cyrus said, whispering now himself. "It will help maintain the illusion." Cyrus could not see Torvald, but he heard him shuffle and he heard the beep the door made as it locked.

They waited for a long minute, another, longer minute, and then yet another one even longer. Torvald's breathing sounded like someone rustling through a refuse bin.

And suddenly the door slid open—no beep, no door chime. Tanner eased over to the bed carrying a thin rattan stick in each hand. From the dimmed light in the hall, Torvald could see Tanner was favoring his right leg even though he was wearing plastic greaves that guarded his shins and knees. When the door opened, Torvald almost let his bladder slip, but he was composed enough to hold his breath as Tanner sidled past him. Torvald took a step from the wall to get closer, but the rubber of his shoe squeaked against the floor. Tanner turned, but only enough to see the glimmer of nunchakus as they swung toward him. Tanner's movement looked like a blur in the light coming from the hall. One moment Torvald saw Tanner's back, the next, Tanner was parrying the attack with the stick in his left hand. Torvald lifted his left leg to kick, but Tanner smacked Torvald's shin with the stick in his right hand.

By then, Cyrus was up, lifting the sheet from the bed with his staff. As the sheet floated above Tanner's head, he turned and kicked Torvald in his chest, sending him back-first to the wall. The light switched on and the door slid shut as Torvald collided with the controls. Tanner faced the bed, but the sheet was coming down, and he only caught a glimmer of Cyrus leaping past him. As Cyrus flew by, he jabbed the staff behind him at the back of Tanner's right knee. Tanner shifted his weight and twisted, blocking the attack with both sticks as the sheet came down over his head and shoulders.

Cyrus landed and grabbed something as Torvald lunged toward the shrouded Tanner with a battle cry. Something hard and round caught Torvald in his ribs, knocking the air from his lungs. The end of Torvald's own nunchakus jabbed into his thigh, but he managed to hold the sheet tightly over Tanner. Torvald tackled Tanner onto the end of Cyrus's bed. As the second blow dug into a rib on the opposite side of Torvald's body, Torvald let the air escape on its own, keeping his body firm to absorb the blow.

A muffled, "Okay, enough," came from under the sheet. Tanner began to twist, but Cyrus's staff came down across his shoulder, narrowly missing Torvald's head. Cyrus dropped his staff on Tanner, and it rested on him a moment. Torvald knocked the staff away with his elbow and struggled to hold Tanner. The staff made a hollow-sounding report as it bounced off Tanner's head.

Torvald looked over his shoulder for Cyrus, but he was already next to him, wrapping Tanner's ankles with a piece of what looked like rope. "What the hell is that?" Torvald asked after dropping an elbow on what he hoped was Tanner's shoulder beneath the sheet.

"Clothesline made from the rigging for that stupid longhouse tent Tsuchiya had us drilling on," each word came out staccato and rushed as Cyrus pulled against Tanner's battered shoulder. Torvald shoved, and Tanner rolled across the rigging line into the floor with his arms tangled in the metal rope.

Something like, "Hey!" was lost in the sounds of shifting mattress and tangled limbs colliding with the floor.

"What are we..." before Torvald could finish and Cyrus could tighten the line, a kali stick jutted out from the sheet and into the inside of Torvald's thigh. Cyrus watched Torvald fall toward the doorway just as Milliken hobbled in with his wooden broadsword. Without missing a beat, Milliken brought the flat of his sword down across what must have been the arm holding the kali stick.

"You scumrakers aren't safe anywhere!" Tanner bellowed as Torvald gathered himself and helped the others finish tying him.

They turned the cocooned Tanner onto his back. The rigging and sheet were now so tight, the shape of Tanner's head could be seen in the imprint. "I'm gonna get you two!" The sheet sank into his mouth with each word and an oval darkened the area with saliva.

"Not tonight you won't," Cyrus retorted. He snatched off his left sock, and just as Tanner uttered the "I..." of his next sentence, Cyrus placed the sock in the impression his mouth formed. Cyrus held it there and pointed at the pillow on the bed. Milliken, as quickly as his bruised hip would let him, grabbed the pillow and tossed it to Cyrus. Cyrus then snatched off the pillowcase and wound it into a twine. The three men tied it around Tanner's head, securing the gag with military precision.

Torvald leaned over to where Tanner's ear should have been. "When you were sitting in my closet waiting to spring your sadistic little trap, did you think in about ten minutes, you'd be getting gagged and gaffled by three so-called scumrakers? Did you? Who's bottom feeding now?"

Cyrus and Milliken looked at Torvald as if he had just opened Pandora's box, only the gods had forgotten to add Hope in the mix of hellspawn that was filling the hollow ship even as his words echoed off the walls. "What?" Torvald asked, almost convincing them of his obliviousness.

"What do we do with him now?" Milliken asked, picking up his broadsword.

Cyrus looked back at the doorway. Dim nighttime hall light streamed. "I have an idea."

Dr. Villichez, nursing a headache for the last three days, had doubled his intake of water per the advice of Dr. Fordham, who was convinced the headache was due to dehydration. This double dosage of water had subsequently tripled his trips to the restroom—especially during the lights-out hours on the ship. The cold and utter silence in his room seemed of little help. Even dispelling the silence with music spheres did nothing. The night before, he had shambled to the lav half-asleep at least four times, and as this was already his third trip, it seemed this night would be no different. A long, lazy yawn struggled to escape his throat as he rubbed his eyes and shuffled to the lav down the path he was learning all too well.

And then his foot collided with something that seemed both hard and pliable at the same time. Villichez heard what he swore was a mumble. As the aftershock of his yawn subsided, he opened his eyes and, even as his pupils adjusted fully, he was not sure his brain had correctly interpreted what he was seeing.

One of the inhabitants of the ship lay before him cocooned in a bed sheet, with either a towel or a pillowcase wrapped around where his head should have been. There was something sticking out from the rope that hog-tied the man. The rope itself looked remarkably like the rigging line the Shipmate had reported missing from the longhouse kit. Dr. Villichez knelt slowly so as not to upset his already complaining bladder and removed the card. Before he could turn it around and bring it into the light he already knew what it said, 'You have been serviced by the cleaning crew. Have a nice day!'

• • • • •

Cyrus, Torvald, and Milliken sat on the floor of the fitness chamber in quiet anxiety. They had not seen or heard from Sifu Tanner since they had left him gaffled and bound in the hallway the night before. They had all come early to face the music, but not knowing the cadence or the tempo formed gooseflesh on their skin.

"You think he's gonna be mad?" Torvald inflected his question with a curious but characteristic blend of oddly mellow anxiety and neurosis.

"Well, you sure talked an exemplary amount of bilge last night," Cyrus said, his own voice quivering.

"Well, you were the one who decided to leave the calling card," Torvald responded.

Suddenly, the door to the fitness chamber opened and Sifu Tanner was standing there hand over fist. He walked in silently as the three men stood at strict attention. His right eye was blackened and swollen, and he seemed to be favoring his left leg. Tanner paced in front of them, taking time to glare at each man in turn as they faced forward, trying not to flinch. Tanner stopped in front of the three men within arms' reach of all of them. In a sharp, swift gesture, he raised his hand to chest height. Each man wanted to recoil but dared not move. Tanner slowly brought up his other hand into a resonating clap. He dramatically brought his hands together, again and again, forming ominous but reverent applause.

Despite their best efforts, looks of confusion overwhelmed their statuesque expressions. With the echo of the unexpected plaudit still resonating in the air, Tanner spoke earnestly, "You all did unexpectedly well last night. Even unprepared, you handled yourselves decisively." Tanner smiled and shook each of the scientist's hand. They all laughed a little, more to expel the tension than to indulge in the humor of the situation.

"I think that was me," Torvald said, pointing to Tanner's black eye. "Sorry."

Tanner walked over to him and met his gaze. What little smile Torvald had left fled as they made eye contact. Consternation eclipsed Tanner's face as he spoke, pointing to the inflamed flesh around his eye. "This one was free. The next one you pay for." He took a step back and levity returned to his face. He clapped a solitary, sharp clap and stood at attention. "It is excellent to see you all here so early because we have a long day ahead of us." He greeted again, hand over fist, and as they all snapped to attention, the door slid open.

Dr. Jang stood in the doorway in a jumpsuit. It was the first time

Cyrus could remember seeing him out of his lab coat since they had first entered the ship on Eros. Anxiety permeated Jang's entire body as he stood at the doorway, apparently not sure whether to enter or run.

"Dr. Jang," Tanner bellowed, "What brings you to this side of physical training?"

He glanced at Cyrus then quickly back to Tanner. "Dr. Chamberlain threatened, well promised rather, that he would inflict bodily harm on me every chance he got until I came to this class to see the havoc I wrought by giving you that card key to get into the rooms."

"You gave him the card key to get into our rooms?" Milliken blurted but was silenced by a fiery gaze from Tanner. Tanner moved his gaze to Cyrus and then back to Dr. Jang.

"Whatever impetus brought you here, we are glad to have you." Tanner smiled. "Fall in next to Cyrus."

As Jang took his place in the line, slightly unsure of what would happen next, Cyrus broke his stance at attention and reached over to Jang. Jang flinched but then realized the gesture was without malice as Cyrus patted him on the back and smiled. "Good to finally have you here," he said and then snapped back to attention. Davidson and Toutopolus trickled in at the regular time. They had been spared the night's onslaught because it had been cut short by Cyrus and his Cleaning Crew. They fell silently into formation and drills as Cyrus explained the dojo protocols to Jang. Jang was beginning to relax until Cyrus explained to him that when the time came today, he too had to pick a weapon and would have to learn to defend himself with it the same way they all did. Jang looked more eager to get to that part of the class than Cyrus had expected.

Jang stood in front of Cyrus, gripping the handle of the bokan with both hands as if he thought he would fall from the ship if he let go. Cyrus lunged forward with his staff and Jang parried, stiffly, but effectively. In an exaggerated arc, Cyrus brought the end of the staff around over his own head, attacking again as he stepped forward. Jang parried again, but this time, his stiffness caused him to lose balance. Cyrus shifted his weight and brought the back end of the staff around into Jang's chest. Jang stumbled but did not fall. The blow had been enough to get Jang's attention, but not enough to send him to the floor. Cyrus stepped back and held his staff at his side. "What happened there?" Cyrus asked.

"You hit me in the chest," Jang answered, rubbing his chest as he centered himself back in front of Cyrus.

"You are too stiff. You have to relax."

"How can I relax if you keep hitting me in the chest?"

"Relax and I won't be able to," Cyrus said, kicking the bottom of the staff with his left foot and spinning it into both hands as he dropped into a fighting stance.

Cyrus lunged forward again. Jang was caught off-guard, and his hands moved the bokan instinctively to his left side, pushing Cyrus's staff to the outside of his shoulder. The heat from the bruise that was swelling across his chest told Jang he did not want to get hit there again. Jang lashed forward, determined to get Cyrus and the staff out of his face. He swung his hands down with fury, bringing the wooden sword down in an arc toward Cyrus's forehead. Cyrus turned into Jang and brought the middle of his staff into the path of the bokan. The two wooden weapons collided with a clap, and Jang, still stoked with adrenalin, pressed into Cyrus.

"Yes!" Cyrus exclaimed, shifting his weight to hold Jang back, "Much better!" Cyrus then stepped down and to his left and Jang's weight carried him past Cyrus. Cyrus swung the end of his staff around and pushed Jang along with a tap on the back. "Don't overextend yourself. Never sacrifice your vertical base for an attack."

Jang gathered himself and turned to face Cyrus again. He was aware of the others locked in mock combat around him, but he focused on Cyrus as he brushed his damp hair from his face.

"You should tie that up next time," Cyrus taunted. Jang turned his head to the side to swing the lock of hair the rest of the way and continued the motion into a lunge. Cyrus side-stepped and blocked the thrust upward with the back end of the staff, but Jang recovered quickly and brought the bokan back down toward Cyrus's neck. Cyrus stepped under again, spun the staff a half turn, and brought the spinning end down on the top of the wooden blade. Jang's momentum carried him forward, and he tripped on Cyrus's foot. Jang careened toward the ground face-first. Cyrus placed his staff under Jang and leaned, hitting Jang in the chest again, but halting his descent to the floor.

"Footing," Cyrus reminded.

Suddenly, as Jang gathered himself again, the door to the dojo slid open. Everyone stopped where they were and turned to see Commander Uzziah standing with his arms folded. Tanner turned to face Uzziah and belted "Ready Position!" Instantly everyone snapped to half-attention and held their weapons at their side—everyone except Dr. Jang who almost fell as Cyrus moved the staff from under his body and shifted into ready position. Tanner waited for Jang to gather himself and for him to attempt to mimic the stance.

"When a fellow martial artist enters the room you greet!" Tanner bellowed and everyone, except Jang, brought their weapons into their right hands and greeted Commander Uzziah in unison. Uzziah straightened his body, brought his open hands slightly to the front then sharply to his sides, slapping his workout pants as he brought his right foot up and then down quickly to the floor. The sound resonated as he bowed ever so slightly, keeping his eyes on Tanner.

"To what do we owe the honor of this visit?" Tanner relaxed his own greeting and stepped toward Uzziah.

"After you guys' fiasco in the hallway last night, Fordham and Villichez asked me to check up on your little soirée and make sure everything is kosher." Uzziah smiled smugly, his eyes calmly surveying the room.

"Join us." Tanner indicated his own kali sticks. "We are weapons training." Uzziah looked around the room at each of their weapons and finally moved over to Dr. Jang.

"May I?" Uzziah requested Jang's bokan. Jang nodded and handed over the weapon.

"Who is my partner?" Uzziah asked, looking around, a confident grin on his face.

"I am," Tanner said, moving toward him, kali sticks firmly in his hands now. Tanner greeted again. Uzziah returned the greeting and launched himself forward as soon as his foot hit the ground. Tanner's right stick clacked against the bokan as he moved to the outside of the attack. Tanner brought his left stick around, toward Uzziah's back, but Uzziah stepped with Tanner's parry and turned into a parry of his own. Uzziah riposted off the parry, angling the tip of the bokan over his left forearm toward Tanner's chest, but Tanner dipped to his left and brought his right stick under and around, pushing Uzziah's lunge to the right. Tanner riposted from his parry and brought the inside of his right stick toward Uzziah's face, but Uzziah stepped forward, following the bokan, and went beneath the attack. Uzziah stepped his left foot back behind Tanner and swung left, but Tanner was already stepping his back foot over. Tanner spun blindly, bringing his elbow around and the kali stick in his left hand into the path of the attack. As soon as Tanner planted his right foot again, he lifted his left knee and extended his leg toward Uzziah's ribs. The Commander exhaled as the kick landed, but continued rolling to his right. He pivoted on his right foot and shifted the bokan to his left hand. Rolling past Tanner's back, Uzziah took a backhand swipe at him, but only connected with wood. Uzziah used the momentum from the parry to flip the wooden sword in his hand into an overhand grip and launched his right elbow at Tanner's temple. Tanner rolled away from the elbow and, as Uzziah tried to follow him, he lifted his left leg in a little hop and caught the back of Uzziah's thigh. Uzziah stopped and stepped back to create some space.

Uzziah stumbled as he stepped, but he completed his turn and lunged back to close the distance. Uzziah swung his left hand like a punch, the wooden blade of the bokan trailing in its arc. Tanner met the attack with both kali sticks and was hit in his ribs by Uzziah's knee. Tanner locked his sticks in a cross around the bokan, and as the Commander lifted his knee for a second attack, Tanner lifted his own knee to his chest and extended his leg. The kick caught Uzziah in his solar plexus and sent him stumbling two steps backward, weaponless.

As quickly as he went back, Uzziah charged forward again, hoping to catch Tanner off-guard. Tanner threw the mass of weapons beneath Uzziah's feet, catching him unprepared. The weapons caught around Uzziah's ankles, and he lost his footing. Uzziah lifted his knees to get his feet back beneath him, but Tanner was already stepping past him, delivering a back fist to Uzziah's upper back. Uzziah careened to the ground in a clattering of limbs and wood. The others could hear the air escape Uzziah's lungs as his torso met the floor and bounced. Uzziah got his arms under his body quickly, but before he could lift himself, Tanner had descended on him and had his arm around Uzziah's right arm and throat, knee pressed into the small of his back. As Tanner pressed the Commander's face into the floor, he moved his mouth as close to Uzziah's ear as he could while maintaining the hold. The Commander's body tensed, but he knew struggling would be of little use.

"Only the Sifu teaches lessons in *this* room, and that Sifu is me!" Everyone stood in slack-jawed awe. "You pay your respect to Sifu, or you will pay your respect to the floor!"

Tanner's chest heaved in and out, his breathing more deliberate than any of them had ever seen as he released the Commander, took a step back, and extended his hand to him. The Commander, his face flushed where it had pressed into the floor, turned slowly. He paused for a moment then took Tanner's hand.

"Now go run and report *that* to Villichez and Fordham," Tanner spat out with more disdain than Cyrus had ever heard in his voice. Tanner collected the weapons scattered across the floor. Cyrus leaned on his staff. The air made him uncomfortable—as if he had been part of the melee. The tension sat heavy on his brow, a swath of perspiration no towel could remove.

Uzziah focused on the back of Tanner's head, and Cyrus tensed, gripping his staff more firmly. When Tanner realized the Commander was not moving toward the door, he turned sharply to face him. Before Tanner completed his turn, Uzziah's hands had already moved to his side, his foot had already come down on the floor, and his head was already bowing. This time he prostrated his gaze, for only a brief moment, then he raised his head, "I would like permission to remain with the class, Sifu," he barked in a militaristic, yet respectful, tone.

Tanner stood, both his sticks cupped into one hand, the bokan in the other, and bowed his head to Uzziah. "If you are going to stay, you will need to pick another weapon because this one belongs to Dr. Jang." Tanner lifted the bokan and tossed it to Jang who, not expecting it, barely caught it. Tanner then moved to the Commander and offered him his hand again, this time in friendship. "Welcome to the class." He smiled widely. "It's been a long time coming."

• • • • •

"Has anyone else noticed there are no mathematicians or philosophers on this ship?" Dr. Milliken asked as he spooned another bite of wheatgrass pilaf from his plate.

Dr. Winberg was quick to chime in with an answer, "That's because there is no room on a pioneering expedition for pseudoscience and people who get paid to talk. Notice there are no lawyers or politicians on this ship either."

However hypocritical the bite behind Winberg's statement had been, Cyrus could see its validity. Everyone had heard this complaint from Winberg before, but it had never been more poignant. He was about to intone his agreement, but Dr. Villichez was already speaking, "A scathing remark indeed, but it is most certainly true. Division of labor is a luxury we can no longer afford. That is, not until we have more fully colonized Asha. So, gentlemen, enjoy your late-night gaming sessions and beating yourselves into a battered stupor while we are festooned on this vessel, for be assured that when we reach planet-side, the renewed adolescence you have experienced on this ship will be ripped from the futile grasps of the unprepared."

An ominous quiet filled the room. Palpable, it filled the lungs and made it difficult to breathe, but uncharacteristic of the unctuous fog it mimicked, vision became clearer, and the solemn faces of each of the scientists became more distinct. Their lives were no longer what they knew; their professions were behind them. They were now men of means. Social standing, academic kudos, and tenure now meant as little as a tick on the back of some world-devouring Leviathan. Their old skills would amount to precisely nil if they could not learn new ones. They would accept this, or they would die.

The rest of the dinner was consumed in reverent silence. Every bite of creatively mingled soybeans, grapes, and wheatgrass was chewed carefully and savored. As they ate, morsel by ambrosial morsel, each man, from pious Christian to blasphemous agnostic, uttered a silent prayer for his own sanity and soul—each of the men genuflecting now under the weight of his choice, in his own way.

• • • • •

When Cyrus entered his room, Dr. Villichez was putting a music sphere on his personal datadeck. As the door slid shut behind him, Cyrus noticed that even in this overly sterile environment, the room had the aroma of aftershave, tweed, and venerable wisdom—just as it should have.

"Isn't the Shipmate programmed with just about any music selection imaginable?" Cyrus asked.

Dr. Villichez didn't look up, focusing a surgical attentiveness on the placement of the crystal sphere. "I prefer the sound of the music sphere. It is more...tactile. It is much more sympathetic than the efficient stream of kilobits that pipes in from the Shipmate's central processor." With the sphere in place, warm, tenor notes of a saxophone streamed into the room as smooth, lilting upright bass massaged the air.

Crossing his legs and cupping his hands together over his knee, Villichez swiveled in his chair to face Cyrus. "Please, have a seat." He nodded toward the empty loveseat in the corner—the only furnishing that had come along with Villichez for the trip. "What brings you here?"

Cyrus sat awkwardly. It wasn't that Villichez made him uncomfortable—it was exactly the contrary—but there was something about him. It was like he knew more about you, the room, about everything, than he put on. With Villichez sitting there, Cyrus found it hard to sit upright. He was, for once, at a loss for words—it was as if he expected Villichez to already know why he was there.

Then, before he knew he had opened his mouth, it had just come out, "Actually, I just wanted to thank you."

"What on Earth for?" Villichez asked, a little bewildered, but patient.

It took Cyrus a moment to fully gauge where his mind was taking him. "Well, I know I haven't been the most manageable of colleagues since we all hatched, and I just want to say I appreciate you taking it all with a grain of salt."

Villichez let out a deep chuckle. Cyrus could picture in his mind sweet-scented tobacco smoke wafting from around a carved wooden pipe with each guffaw. "Dr. Chamberlain, we all sit before a proverbial round table on this ship. I don't see any need to have to *manage* you."

"I see your point, and yet in a way, you do manage all of us. I guess I just want to say, as much as I rouse a rabble here and there, that I do appreciate it."

"Well, in that case, I thank *you*." Villichez made a slight, but evident bowing motion. "But I must say, apart from that business with leaving Dr. Tanner battered and trammeled in the hallway, most of your tirades and endeavors I have found rather amusing, albeit after the wind from your goose flapping has died down."

Cyrus smiled. "Goose flapping?"

"Evidently, in a less...automated day and age, children would chase the rather largish birds around the farm. And when caught, the geese were known to spread their wings and deliver quite a buffeting."

"That is a pretty accurate description of my disposition." Cyrus relaxed into the back of the chair, smiling again, but almost as suddenly as he had loosened, his expression waned, and he averted his eyes to the music sphere. The sphere glimmered as notes of the whispering piano and coquettish bass flirted and danced in the air with them. Cyrus caressed his chin between his forefinger and his thumb as the delicate play of light through the magnetically suspended sphere transfixed him.

"Something the matter?" Dr. Villichez asked, his concern almost as tactile as the music drifting through the speakers from the spinning translucent orb.

"I'm fine," Cyrus pried his attention from the music sphere and turned to face Villichez, who was now leaning forward, his chin cupped in his hand, elbow resting on his knee. "Well, I feel fine as far as I can tell, but my dreams seem to beg to differ."

"Troubling dreams?"

"Not really. Most of the dreams are fairly straightforward. Dreams of life back on Earth mixed in with some odd bits and pieces of this place. You know, typical stuff. It's just that in these dreams...I dunno..." Cyrus turned back to the sphere for a moment as the saxophone stepped between the piano and the bass. It wasn't aggressive, but it was enough to get their attention and have them step aside while he did his own thing. Cyrus replied quicker this time, "It's like things are going fine, but I keep tripping. Every dream things are fine. Finer than they should be. And then I'm tripping again. Every time, tripping over the same emotional thread."

"And how would you describe this thread?"

"I can't really describe it. It's like trying to catch the rain as it falls from the sky —all of it. You can't. And the harder you try, the more frustrated you become."

"I'm not sure I follow. Can you elaborate?"

"I don't know. It's so hard to keep ahold of." Cyrus looked to the sphere again. Now the piano, saxophone, and bass mingled together in a sensuous *ménage a trois* that seemed to fill the room with sapphire and orange hues. Cyrus took in the scent of it, filled his lungs, , and then exhaled it all. He paused under an invisible weight then lifted his eyes to meet Villichez's. "Once, my son asked me to go to a Halloween party a friend from his school was having. Everyone had to dress up. At first, I was reluctant, but after I decided to go as one of my son's favorite cel-shade characters, it wasn't long before I got into it. I recorded episodes of the gram and watched it over and over again just to get the character right. It was amazing how appealing it was to pretend to be someone else for a day." For a moment it seemed the weight would get the best of him, but Cyrus exchanged another breath with the room and was able to lift his head again. "When the call for volunteers for the Ashan expedition went out, it was like being asked to go to that Halloween party again. Only this time, it was an opportunity to dress up as someone else for the rest of my life."

The music sphere continued to spin as the melodic tryst subsided. The instruments were spent, and the air in the room thinned in the afterglow. Cyrus again absorbed as much of it as he could before he was forced to let it go. "It was easier than I expected to leave my daily clothes behind. I can do just fine without the ties, the Laureate pins, the khakis—all of that is flotsam in the bilge bay to me. Problem is, I don't know if I can bear the weight of the costume I chose. The beauty is that I know one way or the other, it's been chosen, and there is no way back, but in the meantime, I feel like I'm standing here naked, in between here and there, and it's just...cold."

The music sphere began to whisper another tale. This one began with the piano again, but it was somber. It was begging for forgiveness for some unforgivable affront. Villichez was nodding either in understanding of Cyrus, or the piano, or maybe both. "You know there's not a man on this ship who has not come to me expressing doubt—myself included. Oddly, or maybe not so odd, you were the last. You know, you were not the only one who came here to escape something, or in search of something new, but it was clear—even from the start—that you were here also in defiance."

"Defiance of what?"

"I believe that is *your* question to answer."

The bass attempted to console the piano to little avail. "Fair enough."

"Besides, with all the work we have before us planet-side, it won't be long before the Damocles lands, and parts of our old lives will return. Perhaps the ten relative years between now and then will reveal some things that seemed timeworn on Earth as welcoming as an old, familiar lullaby."

"Well, I hope you are right." Cyrus began to get up from the chair. He was spent now himself, and the piano's lament was no longer comforting.

"Hope is what this trip is all about, right?"

Cyrus was up now and moving to the door. "Perhaps," he paused and took one last look at the music sphere as it hovered above the datadeck, itself in defiance of the gravity waves that kept the scientists' feet anchored to the side of the ship they called ground. "Well, thank you for your time. I am heading to bed. Maybe sleep will help renew my faith in humanity."

"Maybe it's not humanity you lost faith in." Villichez was up now as well, politely escorting Cyrus to the door.

Cyrus paused and tilted his head slightly toward Villichez. "You know I've never in my life gone to see a therapist."

Villichez put his hand on Cyrus's shoulder and gripped firmly. The gesture was stronger than Cyrus expected but steadying. "And you still haven't. This was just a candid conversation between friends at a round table." Villichez nodded, and Cyrus nodded back with more of a smile than he believed was possible as the door quietly slid shut between them.

ten

—*Anything interesting happen at school today, Dari?*
—*We talked about monkeys all day today. That was interesting, but the most interesting part is why we talked about monkeys all day.*
—*Why was that?*
—*Genivere had an apple, an actual real apple, not dried or anything. She said it came off a tree that her grandfather owned. Well, as she was parading it around the room, a monkey dove through the window, jumped off a desk, and landed on her head. She was screaming and swinging her arms everywhere and dropped the apple. The monkey caught it before it hit the ground and ran into the hallway. They cleared the grounds and searched for that stupid monkey most of the day. Finally, they found it hiding in a closet eating the apple, but it got away again and jumped out another window. Genivere was taken to the hospital for tests they said. She was still screaming when the medi-lev took her away.*
—*Were you scared?*
—*I was too busy laughing to be scared, but a lot of people were freaked out. Afterward, people asked a lot of questions, so Miss Hasabe taught us about monkeys for the rest of the day. She taught about how they were only found in jungle areas a long time ago, but as humans moved into those areas and tore down the trees, they started to move around to other places like the Fringe States where people can't really stop them. She also said that because people killed a lot of the other scary animals that would eat or chase off monkeys, they were able to have a lot of monkey babies. The part I didn't understand was that if most monkeys are from former South America and from Africa, how they got to Los Angeles. South America and Africa are a long ways away. Even for people. She said she didn't know.*
—*Well, they believe monkeys got into New York and Washington D.C. by hiding on planes from South America, but some probably got there from idiots smuggling them here for pets. The story I heard of how they came here is that the monkeys here were grown in pods in a lab, but one day, a group of people who thought testing on monkeys was bad showed up outside a lab to protest...*

—*What's protesting Dada?*

—*Well, it's when you don't agree with something that is happening, and you go in public and complain about it.*

—*Is that a bad thing?*

—*Not necessarily, but these people were particularly angry and weren't thinking very well, and they broke into the lab and let out somewhere between a hundred and two hundred monkeys before they were arrested. Now usually, lab monkeys are sterile, which means they can't have babies, but these people happened to pick a lab that was testing drugs that keep people from having babies for a short time, so the monkeys needed to be able to have babies to be tested.*

—*Why didn't they just catch all the monkeys and bring them back or put them in a preserve?*

—*Because monkeys are just as resourceful as us, if not more so, and they are extremely hard to catch if they don't want to be caught.*

—*But I don't understand why monkeys are so dangerous.*

—*Well for starters, monkeys have long claws and are stronger than they look, but worst of all, they can carry all sorts of horrible diseases that don't bother them but wreck humans plenty bad.*

—*How did they get so diseased, Dada?*

—*I think a lot of the diseases come from people spreading out too far too fast. In the past, when people cut down a lot of trees too fast, they began to discover all sorts of diseases and problems they never had before. Also, people living on top of each other and not keeping places clean helps generate disease. It's basically a side-effect of using the world like a lav seat.*

—*Well, l you can clean a lav seat to fight germs.*

—*I think disease might be nature's way of cleaning the lav seat, only in this case, it seems we are the germs.*

—*Well, Dada, I don't want to be a germ, and I definitely don't want a disease, so I think I'll make sure to clean my own lav seat, so nature doesn't have to do it for me.*

—*That idea sounds like a winner indeed, Dari. But in the meantime, stay away from infested street monkeys, and especially stay away from Miss Hasabe's window if you have fruit in your hand.*

—*Will do, Dada. Will do.*

• • • • •

"How do you feel about leaving the ship?" Dr. Villichez asked. This visit with Cyrus was an official counseling session. "Many have had anxieties and apprehensions over disembarking." Jazz again played in the background, but, Zephyr-like on the sterile air of the ship, the music was decidedly less passionate this visit.

"So you're concerned we're all becoming a too attached to the ship?"

Villichez smiled. "Always analyzing the analyst."

"Well, no reason to worry about me. Leaving this thing is no different to me than leaving anything else."

"Please," Villichez paused to cross his legs, cupping his hands over his knee, "elaborate."

"Guess I just never really felt in-place anywhere. One place is just as awkward as the next." Cyrus looked at the rug beneath his feet and wondered why he had not taken notice of the rug on his previous visit. "I have to say, I feel like I can be myself here." He smiled at Villichez, who returned it. "I guess that's why you're always giving me the stink-eye."

Villichez looked amused then quickly became detached, and his gaze faltered as if someone had called his name from another room. "You know this stink-eye you refer to is not easy to come by. It is earned more than cast. In my country, it is not customary to be combative with those you take under your wing; a certain amount of reverence is demanded by the elder, and a certain amount of...tolerance is expected from those in his charge. Often the indiscretions of the student or child are met with a certain amount of parental vehemence, but that generally arises out of frustration rather than an idea of necessity."

The music took a livelier shift but was still too light to be taken seriously. Cyrus was confused. "I'm not sure I follow."

Villichez shifted his weight, leaning forward slightly. "Do you know why I signed on to this mission?" he paused to take a short breath but did not wait for an answer, "I was in Korea working on the avatar system with Dr. Jang when the Yersinia swept through Manila. It was swift and deadly, and my wife and sons were among the first afflicted. The lab where they worked had been quarantined to protect the specimens and the researchers, but ironically, it wasn't exposure to rodents, or vermin, or even others infected with the disease that got the best of them. You see, we had felt fortunate enough to be able to afford pets, especially our two dogs that helped protect the house from monkey attacks, but evidently, those with pets had been more susceptible to the disease. Ironically, it was the animals that had vigilantly protected us from harm that had somehow become carriers for the malady. By the time the quarantine at the airports had been lifted, my wife, children, and all our pets had already been cremated. Omari, my eldest, a brilliant zoologist, had been such a handful as a child. He was too smart for his own good and too full of fire to be controlled by anyone who wasn't as smart as him. I fancy that's why he had such an affinity for animals—especially primates and predators."

Villichez moved his thumb across the ephemeris on his desk, and the monotonous music stopped, leaving nothing but the hum of the ship. "I am a man who takes pride in his level of patience and diplomacy, but that boy could push me to my limit as fast as flipping on a switch. It was as if that boy had a remote control to my adrenal gland, and he enjoyed using it. But as he became a man, I understood—I was frustrated more by his constant reminder of my own transgressions as a young man than by his indiscretions themselves, and every time he reminded me, an uncontrollable look of disdain would arrest my expression."

The look of confusion was gone, but Cyrus still had no words in response. There was a long silence magnified by the oscillations of the metal and plastic that ushered them through space at a speed that stretched the moment nigh unto its threshold. Villichez looked at the ground, hand clasped across his knee, frozen. It was if he had been left behind by the ship, and only his image remained, while Cyrus, still traveling close to the limits of the universe, was moving too fast to comprehend the reality that surrounded the wizened old man. But he understood. At any speed, the thoughts that consumed the man before him, turning his eyes to the floor, were as real and visceral to Cyrus as the incessant hum in the walls. The weight of it all stooped Cyrus's head as well until Villichez overwhelmed the buzzing with his voice, "You ever wonder why the greatest works of literature or of art center around pain and strife?"

Cyrus only shook his head.

"It's because happiness is easy. We get it. It doesn't need explanation." Villichez smiled as if the next thought lent him strength. "It's misery that needs examining—that needs purpose. I expected to find that purpose on this trip." Villichez's smile was wide now, almost a grin. "So far, I have not been let down."

Cyrus let the words resonate in his ears and settle in his head. There was really nothing left to say. He stood from his chair slowly and extended his hand. Villichez stood and took his hand in both his. Villichez shook it loosely, but it was definite nonetheless. As Cyrus turned to leave, words of his own finally made their way from his head to his tongue. "Didn't feel much like I would expect—the counseling and all."

"Son, I don't think you would ever *allow* me to counsel you. Not unless it was of your own volition. Maybe not even then."

Cyrus smiled and nodded as Villichez patted his hand and released it. Cyrus approached the door, and it slid open to reveal Dr. Eisenhertz waiting, leaning against the outside wall. Cyrus nodded to him, and Eisenhertz returned the nod as they exchanged places in the doorway. As Dr. Villichez greeted Eisenhertz, and the door slid shut, the air seemed lighter than before and a little less cold.

• • • • •

The morning was like any other—except this morning, the ship had been slowed to a speed measurable to the average Novitiate with a datadeck. Everyone was packed into the underused bridge of the ship, and for the first time in two hundred and two relative years, the louvers were open, enabling everyone to take in the infinite breadth of space from a perspective never witnessed by a mortal man.

They had approached the planet from the day side. Set, the blistering orange ball of fusing gas that warmed Asha, lay behind them. Four hours ago, they had run a medium-range scan on the morning edge of daylight. Cyrus, Milliken, and Dr. Qin had examined the data and determined a place to land and set up camp where they would have access to the underground freshwater, and where they could ensure at least twenty years of daylight. Cyrus anticipated stepping out into the open barren of Asha, breathing unprocessed air for the first time in three lifetimes. The ship's suncasters provided white light as energized as sunlight, and the orange rays of Set would most likely be strange at first, but Cyrus looked forward to the familiar feeling of charged photons cascading over his skin from a natural sun.

Commander Uzziah was maneuvering the ship to deploy the communications satellite in geosynchronous orbit over the spot they had selected. Jang sat fixated on the command unit, ensuring the data from Cyrus, Milliken, and Dr. Qin had been properly processed by the Shipmate. Toutopolus sat almost shoulder to shoulder with Jang, huddled over the holographic imager, both visibly shaking with excitement in search of any unforeseen meteorites or debris in the vicinity of the ship.

"Uh, have we deployed the satellite yet?" Toutopolus asked, a barely perceptible vibrato in his voice.

"Dr. Tsuchiya hasn't even suited up yet," Commander Uzziah informed.

The trill in Toutopolus's voice increased as did his pitch, "Then can someone please explain to me why it's floating by about fifty kilometers out?" Toutopolus moved aside to give the scientists closest to him a better view of the hologram. Sure enough, there was a satellite-shaped object about fifty kilometers out in an orbit slightly closer to the planet.

"What the hell?" Cyrus intoned to himself as he increased the size of the object on the imager.

"That's definitely a satellite, but it's not one of ours," Jang added amidst a now audible murmur in the background. He pointed to the insignia emblazoned across the side of the device as Cyrus continued to zoom. 'Terrick,' a hyphen, and the Greek letter rho were now clearly visible on the hologram.

"Son of an uberhound," Uzziah uttered, closely examining the impossible three-dimensional image floating in front of him.

"Uhh…" someone behind them muttered, "Uhh, guys…" Dr. Eisenhertz was pointing at something along the horizon line of the planet outside the window. They all followed his index finger to the brightening glimmer at the far edge of the planet. The sun caught the small metal object in the distance, and it took a moment to register the distance and size of the thing. They could see a proportionally thin tether attached to it, and Cyrus and Dr. Qin instantly knew what it must be—even though it was impossible.

"It's an orbital elevator," Dr. Qin said, more to himself than everyone else.

"What?" Dr. Villichez puzzled, "How the…"

"Hailing all frequencies! Earth vehicle surrender your controls, deactivate all scanning devices and weaponry, and prepare for armed escort and conveyance," a voice with an elusive accent declared over the emergency hailing system with bombast and authority. The imaging hologram zoomed out automatically as the proximity alarm sounded. Two small spacecraft, blatantly designed to intimidate, approached the image of the Paracelsus from either side at menacing velocities.

Even Commander Uzziah seemed daunted in his attempt to gain his bearings. The two attack ships matched the orbit of the Paracelsus slightly below and on either side as the satellite passed beneath the formation. The orbital tether grew on the horizon, and its enormity became apparent as it grew much slower than any object on the immediate horizon should have.

"What should we do?" Fordham asked as a din of bewilderment and panic began to surface around him.

"We should comply. We are ill-equipped to deal with this any other way," Uzziah said, moving his hand to disengage the ship's scanning systems. As the hologram faded, two larger vehicles approached from above and below and then the image was gone. The ship shook suddenly, but the shaking quickly subsided to a low oscillation as the hull vibrated in the magnetic grip of their escorts.

They ushered along in silence as the tethered station, now clearly a dodecahedron, grew on the horizon line. The journey to the station seemed longer and more taxing than the five relative years since they had awakened from their Hyposomatic sleep. Each of them stood before the window of the Paracelsus in absolute silence, watching the impossible unfold before them.

Cyrus ran through the possibilities in his head. The only realistic possibility was that Winberg had been correct. Man had somehow conquered the light-speed barrier in their relativistic lifespan and quite possibly, as Winberg had also proposed, in their original lifespan. The biggest and most pressing question, at least to Cyrus, was if that barrier had been broken before or after the Damocles had been built. The anxiety made the room seem impossibly hot.

"They seem a bit uninviting, no?" someone uttered.

"Something is very unsettling. Why does a colony need fighters? Especially ones they can scramble that quickly." Commander Uzziah folded his arms, watching the window intently.

They moved farther away from the star that illuminated their way as the station loomed before them. They were close enough to see indiscernible movements in the windows like moirés on an antiquated vid monitor. There were four tethers that tapered into the base of the station. The tethers must have been anchored to the ground more than thirty thousand kilometers below. They gleamed in the light cast from behind and arrested Cyrus's attention. Something moved along one of them toward the station. It seemed like a bulge in the cable at first, but the contrast of the polished gray to the shimmering gold of the cord it ran along proved to Cyrus that it was an elevator car. It also proved that even though the station now eclipsed their view of the horizon almost entirely, they still had not witnessed the full magnitude of the thing's size.

As the elevator module moved into the shadow of the titanic orbiter, the glistening tethers, catching and reflecting the orange rays of Set as the Paracelsus passed between them, gave the impression of white hot fire. It was as if the cables had been erected by the gods themselves to keep these strange men leashed to the planet they had chosen as their home. Then, the idea set upon him like a falcon, as swift as it was arresting. "Whoever these people are, they have managed something we could not accomplish on Earth for four hundred years," the awe in Cyrus's voice was magnanimous.

Everyone, stymied in their own right, let the words hang on them until, some seconds later, Dr. Winberg expressed his puzzlement at the comment, "I fail to see what can be more dumfounding than this ordeal as a whole."

The statement was less rhetorical than it sounded, but Cyrus was too transfixed to be annoyed. "The very existence of this station is dumfounding. We could never build an orbital this size—not with tethers like that. This was all impossible on Earth."

"I don't understand, we have the Lunar Tether, the Martian Cable Station, and the Eros Slingshot," Dr. Rousseau interjected.

Dr. Qin understood what Cyrus was getting at, but was not sure where he was going with it. "Those tethers you mentioned are all much shorter; they aren't under the same gravitational stress."

"Nor do they have the same problem of atmospheric corrosion. Aluminum suffices for the thinner Martian upper atmosphere, but these tethers—at least ten thousand kilometers of *each* tether—are coated in gold."

"How can you know it's gold? Any number of metals can exhibit that coloration and luster," the anxiety in Milliken's voice made him seem indignant.

"True, but gold and platinum are virtually immune to atmospheric corrosion. The only coating suitable for Terran tethers is gold. Aluminum, in the atmosphere of Earth, would have to be repaired so often it would render the tether unusable," the amazement in Cyrus voice could not be overshadowed by the angst of the moment.

"Then how did they manage that here?" Dr. Jang asked, leaning on the console, trying to get as good a view of the glinting cables as he could before they were completely consumed by the sheer mass of the station.

"Clearly, such an expense was not an issue here," Cyrus said as a large bay door opened, still several kilometers in front of them. A mist of dust and small debris spread from the opening, catching rays of starlight as it rushed from beneath the door with the escaping oxygen. Then, the humming ceased, and the new, profound silence, incomparable to anything they had heard in each of their lives, engrossed the ship. It was if death itself had enshrouded them, and their ears had failed. The anxious warmth was now gone and was replaced with hard, cold fear.

As their momentum carried them into the mouth of the colossus, lights inside the docking bay came to life. They were ushered closer and could see men in vac-suits in formation around the spot set aside for them. The men were all brandishing weapons.

eleven

—*Did anything interesting happen at school today, Dari?*
—*Not really...*
—*Nothing at all?*
—*Well, there was one thing, but it wasn't a big deal.*
—*It wasn't a big deal? Is that why Miss Hasabe comm-satted me today while I was at the Arcology?*
—*She comm-satted you?*
—*Yes, and she told me about the whole thing, but I want to hear it from you before I say anything.*
—*I didn't think it was that big of a deal. Terry, Scott, and Anthony were playing by the air vent. They had some sweetbar wrappers and were making them hover over it. I was playing with them, and I made a little man out of a stylus tip and put him on my wrapper. I was pretending he was riding on a lev-barge, giving a speech like the Chancellor, but the wrapper twisted, and the stylus tip fell into the vent. The vent started smoking, and it stopped, so we ran to the other side of the room and acted like we didn't know what happened. They had to call a maintenance bot to fix it. It didn't take long to fix, but we lost class time because we had to wait in the hall. Miss Hasabe was losing her mind and screaming at everyone, and when she started asking what happened, those guys told on me.*
—*Is that it?*
—*Well, no, not really. She calmed down a little and asked me in front of the whole class what my problem was, and why I was playing with the vent. It was kinda embarrassing, and I felt bad because I wasn't the only one, so I told her that I wasn't the only one playing with it, but I didn't tell who did it. She asked me if I thought that it was a good idea to do something just because everyone else did, and I told her that every day she's always making me do things because everyone else does it that way. Then, she asked me if everyone was jumping off a bridge, would I jump off too, and I told her that it depended on how high the bridge was, what was underneath it, and why they were jumping off. After that, the class started laughing, and she completely lost her y-drive and flipped out. She left class, and a proxy came in for a few minutes, and when she came back,*

she was still kinda fritzy, but she was at least leveled-out again. She didn't say anything else to me for the rest of the class, so I thought everything was atmospheric again. Besides, I was pretty hot at Terry, Scott, and Anthony for making me out to be the vent monkey.

—I want you to listen to me because I don't want to repeat this again. I don't care if your teacher is off her y and x-axis, you don't mouth off in class again, copasetic?

—But she started it. The way she came at me was sideways, Dada.

—I understand that, and I agree, but still, she writes policy in that room. If she comes at you sideways, you stomach it until you have a free moment, and you comm-sat me, or you accept the consequences.

—Well, what if she's being a bully, and she's dead wrong? What if setting her level is worth the consequences?

—If it is truly worth the trouble, and you feel you're man enough to re-write policy, then when I ask you what happened, you damn sure better be man enough to tell me.

—Fair enough, Dada.

—Besides, I'm sure from now on, she'll think twice about asking questions she doesn't want answered.

• • • • •

As the ship had settled in the electromagnetic net inside the hangar, the armed men had stood around it as the hangar door closed and the bay pressurized. They had surrounded the ship, concentrating on the entrance hatch and cargo bay doors with guns that were integrated into their suits—presumably, so they could be fired in a vacuum. Instructions to lay down any arms and surrender their ship for boarding and inspection had been issued over their comm-link, and they had complied. The soldiers that had boarded their ship were neither hospitable nor gentle. The soldiers had shown complete disregard for the ship and equipment as they had brusquely ushered the scientists from the bridge into the hangar, down a long hallway, and directly into a climber unit. The soldiers had only spoken to bark directions through their speaker units, usually followed by some scathing insult, or to tell one of the scientists to shut up—usually followed by some barely decipherable, but obviously more scathing, insult.

The alarming speed with which the climber descended had been countered by what must have been a gravity wave generator of some sort. The fall to the planet had taken a mere two hours—an impressively short time to travel thirty thousand kilometers in an elevator, but much too long to be shoulder to shoulder, surrounded by surly soldiers with loaded weapons who seemed to have a marked distaste for thier presence—especially when they had no idea what the hell was going on. Jang had remarked to Cyrus that the station was called the J.L. Orbital, as evidenced by a placard in the climber, but he had been immediately threatened with a weapon and told to shut his dung-sucking cake hole.

Now, traveling along the ave in a personnel carrier that had been converted to carry freight rather than humans, wispy apparitions of vapor, too ephemeral to be called clouds, hang over the barren expanse like a cataract. The ave was a wide, unnaturally straight depression, honed to a smoothness that made it look like water in the rays of Set that wavered in the lines of heat rising from the surface.

The personnel lev that ushered them along was deceptively fast and yet moved more smoothly than anything on Earth Cyrus could remember. It was not clear how fast the carrier was moving until they began to pass tall, monolithic spires that seemed to mark each kilometer.

The path led to a second sun that stood at the end of the ave in defiance of the burning ball of orange gas alarmingly low on the horizon behind them. As they approached, Cyrus realized the orange flame they were speeding toward was a reflection of the the star behind them, and that the round ball that reflected it was a dome of some sort. It must have been overwhelmingly large as the ave-side spires appeared at a much higher frequency than its rate of growth.

Even though it was smaller and less dense than the Earth, everything about Asha this day seemed foreboding and unreasonably big. The personnel lev moved past a plateau alongside the road almost as fast as it had appeared on the horizon. Then, there was a pebble that grew to a boulder the size of the craft itself in a matter of seconds. The pilot must have known the boulder was there because he reacted to it even before it had become an obvious obstacle, accelerating the craft on its z-axis, rising momentarily above the precipice of the plateau, then coming back smoothly down to its original altitude.

Jang leaned close to Cyrus, muttering beneath his breath, "Did you notice something strange about that z-shift?"

Cyrus mumbled a negative response through closed lips.

"No hair-rise on the back of the neck. No EM flux," he explained through his own lips, tightly pursed.

"Gravity drive," Cyrus muttered, a little too loud. One of the soldiers, his face obscured by his vac-suit visor, turned to face Cyrus. The soldier lifted the weapon enclosed within the arm of the suit and bellowed through a loudspeaker, "No talking, terrasitic punt-mongrel!"

Momentarily, the heat that flowed into Cyrus's face and centered behind his eyes overwhelmed his shock. He could not take weapons drawn on him lightly, especially with the pretense of intimidation. Even in his anger, Cyrus caught a glimpse of the thin badge over the soldier's heart. It did not display a name, only a metal square with rounded corners and what looked like a hexadecimal barcode with a number beneath it—43235. When the soldier turned, the dome was large enough now to see that the light reflected by the construction was not a reflection at all. Blinding, a pale orange light was being cast from every centimeter of the city's protective covering, but it wasn't consistent. It was hard to look at for very long, but it seemed like the luminescence throughout the dome wavered slightly, and near the lower parts of the structure, the light seemed somewhat dimmer. All of the scientists were forced to turn away or look at the ground, but the soldiers held their positions, the tinted faceplates of the suits sheltering them from the increasingly fierce light of the dome.

When they reached the dome, the light was almost unbearable, and even the interior of the personnel carrier was bathed in it. Most could only keep their eyes open for short periods, while others just kept them closed. Cyrus kept his eyes open for as long as he could, sheltering them with his hand when they began to hurt, and only closing them when the pain was unbearable. When he closed his eyes, streaks of orange and red still danced along the insides of his eyelids.

The gates of the city were large bulkheads that slid open as the carrier approached. There was a long tube with track lighting that was much dimmer than the exterior. Details were hard to catch as their speed and dilating pupils lent too much contrast to the bleached, titian hues that commanded the bleak expanse outside. Then, as his eyes adjusted, Cyrus could see a fine mist dancing toward the center of the chamber in the tracking lights, swirling as it filled the tube. A mist was also pumped into the carrier, which was beginning to slow down.

Bulkheads on the opposite end of the long tube opened, and as they emerged, they were all flabbergasted. The city was large. There were high-rise buildings as well as smaller structures—all with a strange angular efficiency of design. Most of the buildings had windows, but a few seemed to have none at all. The aves were straight and uniform, teeming with levs of various shapes and sizes, and there was even a second layer of traffic several meters above the aves following the same patterns of movement. All of this would have been difficult to take in by a Fringer or someone who lived in a subsistence community, but it was only slightly stranger than the lives they all knew on Earth. The thing that floored their understanding was that inside this monstrous dome that harbored a seemingly cosmopolitan existence from the cruel wasteland outside, it was nighttime, and the stars were shining.

"What the..." Milliken whimpered, involuntarily then immediately hushed.

"The lights of the dome. They must be phase-canceling the sunlight," Cyrus explained.

"Not another word, you Earth-born son of a man-fuck," 43235 was becoming more decipherable and more threatening, but Cyrus would not be silenced.

"Probably been mimicking *Earth* day cycles for decades, maybe hundreds of years."

Soldier 43235 took a step toward Cyrus, and lifted his gun barrel to Cyrus's chest. A harsh blend of anger, fear, and frustration moved through Cyrus, rushing directly to his head and filling his limbs with impetus. Cyrus moved his face as close to the soldier's visor as he could. He could not see the man's face through the tinted plastic, but he didn't need to. Cyrus's words misted the visor as he spoke, "Shoot me, or get the fuck out of my face."

Cyrus could hear the soldier's breathing escalating behind the visor as he extended his arm and pushed Cyrus back with the nose of the gun barrel. As soon as the barrel touched his chest, Cyrus lifted his knee and extended all the impulse in his body into a kick that hit the man's solar plexus, sending him backward against the copilot seat of the carrier and collapsing him to the floor on top of his gun. Cyrus stood fast. He was angry, confused, and rash, but he knew better than to pursue. And then it came—he knew it was coming, just hadn't expected it when it did come. A blow to the back of Cyrus's head sent him down to the floor. Cyrus caught himself, but lassitude overtook him even as the second blow came down between his shoulder blades. As his body settled on the cold metal of the floor, blackness swirled across Cyrus's vision, and as the sound around him became increasingly more muffled, he heard the electronic hiss of, "Welcome to Eurydice, beta-hound," as consciousness faded from his body.

twelve

—Dada, where do uberhounds come from?

—They are bred in labs in hystapods similar to the ones used for extra-uterine childbirths.

—Extra-uterine means outside the mommy, right? Inside is called freebirth, but it's really dangerous.

—Well, 'freebirth' is a term I'd rather you not use. It isn't proper or very nice. It's called in utero birth.

—How do they get the uberhounds to be so strong and scary?

—They have nanoprocessors injected into their brains while they are in the pods to enhance their senses and strength, and so their disposition can be controlled by remote. Rumor is, they may be able to enhance the sense of smell so hounds can even 'smell' parts of DNA.

—Does it hurt when they inject the nanoprocessors, Dada?

—At that stage in life, I'm not sure they would even understand pain. I would think the unnamable shock of spending the very first stage of life forcibly detached from your own kind would be distressing enough.

—Was I born in a pod, Dada?

—Most everyone is these days. It makes it much easier to check for and correct defects.

—Is that a good thing, Dada?

—People seem to think it is.

—What do you think?

—Well, I tend to think our strengths make us good, but our shortcomings make us great.

—I think that when I have kids, I want them to be born the right way. And no doctors tinkering with defects and all that.

—Hopefully, when that time comes, we will have learned enough to just let nature do her thing and to keep our grimy little hands to ourselves.

• • • • •

The throbbing in Cyrus's head and neck stirred him to consciousness. When he came to, he was propped up in a chair in a nondescript room. All the other scientists were arranged in three rows of chairs, while he sat in the center of the frontmost row. Tanner and Davidson sat on either side of him, making sure his body stayed upright. There was a man in a peculiar outfit; he wore a jacket that looked like a blue lab coat cut-off at the hips, buttoned with only the middle two of the four buttons along the front. The legs of the man's pants were completely without pleats or seems, which made them look more like black plastic tubes than fabric. His hair was relatively short and looked as if it had been attended to, but still had no particularly discernable style. The man was flanked by two more men carrying assault rifles who wore khaki jumpsuits similar to early flight suits but lighter in color. Their insignias looked like a barcode, and they had square medallions hanging above them.

"Now that all of you have joined us, we can parlay on the problem at hand," the man in blue and black said, pacing the floor with his hands clasped behind his back. "But first, allow me to introduce myself. I am Torus Balfour Denali," he paused as if he were awaiting recognition. Cyrus, head pounding with the beating of his heart, could not tell what part of his name, if any, was a title until he noticed the thick-rimmed oval ring clasped to the man's insignia badge—'Torus' was a contrast to the squares worn by the members of his entourage. When no acknowledgment came, the strange man continued, "I am commander of the Archons of Asha, and I believe you are espions and that you should be treated as such." He paused again as if he expected a response other than confusion. "However, hospitality has been demanded of me by the Praetoriate. It is their desire that I show you the utmost courtesy while your sudden 'appearance' is investigated. It is their belief that the war was over too long ago for a reconnaissance operation to be of use, but I find your appearance so close to the Advent of the Defiance to be entirely too ironic."

"There was a war?" someone behind Cyrus blurted. The outburst was so sudden it rang through his ears and settled with pounding authority in his temple.

Denali scoffed with an expression that looked like he was about to hock and spit. He then waved his hand through the air in an almost unconscious gesture as if he was slapping the air with the back of his hand. "I will not trifle with your feigned confusion." He looked as if he were about to spit again. "Quadrad Chaldea will regale any queries you port to have." Denali made another slapping motion and left as the guard to his right moved forward.

"I may have orders to gale you out, but you can all punt off as far as I am haunted." the soldier mimed the same hand motion Denali had made, only less theatrically. "So to your first que-ree, the war started in the first gyre and was finished by the Defiance of the Knight of Swords on eight DC, Murioplex, twenty-five gyres from. Some think what the Sword Scourge did was overstrong, but if you query me, I wage you terrasites were arreared too long." He basked for a moment in the light streaming from the bands in the ceiling, proud either of his words or what they meant. Whatever conceit was inherent in his delivery was lost in the quagmire of confusion on the faces of everyone in his audience.

Tanner leaned over to Cyrus, who was holding the bruise on his head and mumbling figures to himself. "Whoever these people are, they have been here hundreds of years..." Tanner said softly into his ear.

"Yeah, the tech is much more advanced." Cyrus winced.

"And the language is almost a creole. Even British English and original American English weren't this different up until just before the Uni."

"Well, they weren't six hundred light years apart either, but..."

"You que me or you finish the jatter, dexter!" the guard interrupted, folding his arms as he stood. He moved closer to Cyrus. "You are the punty breed-hound that put the gork to Colfax." He moved within arm's reach. "If they dint order me to coddle, I would strong-arm you rightforth."

Cyrus took his hand from his head, rolled his shoulders back, and flared his nostrils as he met the eyes of the soldier Denali had called Chaldea. Tanner could almost feel the fury building in Cyrus again as if tendrils of some invisible electromagnetic current were stretching out of Cyrus's eyes toward the strange man before him. Cyrus was almost lifting himself from the seat with his anger when Chaldea retracted.

"Scrabbling like a feist-monkey only vinces you more the spions, but I gale you this; I won gork out like that sunfried Colfax. You tuss with me you get finished, complete. If I were you, I would process that rightforth, dexter." Chaldea gestured, and the door opened. Six armed men with triangles on their badges entered the room and ushered the scientists out in two groups. Cyrus, Tanner, Villichez, Toutopolus, Jang, Winberg, Torvald, Cohn, Uzziah, and Murphy were corralled and shuffled in one direction, while Milliken, Davidson, Qin, Fordham,

Eisenhertz, Tsuchiya, Murphy, Koresh, bin Hassan, and Thompson were marshaled in the other.

Cyrus's group was set up in a room that looked like a barracks. It was a long, somewhat narrow room with five bunk beds lining the wall on one side and a long window with a view of the city on the other. There were two footlockers at the end of each bunk and a rather large, and completely out of place, holostation in the corner of the room furthest away from the door. Opposite the sliding entrance door was an antiquated swinging door that led to what must have been the showers and the lav. After they all shambled into the room, the door closed behind them, and they were left to their own devices without any instructions or explanation. After their exhaustion began to overtake their confusion, they began to settle into various bunks. Cyrus made an attempt to do a few push-ups to quell his frustration, but they only made his head pound more fiercely. Finally, he settled on the bottom bunk closest to the lav and holostation.

Jang settled next to the window, watching traffic speed by below. They were about seven stories up as far as Jang could tell. The elevator they had been packed into had the numbers covered, and the soldiers had sheltered the buttons when they pressed them. The elevator was a large one designed to move freight, but it had been too cramped to get a good idea what button had been pressed. Now, Jang could see that they were about twenty-five meters above ave level. Upon closer inspection, Jang realized the floors must have been slightly higher than those on Earth because on all the buildings he could see, what his eyes told him should have been seven stories appeared to be only slightly larger than five.

After his head had convinced him it would explode if he did another push-up, Cyrus went over to the holostation and turned it on to pick up the broadcast stream. Remarkably, even though it was considerably larger, had a higher resolution, and projected directly onto the floor, the hand gestures to operate the holostation were very similar to those on Earth. A few of the scientists sat together on the bunks, but no one said much of anything. After about an hour of lumbering around, the door opened, and three soldiers brought a clear plastic container of food for each of the scientists. There was cubed steak, rice, and tomatoes on a bed of lettuce, as well as a cup of water glued in the corner of each. The soldiers handed each scientist a container, then grabbed Toutopolus rudely, shuffling him out the door with his dinner.

Cyrus, in the middle of shoveling a forkful of tomato and lettuce into his mouth, watched as they took Toutopolus. A few of the others had noticed Toutopolus's abduction, but most were too exhausted to protest as they turned their attention back to the first food they had seen in uncountable hours. Cyrus noticed Tanner bowing his head over his container of food for much longer than normal. Cyrus picked up his own food, dragged his feet over to the bunk Tanner had chosen, and opened his dinner as he sat down.

Tanner looked up from his prayer to find Cyrus shoveling chunks of steak into his mouth. Cyrus noticed Tanner had finished his vigil. "Tastes strange. Really slimy," he spoke between exaggerated chews.

"That's because you haven't had real meat in two hundred years," Tanner said as he opened his meal. "Any idea what they're doing with Toutopolus?"

"I was just about to ask the same thing." Cyrus chewed another bite of ground steak. "Meat's pretty grimy if you don't eat it for a while, huh?" He swallowed. "I think they're probably *querying* him now about all this *espion* nonsense."

Someone in the room began sobbing. Tanner swallowed, then looked at Cyrus for a long moment as he stared at the holographic images on the floor. "I thought you hated the holocast stream."

"I do. But it's the fastest way to find out anything. Everyone here seems bent off their runner—too bent to fill us in."

"One way or the other we're going to have to adjust." Tanner looked at his food, hands on his knees. "This is the deal, huh?"

Cyrus shook his head. "Just trying to figure out what the timeframe is. I keep wondering how I can keep Darius from cruising up on this snag a year from now."

"After they find out what happened, they could let us go."

"So far, they don't seem like the letting-go type." Cyrus shoveled in a mouthful of rice and chewed quickly. He spoke through the food as he stood, "I'm gonna gather some more recon."

Cyrus walked back to the holostation to find Jang propped up in front of it, his lunch devoid of rice and vegetables, with only a small bite taken from the steak. As Cyrus walked, he noticed Dr. Cohn curled up on a bottom bunk, whimpering with his sheet over his head.

Cyrus could feel the same pressure that was flowing through his body when he kicked Colfax 43235. It strangled his mind into its least common denominator, but it motivated him and made him impetuous. It took every ounce of his intellect and reason to keep him calm, but he needed focus now more than piss and vinegar, and another outburst like the one on the personnel carrier might get him shot.

Cyrus knelt next to Jang, who was cycling through streams on the holostation. He settled on a stream that must have been dedicated to children because there were grown men grinning unrealistically and prancing around in single-colored outfits. Jang fixated on the ridiculous scene as the men began singing numbers and counting various fruits, some recognizable, some strange versions of the familiar. The fruits bounced around the floor of the barracks in bunches as the men counted in sing-song voices.

"I'm processing," Jang said before Cyrus could ask, then fell back into his trance. Cyrus ate more of his dinner and looked around the room. Winberg was rocking himself on a bunk next to Villichez, speaking too softly to be heard. Cyrus couldn't help noticing that it was the quietest he had ever heard Winberg speak. Commander Uzziah was standing in the corner beside the lav door with his arms folded. Cyrus could tell he was absorbing every nook and cranny of the room. Torvald stood at the window, transfixed at the scene outside. His food was untouched, and his body was limp against the window itself, which seemed the only thing that kept him from blowing away like a discarded wrapper on a desolate, windy ave corner.

After what seemed like a half hour of little change, Dr. Murphy screamed from inside the lav and came running toward the door, his pants draped awkwardly beneath his waist. When he reached the door, the cuff of his pants leg caught underfoot, and he tumbled toward the door and crashed against it face-first. His body bounced, but he lunged back at the door and began pounding on it and screaming, "What the hell is going on? Tell us what is going on!" over and over again.

Villichez made an attempt to calm him, but it was of little use. Finally, after about five minutes, some guards came into the room, and Murphy collapsed to the floor in a sobbing, exhausted heap. The soldiers entered, and everyone expected them to attack Murphy or haul him away, but they merely pushed him to the side. They returned a spent Toutopolus and moved directly to the bunk of Dr. Cohn, who seemed to have run out of water to fuel his tears. Cohn was repeating a verse to a song in Hebrew softly to himself when they snatched him from his bunk. He seemed like he was going willfully until he reached the door and saw Dr. Murphy, now silent, slumped uncomfortably against the wall. Dr. Cohn stopped, focused on Murphy for a moment, then began thrashing wildly and muttering in Hebrew. One of the guards reeled from being smacked in the face by a flailing elbow, but two others grabbed Cohn's arms at the wrists and twisted them painfully behind his back. Cohn dropped his weight like a veteran tantrum-thrower and stiffened his legs, but the guards wordlessly scooped his legs from under him and took him away.

Everyone was silent after the spectacle. Villichez, somehow composed through all this, moved over to the bunk where Toutopolus sat and put his hand on his shoulder. Cyrus went to move closer to where they were so he could hear what had happened, but Uzziah stopped him. "They are watching us," Uzziah said, pushing Cyrus toward the holostation where Jang still sat mesmerized.

Uzziah ignored Jang and moved his hand, signaling the holostation to its maximum volume. Jang stayed focused on the holographic figures moving on the floor. Uzziah turned his back to the holostation, looking toward Villichez and Toutopolus, but he stepped so that his mouth was very close to Cyrus's ear. Cyrus stayed focused on the holograms on the floor as Uzziah spoke. "They took the one that was hysterical. There were two that had obviously broken, but they took the least violent," he mumbled.

"What does it mean?" Cyrus muttered under his breath as if he were speaking to Jang kneeling on the floor in front of him.

"It means they still think they are fighting a war. But whatever it is, the rest of the city seems unconcerned. Something very odd is happening here."

"Beyond the fact that none of this should be here?" Cyrus's attempt at humor was smothered by the tension in his own voice.

"I think I got it!" Jang yelled, hopping to his feet and alarming both Uzziah and Cyrus into defensive positions.

"You've got what?" Cyrus said, relaxing his guard, but falling a step away from Jang.

"The names of the *Dhekad*. They are like months but shorter. The names are like transliterated Greek numbers. *Dhekak* is the first. *Murioplex* is when that Chaldea idiot said this Defiance thing happened. *Aekatomuriox*, the current *Dhekad*, is the sixth. So it's my guess they are all named after the respective 10-base Greek numbers, or at least variations on them, which would imply that each one is only ten days, or Dome Cycles, long. My guess is, that's the time it takes for them to complete one phase-cancelled sunrise and sunset. Their years are called *gyres* and, as far as I can tell, are made up of ten Dhekads and are one hundred DC." He was so excited he did not pause to breathe during his oration.

Cyrus stopped, the muscles in his body froze suddenly as if some visceral part of him knew something his brain did not yet comprehend. "Wait, did that program say what gyre it is now?"

Jang looked confused, as if he had been following a line of breadcrumbs, and the trail in front of him had just been blown away by some unexpected gale. "Uh...three DC, Aekatomuriox, two thousand, two hundred and sixteenth gyre."

Cyrus rolled his eyes to the ceiling and mumbled to himself, rolling numbers through his head as quickly as he could without jumbling them. After a few seconds, he paused, quickly checked his figures in his head again, and then looked back at Jang. "That would mean the war happened about 607 Earth years ago. Good lord..."

"But we have no idea how long after settlement the war started," Jang added.

"I don't think these hound's wives are gonna offer up that information from the looks of it either. We'll have to take shifts on the gram until we can figure it out."

"Sure," Jang moved back toward his perch, but then stopped and turned back to Cyrus, "Out of curiosity, why the urgency?"

"The only way this could be here is if someone developed faster-than-light technology—most likely some form of continual-phase shift. The question is more *when* than how."

"Still not sure what that has to do with what they are doing to us and when it will stop."

Cyrus was calm, but his eyes, as focused and still as they were, seemed as if they were staring not at Jang, but into some horrific place that humans did not belong and were not welcome. "Well, it has very little to do with us all directly, but it has very much to do with me. So if you don't mind, for the sake of the others, could you please humor me? Because if I don't find out what's happened to my son soon, I'm gonna set as much of this place on fire as I can 'til they shoot me—and if me being shot doesn't affect you, I'm sure the fire will."

thirteen

—*I have something to tell you, Dada.*

—*What's that Dari?*

—*Well, uhh...Uhh, never mind.*

—*Come on Dari; you can't tell someone you have something to tell them and then tell them never mind. That's foul.*

—*Well, okay, but promise you won't get mad.*

—*How can I promise you that? The simple fact that you feel the need to ask me to not get mad means you believe whatever you have to say most likely* will *make me mad. That's like asking someone to promise to not die just before you stab them. I have very little control over the emotions generated by what you haven't said yet.*

—*Well, that's why I don't want to say it.*

—*Hmm. Remember when we were coming down the ave after I picked you up yesterday, and that guy in the bright green lev turned in front of us against the arrow?*

—*Yeah, that was scary.*

—*Why was it so scary?*

—*Because he stopped right in front of us, and you had to tweak the x-axis not to hit him. We almost slid into the ave going the other way.*

—*All because the guy decided halfway through his mistake that he was being a test dummy.*

—*But what does that have to do with me?*

—*Listen Darius, and I'm gonna say this so you remember it. You can't be half a fuck-up. Sometimes, when you start something, you just have to finish to keep things from being worse. Things were screwed up the moment you decided to do what you did. So if you start to say something that might put someone off their x-axis, own up and finish it.*

—*Dada, I lost my ephemeris today, and I can't do my homework until I get a new one.*

—*Then we have to get you a new one before the gallery closes so we can get it primed and logged in today.*

—*You're not mad?*
—*No, I wish you'd take better care of your things, but no, I'm not mad. I would have been mad if I had to hear it from Miss Hasabe though. I swear that woman calls me more than your mother does. Your mother's going to begin to think she and I are having an affair.*
—*Uhh...*
—*What now?*
—*I don't know about mommy being scared of an affair, Dada. Cuz mommy's real pretty, and Miss Hasabe looks like a shaved monkey with a wig.*
—*Dari! That's not a very nice thing to say.*
—*You can't be half a...well you know.*
—*Boy, your antics are gonna get us both into some serious trouble.*
—*Well, when it happens, I'll try and give you as much early warning as I can.*

• • • • •

The room was beginning to smell like a locker room. Eight DCs had passed since they were brought here, and they had only seen the cleaning bot once. Jang believed the bot came in five-DC cycles, at the beginning and middle of each Dhekad. Even if the bot had come in two-DC cycles, it would be impossible for them to remove the stench of anxiety and misery that thickened the air, making breathing deliberate. It didn't help that many did not shower for fear of surveillance. To some it didn't matter, others got over it as time passed, but a few could not get beyond the idea of being watched every moment. Torvald would walk around normally and occasionally watch the holostation, but he would shiver periodically as if a draft had passed over him. Eventually, he would huddle up in his lower bunk, concealed by his blanket and the shadows. The showers themselves were like an ice bath. Uzziah remarked that the settings for hot water only worked marginally, probably to keep them from obscuring the gaze of their observers with steam. This theory seemed to prompt Murphy and Cohn to avoid the showers completely. The showers were not as cold as they seemed, but the knowledge of being watched with scrutiny while naked lowered the temperature for most of them dramatically. As far as the level of hospitality, nothing changed. Periodically, someone would sit by themselves for too long, or would talk too much about their life at home, or would stare at the wall or outside the window too long, and would get scooped up by guards. Villichez had unaffectionately named the guards the Flying Monkeys, as after seeing a hologramized version of The Wizard of Oz, they had become a frequent subject of his son's nightmares. Cohn and Toutopolus had been taken twice, and Murphy, Tanner, and Jang had all been taken once each. Tanner and Jang had both been taken—Jang literally while he was asleep—and had been left in empty rooms for hours without being asked any questions. Everyone's actions, in turn, became calculated and, as far as Cyrus could tell, no one slept until his body shut down from exhaustion.

A tap on his shoulder turned Cyrus's attention away from the hologram. "My turn," Jang stood behind him, his lab coat draped around his shoulders in a way that made it look like a cape. "Find out anything?"

"Not really. They keep talking about the mass migration to Druvidia that's coming up. Evidently, getting living space there is a big deal, and I guess new construction has been going on there to accommodate a large population."

"Must be taxing having to move every generation to run from the night. Wonder why they don't just make dome cycle lights that turn inward."

"Well, these, I'm sure, run off the power of Set itself; I can't imagine the energy source required otherwise."

"I guess they do have a ginormous free fusion reactor...say, you know, I forgot to tell you earlier, there was a cast about the development of the faster-than-light drive last night, or night cycle rather. They were talking about the first ship to colonize here. The Anemoi I think it was called."

"They say how it worked?"

"Something about reaching 50% of the speed of light then turning the gravity drive in on itself. Causes space-time to ripple and uses Laurel contraction or something like that..."

"Lorenz contraction."

"Yeah, that's it. Well, they said the gravity squeezes the ship to a size small enough to kind of fold into space-time and unfold in another place. Time lapses, but it is measured in seconds, not years. I'm sure it's more complicated than that, but the cast was written for Novitiates."

"Probably has something to do with building more efficient gravity drives. They have obviously made ones smaller that are less demanding of energy."

"Like that personnel lev we rode in on. That thing wasn't EM."

"They say when they developed it?"

"I think they said it took around thirty gyres on Earth to develop it and implement it into the first ship. Thirty gyres—a little more than eight years I guess."

"Pretty big project," Cyrus stood, stretching out his legs momentarily before standing fully erect. He arched his back and his shoulders blades until there was a slight pop from his spine. Jang pulled his lab coat over his shoulders and sat Indian style, his usual position in front of the holovision. "You get much rest?" Cyrus asked as he turned to walk away.

"Nope, been hard to sleep since I got waylaid. I catch ten to twenty here and there in fugues. I'm starting to see people standing behind me. I'd be a complete lab rodent right now if it wasn't for my shifts on this thing." Jang indicated the hologram as an advertisement for upscale living space in Druvidia displayed a somewhat Spartan but spacious dwelling. Cyrus nodded and returned to his bunk.

Villichez stood looking out the window as Cyrus sat down next to him. The dome was dimming almost imperceptibly, giving the impression of a sunset in a moonless sky. The artificial twilight was convincing except for the corner of orange sun peeking from behind a building at the end of the ave, fading with the darkening dome rather than descending below the horizon as it should.

"The speech patterns in this place are becoming marginally understandable, no?" Villichez scanned the ave outside, looking at the other building, in hopes someone might be there looking back.

"Seems to me, the more proper speech, like from the newscasts and children's casts, are more like standard Commonspeak than the colloquial speech in this facility. I find the educational and informational streams considerably easier to understand," Cyrus said, rubbing his thighs deliberately and stretching out his fingers to their limits as he kneaded his legs with his palms.

"Discover anything on your shift?" Villichez didn't take his eyes away from the city milling beneath them.

"Not really. Even though it was the newscast, it seems like not much happens here. This Defiance thing seems to be the most interesting thing around." Cyrus rubbed the fingers in his right hand until two of his knuckles popped. "Someone did steal some sort of military vehicle. They blamed it, like everything else wrong the last few Dome Cycles, on some gang called the Apostates. Other than that, it was normal, just your usual robbery or violent act." Cyrus twined the fingers of his hands together and then untwined them.

"Disturbing that we find robbery and acts of violence normal, don't you think?" Villichez stayed focused on the dimming sun, no longer too bright to look at directly.

"Well, jealousy and anger, however base, are natural human

emotions. Our responses to them would also have a range of normalcy and a threshold. A threshold that, I would think, exists on both sides of the bell curve. For every depraved action, there should be an overly tolerant, or equally base, inertia. They have to both exist for motion in any direction, but we tend to select them arbitrarily and to our own tastes." Cyrus was more alert now, his fingers no longer needing to move to engage his mind.

"I'm not sure I follow your meaning," Villichez turned from the window to face Cyrus.

"You see, it is not unheard of for a renegade monkey who is denied alpha status by a stronger monkey to steal the female offspring of the alpha monkey and raise it himself—not as its offspring, but as a mate so that his own offspring might be stronger. If a human had even the desire to do this, you would log a great deal of hours in your appointment book. If he actually went through with it, we would throw him into the deepest, darkest nook of the most horrid prison we could find. And yet, zoologists turn a jaundiced eye to it, reading it off as natural, so long as it's a monkey that's doing it. No one throws the monkey in jail. We just log it, categorize it, and keep moving. I know this example is extreme, but there are a great many responses to emotion that are not as extreme but fit the same paradigm that humans and monkeys share. But people like Winberg and the Meritocracy believe they somehow are unsavory for men, or rather affluent or educated men, to indulge in."

"But, human beings, my friend, are not monkeys."

"Given our current circumstance, I strongly beg to differ." Cyrus smiled. Villichez opened his mouth to answer but whatever he was about to say was shattered into oblivion by Jang's excitement.

"Look! There's a cast on that Knight of Swords guy," Jang reported, raising the contrast on the hologram so everyone could see. Everyone who had the slightest of their wits about them focused on the images that spread across the floor.

"...first Grand Mobius of Archons fronted the plight in the defense of Asha. Aerik Kazamesh, who became known as the Man of Swords, levied on the first vessel from Earth forty-seven gyres before the first. He helped design the Eurydice Dome and was given the title of Prefect of Stone while the first Prolocutor, Rex Mundi, was overseeing the construction of Druvidia." An image of a city-sized dome under construction spread across the floor in front of them. Construction levs lumbered around the structure, carrying building materials and manipulating parts of the dome with mechanical arms. The image faded, revealing a recording of a considerably older hologram. A man wearing a white linen robe was speaking in remarkably clear Commonspeak, with no trace of the accent the scientists had been assaulted with since their ill-fated arrival.

"When Prolocutor Mundi refused to allow any more levies from Earth and began violently turning away more persistent ships, Kazamesh was appointed Grand Mobius. He then established the Archons of Asha to help defend against the Terran backlash."

"A quiet and private man, Kazamesh refused public interviews and only regaled queries through surrogation. Although his surrogations were always quip and keen, he proved shrewd and ruthless at military strategy. His strategies turned back attack after attack from Earth." An image of a man wearing a more Earth-like version of the uniform Denali had been wearing faded from view, and the image was replaced by holograms of several smaller fighters attacking an ominous warship in a four-point pincer formation. Suddenly, what looked like a small asteroid sped in from some place off the hologram and collided with the warship in a place where the fighters had been concentrating their fire. It tore a hole in the side of the warship and metal, flame, and what could have only been bodies vomited from the scar. As the flames dissipated into the vacuum, the image faded again to reveal another image of Kazamesh in uniform, now holding some sort of card.

"When asked how he continued to win battles with minimal losses, he jatterly remarked that he used a set of Tarot cards given to him by his mother. This earned him the moniker 'Knight of Swords,' which he embraced." The hologram grew, filling the floor with the image of a Tarot card. The card showed a knight, sword in hand, charging on his horse toward some unseen foe. The card rotated once slowly and then dissolved into more scenes of interstellar battle. Extraplantetary lasers extended from Ashan frigates, ripping into large Earth warships. The warships fired volleys of missiles so numerous they looked like clouds of smoke. Electromagnetic disrupter fields around the warships gave off flashes of purple and red as they diffused many of the lasers, while frigates and fighters evaded or launched countermeasures. It looked like the later levels of Conquest of Ages, but was both quieter and yet more sinister.

"Earth began to send more vessels, and it seemed the war would press on for hundreds of gyres, but the invention of the Whisper Node gave Asha the edge over the oppressors. The ability to communicate instantly over any distance gave the Archons the ability to attack Earth directly." What must have been scientists and engineers, not in lab coats, but in light blue jumpsuits, posed next to an odd cubic machine that looked like a food processor. The scene switched to an image of a land dock where frigates and other engines of destruction were being assembled.

"Resources were plentiful, but with the construction of Jacob's Ladder and the Druvidian Project, ship construction was limited. Prolocutor Mundi suggested the forces regroup and fortify, but the Man of Swords had devised one final attack." A computer-generated image of a carrier ship, seemingly weaponless, appeared on the screen. It rotated slowly as it hovered above the floor. The side of the ship melted away to reveal its insides, giving an impression of scale. It was a smaller, extremely Earth-like ship that looked much like the Paracelsus.

"In defiance of the orders of the Prolocutor and the Praetoriate, the Knight of Swords launched Mjolnir, a faster-than-light craft retrofitted with a near-light drive. In a most devastating attack, he ordered Mjolnir to unfold just outside Earth orbit, traveling at 98% of the speed of light." An image of the northern hemisphere of Earth appeared, and just above the North Pole, there was a glimmer that erupted into what looked like a laser beam. The beam flashed for a fraction of a second then erupted in an explosion in the Arctic Circle. Even though the hologram played out in slow motion, the explosion spread faster than the eye could see, filling the floor with a flash of white light. Cyrus wanted to shield his eyes as Jang and Villichez did, but he looked on, enduring the pain of his pupils shrinking to pinpoints.

"The impact with the polar ice cap must have caused great destruction. The decisive blow finished the war, but little is currently known of the Terrans' fate as no word has been heard from Earth in the 2200 gyres since the Defiance." The hologram, which had remained inactive since the explosion, now faded into a tribunal. There were three figures sitting behind a large table on a rostrum. They each wore blue hoods that completely obscured their faces. A small diadem rested on each hood. The symbol of an eye surrounded by six wings in an aster graced each diadem. A man stood before the tribunal, hands clasped behind his back. He had the same stature as the image of the man they had called the Knight of Swords, but this man's hair was less perfect, his clothing more ruffled, and his unkempt beard obscured his features. The hologram focused more on the tribunal than on the man.

"For his crimes, the Knight of Swords was sentenced to death, but was pardoned and exiled by Prolocutor Mundi. At his adjudication, the Sword Scourge, when asked if he had any remorse, regaled that there was only one man in the universe he had to answer to, and he refused to say anything else. Upon his exile, the Sword Knight's charisma left a lasting legacy. Even rightforth, the message of the Knight speaks to youth and has resulted in the formation of the Apostates of the Sword, a radical group that spreads mayhem and confusion throughout the city. There are even rumors that the bunker where the Knight was exiled has been inhabited for several gyres by the Apostates. However, that rumor is unconfirmed as the location of that bunker is unknown. The Advent marks the DC where light from the explosion of Mjolnir can be seen in the darkened dome. There will be a full DC darkening, and all ave traffic will be stopped for one full hor in observance of the Advent of the Defiance."

"What the hell is a *hor*?" Winberg bellowed.

"It's an hour, just with the accent," Jang replied as someone from the back of the group shushed them both.

Cyrus could barely hear them. He stared through the three-dimensional scenes that played out on the floor. The shapes and colors blurred, the sounds became muffled, and everything obscured until neither images nor sounds held meaning for him. His vision faded until only the numbers in his head were real.

Forty-seven gyres since the first.

He rolled the number around in his head and divided it by three point six five.

Twelve point eight or so. It was close to thirteen years between the first ship landing and the war.

The war had begun about six hundred seven or six hundred eight years ago and ended a little more than six hundred years ago. That was why the light was reaching Asha from the explosion in the next few Dhekads.

Outside of relativity, the Paracelsus had left earth six hundred thirty-one years ago.

Which meant it was only a little more than ten or eleven years before the faster-than light ship could have been launched.

But, according to Jang, the FTL technology took eight years to develop. In Cyrus's experience with Jang, he had seldom, if ever, been wrong with his figures—especially not simple ones.

Eight years. They had begun developing the faster-than-light technology four years after the Asha expedition had left. If Cyrus had not heard about it before, it meant that it had begun development not too long after it had been proposed—which would have been no later than a year before...

...there was no way the Uni could have spared the expense of two interplanetary expeditions, was there? No, not when a more efficient method was less than a decade away.

Which meant, by typical Uni protocol, the production of the FTL ship would have preempted the launch of the Damocles. Cyrus asked again just in case *he* had been mistaken, "How many gyres did it take them to develop the FTL ship again?"

There was a pause as if it took a moment to translate Cyrus's question, then finally Jang realized and answered, "Thirty."

Thirty. The word solidified in the air—scorching at the surface, and yet impossibly cold at the core. It was a comet that invaded Cyrus's atmosphere, eclipsing his sky. Then, defenseless, his eyes sank below the horizon as the comet, with all the impact of a myriad of nuclear weapons, collided with his own world, knocking it off its kilter.

Tanner could see, at that moment, Cyrus's dark days expanded to months, years, a lifetime as his entire world teetered sideways. The renewed life Cyrus had engendered in himself the last five years sank through the cracks, hiding beneath the surface; the lines in Cyrus's face became clearer, his cheeks quivered, and Tanner knew a thick ocean of isolation and self-hate was filling the void beneath, faster than his hand could reach Cyrus's shoulder. It was a futile attempt at comfort, but he left it there anyway.

Cyrus retreated wordlessly, walking with hard-mustered dignity, a barely perceptible drag in his step. The others seemed oblivious. Tanner himself would not have figured it out by now. He only knew because Cyrus knew. And even though Cyrus had not said anything, Jang himself was clearly working through the figures in his head, and those among them that had relatives on the way would also soon realize, in their own time, that they were never going to see their families or friends again.

fourteen

—*I got something to tell you Dada, but I don't know if you will get upset.*

—*Well, you won't know until you tell me right, Dari. What is it?*

—*I just want to say...I love you, Dada.*

—*Dari, why would you think I would get upset at that?*

—*I dunno, Dada. Just cuz you don't ever say it.*

—*Oh, Dari. Sometimes I work so hard to show it I think I forget to say it... So many people say it and don't mean it—to get whatever it is they think they want. I just want it to be true. Whether or not it is said is secondary, but you should never be ashamed of saying it or showing it if you mean it.*

—*Like when people ask how you are doing? They say it all the time, but they don't always mean it. Sometimes it's enough just to know the other person wants you to be doing good.*

—*Yeah, exactly.*

—*That makes sense, but it's still nice to hear it sometimes.*

—*I suppose I can see that. Do you ever feel like I don't show it?*

—*Never to me, but maybe mommy sometimes. I think sometimes mommy doesn't see it.*

—*Maybe, Dari.*

—*Do you ever talk with mommy like this?*

—*I used to.*

—*Because this is when I see it the most—when we talk, you know, like man-to-man and stuff.*

—*Well, it'd be kind of hard for me to talk man-to-man with your mother.*

—*Maybe you should try.*

—*You know, maybe I should.*

—*Know what, Dada?*

—*What's that Dari?*

—*You may not be very good at saying it, but you are good at showing it I think— in your own way.*

—*Well, good at showing it or not, I do love you, son.*

—*I love you too, Dada. Can you promise me something?*

—*Sure.*
—*When you have that man-to-man talk with mommy, tell her you love her too. Okay?*
—*I will Dari. I will.*

• • • • •

"Must be hard stuck in this chimp hovel without your Bible." Before he spoke, Cyrus waited until Tanner had lifted his head from his prayer.

Tanner looked at Cyrus and smiled through the weary lines of his face. "Well, I wouldn't think much of myself if I didn't carry it around here." He pointed to his temple, leaving his index finger at the side of his head for a long moment.

Cyrus laughed. He seemed more amused at his thoughts than at Tanner's actions.

"What's so amusing?"

"The soul of the academic dies hard. It seems like most would have pointed to their hearts."

"Well, I think if more people carried the Word in their heads rather than their hearts, holy wars and religious persecution wouldn't exist; at least not to the levels it has throughout history."

"No kidding."

There was a long pause until Cyrus yawned and buried his face in his hands. As he exhaled into his palms, Tanner thought he heard him mumble the words, "I'm planning on getting out of here."

Tanner paused again then continued, "Unfortunately, too many walk with the Word, but don't understand it. The upside is that I believe there are many who understand the Word, and who walk with guidance, even without the indoctrination."

Cyrus was sure Tanner had heard and had understood him. "You know me. Even without rules or a plan, I wouldn't even take the slightest shuffle forward without guidance." Cyrus looked at Tanner until he met his gaze. Tanner's eyes were unwavering, so Cyrus continued, "But even a man with ample guidance needs help from his friends to stay on the path."

"Well, you know me too. I believe there is no path other than the path where you are needed. Life is full of hard choices. A life full of easy paths, to me, is no life at all. But, just like many men choose the easy path just because it is easy, a few choose the path of most resistance for the resistance's sake. I can follow a man down that path so long as he knows it only leads to disaster, and he accepts the responsibility."

"Well, there is no longer anything for me down the easy ave. I made that choice a long time ago. I just wasn't able to see the full scope until now. But I think I remember that somewhere in that Book of yours it says that not being able to see the end of the path doesn't necessarily mean you shouldn't follow it."

"Yeah, well who knows what is at the end of that ave?"

"Well, maybe it's a bright light. Maybe it's more misery. Maybe it's another choice. But one way or the other, whatever is at the end is yours and no one else's. I think that is worth the trouble, no matter what that trouble is."

"Amen to that." Tanner extended his hand, and they shook firmly in agreement, and then, as they released, Tanner focused on Cyrus. "Out of curiosity, who else agrees with your philosophy?"

"Well, you remember Dr. Azariah?"

"The military kinesiologist?" Tanner made a point of not looking at Commander Uzziah, who walked by as they spoke.

Cyrus didn't look up either. "Yeah, the obnoxious coxswain for the Arcology of Haifa," he said, intentionally loud enough for Uzziah to hear.

Uzziah grunted, mumbled something unintelligible under his breath, then knelt next to the holostation, still within earshot. Cyrus continued, again loud enough for Uzziah to hear, but not loud enough to be obvious, "Well he started the whole dialectic. He suggested I set up a symposium with Dr. *Cheat-ham*..."

Tanner paused for a moment, searching his memory. "The keycard guy?"

"Yeah, that one. Cheat-ham said he knew of a professor from some place in Greece, you know, the guy who wrote that 'City of Tightrope Walkers' book. Well, that professor was a little miffed with the opposition, so he wanted to write a treatise as well."

"A good didactic rant can be cleansing."

"Well, I didn't get to set up anything before departure, but I know there are at least three others on the other ship that are always up for a bit of *cleansing*."

Tanner laughed, but Uzziah turned with a disturbed look on his face. He met Cyrus's eyes for only a moment, but his concern was evident.

Then, Cyrus turned back to Tanner, his brow was furrowed and his jaw tense—the same look that he wore when he was sparring. "Before the cleansing, I need to plant the seed," he breathed into his nose deeply then exhaled, "and I need to do it now."

Cyrus extended his arm forcefully and grabbed a handful of Tanner's shirt just below his throat. Tanner was almost startled at the abruptness of the assault, but had he not trusted Cyrus implicitly, his hand would never have reached his chest. Tanner looked down at Cyrus's hand then back at Cyrus. "What the fuck do you want from me?"

"Your cooperation!" erupted from Cyrus's mouth as he twisted the shirt in his hand, pulling Tanner in closer.

"I'm going to ask you once and only once to take your grimy paw off my shirt," Tanner said brusquely.

Uzziah stayed focused on the holovision. He had an idea where this was all going, but he had to let it play out. Villichez and Winberg, however, turned their attention away from the images on the floor, and Villichez began moving toward Cyrus. Tanner saw Villichez moving toward them with his hand out. Villichez parted his lips to say something, but it was too late. Tanner was already slapping Cyrus's hand away with his right hand and bringing his left around in a fist.

Tanner punched Cyrus and knocked him off the bed to the floor. Tanner then lunged from the bed and launched his left foot into Cyrus's ribs, adding to Cyrus's momentum and sending him rolling toward Villichez. "You're gonna get us all killed, you stupid freebirth!"

Villichez moved to get between them, then hesitated. That was not an insult he had expected to come from Tanner. Something was off. Besides, from what he knew of their relationship, it was not like Cyrus, even under duress, to take a threat from Dr. Tanner lightly or to take a beating with no effort to fight back.

In the time Villichez hesitated, Tanner had kicked Cyrus again, and Cyrus was coughing, curling himself into a ball. Something was wrong about this entire display. "Give it up! This whole hound-fucked fiasco is over, get it, over!"

Tanner moved to kick Cyrus again, but was snatched off his feet by Uzziah, who turned, stepped through the hologram, and pinned Tanner against the wall. Tanner kicked his legs out but missed Uzziah entirely. Uzziah held him there against the wall, forearm pressed against his chest. As the two of them looked at each other, they understood completely. Neither of them wanted to show their hand to whoever might be watching, but they both knew the other was not fighting at the fullest of his potential.

Villichez tried to look after Cyrus, but Cyrus slapped his hand away. Jang and Toutopolus stood around also, offering helping hands, but were met with the same resistance. Winberg chuckled, but a glare from Villichez quickly stifled it.

And then the door opened. No one could have seen it because his face was buried in his forearms, but Cyrus smiled. He didn't look up, but the hurried footsteps moving toward him told him his plan was working. Hands grabbed him, lifted him up, and he stayed curled up like a prawn as they hauled him out of the room like luggage.

They didn't bother with Tanner or Uzziah. Uzziah let Tanner drop and mumbled, "Later for us," without parting his lips. Tanner brushed himself off, looking to the floor and coughed, spitting out a guttural, "*Ani yoda'a*"; 'I know.' Uzziah stood and paused, he must have been fazed by the Hebrew, but he didn't show it. Besides, it was not unexpected from Tanner given his field of expertise. Tanner stood, rubbed his chest, and stepped out of the hologram. Uzziah gave him a brisk pat on the back then nodded. Tanner returned the nod then shuffled his feet over to the bed, evidently ashamed of his outburst. When he reached the bed, he pulled himself up to the top bunk and buried his face in his pillow.

● ● ● ● ●

Cyrus took in as much as he could from the view through his forearms. He remembered this hall clearly because they had been ushered down it from their 'debriefing room.' It was easy to count the men's steps as they carried him because he bounced with each one. After the twenty-third step, the men turned to the right. Cyrus whimpered a little to himself and then let out a quiet, but wrenching, sob. He sniffled to add authenticity, and in the moment it took him to recover, he tried to take in as much of the hallway as he could. The dim orange of fading sunlight filled his vision, indicating there was an atrium or a dais that overlooked the glass façade of the building. It could have been the rear of the building, but that was not likely. The scientists had been led down this hall on the first day, but they had been brought around the back side of the hall. Cyrus wished he had been conscious upon his initial entrance, but there was not much that could be done about that now. There were another twenty-five steps, another right turn, ten more steps, and then the men pressed an access button to open a door. The door slid open, and a sliver of light poured in through the opening. There was only a single chair in the center of the room. The soldiers plopped him into the chair like a sandbag and left wordlessly. The descending door shrank the sliver of light until he was left shrouded in darkness.

But the darkness made it easier for him to think. They had carried Cyrus past three doors—one in the same hallway as their room, one that was across from the dais, and one just before they had tossed him in here. An observation room must have been the room opposite this room, and the other interrogation room could very well have been the room immediately next to this one. The soldiers watching them did not need to be immediately next to the interrogation rooms to monitor the scientists, but proximity would ensure a certain amount of security. As far as he could tell in the short time the door was open, there were no windows or two-way mirrors in this room, but there could easily have been some form of microscopic fly-eye cameras embedded in any, or even all, of the walls. They could be monitoring his body heat to note his position and bodily changes, and they could have embedded microphones anywhere in the room. No doubt, they were still watching him very closely because they had scooped him up almost immediately after Tanner's feigned outburst, which had been such a remarkable performance that the memory of it still resonated in Cyrus's jaw and temple.

However calming, the darkness became unnerving as soon as Cyrus realized he was no longer aware of time. The darkness was persistent and smothering, and Cyrus began rocking back and forth in his chair to push back the veil of despair. He lifted the legs off the floor as he rocked, and he let them fall back again with resounding, metronomic clicks. The darkness unsettled him, but he only gave into the anxiety to set the bait. He rocked back and forth for the ruse, then for comfort, and, as time pressed on without him, he rocked because his thoughts began to turn against him. He knew he might not ever get out of this place. They could decide to kill every last one of them. They could even begin subjecting them to physical torture. The men holding them didn't seem the type, but who ever did? But captured, tortured, experimented on, or set free, the one thing that was beyond debate, was that he would never see Darius again. His son was lost somewhere in the past that he had so recklessly left behind on the hopeful breaths of a capricious dream—an ill-wrought prayer on a foolish plight to escape his own demons—demons that refused to be left behind. Demons that sat with him now, in this very room, whispering his every transgression into his ear even as he tried to rock them away—and they were not wrong.

And the tears came—as real as the chair he was sitting in. Real as the sound generated by the rhythmic collisions of plastic against concrete. Real as the icy hand that now gripped his chest from the inside, making it hard to breathe and to think.

Then, Cyrus wanted nothing more than to lash out at the real enemy—not Soldier 43235, not the Flying Monkeys, not Dr. Winberg, not Torus Denali, not Feralynn. His most loathsome enemy was right here in the room with him, and he wanted to tear his heart out with his teeth. But he was beyond reach or reproach. So Cyrus arose, his indignity shaping the merciless darkness into a form befitting his adversary. He snatched the chair from the floor and swung it, then he brought it back at his assailant, but the demon was elusive. Cyrus spun and swung again, then spun back the other way, but the chair slipped from his hands and careened into the door.

Then, as he took a step toward the door, his legs gave under the weight he was carrying. He had carried the burden for too long, and they could take no more. He fell next to the door and slid down the wall into a heap on the floor. Sobs wracked his body, and he clawed at the door, and it seemed, for a moment, that something on the other side of the door clawed back.

But the sound had been more brushing than scraping. He pressed his head closer to the wall. The blood pounding through his temple made hearing difficult, and he couldn't tell if the sound was gone or if his own internal workings were obscuring it. He took in a deep breath, held it, let it out, and he focused. He had reached his lowest common denominator. The sum over all his histories had been reduced to one and only one choice—he would destroy everything and everyone in this building before he destroyed himself.

But flopping about like an anaphylactic test rodent would not help one bit. He needed focus because his captors had gone way beyond the limit marker. He wasn't going to be their test monkey one second longer; the poking and prodding was over. He had considered it, tested the water, but now they had cemented it for him—he was leaving, and he was taking his friends with him.

Cyrus pulled in another breath, and then he heard it—faint at first, but then louder. Smack, smack, shuffle, smack. It was muffled, but it was there. Then, he realized his ear was over the door sill, and what he was hearing were footsteps in the hallway.

The cold hand inside his chest began melting, and clarity rushed into his mind again. He continued to breathe deliberately, trying to keep his heart rate up in case they were listening and monitoring him through infrared. As he breathed, he listened, and he calculated. This building could very well have been a military structure, but it was not designed to house prisoners. People moved about the halls freely.

He remembered that some stories of being taken by the Flying Monkeys included a room with a table, which meant most likely there were two interrogation rooms. Everyone had been taken around this corner, either the back way or the way they had brought Cyrus—which meant *all* the scientists, not just the ten in *his* room—were most likely in the same area. He needed to put it to the test, but he could do that very easily, and he could cut two marks with one laser in the process.

He began sobbing louder and scratching and beating on the door until one sob wracked his entire body. He whimpered dramatically then screamed, "Let me out!"

He thought about how he had felt just moments ago. How he had wanted nothing more than to bring it all to an end. How even though his sins were his own, his attitude toward himself had been engendered by the men that kept him against his will. This sent his tantrum into a frenzy.

"You infested fuck-holes are gonna pay! Every last one of you! When they get here, you'll all be sorry!" He let his sobs overwhelm him, sank to the floor, then, almost as soon as he hit the floor, he lunged at the door again and banged on it repeatedly. "You hear me, you Fringe-whore fuckmongers!"

"The Vanden Mittoren will be your downfall! You can't keep us here forever! Dr. Milliken is too important to the war! You will drown in the blood of your fucking children before the Vanden Mittoren are done!"

Then he collapsed, his cheeks fluttering, nostrils still flaring, sucking in the tears that had not had time to dry, sending quiet spasms through his body as he coughed into his arms, curled into a ball, but keeping his head next to the door seam. He sat there sobbing, not sure himself if the sobbing was real or feigned. The pain, however, was very real. Maybe the sobbing was an exaggeration of what he felt inside. If it was, it was too long coming. Either way, the whimpers and gasps continued as he tried to take in the muffled sounds from the hall over the throbbing of his own blood and exasperation. And he stayed there, curled in a ball, no sound but his own lament, for impossibly long minutes.

He tried to glean how long he had been there, but seconds, minutes, even hours, were now blended into an inchoate haze. The darkness held him in confinement. He was trapped in a fugue. His stupor turned him in on himself repeatedly, and he was left there tessellating into his own dread. Time and space warped as he collapsed in on himself, and the sobs became very real again as he approached his own event horizon. Then there was a sound, and a point outside of his own existence blue-shifted into his mind with alarming clarity. Even there, on the threshold of despondency, it was clear a door was opening in the hall. He focused on reigning in his emotion and making way for the sound waves that squeezed, contorted and muffled, through the seine of the door seam.

There was a pattering, like the clambering of a spider in a child's nightmare, then a barely perceptible murmuring—the words were indistinct, garbled, but the anger in them was clear even through the filter of the seam. Then, there was another pattering, more erratic this time, which grew louder. There was some clambering then another whoosh like the first. This one was louder, and a slight tremor went through the wall—a shiver that would not have been discernible if Cyrus's head had not rested against the door frame. Then, there was another whoosh, another pattering, and he was alone in silence again.

Cyrus lay there for what seemed like only a moment, breathing deliberately but calmly into his nose and out through his mouth, slowing the unreliable expanding and contracting of his lungs into a voluntary, but relaxed, quiet. Breathing like this eased his heart rate into a steady rhythm, stilling the pounding in his temple. As he lifted himself, he realized his legs had lost most of their feeling. As he stood, his knees wobbled, and as the blood rushed down into his legs with a tickle, the precariousness of his stance became evident. As he shambled toward the chair, it felt as if all the blood that had not rushed to his legs had settled in his bladder. He picked up the chair and set it on its legs again. He put up a concerted effort to sit down gracefully, but halfway through his descent, his leg gave, and he plopped clumsily into the plastic seat. He propped himself upright, focusing his awareness on his toes, his knees, his elbows, his shoulder, then he flexed the muscles from his neck down to his toes and back up again. His body protested at first, but as his blood began to circulate again, his mind became clearer. The noises in the hall could mean many different things, but the timing was too convenient to have been much of anything other than what he suspected. As far as he could tell, this whole operation was a puppet show—a fiasco orchestrated by men and women who had never known anything of violence or true combat other than the occasional skirmish, riot, or melee. Most likely their fathers, their grandfathers, and even their grandfathers' fathers had never seen anything more. Cyrus had no illusions that his own background was any different, but this put the men who kept them on decidedly different terms in his mind; he might not be any more experienced in conflict than them, but their methodology and ignorance made them easy people to predict and exploit.

fifteen

—*Do you believe in God, Dada?*

—*Yes, Dari, I do.*

—*Then why don't you ever go to church with me and mommy?*

—*Well, it's mostly because of how I think a god would have to be. I don't really like the way churches anthropomorphize God.*

—*Anthropomorphize. Miss Hasabe taught us about that. That's what they do in fables when animals wear clothes and talk and act like people.*

—*Yeah, and they usually have the worst, least admirable characteristics of people. I can't understand why God would be as petty and mean as He is portrayed.*

—*So what do you think God is?*

—*I dunno. I think God is less like a person and more like an idea. Like trying to explain abstract art to a blind man; the more you explain, the further you get from the heart of the matter.*

—*You know, sometimes in church, God sounds more like Santa Claus. Like he has a naughty list and a nice list, and people go to the altar thingy and sit on his lap to ask for gifts.*

—*You're right, but I don't think it should be like that. I think God is in us all, and when we are naughty, deep down, we know we are falling off the list—our own list—and we either react to it, or we let it tear us apart.*

—*Yeah, I usually know I'm being a knucklehead when it happens. Even if I'm not sure, I have a feeling, like if I take one more step, I might slip, but you and mommy still love me even when I slip, even when it's real bad. The thing I don't get is why the Santa Claus god doesn't love the people who slip up.*

—*Well, that's the trick. If God doesn't 'love' or 'hate,' then I think 'falling off' is just people using God as an excuse to pass judgment on and belittle others.*

—*Yeah, but the pastor is closer to God, right?*

—*See, that's the catch. You should never set any man above you, no matter what he claims to be, nor should you expect any man to set another above himself.*

—*Well, what about Miss Hasabe? I have to answer to her all the time—and you and mommy too.*

145

—*Respect and reverence are two different things, Dari. A man of integrity always answers to the people he respects, like it or not.*
—*What if they don't respect him back?*
—*Make sure you hear these words and hear them well, regardless of what you do, what you say, who you respect, and who you do not, at the end of the day, above all else, you have to answer to yourself and yourself alone—and the mirror accepts neither lies nor excuses.*

●　●　●　●　●

"What was that little stunt you pulled yesterday?" Winberg's voice was usually condescending, but today, as Cyrus sat battered and bruised on the floor next to his bunk, Winberg's tone had gone way beyond the outer marker.

"You see, it's this new exercise called minding-your-own-goddamn-business." Cyrus looked up to meet Winberg's eyes. "You should try it sometime."

"Well, your nonsense might have been passable on the ship, but down here, it's gonna get someone killed. I'd say that puts it right in the 'my-goddamn-business' category."

"Then you watch your own back, and I'll watch mine." Cyrus stopped, but as Winberg was about to open his mouth, he continued, "Seems to me like that might be easier for you if you get out of my face." Cyrus stood, but Winberg grumbled and walked to the window to look into the artificially darkened night sky.

Cyrus sat back down and extended his leg beneath the bunk to stretch it. Tanner, eyes puffy from limited sleep, leaned over from the bed, "A bit high strung are we?"

"I don't like the bend in his keel." Cyrus reached his hand beneath the bed to stretch his leg further.

"I hadn't noticed." Tanner smiled. "He does have a point though. This could get out of hand."

"As far as I'm concerned, it already is out of hand." Cyrus slid his leg out of the stretch but kept his hand beneath the bunk. The muscles in his forearm continued to tense and relax, and his body stayed turned more toward the bed even though he focused on Tanner.

"Maybe they will sort this out sooner than we think," Tanner said. The inflection in his voice was wispy as if he barely believed it himself.

"You and I both know better. This whole operation is a lampoon. They keep playing with us. If they listened more carefully, they could hear the truth. But I don't give a damn whether they hear or not. Bottom line is, I'm not staying here to rot while they 'sort it out.'"

"And I would not expect you to. I'm just saying, don't jump into the fire just because you're mad."

"What other reason is there to jump in a fire? They keep at us like they might get somewhere, but they are too monkey-minded to see there is nowhere to go. I'm not gonna let them play with me until they get tired." Cyrus knew the holovision might not have been loud enough to mask his rant from his captors, but he didn't care.

"Your brand of bluster does not normally come without impetus, but I am curious. How are you going to achieve this egress, and where do you plan on going? We are in a giant hermetic dome somewhere in the middle of a planet-wide desert." Tanner could see the corners of Cyrus's eyes quivering.

"You don't have to go along if you have doubts. Just don't get in my way." Cyrus clenched his teeth and kept his voice down, but his tone was biting nonetheless.

"Doubts? Why would I stay here? Besides, I'd follow you into the fires of hell if it came down to it because I know you wouldn't take anyone else into the fire rashly."

Cyrus's anger was no longer directed at Tanner, but the fire still burned within him. His fury lapped at the walls of the material flesh that tried futilely to contain it. Tanner and Cyrus sat there for a while, wordless. Cyrus continued to stretch, his hand still under the bunk, until finally Tanner began doing push-ups next to him. After his sixtieth push-up, Tanner sat up facing Cyrus, taking in deep breaths. "Have you noticed it's a lot easier to do push-ups here? For a while, I thought it was anxiety until I realized it was harder to do jumping-jacks because the rhythm was all off."

Cyrus turned from the bedside, pulled his knees to his chest, then cupped his left hand over his fist as he pulled his knees into him with his forearms. "Remember Asha is smaller and slightly less dense than Earth. The gravity here is about 87% of Earth's," he grumbled through the words, but the tension in his voice was subsiding.

Cyrus's eyes were still ablaze, but now they were more focused. It was clear he was calculating. "You still want to leave?" Tanner asked, keeping his voice down.

"It's more a *when* than a whether-or-not at this point. I just need to sleep on it a few nights to get my head in order." After that, Cyrus crossed his legs, spun out of his crouch into a standing position, and then sat on the bunk with a creak. He kept his right hand in a fist over his chest, concealing the bolt he had surreptitiously removed from the bed. He then settled into the pillow, the bed thumping lightly against the wall as the missing bolt allowed it to move under his shifting weight.

• • • • •

Cyrus sat next to his bed facing the wall, using the leg of the bed frame as leverage in his leg stretch. He kept his left hand on the leg that rested under the shadow of the bunk, apparently rubbing his ankle. Someone put a hand on his shoulder. He turned to see Villichez stopping slightly behind him. "I had been meaning to tell you, but I kept forgetting. I took the liberty of taking over your holovision shift in your absence."

Cyrus relaxed his stretch and adjusted his left sock to stash the bolt he had removed again this evening. He turned to face Villichez, continuing to stretch once he rotated. "Discover anything?"

"Actually, there was quite the interesting history program in the middle of your furlough. It discussed some of the origin of the civilization on this planet."

"Like what?" Cyrus spread his legs slightly wider, but he focused on the old man as he sat on the bunk next to him.

The bed creaked and shifted against the wall as Villichez's weight settled. "Well it was mostly an articulate, but one-sided, rant about the iniquities of Earth and how the emigration to Asha left most of those shortcomings behind. It mostly talked about how the sampling of the first expeditions to the planet eliminated religious and racial prejudices, which were further avoided through the ban of leviance from Earth after a man called Prolocutor Mundi was elected leader of Asha. Basically, the only languages that survived the exodus were Greek and a form of Commonspeak called Ashan. It also seems none of the original colonists held much stock in religion."

"Well, that makes a lot of things make sense. Although they seem to be, as far as I can tell, exceptionally ignorant of life on Earth, most casts that I've seen show Earth as populated by idiotic monsters." Cyrus relaxed his stretch then shifted into another one.

"It seems to me they replaced the hatred they left on Earth with a hatred for the place they left it. The cast suggested the citizens of Earth were parasites that had raped the planet into a stagnant wasteland, and that Ashan civilization was more evolved, for lack of a better term, because it arose in a wasteland rather than degenerated into one. It seems this hatred manifested itself into a riot in the midst of the war that caused most documentation from Earth to be destroyed, which over the course of the five hundred plus years, I'm sure has directly resulted in the ignorance you speak of."

"What kind of moron destroys information?" Cyrus scoffed.

"In my experience, it is usually the kind that never really used it to begin with."

$$\bullet \quad \bullet \quad \bullet \quad \bullet \quad \bullet$$

Davidson closed his eyes, but the tap, tap, tap, tap, tap...tap, tap, tap, *tap*...penetrated his skull, arrested his brain, and drew him back to consciousness each time he tried to sleep. It had been more sporadic the dome cycle before, but now it seemed to persist the entirety of the city's artificial night. It had started two days before, when Milliken had been dragged off for hours and had been asked inexplicable questions about some imminent attack. Horribly confused, Milliken was of little use to them, but he had received a righteous beating for his trouble nonetheless. In the fray, Milliken managed to put one of them down with a kick to the groin, which had only exacerbated his flogging.

The sound made Davidson restless. He stirred, tossed, and looked around the room, but no else seemed to hear it. Some seemed restless themselves, but no one seemed agitated beyond their wits.

Finally, he appealed to the darkness, "Milliken, are you awake?"

"Yeah," wafted up airily from the bottom bunk.

Davidson hopped off the edge of the bunk. His body was wearier than he had expected, and his knees could barely take the shock. He plopped down on the side of Milliken's bunk too hard, and the metal frame sent a jolt through his thighbones. "You hear that noise?" Davidson asked beneath his breath.

"Yeah."

"Is it keeping you up too?"

"I haven't been able to sleep since I got gaffed. I can barely hear the sound."

"Every time I almost get to sleep, it starts pounding through my head. It's driving me insane." Davidson realized it was harder to hear when he focused on keeping his own voice down. He leaned toward the wall to see if it was still there.

"Maybe they are doing it to try to break us?" Milliken proposed, clasping his hands over his chest.

"I don't think so."

"It sounds a little like IPA signal code." Milliken sidled closer to the wall. He knew their captors were probably monitoring them through fly-eye cams and mics and probably also through infrared, so he tried to make his motions as natural and subtle as possible. "If it is, it's kinda choppy. It's been going on for so long the ball-biters must not be able to hear it."

Milliken sat deathly still in the bed. Davidson tried to keep from moving, but his body seemed to be shaking at a steady oscillation. It was hard to hear the tapping in the wall over the pounding of blood through his temple, but he knew the moment he tried to go back to sleep, it would be all he could hear. Then, as his breathing began to settle and his nerves began to calm, he could hear the pattern despite the aberrant rhythm. Tap, tap, pause, tap tap. Tap, tap, tap, tap, *tap*. Pause. Tap, *tap*, tap, pause, tap. Tap, tap, tap, tap, tap. *Tap, tap*, pause, tap, *tap*. Then shakily, it repeated.

Milliken began to mumble to himself, "Vuh... Vuh... yee." He stopped, counted under his breath, then mumbled again, "Vee guh ay... ay tsuh."

"*Wie gehts?*" Davidson answered. It was German, or so it seemed. "How are you?" he translated, letting his words drift out on a gasp to avoid the room's microphones. Davidson slid closer to Milliken's head and the wall but did not turn. If someone was watching them, he did not want to call attention to himself. "Can we send?" Davidson said into his hand, not sure if even Milliken could hear him.

Milliken was still. Davidson was about to repeat himself when he heard Milliken whisper, "Yeah."

"*Nicht gut, und du?*" Davidson said into his hand. Not good, and you?

Milliken stopped for a moment, mumbled, counted to himself, then turned on his side facing Davidson's back. Somehow he used the hand supporting his head to tap the wall lightly. Tap, pause, tap, tap, tap. As soon as he started, the tapping on the other side stopped. Milliken continued. Tap, tap, tap, tap, *tap*. *Tap*, tap, *tap*, pause, tap. Pause. Tap, *tap*, tap, pause, tap. Tap, tap, tap, *tap, tap*. *Tap*, tap, *tap*, pause, tap.

There was a long pause. It seemed like the silence that filled Davidson's head had not existed in weeks.

Then, another series of taps, longer this time and in an awkward rhythm, came back across the wall. Milliken counted to himself a few times, then reported, "Vuh ay-ur d-uh. Yee kuh. Buh eh suh er. Zuh eye een. Ah muh. Duh eh-r. Eh duh vuh ih-n tuh."

"*Werde ich besser sein am der* Advent. I'll be better on the Advent."

Milliken expressed his bewilderment, then nudged something into the wall on his own accord. There was another pause, then another series of taps. *Wir gehen aus.*

"We are leaving," Davidson translated.

So it was a code, and someone in the other group was planning an escape on the Advent day they kept mentioning on the holostreams. But who was it?

"*Wer ist dass?*" before Davidson could translate, Milliken was already sending taps.

The taps came back quicker this time. "Cyrus," Milliken mumbled, almost laughing. Then, to Davidson, it all made sense. The Vanden Mittoren Milliken was questioned about was not the name of a faction, it was a warning in German—*Wanden mit Ohren*. Walls with Ears. Davidson began to say something else into his hand, but Milliken kicked to shush him—more taps were coming.

"*Bringt der* Cleaning Crew *zusammen*," Davidson deciphered from Milliken's broken linguistic transliteration. Bring the Cleaning Crew together.

"Why? *Warum?*" Davidson asked through his hand. Milliken tapped.

More taps returned. *Ich brauche ihnen*. I need you. The 'you' was plural. *Bis spaeter*. Until later.

I need you—plural. Cyrus did not know that the only members of their 'Cleaning Crew' that were in this room had already assembled to decipher his code. Both Fordham and Davidson knew German, and even if Cyrus had not known that, Tanner, who seemed to know everything about everyone—at least what was in their dossiers—did. Guessing that someone in this room knew how to IPA signal was a risk, but given so many scientists in one room, it was likely. If ships relied on it for distress beacons across a solar system, why wouldn't it work across a wall with a group of overachieving academia on the other side? It had been a gamble, just like most everything noteworthy Davidson had seen or heard of Cyrus doing since he had met him, but the gamble had worked. Now, the fatigue Davidson had collected through days of sleep lost to the taps in the wall seemed a paltry sum to pay for the relief that now began to fill him. Without another word, Davidson climbed back up to his bunk, and for the first time in innumerable nights, dreams came easily.

⬤ ⬤ ⬤ ⬤ ⬤

The bed squeaked softly with each arch of his back, rapping lightly against the bunk wall in rhythm with each sit-up as Cyrus used the bed frame for leverage. He didn't know whether it was because his mind had begun to accept his surroundings, or because he was more relaxed now that he had taken active measures to change those surroundings, but Cyrus could now sleep—albeit only during light hours. Sit-ups and a shower now relieved the stupor that had been left behind by his unexpected but duly needed siesta. They also justified his bed creaking and tapping through the night in case their captors had been listening.

After his last sit-up, he left the bed and made his way to the shower. The scientists who had overcome their aversions to being watched customarily left their clothes near the entrance to the shower upon entering. The soldiers had been bringing changes of clothes every other day now, and the clothes the scientists had worn were taken away, most likely for cleaning, but more likely for inspection. The idea of sitting around in wet clothes that would be replaced anyway had begun to seem like an unnecessary plea for illness, especially since their bodies had very little practice in the last five years with fighting off disease. And who knew what diseases these posturing, self-indulgent, half-wits had engendered and cultivated in their little hermetic dome.

Cyrus stepped out of his jumpsuit at the entrance to the shower alcove. He knew Toutopolus would be there because he had seen him come in earlier.

"Finally got some sleep?" Toutopolus asked as Cyrus stepped up to a showerhead to his right, leaving a stall between them.

"Yeah," Cyrus answered, turning on his shower. Cyrus felt the water cascade across his face and his now full beard. "Can't seem to sleep at night though."

There was a long pause. Out of the corner of his eye, Cyrus noticed Toutopolus's soap bar had dwindled almost out of existence. Cyrus picked up his own soap bar and held it out for a moment. He hadn't seen soap bars since he was a Novitiate. Ironically, the Uni had declared bars of soap unsanitary, and all soap had to be distributed in liquid form in tubes or bottles. Cyrus manipulated the soap bar in his hands, poking at it to test its consistency.

Cyrus turned the bar over as he spoke, "I used to love bars of soap, but I could never use them after they were whittled down to about half. My mom used to hate how I left half bars all over the shower and would declare there was no more soap left. She preferred bars herself, but I think she said a silent prayer the day the Uni did away with them altogether." Cyrus turned the bar around in his hands, reveling in the nostalgia.

"My father made me use the soap until it disappeared. We didn't have all the fancy liquid soaps and creams until the Uni formed, and my father ran our house like he ran his barracks."

Cyrus picked up another bar of soap from the stall between them. He then took a step toward Toutopolus, extending his original bar with his left hand. "Perhaps you should use this fresh bar though. Fresh bars always lather up better." Cyrus wasn't sure he had put enough emphasis on the right words. At the same time, he was afraid that if he put too much emphasis on the right words, whoever was watching them might pick up on his subterfuge. Toutopolus took the soap, and Cyrus went back to the stall and began to sing. It seemed odd to Toutopolus, and yet, at the same time, it seemed appropriate.

Gonna lay down my burden, down by the riverside.

Toutopolus was sure he had heard the song before somewhere. He knew the tune, but not the words. He thumbed around the soap Cyrus had handed him. There was a certain comfort that came when a new bar of soap was opened. He had not opened one himself since he was a small child, and the ones he got to open, thanks to Kyrie Lokhage Nestor Toutopolus, were few and far between.

...down by the riverside.

...but this bar was strange. This bar had something etched into it, but he didn't remember any kind of imprint on the bars he had used here previously. Toutopolus turned the bar over in his hand, making an effort not to be obvious. There was just enough light inside the shower, and the bar was just the right color, which made clear the grooves that had been gashed into the soap by ungroomed fingernails.

...down by the riverside.

'Advent—when hell brks get 2 nxt flr' and a down arrow. It was confusing, and it was poorly rendered, but Toutopolus was sure he understood. There was more method to Cyrus's outbursts and rants than it seemed—as always.

Gonna lay down my burden, down by the riverside.

Toutopolus began to lather himself with the face of the soap containing the writing. He didn't know exactly what was expected of him, but just the idea was as refreshing as the lather from the full bar of soap. Something was going down on the Advent, and when all hell broke loose, Cyrus needed him to get to the second floor down.

...ain't gonna study war no more.

Toutopolus smiled as he felt the words melting into his skin and the tones of Cyrus's song still echoed through the tiled walls of the shower. He still couldn't remember where he had heard the song before, but wherever it was, he had enjoyed being there.

Cyrus emerged from the shower with his hair and beard still damp. Tanner could tell it was frizzing up even as it was beginning to dry. "I didn't know you could sing," Tanner remarked as Cyrus moved to the floor beside the bunk. Cyrus began stretching again, pulling his knees as tightly to his chest as he could.

Cyrus held the stretch for a ten-count and released before he answered, "I usually only sing when I'm by myself—and not that often."

"Interesting choice of song."

"My mother used to sing that song. Usually when she thought no one was listening. I always thought it was pretty odd when I was a kid. It wasn't until I had left home for the Arcology that I realized she only sang when the stress of trying to provide the best she could seemed like it was all over her head." Cyrus pulled his legs to his chest again, counted to himself, then relaxed. "It's funny. I always thought my mother was invincible, you know, a fount of limitless power."

"I think, in a way, every child does—or rather, it's a sad person who goes through childhood knowing better." Tanner flexed his arms, testing each of the muscles from his wrist up to his shoulders and then back again.

"Yeah, you're right. When my mother's health started to fail, I realized the times she sang that song were when she wasn't sure she was going to make it or when she didn't know everything would be okay—even when she said it would be—because she *was* vulnerable. There *was* a limit to her power, but she would be damned if she let anyone who depended on her know it. Oddly enough, the thing that struck me the most was after I matriculated out of the Arcology, when the emphysema finally overwhelmed her, she *didn't* sing that song. Not once. It was like she knew, somehow, that things would be okay."

"So, why do you sing it?" Tanner asked, stretching his arms behind his back. At first, he was worried his tone sounded facetious, but Cyrus must have known because he simply responded without challenge.

"Because back in that room, in the darkness, I realized even after years of matriculation, there isn't much I *do* know. And I don't know what *that* means."

"Maybe it means life isn't over yet." Tanner smiled, and Cyrus returned it as Torvald walked over to him and Tanner.

"I can tell something is up, but I don't know what it is," Torvald said, his voice shaking from not being used for most of the duration of their stay in the room.

Cyrus was surprised to hear Torvald's voice again but was more thrown by the timing. Cyrus had still been trying to find a way to approach Torvald without alarming their captors, but neither an idea nor an opportunity had presented itself—and Cyrus had already played too many of his cards today. "I'm not sure what you're talking about," Cyrus made a point of avoiding eye contact with Torvald as he continued to stretch; he wanted to tell him about the plan, but for now, Torvald would have to wait.

"I gotta know something," Torvald added, his voice still shaking. "I can't take it here anymore. It's too...sterile." That was an interesting choice of words given the stench in the room, which was only evident as they woke, assuming they had actually been able to sleep.

"We're all stuck here," Cyrus added, without looking up, "There is nowhere to go. Nowhere." Cyrus needed Torvald to back off. Perhaps, tonight, Cyrus could communicate something to him in German—something quick to at least calm his nerves—but he couldn't do it now.

Even though Torvald had spoken very little since they had been here, he had maintained a certain level of composure—perhaps that was why he was the only scientist in the room that had not been taken by the Flying Monkeys—but the last word in Cyrus's sentence apparently had been the drop that broke the dam wall, and soundless tears suddenly flooded from Torvald's eyes. Cyrus wanted to keep his eyes away from Torvald, but he could feel him retreat into place in his mind he had managed to avoid up until now. Cyrus stood, moving closer to Torvald, but he took a step back as if Cyrus had missed the opportunity for consolation. Torvald waved his hands in the air between them, shaking his head as he took another step backward.

Cyrus leaped forward, quickly covering the distance between them, stumbling slightly as he inadvertently brushed across Tanner's ankle.

Torvald stopped Cyrus with his hands.

"*Etwas kommt,*" was all Cyrus could manage to mumble before Torvald tripped over Jang, who was kneeling in front of the holovision, and fell backward onto his butt, sobbing uncontrollably as he hit the ground.

Then the door slid open, and two Flying Monkeys rushed in. One soldier moved directly at Cyrus, and Cyrus almost kicked him, but he held back the instinct. He needed to stay calm. It was too close to the Advent, and he couldn't risk the plan that had already been set in motion.

The second soldier, one Cyrus did not recognize, grabbed Torvald in a sleeper-hold and lifted him by his neck. The advancing soldier looked up and smiled, and Cyrus saw it was Soldier 43235 just before getting shoved to the ground. Then 43235 turned, grabbed Torvald's flailing ankles, and they hauled him out of the room.

• • • • •

The tapping in the wall had ceased to have any discernable pattern for the last night cycle or two, but now it coalesced into a choppy, but salient, five-beat pattern. So as not to alarm anyone who may have been listening, Davidson waited before he got down from the bed. He wasn't sure how long he had waited, but by the time he descended to the bottom bunk, Milliken had transcribed the first line of the message.

"*Ist der* Crew *zusammen?*" Is the Crew together?

"*Ja.*" Milliken had already responded, utilizing what little German he knew.

"*Ich brauche ihnen zu etwas machen fuer mich.*" I need you to do something for me. The message repeated until Davidson had descended and translated it. He gave Milliken the answer.

"*Was?*" What?

"*Am* Advent, *brauche ich Hilfe.*" On the Advent, I need help.

Before they could send another 'What?' the next message came through. "*Wenn koennen ihnen, fahren der* Crew *zu* the dock." In the end, either Milliken's transcription or Cyrus's German had broken down, but both Milliken and Davidson understood the message: When you can, get to the dock. It was an ambiguous request, and they had very little idea how they could help, but at least it gave them something to look forward to other than more psychological torture.

• • • • •

Cyrus had not seen Torvald in three DCs, and it was already the dome-darkening the day cycle before the Advent. For the last three dome cycles, Cyrus had still been able to sleep during light hours, but each time he awoke with the image of Torvald's face just before the Flying Monkeys took him away. Torvald was a grown man, hearty and stalwart, but he had not been able to take the unexpected change in events and the captivity very well. And worst of all, Cyrus had not been able to help him when he needed it. And now, if he was not in the other room, it would be too late. Cyrus had attempted to ask about Torvald's whereabouts through the wall, but he had received no response, which also worried him. He could not think of anything he could have done that might have showed his hand, but Cyrus could not shake the notion that these goons, as sophomoric and gullible as they seemed, were on to him.

sixteen

—Dada, do you ever get afraid?
—Yeah, all the time, Dari.
—You don't ever look like it. You never panic. It's like nothing ever bothers you.
—Well, panic and fear are two very different things. You know how they say there is a fine line between bravery and stupidity?
—Yeah.
—Well, what's the difference between a brave man and a stupid man?
—Is it the outcome?
—There are plenty successful idiots, and plenty of brave men that failed.
—What is it then?
—It's the fear. The stupid man jumps in headlong, never considering the consequence or the risk. A brave man calculates the risks, knows what he stands to lose, and goes in anyway.
—So the brave man never panics?
—No, everyone panics on occasion, but the brave man doesn't let it get in the way
—So you're saying, if I want to be a brave man that people look up to, I should always do what I believe is right no matter the outcome, and I should see it to completion no matter how I feel.
—Precisely, and after that, if it's absolutely necessary, you can fall the hell apart on your own time.

• • • • •

The manacles on Cyrus's wrists were cold and restricting, but they were loose enough to keep his mind from racing as fast as his pulse. They had cuffed everyone's wrists in front, but evidently Cyrus had been perceived as a greater threat, so his wrists had been restrained behind his back. The Flying Monkeys had made a show of the small remote key that opened and tightened the restraints before ceremoniously handing it to Soldier 43235. Cyrus and his bunkmates

157

were then ushered from the barracks room in a single file line toward the front of the building.

Soldier 43235 and Quadrad Chaldea, the soldier that had 'debriefed' them on their first day, walked on either side of Cyrus. Cyrus's heart was beating so hard he was sure they could hear it. Torus Denali himself walked directly in front of Cyrus, and Denali, Cyrus, and his escorts all walked in the front of the line of scientists toward the front of the building. The orange light that had flooded through the façade had been replaced with a veil of darkness. Most of the ambient light outside had also been extinguished, and the glare from what little light emanated from the city made the glass look as though the entire building was submerged.

They lumbered toward the dais at the front of the building. According to Tanner, who had been conscious when they first entered the building, they had been brought up to the second level of lev traffic and had been ushered in through a docking bay high above ave level. Tanner said the docking bay level was only one level below where they were bunking, so there was ave traffic one level below them and another level of traffic on actual ground level, four to six levels below their bunk level.

If they kep to their normal modus operandi, the Flying Monkeys would keep the scientists separate. The question was, would they take them in groups to the same elevator, or would they, in the interest of time, take them to the separate elevators simultaneously? Or would they take one group, and then the other, and if they did, which group would be first?

...at this point, it didn't matter. The ball was already rolling, and any second now, it would plunge over the precipice. Cyrus just hoped everything fell into place, and most importantly, that everyone stayed focused. But he had faith in them.

As they reached the dais, Cyrus could hear the garbled voices of men beneath them funneling into the lobby. That was when it began.

There was a pop like someone had dropped a closed glass bottle, and then there was an odd crackle and a prolonged hiss. Winberg and the two Flying Monkeys that brought up the rear stopped. One of the men grabbed Winberg, while the other went back to look at the room the scientists had been kept in. Winberg managed to peek around the corner to see the images from the holovision contorting under bluish flames that erupted from the wall behind it. The flames turned reddish orange as they moved across a bed sheet that had been left on the floor inside the holovision image. The flames spread across the sheet to a bed and to the wall.

"Someone stop him! He's going to get us all killed!" Winberg belted down the hallway.

Fucking Winberg. What was he playing at? Why couldn't he mind his own goddamned business? But Cyrus went on anyway. Soldier 43235 attempted to grab him, but Cyrus purposefully tripped over his own feet. He stumbled into Chaldea, and they both fell. Cyrus landed on his butt and exhaled, pulling his knees into his chest as he had practiced for several DCs now. He looped the chain connecting his cuffs under his butt and behind his heels, but it caught on his right foot.

Soldier 43235 reached for the remote. He fumbled to find the number code of Cyrus's cuffs, but he instead pressed the button to select all the units, then pressed the button to tighten the chains.

The chain twisted Cyrus's body to the side as it constricted, but he instinctively kicked it with his free foot. The jolt sent a frozen shaft through his body as the arm he had dislocated a few years before slid out of its socket. For a moment Cyrus's vision went hazy, but as he continued to spin on his hip, he realized both feet were free and his cuffs, which were now tightened to only a few centimeters apart, were now in front of him.

Cyrus kicked 43235's knee, buckling him to the ground, and hopped his torso off the floor, landing on his feet. He felt the shock of the landing in his shoulder as his arm drooped uselessly at his side. Denali was two steps away, moving toward him, and Cyrus could hear Chaldea behind him now. Soldier 43235 was prone between them, but it wouldn't make a difference for long.

Uzziah had worried that he had not pushed the shaved-down bolt Cyrus had slipped him far enough into the inlet slot of the holovision. The slot was much like its predecessors on Earth. It was designed to accept a video signal from an auxiliary device and to provide power to the device through a node nestled at the end of the circular input. He was worried that the bolt had not gone deep enough to reach the power coupling, but the commotion that erupted behind him allayed his fears.

When Dr. Winberg yelled, Uzziah did not even turn around. He kept his eyes on Cyrus, who had dropped to the floor, stumbled two of the guards, although he seemed to have hurt himself, freed the cuffs from behind his back. The two guards next to Uzziah split, one moving toward the fire, the other toward Cyrus. As the guard moving toward

Cyrus turned his back, Uzziah clasped his hands together and launched his left knee into the soldier's tailbone. As the guard stumbled, Uzziah brought his elbow around into the base of the soldier's skull. The guard collapsed as Uzziah yelled to Tanner *"La madregot!"* To the stairs! Uzziah knelt as the other guard began turning. Uzziah had grabbed the fallen guard's weapon from the floor by its barrel and spun, bringing the metal stock of the assault rifle across the second guard's temple.

Tanner was already moving as the man collapsed. Jang followed him, and Uzziah moved behind them both. Uzziah didn't know what miracle Chamberlain was going to work to loose his chains, but chains or no, he and Tanner had to get Jang to the stairs and to the bottom floor.

Toutopolus was so nervous that he didn't notice the confusion that had erupted around him until someone bumped into him and crumpled at his feet. He realized his chains were tighter than before, and he remembered Cyrus's words; *when all hell breaks loose, get to the next floor down.* It seemed like an alarm should have been ringing. This was an emergency. Why were there no alarms? Emergency drills through Laureateship, even all the way back to Novitiateship, taught him there should always be alarms and order—and an obvious way out. The rules were odd but simple: no one responds to 'rape' or 'help', but everyone is afraid of 'fire'; the elevator is not safe in an emergency, so always take the stairs; stairwell doors always swing, never slide. He debated running back the way he had come to the freight elevator, but he had seen Tanner, Uzziah, and Jang rushing through a swinging door, so he followed them because when all hell breaks loose, he needed to get to the next floor down; but the elevator is not safe, and stairwell doors always swing, never slide.

Denali rushed right into Cyrus's hands both figuratively and literally. Cyrus looped his cuffed hands over Denali's head. Denali tried to duck, but Cyrus brought his knee up into his armpit. Cyrus glanced over his shoulder and saw Chaldea raise his rifle butt. Cyrus shot back the leg he used to knee Denali and caught Chaldea in his solar plexus. Chaldea's knees buckled, but he stabilized himself by bringing the rifle butt to the floor. As he pushed himself up, Cyrus brought his foot down and across the improvised kickstand. As Chaldea fell over the rifle, Denali reached for his sidearm. Cyrus lifted his left leg, stepped down onto Chaldea's stooped shoulder blades, and still holding onto Denali's neck, vaulted over the wall of the dais.

Davidson stayed close to Milliken but had no idea what signal he should have been looking for. The ride down the freight elevator had seemed longer than it should have been even though they only went down one floor. They were being led back to the lev dock they had set down on originally to watch the Advent. Davidson and Milliken were at the head of the group of scientists, moving toward what must have been the front of the building given the amount of glass forming the wall. The guards that had applied their restraints led the procession. The one that had pulled Milliken's hands behind his back and had clasped the cuffs around his wrists had called him a pill-kicking puntmongrel. The smirk on Milliken's face, even as his arms had been cranked uncomfortably behind his back, told Davidson that guard must have been the recipient of Milliken's groinal assault.

Everyone else's hands had been clasped somewhat loosely in front of them, and the guard now walking to the left of Milliken's favorite guard was carrying the remote to the cuffs. If Davidson could somehow get the remote, he could free everyone. But how could he possibly do that? His kung fu was good, better than he had ever imagined it could be, but he had never used it for anything other than sparring. Besides, even if he could release everyone's bonds, what good would it do? He knew Cyrus had some sort of plan, but he had no conceivable idea what it could be.

They were only a few feet away from the bottom of the dais when the clamor above began. Then almost simultaneously, the soldier with the remote received a message in his earwig radio, and the cuffs on their restraints began to pull together. There was yelling, a grunting, and a sound of metal clattering against concrete. It sounded as if someone had released an uberhound in a conference room.

The guards turned and raised their guns. The remote guard looked over them, training his barrel on the whole group, but Milliken's guard smiled and kept his barrel trained on him. Davidson didn't know if this was the signal he was supposed to be looking for, but there definitely was not much he could do at the moment, so he raised his hands above his head and hoped there was a better signal coming.

Torus Denali's back arched over the rail of the dais as his throat, caught by the chain on Cyrus's restraints, stopped Cyrus's descent to the lobby floor. Cyrus's right arm felt like it was being ripped from its socket. He leaned to his left, hoping to relieve some of the pressure as he looked at the ground beneath him. As he looked down, his heart dropped into the pit of his stomach. He had expected the floor to be three meters above the lower level, but it was more like four. There were agitated soldiers barking orders below him, and there was the din of general chaos above him as Denali clawed at his hands and cuffs. Before he had vaulted over the edge, Cyrus had seen Tanner and Uzziah scuffling as well, but he had no idea where Toutopolus, Torvald, Davidson, or Milliken were. Cyrus felt the flesh of Denali's neck shudder and shift, and he heard a hacking sound. Droplets of either spittle or vomit cascaded across Cyrus's forehead. There was another set of hands scraping at Cyrus's now, and he heard someone yell, "Punt it, just do 'em all!" There was a short pause and another voice indecipherable in the calamity. Cyrus looked at the ground, again hoping that he had bought enough time before he had jumped. Then he heard, "All of them! Now!" and he knew it was too late.

Toutopolus threw open the door from the stairwell and rushed through into a mire of confusion. The state of affairs in the downstairs hall was very different from upstairs. Scientists stood confused, guns trained on them from all sides as Toutopolus barreled out the door into one of the guards. The guard stumbled, tripped over someone's foot, and hit the ground hard as all the other guards trained their guns on Toutopolus. Perhaps Cyrus's plan included him being bait—he was fine with that—but that wasn't what it sounded like. It had sounded like he needed to get Cyrus help before something bad happened. But now, as Toutopolus raised his chained hands above his head, it looked like all he was going to get was orchestra seats at an execution. *What the hell were we thinking?* ran through his mind so clearly he was sure he had spoken the words aloud. Five years of kung fu training and they thought they could escape from a military base with a harebrained plan organized in showers and through walls. Then, his bladder released and cemented the whole notion creeping up from the base of his brain; this was not going to end well.

Cyrus looked up from the ground and heard voices approaching from somewhere near the façade of the building behind him. Sound seemed to not travel as well here as it did on Earth, or at least as it had on the Paracelsus. It was hard for Cyrus to remember anything about Earth in detail, especially hanging here from a man's neck four meters from the floor with guns most likely trained on his back. Then he remembered the one Earth detail most important to him at that moment.

Gravity.

Earth's gravity was about one and one-sixth the gravity of Asha. A healthy grown man could drop from about three meters on Earth and catch himself, but here...

...and his restrains released before he could complete the thought.

The corners of Milliken's eyes twitched as his frustration fumed toward the soldier smiling in front of him. Euston was what they had called him—at least that was what it sounded like the day Milliken had buried his foot into the man's crotch. And now, with a haughty grin across his face, this Euston silently dared Milliken to make a move. Then something came crashing through the door next to them.

Something slid across the ground behind Milliken, but the rancor seething from his eyes had filled his whole world now. Nothing existed but Euston, Euston's rifle, and the odium that swirled around them. Milliken, weeks earlier, had wondered what had run through Cyrus's mind when he had attacked the trained, armed soldier on their conveyance to this city. Now Milliken had trouble understanding how any self-respecting man could have done anything else.

And then the cold strain around Milliken's wrists loosened, and as Euston's eyes averted to the clatter on the floor behind Milliken's feet, Milliken hands, now without restraints, thrusted toward Euston's weapon and throat.

The ground moved up toward Cyrus with alarming speed, and yet the fall seemed impossibly long. His muscles loosened, and as his feet touched the floor, Cyrus allowed his body to compress, and he absorbed the shock in his legs and gluteus as he grunted and braced himself with his left hand. Then, even as the tremor passed painfully through his shoulder, he gripped his right wrist with his left hand, restraints still dangling, and he rolled toward the first soldier he saw.

It took a moment for Davidson to recognize what dropped from the sky and rolled toward them. It wasn't until his cuffs bounced off his head that he realized somehow, impossibly, Cyrus had done it.

As the soldier in front of him turned toward the strange splat and grunt at the edge of the lobby, Davidson knew what help Cyrus needed—but his knees locked, his body numbed from the waist up, and he just stood there, hands above his head, anxiety vibrating his right cheek in pulse with his erratic heart.

As the wet warmth spread across the front of his pants and down his thighs, Toutopolus took in the chaos. With guns trained on him and alarm on the guards' faces, he expected to reel backward as gunfire tore into his chest. What did not expect was a flailing Cyrus to drop down like a spider at the end of the hall as his restraints released.

Then, as the guard he had tackled at the door began to rise, Toutopolus thought of his three daughters whom he would never again hear giggle until they shook and fell. He thought of his wife who would never again smile and kiss him to shush his rambling ad infinitum about some new nanotechnology. It was not the first time this lament had arrested his thoughts in this place, but it was the first time he realized his captors, these fucking guards, especially the podwaste motherfucker crawling to his feet in front of him, were to blame. He caught one loop of his cuffs in his right hand, and with force enough to reverse the fabric of time itself, he tried to kick through the motherfucker's head.

Milliken had wrapped the fingers of his right hand around Euston's neck and pressed his thumb hard just beneath the jawbone as Sifu had taught him. Something or someone smashed into the soldier to his left as Milliken twisted Euston's neck to the right while pulling his rifle in the opposite direction, and he drove his knee twice into Euston's groin. Euston's rifle fell to the floor as Milliken brought his hand back in a fist into Euston's ribs. Euston's body buckled from the attack to the groin, and out of the corner of his eye, Milliken noticed Cyrus was on their floor lying on top of another soldier. Milliken dug his unkempt nails into Euston's neck and raked as he ducked under his arm, stepped his right leg behind him, and flipped him.

Euston landed face and chest-first on the ground, and Milliken was already moving to finish him when he noticed two guards across the lobby with their guns trained on him.

Dr. Winberg could barely believe his eyes when Cyrus leaped over the edge of the balcony using the Ashan commander's neck as an anchor. The guards scrambled around as anarchy was loosed upon the hallway. Arms, legs, elbows, and knees swung wildly as bodies dropped, and scientists and guards alike moved about like roaches from an overturned refuse bin.

So this is how Dr. Chamberlain is going to get us killed. The fire was now spreading toward the hall at an alarming rate. Water began cascading over them as four guards rushed up from behind with extinguishing units. As the men approached, and as the two original guards who were still conscious moved to follow whoever had escaped in the stairwell, Dr. Winberg saw his chance.

"I can help you!" he yelled above the cataract and chaos. "I know his plan!"

Torvald knew something was coming, but he had no idea it was coming like this. He had spent two dome cycles alone in a darkened room with only a table and a chair. He had spent most of the time curled up beneath the table, locked in a repeating memory of life in Bonn. He expected to remember his fiancée, Siobhan, and he had continuously tried to revisit images of the thick red locks of hair she could never keep from tangling, her skin so pale it would freckle the moment sunlight graced her body, and her laugh that, despite being a masculine laugh, turned him on to her more than any other of her outward traits. But every time he tried to think of what Dr. Villichez referred to as 'enchanted thoughts,' he always returned to the same vision—riding on the Bonn sub-lev from end to end the day before his fifteenth birthday. It had been the week of Karneval, and the doorman at the bar where his surprise party was supposed to be refused to let him in because he was eight hours too young. His best friend Jörg had to tell him about the surprise that was never sprung. For a full night, he rode that same sub-lev again and again, complaining to Jörg, who stayed with him the whole time. That image continued to run through his mind even after they removed him from the dark room and placed him in with the other room of scientists. Davidson and Milliken had tried to tell him something, Davidson had even spoken to him in German, but all he managed to understand was a paraphrase of what Cyrus had told him before he was gaffled, 'Something is coming.'

That image of that sub-lev ride was still in his head now as the orderly line in front of him disintegrated into bedlam. It felt as if his insides had been tangled up in a rigging line, and now two mag-levs were tugging at either side trying to free it. Only moments earlier, his wristlocks had tightened, but that had seemed like only part of the routine, and then something fell from the roof in front of the chaos, and his wrists were freed.

Then, hard metal collided with his shoulder and reinforced this demand for his attention. He stumbled from the blow into a guard and was shoved back the other way. Then, Torvald surprised himself as he spun and brought his leg around in an arc incident with his assailant's head.

The guard, unprepared, took Torvald's heel to his face and dropped straight down. A rifle butt rubbed against Torvald's scalp, but he swept the other guard's legs, and as the guard hit the ground, Torvald stomped down on his torso with enough force to send a shock up his own leg. He then stood there stunned with vision blurred, frozen on the man's chest like a hunter with his trophy as the scrapes on his scalp and shoulders protested against the cold washing over him. Eisenehertz, Rousseau, and Qin were cowering and staring at Torvald in awe. Torvald saw past them to the two khaki forms moving through the rabble toward some tussle at its front. There was a bizarre hissing above him, and he heard the soldiers yell "Desist!" and he knew Cyrus was in danger.

Had Cyrus known the level and intensity of the pain that would wash over him as he lunged, dislocated shoulder first, into the back of the unsuspecting guard, he might have chosen another course of action. But now, his knees gave out beneath him as the sickening pop from his shoulder resetting still resonated in his ears. It felt like his spine was ripped out of his side. The ground engulfed him, a thick black frost spread through the void left by his seemingly excised backbone, and Cyrus wondered if the man he had checked into the wall had managed to maintain his own consciousness...

...the warmth of a jaundiced sun was an alarming contrast to the apathetic chill that had brought him here. He was moving quickly as if he was riding a mag-cycle, but the movement was too bumpy, more organic. Maybe it was a nanohorse. Either way, the sense of urgency rushing through his veins like a poison made the nature of his conveyance irrelevant—whatever he was riding was not fast enough.

He rode faster and faster, but it was still not enough to appease his anxiety. His destination was a small point on the horizon, barely visible in front of the setting sun, but he instantly knew what it was. It was a little girl, but she had the face of a woman, and she wore the look of a mother in mourning for her child.

And the clouds began to coalesce and swirl in the sky behind her, but she was oblivious to their formation or their intent. He harder as the clouds continued to form—thick, unctuous billows that seemed to issue from despair itself. Talons formed, and then sinewy arms, and then a ghastly visage that eclipsed the pallid sun. The form reared back, the girl still in either ignorance or apathy, and Cyrus still too far away. The creature lunged forward, teeth bared and mouth gaping, to devour its prey...

...but Cyrus was snatched from his mount by his neck, and the surreal horror before him faded and gave way to very tangible disorder.

Toutopolus pulled Cyrus to his feet by his collar, but had been too focused on the resuscitation to see the rifle butt that smacked against the side of his head as someone yelled "Desist!"

Cyrus stood into a kick, but his vision and balance failed him. He stumbled and only managed to kick the barrel of the soldier's rifle.

But that had been good enough to knock the guard off balance. Toutopolus moved, clutching the side of his head and revealed another guard training a gun on them both. The ground was still wobbling beneath Cyrus's feet, and when he moved, he stumbled into the off-balance guard, and they both clambered to the floor in a sprawl. As he fell, Cyrus brought his forehead down hard on the guard's nose.

Cyrus rolled onto his back, still on top of the guard, and found a gun barrel aimed at his head. "Move again, and I finish you!"

Uzziah pushed past Tanner and Jang on the second landing. By the time they reached the fifth floor, two floors down from where they had started, their chains had fallen away, but Uzziah kept holding the rifle like a bat. He could use the weapon as had been intended, but it was clear these men had been ordered not to shoot, so he held it like a polearm because a man wielding a rifle as a Kantistyka racket was less likely to elicit unsanctioned gunfire.

They reached the fourth floor, and the door opened in front of them, but Uzziah kicked it back and had kept running, pulling Jang along with him. Tanner scuffled with someone at the door when it opened again, but he somehow barred the door and continued to follow.

Dr. Rousseau moved out of Torvald's way as he rushed forward, but he had to shove Dr. Eisenhertz to the ground. Someone had yelled, "Move again, and I finish you!" and Dr. Qin moved between Torvald and one of the soldiers. As Torvald rushed toward them, and the soldier turned, Qin crouched down, covering his head. Torvald launched his own body over Qin and threw a left punch at the soldier's head, using the loop of the cuffs as metal knuckles. The soldier turned his temple directly into the attack and crumpled as Torvald landed on top of him. Then, unexpectedly, something from the soldier's utility pack jabbed into Torvald's side, knocking the breath forcefully from his lungs.

Toutopolus flipped the man onto his back with the kick. The man tried to spin on his back and bring his leg around to clip Toutopolus's feet, but Toutopolus had fallen for that move too many times. Toutopolus jumped and brought both feet down on the soldier's midsection. Toutopolus stumbled off the soldier's torso and toward another soldier that had turned his back with his machine gun hanging from its shoulder strap. The soldier reached for some other device and yelled, "You fit to fry espion!"

That was when Toutopolus tripped on Davidson's ankle.

Davidson still could not make sense of the debacle that was playing out around him. Bodies were spinning, flying, and falling everywhere. As he became dizzy, he realized that he had not been breathing. He had heard the words, "You fit to fry," but he was still trying to clear his vision. Then something clipped his Achilles tendon and sent a sharp twinge through his entire body that shocked him to his senses. He saw through the chaos of the melee in front of him—there were two soldiers across the lobby neglecting their machine guns to reach for something else to gun down Milliken who, with the bellow of some enraged creature, blindly charged at them.

The soldier stood outside of Torvald's reach, and he pulled a small black box from his utility belt. Torvald coughed and noticed that Davidson was the only thing in the hall that seemed to not be moving. Everything else was spinning around him as if Davidson was the center of balance in a universe that refused order. Then, as the soldier pointed the black box, Torvald realized Davidson was, as these jackmonkey Ashan soldiers would put it, finished, complete.

But then, a comet from the chaos assaulted the stable center, and Torvald saw Toutopolus, like a Fringe cat in a wildlife holostream, curl into a ball and bowl into the legs of the soldier with the black box. A tiny bolt of lightning burst from the box, but went upward, dissipating into the ceiling as the guard fell, his limbs flailing awkwardly on the floor. Torvald rolled from the man twitching beneath him, and he noticed Cyrus was still in danger.

"Get up, rightforth!" the soldier standing over Cyrus bellowed as he ignored the calamity around him. Cyrus looked down the barrel of the gun, and he felt the heat well in him again, eclipsing the throbbing in his shoulder. Then he saw the earwig radio in the soldier's ear. They were all connected, and yet, in the midst of this nonsense, not a single shot had been fired—not even into the air. So Cyrus leaned forward as if he were about to stand from the bloody soldier writhing beneath him, and he kicked the soldier's knee.

Torvald launched himself from his crouch toward the soldier standing over Cyrus, but Cyrus kicked, and the soldier's body came back toward him. Torvald landed another metal-knuckled punch at the base of the soldier's skull, snapping his head forward. As he fell, Torvald noticed another black box, like the one that had been pointed at him, on the man's belt.

A world-class sprinter could cover thirty meters in a little less than three seconds, but Milliken had a larger distance to cover in less time. The thought crossed his mind then dissipated in the fury that still fueled his body and launched him toward the guard across the lobby. The guard pulled something black and cold-looking from his belt and pointed it at Milliken.

Davidson hurled himself after Milliken, screaming as he charged toward the second guard across the lobby. The guard pulled the black box from his belt, and as Davidson screamed, the guard turned his attention to him. There was a flash, and Davidson's vision went blank. He felt his chest stop moving forward and realized he could no longer feel his legs. Then the feeling in his arms and fingers was gone, and then, finally, he felt nothing.

Milliken saw a thin bolt of lightning streak from the black box of the guard to his right. It had halted the screaming of whoever had followed him out of the brawl into the lobby. He didn't know what it had done, but he was sure he didn't want to find out, so as the guard turned his eyes back to him, Milliken leaped forward and dropped.

Torvald saw Davidson get zapped by the bolt of lightning that shot out from the soldier, and it felt as if his own heart had stopped. Davidson twitched as static electricity crackled through his body, but now, Torvald had one of the black lightning boxes in his own hand. He saw Milliken drop to the ground, slide, and clip a soldier from his feet. Torvald lifted the box and pressed the green button, hoping simultaneously that he was pressing the correct button and, for Davidson's sake, that the bolts that issued from the box were not lethal.

Cyrus elbowed the man writhing beneath him, hopped to his feet, and kicked him in the side of his head, then turned as Davidson collapsed, a sparkle of electricity dancing across his chest. The soldier that zapped Davidson looked nervous as he tried to pick his next target. Another soldier fired a bolt over Milliken and left a blue scar in the air as Milliken's momentum carried him into the soldier's legs. There was a loud pop as the man collapsed, attempted to brace himself with his arm, and failed. The soldier's head smacked against the tiled floor as the sickening snap from the man's shattered arm still resonated through the lobby. The left soldier, realizing he was about to be flanked as Milliken rolled to his feet, was stymied, and he turned back to his right quickly to aim the box at Cyrus.

After losing consciousness once, even for a moment, Cyrus knew that above all else, he had to stay on his feet if they were to make it out of here. His eyes focused on the soldier's shoulders because the shoulders always move first, but the soldier was too far away, and his uniform was too baggy. As Cyrus dove to his right, he wasn't sure if the soldier was about to press the button, or if he had already pressed it.

The box had begun humming in Torvald's hand, and in the time before it discharged, Milliken had taken out his guard, and the other guard had turned, aiming his box at Cyrus. Cyrus stood directly in front of Torvald, blocking his shot, and Torvald felt a bitter heat in his throat as his stomach compressed. Cyrus dove out of the way, drawing the other guard's attention. Then, as Cyrus rolled into a ball, Torvald's box discharged, sending a bolt into the ribs of the guard just as he fired. The guard's body twitched violently then stiffened and fell as his bolt streaked toward Cyrus.

Cyrus rolled past Toutopolus as he heard the snap of static almost simultaneous with the blue flash in the corner of his eye. He was sure he was going down, but as he dipped his shoulder and flattened across the floor, he saw the hair stand on the already unconscious soldier next to him, and he could smell the metallic twinge of ozone as tendrils of dissipating current danced across the body of the soldier that had inadvertently shielded him. Cyrus rolled backward stood, flattening against the wall. Everyone he had involved in the plan was up except Davidson. Rousseau, Tsuchiya, and Koresh were down, and Qin was huddled in the corner shielding his head. Bin Hassan stood frozen in place yelling in Arabic.

"Get Davidson and head to the dock!" Cyrus yelled.

"What about the others?" Toutopolus asked.

"Just get to the dock." Cyrus heard footfalls coming down the stairs. "Go now goddamn it!" He knew the soldiers could probably hear him, but the roar of the sprinklers should have muffled his commands. Besides, it probably would not matter anyway.

Cyrus launched himself off the wall toward the stairwell door. Torvald turned, tossed Cyrus the black box, and yelled, "Charge it first! Green fires," and then turned to help Davidson.

Winberg sat in a surveillance room on the same floor as the barracks. A series of holomonitors displayed the escape attempt as it unfolded. What initially looked like an imminent slaughter now looked like a possibility. Winberg could see these soldiers had no idea what they were doing. The only one who seemed to understand how to quell more than a riot of belligerent teens was Denali, and he was now on his way out on a gurney.

These men wanted to believe this band of wayward and confused scientists were spies, and Dr. Chamberlain was doing a good job of convincing them of such. Hell, with the exception of some awkward hesitation here and there, Chamberlain and his cronies looked like they had been trained for this sort of thing. And so far, it was all working in Winberg's own favor.

Denali seemed sharp, but it seemed like a distinct lack of demand for real soldiers had reduced the acumen of his charges to that of mere peacekeepers. This particular melee was, in fact, chaos, but the chaos had been orchestrated; Dr. Chamberlain was more than renegade chimp jockeying for belly room. Winberg could even say he respected him as the escape played out. He still despised the man's lack of refinement, but he could see an inkling of what made these men, who had been soft-cultured in the halls of academia, fling themselves at armed soldiers as if the mere fact that Chamberlain said they would be okay made it so...

...but sitting here, hearing the second-in-command issue the order to lock down the louvers and release the uberhounds, Winberg knew it would *not* be okay.

When Winberg had offered his assistance to the Ashans, he had been fully prepared to further his own aims at Chamberlain's expense. But now, he could see Cyrus was not as reckless as he wanted to believe, and he felt like a coward for not having seen it sooner. "No, that's exactly what he wants you to do! You'll be playing right into his plan!" Winberg belted as he lifted his hand to halt Quadrad Chaldea.

"*Yamina!*" Go right, Uzziah had yelled at the bottom of the stairs. Tanner threw open the stairwell door, and every hair on Tanner's body stood on end as a bolt of lightning streaked between him and Jang. Uzziah had already gone through the door, hurling the rifle at whoever had fired the bolt. There were two guards positioned several meters away in front of the door, and another bolt flashed behind Tanner, but he was already across the doorway. Tanner spun and charged through opposite Uzziah.

Uzziah launched a left, and as the guard lifted his hand from his rifle to block, Uzziah kicked him in his ribs. The guard stumbled backward but stabilized himself and then stepped forward, swinging the butt of his rifle around in an arc. But Uzziah had anticipated the attack, and he lunged forward himself, landing beside the man outside the swing of his rifle. Uzziah blocked the follow-through with his right hand, pulled the man toward him slightly by his elbow, then turned, driving a knee into the man's kidney. As the man's body buckled, Uzziah was already behind him, pulling his right arm behind his back into a chicken wing. Uzziah gripped the man's left hand over the handle of the rifle and pulled the rifle back into his throat. How unfortunate for this man, Uzziah thought, that we are both left-handed. It was, however, fortunate for Tanner, Jang, and himself, because it was going to be their way out of here.

The man lifted his rifle as Tanner vaulted out the door, but Tanner moved to his left, grabbed the rifle barrel with his left hand, and pulled as he brought his elbow up and across the nose of the soldier. The soldier stumbled backward, blood erupting from his nose, but held his footing. Tanner spun, bringing the back of his left elbow around into the man's face again. The man crumpled, and Tanner finished his spin, clubbing his right fist across the back of the man's neck. Tanner turned and prepared to dive behind cover, but he saw Uzziah using one of the guards as a shield and covering the two men in front of the door. "Drop your weapons!" Uzziah ordered. "*Tikra le* Jang, *kach ekdach, ve lech!*" he said to Tanner. Get Jang, get a gun, and go!

Cyrus stood to the right of the stairwell door as heavy footfalls echoed through the stairwell. He shifted the black box into his left hand and pressed the blue button. He was short of breath, and he was on edge, but with at least four men coming down the stairs a meter or so away, he needed that edge because it kept him sharp, and most importantly, because it incensed him into doing the egregiously stupid thing he was about to do.

As soon as the door creaked, he launched himself into the mix. In their midst, it would be hard for them to get a good hit, but easy for him. He slammed into the guard that was entering first and checked him against the door jamb. Cyrus kicked the door into the soldier still holding it. Cyrus could see the other two were still on the landing, caught off-guard by his advance, but now they were steadying themselves for a shot with their lightning boxes. The soldier against the jamb kneed Cyrus's midsection, and Cyrus felt his insides convulse. He began to tense the muscles in his abdomen to hold back the convulsion, but then he let it release. He threw his head forward as his body wretched, driving his forehead into the guard's nose as vomit erupted into his own mouth. He had eaten only enough to ensure his blood sugar levels could sustain some effort, and now the acidic chyme from that food burned through the back of his throat as it filled his mouth.

The other guard had recovered from the door hit and was now bearing in on Cyrus. Cyrus spun, bringing an elbow across the temple of the guard next to him as the other guard reached for his throat. Cyrus blocked the man's advance, but grappled his wrist and yanked him in. The man followed with a right, leaving his rifle to rest on its strap, but Cyrus ducked. The attack caught the guard behind him, who had been dazed by Cyrus's initial attack. Cyrus kneed the advancing guard's ribs, and as the air in the man's lungs widened his face and eyes, Cyrus expelled the vomit in his mouth into them and brought his left elbow back into the face of the man behind him.

Cyrus spun the soldier in front of him into a chokehold as he flailed at his stinging eyes and nostrils. Cyrus fired the black box under the man's arms and caught a guard on the landing in his chest as another bolt streaked out toward him. The bolt caught the flailing guard in his stomach and Cyrus pushed the man's body aside as static yanked at the hairs of his beard. Cyrus bounded up the stairs as the last soldier dropped his black box and, forgoing his rifle, lifted his leg.

Cyrus jumped to the right and realized he was several centimeters higher than what he or the soldier had expected. Cyrus rebounded from the wall and extended his body to punch, but even off-guard, the man was quick enough to block. Cyrus landed and kicked, but the man turned, catching Cyrus's shin with the side of the metal rifle. A splitting shock shot up Cyrus's leg and into his groin, but he ignored it and fired a jab then a body punch. The man blocked both and followed by lifting his knee. Cyrus side-stepped and they faced each other again with the stairs to Cyrus's right. Cyrus was sure he could beat this man—Milliken was this fast on a good day—but there wasn't time for this. The man threw another jab and Cyrus blocked, but as the man followed with his right, Cyrus knew what had to be done. He stepped in, let the punch hit him, rolled with it, then grabbed the guard's collar and pulled the man back on top of his foot, flipping the man over him and launching him down the stairs. Cyrus rolled to his feet and bounded up to the next floor.

Tanner ushered Jang through the front of the building, covering the outside with the assault rifle as they barreled through the glass door. Tanner would have preferred a staff or a sword, but this clunky, callous piece of metal would have to do. As the door closed behind them, Tanner saw spots as his eyes adjusted to the artificial night outside the building. There was a writhing mass of people gathered on the opposite side of the ave, and there seemed to be guards scattered among them. These guards appeared to be more municipal than soldiers, and they seemed unaware of the chaos inside the building.

Tanner followed the eyes of the throng upward to the convoy of levs and lorries floating by several meters above their heads that were converted into various shapes. A dragon-shaped lev approached, spewing flames and inciting cheers from the crowd. Jang said something like, "How are we gonna get up to them?" but Tanner had already flipped the assault rifle onto his back and was leaping onto one of the titanic statues that flanked the entrance to the building. When Tanner reached the arm, he had only a second to position himself to jump onto the back of the float. As he landed, Tanner swung the assault rifle under his arm. He caught it clumsily, but with enough authority to scare the men riding on the back of the float into submission. Tanner checked over his shoulder to make sure the sniffers on the street were still preoccupied with the crowd. He was not comfortable with his current position, but he was much less comfortable in the custody of half-wits. After the men on the float sat with their hands above their heads, Tanner leaned the assault rifle barrel into the window. "Set it down over there, or I finish you!"

As the lev descended to where Jang was standing, Tanner kept his eye on the men on the float to make sure they didn't have any twinges of heroism. Had he really been reduced to a common levjack? No. These men would go home to their families, and eventually, they would get over whatever shock they were feeling at the moment. There was no guarantee whatever life he might have outside the custody of his captors would be better, and there was no guarantee that he would not be captured again, but at least, on the outside, he could have the illusion that his fate was his own—an illusion that these frightened men in front of him already had. So, as the lev set down next to the entrance, and Uzziah, assault rifle blazing, came backpedaling through the front door, Tanner swallowed his distaste for this whole situation.

By the time the magistrates monitoring the parade had figured out something was amiss, Jang was already raising the lev to the upper dock at a speed that pinned Tanner and Uzziah to the dragon's back.

Torvald and Toutopolus scooped up Davidson and were already through the doors to the dock when they heard the barking. Toutopolus fumbled the black box and almost dropped it before pressing the blue button to charge it. Then, as the uberhounds fanned out in the lobby to flank them, Milliken stepped back into the building, and he had a rifle.

Milliken had been raised in Navarre, an autonomous province in Spain next to the Basque lands of Euskal Herria. Navarre had been reluctant to join the Uni, and Euskal had vehemently opposed unification. In an attempt to get them to come crawling to the Uni for help, Spain had introduced monkeys into the ecosystem of the Basque lands that resisted. His father ran a chicken lab on the Euskal border where chickens were pod-raised for research and consumption. The lab had good countermeasures against rodents and vermin, but Fringe monkeys learned fast, and they were persistent. Assault rifles were outlawed by the Uni, but it didn't matter so close to the Fringe. Milliken had learned at an early age how to use one, especially against groups of attacking animals, and here, as he had disengaged the safety, he remembered to aim low, two steps in front of the rushing animal, and he pulled the trigger.

Milliken fired three short bursts and put one of the animals down, but the other two, apparently programmed to respect guns without startling, recoiled and then fanned out to flank. Milliken took out the hound to his left before it could angle in.

Toutopolus noticed a soldier on the dais taking aim at Milliken. Whatever cease-fire had been issued was most certainly lifted now. Toutopolus took aim, not even sure how to aim with this overgrown lev bay opener.

Cyrus heard muffled gunfire as he rushed the door. He told himself he should turn around and go back to the dock, but he kept moving toward the door as he pressed the blue button on the black box.

Villichez watched the guard in front of him, Colfax he believed, focus on some order from his earwig and then flip a switch on his rifle. The soldier next to him flipped the same switch on his weapon and tensed as another cadence of gunfire rang out. The soldier that took aim over the edge of the dais suddenly flew back toward Villichez, a sparkle of blue dancing across his face and neck.

Then, the door to the stairwell flew open.

Cyrus dove at the floor as soon as he opened the door and heard a volley of gunfire. He could feel the swirling air rent by bullets coursing over him as he turned and landed on his side. His momentum carried him through the water on the floor, and he expected his body to erupt in a fit of convulsions as bullets tore into him, but the volley missed its mark. Then, as he flattened himself to the ground, Cyrus realized what mark it had found.

Villichez's body shook and then froze. To Cyrus, he looked like a man who had just had all his loved ones snatched away from him, watching in still horror as they were ushered merciless into the sunset, never to be seen again. Or maybe that was what he himself felt. The air was oily, and things moved in the gel as if gravity itself was stunned. Even the water cascading from the sprinklers seemed to fall slower, each drop discernable as it struggled to push its way through the aspic air. Villichez fell in a shower of his own blood, which stubbornly mixed with the deluge. He outstretched his arms to Cyrus, but he could not reach him.

Darius, Xander, the Arcology, even Feralynn, and now Villichez— the weight of everything he had lost since he had arrived on this barren lavpool kept his fist clenched, nails digging into his right palm as the corner of the black box pierced his left.

"*Anák na laláki*," Villichez muttered, and then his gaze turned inward. The ground hungrily pulled Villichez down, and Cyrus felt a pressure in his own chest as Villichez's blank stare met his on the ground. The gel made the senses unreliable. Sight wavered, sound muffled, touch and smell distorted, and Cyrus felt more than heard the cry that erupted from his own center, guttural and deep, as he turned to face 43235, smoke issuing from his rifle barrel in brazen lack of remorse.

Soldier 43235 was over him now pointing his gun and yelling something that Cyrus neither could nor cared to hear. Cyrus felt the heat from the gun barrel despite the half-meter distance. Cyrus pushed himself forward on the ground, and he kicked the barrel upward as 43235 fired again. The mire around them muffled to report as Cyrus jammed the black box into the inside of 43235's knee and pressed the green button.

The jolt knocked Cyrus's hand away, numbing it, and the box disappeared into the falling water. Cyrus stood and snatched the rifle away from 43235 as he collapsed over his weakened knee. The soldier lifted his hands to defend himself, but Cyrus was already stepping past him to flip him with his own rifle strap. Villichez's murderer scrambled to get back to his hands and knees, and he coughed, spraying water from his nostrils as his weak knee gave way. He floundered as he reached for a black box attached to a fallen soldier's belt. Cyrus saw an errant set of manacles on the ground and the remote on 43235's belt. Cyrus dropped the rifle and kicked 43235's supporting arm from under him. He fell as Cyrus moved beside him and snatched the remote from his belt while simultaneously scooping the cuffs from the floor. Cyrus extended the chain between the cuffs with the remote as 43235 crawled and grabbed the black box, but Cyrus looped the chain of the cuffs around his neck as he rose. Cyrus clasped the wristlocks and lifted 43235 by his neck. He pushed 43235 against the wall with his forearm and looked him in the eyes as he pressed the button to tighten the cuffs.

"It's not the same when you have to earn it, is it?" Cyrus yelled into the soldier's face as 43235 frantically scratched and scraped at the chain tightening around his neck, gouging his own flesh in an attempt to tear the restraints away. His tongue slipped from his mouth, and his body twitched in a spasm, and then there was a sound like someone dropping a wet rag, and his body went loose.

Cyrus let the body drop and, as his hearing became clear again, he heard barking, this time closer and moving toward him. Cyrus snatched up a rifle, and as he ran to the stairwell, he heard more footfalls than he could count. Cyrus heard the whoosh of a door sliding open in the hallway at the edge of the dais And realized he was about to be surrounded. He lifted the rifle with his right hand, and as the barking closed in on him, he ran toward the dais. As he cleared the corner just before the edge of the dais, he squeezed the trigger of the rifle, and he saw khaki forms duck and dodge as he fired and launched himself, for the second time, over the edge of the balcony. As he fell, gunfire issued after him. Splinters of plaster and concrete fell with him as the ground rushed up again, even slower this time. He rolled as he landed, and as he came to his feet, he saw metal louvers at the entrance slowly closing. Cyrus looked over his shoulder and saw two uberhounds clear the railing of the dais after him. Then, gunfire sounded from in front of him, and he instinctively shielded his face before he realized Milliken and Uzziah had stepped inside the closing louvers and were firing past him to cover his retreat. As Cyrus reached the doors, Uzziah and Milliken backed through the closing louvers, and they leaped onto the back of the float. Toutopolus patted Cyrus on the back and smiled, but Cyrus had difficulty returning it. "I can't believe we made it!" Toutopolus exclaimed.

"We're a far cry from safe here," Uzziah said as he checked the magazine on his rifle. Jang pulled the float away from the dock hastily, in response to the ominous looking assault-lev rounding the corner of the ave behind them.

seventeen

—More trouble at school, Dari?

—When isn't there?

—Terry or Genivere?

—Terry.

—So what now?

—He took my Monster Mashup holodeck card.

—Well I told you not to take your games to school.

—Come on Dada, I don't need a lecture right now. I already know.

—You tell Miss Hasabe?

—Yeah, she said the same thing you did about having it there in the first place, cuz Terry said he didn't have it. Problem is, I told him if he didn't give it back, I'd pop him good.

—So?

—So, I don't know. I'm scared.

—Well, I don't know if you poppin' people because of something you could have avoided is on the axis, but maybe I can answer your question with a story.

—Okay...

—So this monkey walks into a toy store one day, and the manager asks if he can help him.

—Wait, why's the manager talking to the monkey? Why doesn't he just tranq him?

—Because it's a fable. You remember, anthropomorphization.

—Oh yeah, well, I don't like talking monkeys very much.

—Well, neither do I, but that's the story I got. Savvy?

—Savvy.

—So, the manager asks if he can help, and the monkey says, "Yeah, you got any sweetbars?" And the manager says, "No, sorry, we only sell toys." So the monkey says, "Okay," and leaves. The next day, the monkey comes back to the store, and he sees the manager and asks, "Got any sweetbars?" The manager is baffled but not sure it's the same monkey. He replies politely, "No, we don't have any sweetbars." And the monkey says, "Okay," and walks off. So another day goes by,

179

and the monkey comes in again, sees the manager, and says, "Hey." But this time the manager recognizes him and braces himself, already prepared to be irritated. "You got any sweetbars?" the monkey asks again, and the manager loses it. "Look we don't have any sweetbars, we didn't have any yesterday, and we're not gonna have any tomorrow! If you want sweetbars, go to a bakery!" So the monkey says, "Okay," and goes on about his business. So two days go by, and the manager thinks he's seen the last of the monkey, but on the third day, the monkey shows up again. He catches the manager talking to an employee and tugs on his shirt, "You got any sweetbars?" And the manager completely loses his y-drive. "Look you stupid monkey," he says, "if you come in here one more time and ask for sweetbars, I'm gonna nail you to that wall right there!" The monkey looks at the wall, then calmly looks back at the manager and says, "Okay," and walks off. Well the next day, the monkey shows up again, and the manager's head fills with steam on sight. "What?" he yells as soon as he sees him. "You got any nails?" the monkey asks. "No, we don't have any stinking nails!" he yells. So the monkey looks at him, right in his eye, smiling, and asks, "You got any sweetbars?"

—Ha, that's funny, but I don't get what it has to do with me and Terry.

—Well, what's the moral of the story?

—That toy stores should carry sweetbars and keep out monkeys?

—No, smarty pants. The moral is you shouldn't make a threat you're not prepared to keep, or monkeys will take advantage of you.

—Isn't a threat you can't keep called a bluff? Don't people do it in poker all the time?

—Sure they do, and lots of them lose when their cards are called. Point is, a man should follow through with his threats, or he should keep his mouth shut.

—So you're sayin' when I see Terry I should pop him?

—No Dari, I'm saying there's nothing worse than a man who doesn't do what he says he will, and he, and only he, has to live with the misery that comes with being that man.

• • • • •

"**Maybe we should have procured a more solid vehicle** than a parade float," Uzziah said as he held his sight on the hovering tank lumbering after them.

"If you see a better vehicle, you're welcome to go get it!" Cyrus yelled over the wind coursing between them as they sped down the ave over the heads of onlookers who seemed to think it was an elaborate stunt. Jang handled the vehicle as if he had been driving parade floats his entire life. And his instincts were good, probably honed from more than one mishap involving the Seoul municipal police. He kept the lev low, only a few meters above the people on the ave, and he hugged the corners tightly, taking a corner whenever the assault vehicle got too close. There was no way the pilots of the assault-lev would risk using heavy munitions in this environment, but as one of the nodes on the front of the tank began to glow, Cyrus realized the pilots felt their planetary lasers would cause acceptable collateral damage.

"Get down!" Uzziah yelled, pressing himself to the stucco deck of the float. Tanner and a dazed Davidson rode in the cabin with Jang, while the others, on the back of what must have originally been a flatbed lorry, flattened themselves into the sculpting that had transformed the craft into an Eastern dragon. A line of orange light stretched from the node on the tank behind them and sliced over the vehicle. Jang dipped closer to the crowd as the razor of light clipped the tip of the craft's tail. He swung left around a turn as a second laser stretched over the right side of the float.

Tanner stuck his head out of a hole in the side of the dragon's chest. "What now?" he yelled over the wind.

"Get to the gate!" Uzziah yelled.

Tanner nodded as Cyrus looked around. They sped over another cheering mob as the tank rounded the corner behind them. The four large caliber guns of the assault-lev's artillery cannon followed them as the turret stood in place; there was no way they would use them here, but as soon as they got into the open...

Cyrus found a panel on the back of the dragon's neck and pressed one of the buttons, and the float shook as a roar sounded. He pressed the button next to it, and bluish flame erupted from the dragon's mouth, eliciting another round of cheers and plaudits from the crowd.

"Should we fire?" Milliken asked, keeping the tank in his own sights as best he could.

"Won't do much good!" Uzziah yelled back.

The lasers fired again, but Jang pulled around another turn, leaving the lasers crossing beneath the float. Toutopolus slipped, but Torvald caught his shoulder before he could roll out of his nook.

"Are you a marksman?" Cyrus asked, tapping Uzziah on his shoulder.

"What? Yeah, best in class. Why?"

Cyrus lifted a tank marked 'combustible' and pointed back to an open compartment in one of the rolls of the dragon's body. "Two more of these!" he yelled.

Cyrus left the canister in the cranny behind Uzziah and crawled back to the front of the converted lorry. He banged the flat of his hand against the body of the dragon where Tanner had popped out his head. Tanner's head craned out the little window, and Cyrus leaned forward.

"Take another turn and slow down!"

Cyrus grabbed the other two canisters from the compartment and crawled back to where Uzziah sat. Milliken sat on the opposite side of the dragon's body. "Okay, after the next turn get ready!"

The dragon accelerated, and just as the tank loomed around the corner, Jang dipped left again and slowed. Cyrus readied himself, grasping the handholds along the top of the canister. Jang rose to a level halfway between ave levels as the people beneath them looked on. For the first time, Cyrus noticed all the adboards displayed the same image. The man they called the Knight of Swords was giving an impassioned speech. A transcript ran beneath him in subtitles, but there was no time for reading. Cyrus hunkered down as he saw a hint of gunmetal peek from around the corner, then he stood and heaved the gas canister at the tank. The canister spun through the air, and, just as the node of the tank peeked around the corner and lit up, Uzziah fired a burst from his rifle.

The canister exploded in a blue fireball in front of the node, and Jang hit the throttle again just above the lower ave as a laser stretched across the street over them.

Tanner's head poked from the window again, "We can't keep this up all day!"

"I know! I know!" Cyrus yelled back, losing his balance as they rounded another corner. As they came around the corner, they were met with another cheer. On a large adboard just above them, the image of the Knight of Swords faded into an image of Earth, solitary and frozen, gibbous in the rays of a sun Cyrus would never feel the warmth of again.

"Move up! Move up to the base of the board!" Cyrus yelled to the cabin. Torvald leaned over the left side and relayed the message. The float rose, and Cyrus leaped off the float onto the catwalk that supported the board. He held the remaining canisters in each hand and placed one next to a support of the board.

"There's no time." Cyrus screamed over the wind and crowd, "Go to the edge of the block! Fire as soon as I am clear!"

A laser fired through the head of the dragon and the tank strafed sideways into the large ave firing the second laser between the adboard and the float as Jang pulled away. Cyrus ran to the opposite end of the sign as the tank lurched forward and set the last canister at the end. He had noticed that the building behind this one was terraced, but he had no time to gauge distance. He hoped he had not made a mistake as he sprinted to the end of the catwalk. As he approached the safety rail, he saw there were about four meters between the two buildings and the terrace was about two meters below. He leaped up at the end, braced both feet on the rail in a crouch, and extended his body with all the might in his legs. As he stretched, pulling his legs beneath him, he heard the report of automatic fire and then felt the shockwave of the exploding canisters as the air around him warmed abruptly. As soon as he hit the landing, he rolled again, but his ankle and shoulder cursed him for it. There was a horrible screeching and hissing, and the building shook beneath him as if some mythical beast had been loosed by the gods themselves. Cyrus pedaled out of his roll, but he staggered into the side of the building. His shoulder kept him upright, but the contact sent a fog through his body. He coughed and spat, letting the wave of fear that rushed over him overwhelm the pain. The float was about eight meters away. Cyrus looked over his shoulder as he ran and saw the adboard come down over the tank in a shower of sparks and metal. The ground rumbled as the sign pushed the tank into a building at the head of the block. Cyrus felt a burn in his chest and coughed up something that was too thick to be phlegm. His legs burned, and his ankle throbbed, but he pushed himself to the end of the building just as Jang made the turn. Cyrus flung his body into the air for what, hopefully, one way or the other, would be the last time.

Uzziah had known exactly what Cyrus was up to when he had jumped onto the adboard platform, but he was still surprised at the result. This entire escape plan seemed like a colossal zoo fuck, and yet, it was unfolding better than some missions he had seen planned out in war rooms; and mostly due to the fact that the man that had been at the reins threw *himself* at the toughest problems and just brought anyone willing along. And now, struggling to keep his feet beneath him, Cyrus dove and stretched out his hands as the float turned. Uzziah and Toutopolus both lunged and caught Cyrus's shoulders, dragging him into the float on top of them. Cyrus wailed as he landed, flopped like a dying fish, and then he slowly rolled onto his butt, holding his left shoulder as if he was shot. "Thanks," he huffed through a veil of sweat as Jang piloted the float into a wide clearing at what must have been the center of the city.

There was a large crowd amassed here, focused on an ominous screen that had been erected on a stage in front of some sort of monument. At each of the four corners of the monument was what looked like the bow of an interplanetary attack ship. Around the square, five other adboards showed identical images of a lone earth against the desolate backdrop of space. There was a countdown timer beneath the image and a white-outlined box in the upper right corner that showed a zoomed image of where the earth lay in the dome-darkened sky.

And then Cyrus could saw it was not a monument at all but the nose of what at one time had been an ominous warship. As the timer ran to zero, the screens flashed white except for the highlighted box, which remained dark as a white aster formed at a point slightly off center. There were no cheers, no gasps, no applause—only the rush of the wind and the whirring of the float's grav drive as Jang sped through the square.

Cyrus nursed his shoulder, and when the flash finally faded, the Earth was still there, but there was something about it that was different. The orbital telescope's digital interpretations of six-hundred-year-old light waves whispered to them as they passed. *The world you knew is gone—and you can never, ever go back.*

They moved out of the center square into deserted aves. Jang shuttled the float onto the central thoroughfare with a maneuver that sent a jolt through Cyrus's body. Tanner leaned out to ask, "So how do we get the bulkhead open?" but then, "What in the hell?" rose from the opposite side of the cabin. They all faced forward, and as the smoke in front of them spread, they saw the bulkhead had been blasted through—from the outside.

Then a low hum behind them arrested everyone's attention, and the tank they had left behind, dented and scraped from its collision with the sign and building, pulled into the deserted ave behind them. The large assault guns trained on the rear of the float as it was bathed in spotlights.

"Your little feist-run is finished. Power down your vehicle and surrender!" echoed from the tank through the empty ave.

"I can make it!" Jang reported.

"I dunno," Cyrus mumbled to himself, but the craft was already lurching forward.

"You will receive no other warning," the high pitched whine of the larger guns spinning up could be heard through the threat echoing behind them.

And then the float stopped hard. Everyone lurched forward. Cyrus protected his shoulder, but his ankle twisted and gave as another tank descending from behind a building at the end of the ave in front of them.

184

And for a moment they were all frozen in time. As improbable as their escape had been, it had never once felt impossible—until now. The tank in front slowed its descent and then stopped, half concealed by a building. They heard the whirr of the gun turret on the tank behind them, and Uzziah said, "Wait a minute." And then the air crackled and split as the heat from tracer rounds sped over them like the tail of a scorpion.

Cyrus thought he was dying. Sound no longer existed, and all he could feel was heat. Then, suddenly, it felt as if the ground itself rippled and rushed up into the bottom of the float as the world shook behind them. Cyrus turned to see the tank behind them explode in a shower of flames and scorched metal as it smacked into a building and slid down the façade into the ave.

By the time the world stopped shaking, the second tank was positioned in front of them above the ave, its cargo bay open. Strange figures inside beckoned for them to move forward. "What are you waiting for, an epiphany?" echoed from loudspeakers in front of them. Jang rushed forward as the tank began moving toward the open bulkhead. The quad guns above the tank fired into the guardhouse beside the gate as soldiers ducked back inside. Jang pulled the float inside just as the tank cleared the first gate. "Are we winning?" erupted through the tank from loudspeakers.

"Yes!" the men and women around them retorted, raising their hands triumphantly in the air. Cyrus recognized them instantly— Apostates.

Cyrus climbed from the back of the float confused, hurt, and unsure if he was any better off than he had been yesterday.

"Yes we are!" a wizened man reported into the remote mic in his palm as he emerged from the band of men to help Cyrus from the float. He tucked the microphone away in his clothing and extended his right hand. "I believe this is how you greet each other, yes?" His handshake was awkward but firm. "You are Doctor Cyrus Chamberlain. I am Paeryl of Nine."

Cyrus was staid. "How do...I mean...why?"

The old man in front of him looked confused by his reaction.

"Wait, he doesn't know," the older man paused, looked at the men behind him, and then rubbed his chin. "But how could he know?"

He grabbed Cyrus by his right shoulder. "The Knight of Swords, our patriarch," he paused histrionically but with a genuine smile of reverence, "he is your son..." There was a look of contentment in the aged man's eyes. It was the look of gratification a man has after returning from a long journey. "...and he left something for you."

• • • • •

When the louvers on the sides of the tank finally opened, they were moving through a mountain pass. They had passed through a group of men and women that seemed to be guarding the pass and into the clearing on the other side—their Domicile as Paeryl had called it.

The scene was desolate, the level of squalor was abject, and upon first inspection, both sympathy and disgust welled up in Cyrus like a fount. But as they moved through the arid valley that couldn't even be called a village, and as the denizens themselves left their tasks behind to come see the haggard procession, Cyrus saw something else. The naked children and tattered, scanty clothing of the people looked like those from the holoscans of Fringe communities waiting to be admitted into the Uni. The first thing Cyrus noted that set them apart, however, was their demeanor; they did not possess the disease-wracked grimaces of the destitute Fringers. They did not shamble as they moved to the carved path that served as an ave through the center of the valley. They were remarkably alert, energetic even, and they seemed...content.

The light from the sun low on the horizon, pallid as it filtered through the mountain tops, cast a green glow on the exposed skin of the villagers. They all seemed ecstatic, almost exultant, as they bustled to get a glimpse of the passengers within the assault-lev as it passed.

Tanner leaned over to Cyrus just as he noticed another major difference between this place and the images they had seen of the Fringe. "There are no structures here."

Before Cyrus could respond, Jang chimed in, "This is a very different scene than the holocast rendered. They don't seem like terrorists."

The men and women in the assault craft laughed and joked with each other on the other side of the cargo bay door. Cyrus could make out the words, but the meaning was unclear. One of the men watching them left another man and woman and sat on the floor of the cargo bay between the window and the scientists. He was bald, was thin but muscular, and seemed slightly taller than the other men. He folded his legs, sat on the floor of the cargo bay, and just looked at Cyrus as if a holocast was playing on top of his head. Cyrus looked around, pretending not to notice, but after a few minutes, he could not quell the crawling beneath his skin. Cyrus faced the bald man, who smiled a wide, toothy grin, looked at Tanner for a moment, and then turned his eyes back to Cyrus.

Cyrus returned the smile, but it felt like it slipped across his face.

"Look at them," Cyrus heard Tanner speak softly into his ear, "They seem to have little concept of privacy."

They moved closer to the opposite side of the valley as Milliken limped around from window to window holding a med-patch on his head. "What are you building?" Torvald asked him as he hobbled past the third time.

"I don't think this is a valley," he winced as he craned his neck into a position that, judging from his expression, must have brought more pain than expected. "I think it's a crater."

Then they moved into the only crafted structure they had seen since they had left Eurydice. It was both odd and mildly disturbing how comforting the sight of concrete and steel was to Cyrus as they entered the construct. The lev set down smoothly, and the men and women all emerged from the door behind Paeryl. "Shall we proceed?" Paeryl asked, spreading his arms in an inviting manner. "There is much before us." The man was calm but obviously excited.

A man and woman opened the cargo door, and Torvald leaned between Cyrus and Tanner as they waited. "You notice this Paeryl guy is the only one who has spoken to us?"

"I don't think the others are allowed to," Tanner said as quietly as possible. They were beckoned to leave the lev, and they found themselves in a large garage. There were various types of vehicles, but none with any kind of markings that would indicate they belonged to a specific group—especially not the Apostates.

They were led into a hallway, and as they reached its end, Paeryl pulled Cyrus into a side room. "You must remove your footing," he said matter-of-factly.

At first, Cyrus was bewildered, and then, as Paeryl's eyes lowered and he removed his own shoes, Cyrus understood. Cyrus nodded to the others and removed his shoes and socks. As each of them bared their feet, they were led through the doors at the head of the hall. They all entered, Paeryl, and then Cyrus and the scientists, with only a few of Paeryl's entourage behind them. The rest remained outside even though they had also removed their shoes.

Inside was a room that could easily have existed on the Paracelsus. Computers, holographic imagers, and holomonitors were spread throughout the room. There were workstations that looked familiar and other devices that did not. There were doors like the ones they had just entered that lead to other parts of the complex, but they were being led to a raised platform about fifty meters directly across from the entrance. "We have been the stewards of this facility for ages, and the Riddle of the Gate has perplexed us sinceforth. Our Doctrine tells us that *you* can unlock this door that shall reveal our fate."

Paeryl seemed like a quaint old man, and to his men, a revered leader, but his rhetoric was a little creepy. Cyrus never liked undue supplication, especially when it was directed at him. And even if what Paeryl said was true, even if Dari had somehow been the progenitor of this odd band of rebels, Cyrus had absolutely no idea what they thought he, as a father six hundred years too late, could possess that could enlighten them. At the center of the room, Paeryl raised his hand in a gesture, and the rest of his entourage stopped where they stood. "Go," he said to Cyrus, "It is for you."

Milliken moved to follow, but Tanner and Uzziah both stopped him. The scientists stood with Paeryl's band as Cyrus moved unsteadily across the last several meters to the ominous circular gateway. At the end of the room, he walked up the stairs to the platform. As soon as his naked feet touched the platform, a holoprojector spread letters across the air in front of the metal iris that had barred egress into the deepest section of the complex for hundreds of years.

Cyrus stood, awestruck by the amber letters that spread in front of him. "When you find yourself where even fools fear to tread, who will rush in to save you?"

Cyrus could understand why they had been baffled. Not sure exactly why he had been brought here, it had taken him a moment to process the answer, and there was no earthly or Ashan reason why these people should know a detail from a story he had made up too many years ago. His fingers were unsteady as he pantomimed the letters 'a,' 'r,' 'y,' 'a,' and 'l.'

The large iris before them dilated, revealing what looked much like an Earth living room and also revealing what at first seemed to be a reflection. Then, as his perception of depth shifted, Cyrus realized that, despite the same beard, the same long, coarse hair, the same posture, the eyes were very different, and they were unmistakable.

Cyrus looked upon his own son. He opened his mouth in an attempt to speak, but words had become both useless and impossible. Then, the weight of revelation proved too much. His legs could no longer support the burden. Whelmed to his knees by the sight of the man standing before him, the room seemed to turn in on itself. And there, as he reached out to his son for the first time in too many years, Cyrus wept.

part two

Nothing is at last sacred but the integrity
of your own mind.
Absolve yourself to yourself,
and you shall have the suffrage of the
world.

RALPH WALDO EMERSON

eighteen

—*Did Dr. Postlethwaite comm-sat you today?*

—*No, why? Does this have anything to do with that holodeck game?*

—*Yeah. Well, yeah and no.*

—*Explain.*

—*Terry told the Disciplinarian that I threatened to pop him one, and the Disciplinarian referred me to Dr. Postlethwaite's office. So we get to his office, and he starts railing me like I shot the Chancellor or something. And Terry's sitting there all smug and smiling like an overstuffed rat. And Dr. Postlethwaite just keeps at me about my attitude and Miss Hasabe's eval and being combative and how I'm now becoming violent, and I couldn't take it anymore.*

—*So what happened?*

—*I popped Terry right in his fat, cheese-puff grin.*

—*What? In the office?*

—*Yeah, right in the middle of some blah-blah about me bringing down the character of the whole class.*

—*Why?*

—*Cuz, I'm not gonna sit there and take the blame and just soak in it when I didn't do anything. I told Miss Hasabe there was gonna be a problem, but she and Disciplinarian Khoury and Dr. Postlethwaite didn't wanna listen. I'm sorry Dada, I'll be the bad guy, but I ain't gonna be their escape goat.*

—*Scape goat.*

—*Whatever it's called, it ain't me.*

—*So how am I supposed to handle this?*

—*I dunno, Dada. You do what you gotta do, but I'm not apologizing.*

—*Well, I'm glad you told me before they called.*

—*I don't think they're gonna call, cuz they didn't listen, and they know they messed up. Dr. Postlethwaite didn't know what to do after I slugged Terry. Terry started crying, and he just sent us back to class. Maybe he knows if they had listened to me, none of it would have happened, and so he's scared to call you.*

—*I'm sure that's not too far from the truth.*

—So am I punished?

—Well, what do you think your punishment should be?

—I don't think I should get punished at all. This whole monkey hunt is punishment enough. But if they had listened to me when I told them, it never would have come down to this.

—Well, maybe your punishment is learning this lesson the hard way.

—What lesson is that? That principals are just as water-headed as school bullies?

—No, that no one listens to the man on the rostrum, not even the ones that agree with him.

—What the heck is a rostrum?

—Dari, mad is as it is, but you mind your tongue around me.

—Sorry Dada, but what is a rostrum?

—It's those raised platforms like the Chancellor always stands on to give speeches. I think in ancient Rome, leaders used to stand on platforms made of pieces of the ships of their enemies. Either way, people cheer and praise, or they boo and hiss, but they never hear what he's saying, they usually only hear what's already in their heads, and they don't believe it until they see it or feel it. By then, it's usually too late. So maybe next time, find a better way to solve your problem; if there is one.

—I don't know what better way I could have done it, Dada.

—Then, you'll just have to live with the consequences, whatever they may be. I'm gonna comm-sat Dr. Postlethwaite and see if we can't get this all sorted out. In the meantime, just keep your distance from that Gallager boy before he gets your Novitiateship revoked.

—I'll stay away as best I can, Dada.

—So, we savvy on this?

—Kinda savvy. Still burns me up a little. I see what you're saying, but it still don't sit straight.

—Well, bounce it around until it does.

—It's bouncing, but it still comes up sideways. I mean, I'll do what you say, but I'm never gonna be anyone's scapegoat or e-scape goat ever again. And if they try and make me, I'm gonna stand on the rostrum and yell so loud even deaf men will hear me.

• • • • •

Cyrus breathed in deeply, and then held it, savoring the taste of consummate disbelief. "How?" he asked, ignoring the sliver of pain that spread across his torso as his lungs contracted.

Darius stood from his chair and walked over to Cyrus as the iris closed behind them. "I am deeply sorry, but I am not as I seem. I am merely an apparition of your son. A product of a computer system left behind to await your arrival."

Cyrus looked through his tears at the room. At the back wall, there was a processor unit about three meters wide and a meter and a half high. It was an impressive piece of hardware; even the advanced Agamemnon unit on the Paracelsus, which controlled every function of the ship, included two redundant backup systems, and housed at least one copy of every accessible written work ever rendered to page or datadeck, was only about the size of a seat cushion. *What could possibly need a processor that large?* Cyrus thought to himself until he noticed the umbilical that led from the processor to the wall.

"You're an avatar," he expelled, draped in a veil of disappointment.

"Your son manipulated the interface created by your colleagues Dr. Jang, Dr. Winberg, and Dr. Villichez to accept freeform entries. He used the processor as an ephemeris and vigilantly made entries every day."

"Every day?"

"It was easy. He combined the system with the avatar they had made of *you* when you left Earth. His vigilance has afforded me more than a few of his personality traits. Most importantly, it has afforded me the privilege of getting to know you," the image bowed melodramatically but it seemed oddly sincere.

"But why?"

"Because he—I, if you don't mind—need your help. Something is amiss in this place."

Cyrus picked himself up and moved to the chair diagonal to where the image of Darius had been sitting. Cyrus waited until he was seated to speak, "Well, I have had more years of disillusionment than most mortal men have ever been afforded to help me learn to stop expecting to see what I expect to see." The sheer length of the sentence burned across his protesting sternum, but he continued: the pain was sobering, "I have seen more today than in even all those years. It seems that precious little could surprise me more, and yet, I feel like I should know better."

"There is something much larger than any of us going on here. I don't know how far it goes back, but I know it goes back, at the very least, to the beginning of our time as colonists here on Asha." The Darius image moved closer as he spoke.

"Explain." Cyrus reclined to relieve the pressure on his exasperated muscles and joints.

"You know how the holocasts say I was exiled?" Darius's likeness moved back to his chair and sat. His movements were graceful, dignified, and it made it hard for Cyrus to not see this trick of photons of light and manipulation of sound waves as the son he had learned to love and admire as a better man than himself.

"Yeah, because the Knight of Swords—because you—were sentenced to death for the Defiance."

"Well, you see, the interesting truth is that no pardon was ever issued. I was supposed to die on the first anniversary of the Defiance, but I escaped with the help of some Quadrads that remained loyal and some sympathizers—all prisoners. We fled to the first place where we could find shelter."

"So you built this bunker here?"

"No. We *found* this bunker here."

"Some other colonists built it? What for?"

"No, stranger than that. It was too old for even that. When we analyzed the valley, we realized whatever this bunker was, it had been built *before* the crater was created. It had been a part of some existing structure that was destroyed by whatever created this impression in the surface."

"So you're telling me something or someone built this base before humans ever got here?"

"Precisely. Our equipment, even the stuff we stole later, wasn't good enough for us to glean exactly how old this structure was, but in our efforts, what we did find was that somehow this structure housed everything we needed to survive in these impossible conditions."

"Maybe, it's low blood sugar or the overall weight of the day getting to me, but I don't follow."

"As we searched the system of caves connected to the bunker, we found an immense vein of coal, and we stumbled across what we call the Eos."

"The Eos?"

"It was the source of our awakening, our realization that the Ashans, even though they had left the wastefulness of Earth behind, had gone well beyond the limit marker in their arrogance. They were no more attuned with the universe than the enemy they had dubbed 'terrasites'; they were just as materialistic, just as clumsy, and just as useless as the people of Earth, despite the fact they managed to live on uninhabitable ball of rock."

"What could you possibly have found in that cave that makes all of that less a tirade than it sounds?"

"The Eos is a pathogen. We have had difficulty studying it because we have never had the proper knowledge base, but what we do know is that it lies dormant where a freshwater tributary to the ocean passes through a cavern we call Plato's Cave. It infects the host organism as the organism enters the cave—the first of us to enter the cave became acutely ill, feverish, even convulsive. When the host would awaken, his or her thirst would be voracious, but those afflicted, would recover very quickly. We found, when they emerged, the disease had given their skin a greenish discoloration. It became clear very quickly that their metabolism had been drastically altered. So long as those infected were exposed to frequent sunlight, they did not need to eat, their level of excretion was profoundly diminished, and sleep became more of a luxury than a necessity. It also pretty much eliminated menses in our women. But if they were out of sunlight for two days, they began to waste away. One man became trapped in one of the bunker rooms during a power outage. He had already been researching inside for a day and a half. It took us another full day just to get the door open. When we found him, he was just a desiccated husk. Evidently, stress and lack of water accelerates the degeneration."

Cyrus mulled over the words in his head. He had been convinced that nothing more this day could surprise him, and although he was not taken aback by disbelief, the awe the words inspired kept him floored. "But the sun sets on this bunker every twenty-five years."

"And every twenty-five years, these people migrate, just as the Ashans do. There is another valley, across the equator, called Avalon, which they migrate to when Set moves on. The Hierophants, like Paeryl, maintain a greater knowledge of technology than the others in the society, and they pass that knowledge down to their acolytes. They carry phylacteries as ceremonial ornamentation that allow me to gather information in the time that they do not reside here in Xanadu. However, the Echelon, the Ashan force that was organized to deal with us, does not know the location of this bunker, but they know the paths we would have to take to get to Avalon, and Avalon itself has been compromised."

"So you know all this because you watch over them?"

"I gather information. Watching over them would imply that I could do something to help them. I, unfortunately, in all my knowledge and wisdom, am woefully inert." A look of sadness spread across the face of the image before him, but then it quickly returned to the solemn expression from before.

"But these people here are your descendants, correct?"

"Well, yes and no. We liberated the families during one of the migrations. These people are *their* descendants."

"Do they know you are here? I mean, all this," Cyrus indicated both the holographic image of his son and the processing unit in one sweeping motion, "What should I call this?" Cyrus was calm, but the awkwardness and inability to grasp everything at once lent a clear air of frustration to his words.

"Well, your son named the neural processor that facilitates my programming the Xerxes Mark 917, I call myself Darius Prime, but honestly I would like you to call me Dari."

Cyrus shook his head. It was a subtle motion that seemed a half-hearted effort to dispel some bug or web that refused to stop pestering him. He continued as if the last statement from the machine did not exist, and never would.

"But it seems like they almost deify you. What is the link?"

"The link is I brought them here, away from the detachment to the only thing of any relevant importance."

The hypocrisy of the statement rang through his mind like a peel from a distant carillon; and yet he understood. It was not the technology that was the problem, no more than a knife, a spear, or even a gun is a scourge by itself. All of these things could be used to feed, to heal, to protect. It was when the fear of these objects overwhelmed those who did not wield them, and when the necessary reverence to those objects was lost by those who did, that they became instruments of destruction. Cyrus remembered something Tanner had said in the dojo once, 'no one appreciates breathing until they can't do it anymore, and then its importance becomes lucid.' Technology made things easier, but when things became so easy we were no longer reminded what life was on a daily basis, people remained detached until someone died; and even then, whatever epiphany they were afforded, was fleeting. Wasn't that why he was here in the first place? He could no longer play the role of the colonist, or the pioneer he had expected to become, but ultimately, how was this any different? It was all fresh, it was all new, and in one day, every aspect of his very soul had been harrowed; and not only his breath, but the systolic rhythm of his heart, the life that he had narrowly escaped with, stood brazen and naked before him.

Perhaps something changed in his heat signature or his stature or the pause was longer than Cyrus had realized, but the image continued his point without a response, "I watch them through the fly-eyes and the phylacteries. They carry on the traditions they have handed down and developed throughout the centuries, some generated by me, but most of their own design. Maybe because they need a past that isn't the opposite Eurydice of or Druvidia, or maybe it's just because they see something we are too stubborn to recognize. Either way, they have an affinity for melodrama, but they don't worship me. They are too simple for that. I may be a martyr or a progenitor to them, but they unequivocally worship the sun that grants them life and hope in an environment that seeks to destroy them. Without it, they would certainly perish, and they are not too haughty to acknowledge that."

The figure before Cyrus was an apparition, a zephyr, but he wanted to believe because he had lost so much. But the day weighed upon him like a yoke—a halter that dragged the Herculean weight of his life's transactions behind him like a plow. Cyrus exhaled again, relishing the air he took in to replace it, even as his right side protested. "Can I ask you something?"

"Anything."

"Did you do the things they said you did?"

"Yes."

"Why?"

"Because the war had started, and the job had been given to me to win it, not to play with Earth until they gave up. I struck when Earth felt they could wait us out."

"But no path is that simple. Nothing boils down to just one base. At least not a base we can spit out in one sentence."

"True again. Which leads me to why I need your help."

"Explain."

"Uncle Xander pulled some strings and made sure he and I received a charter for the Anemoi. When we got here, I worked as an instructor in Earth history for a few gyres before the levy sanction. The society of Eurydice proliferated to the point where migration upon sunset would have been a problem. The leviance from Earth was first stopped because of population problems. There was an abundance of resources and ore, but we could not produce accommodations fast enough. Earth was wrenching on the throttle to levy more people, but we had to slow down. I was advisor on Uncle Xander's Council of Nine, under Rex Mundi, who was personally supervising the surveying of potential Druvidian sites because he had been an eminent environmental engineer on Earth. Right about when production began on the Druvidian project was when things began to go sideways. Uncle Xander was summoned to one of the survey sites but was killed in an excavation accident. After that, all Druvidian construction projects were halted, and accusations of sabotage from Earth began to spread. There was a research ship called the Zephyrus. It was a star skimmer class ship built with newer gravity drive technology that was strong enough to counter the gravity well of dark stars. The intent was to use it to study a not-so-distant neutron star, but the ship was decommissioned, and the technology was taken by the Ashan government to engineer faster ships. Everything about the situation seemed off-kilter to me from the start, so I signed up as a military advisor. I organized the Archons, and after notice was taken of my strategic abilities, I was appointed by Rex Mundi as supreme commander of Ashan defense."

"Why do you think Earth would sabotage Xander's expedition?"

"Well, the common belief was that they wanted to halt our progress so that upon sunset, we would be forced to allow transports from Earth in order to rapidly colonize the sunside. From the onset, it seemed like keelrot to me. I personally believe Mundi had Uncle Xander killed—his death was too convenient for what Mundi was trying to do."

"What was that?"

"Engender a schism against Earth."

"So why did you go along with him?"

"Because going along was the only way I stood a chance of getting at what was going on at all. Life in Eurydice, however cosmopolitan, was still difficult, and Mundi had developed himself into a full-blown cult of personality. Besides, the Uni had begun to treat Asha like an imperial colony. They had started shooting down barrage ships like a cranked out Dad slapping his kids. That alone was hard to abide. What side to be on was easy to decide, but it quickly became clear to me there were other problems. Firstly, the Druvidian project was going a little too slowly for all the resources we were putting into it. Secondly, I'm fairly certain Rex Mundi was an avatar."

"What made you think that?"

"Well for one, his name was as arrogant as it was trite. King of the World? In a society dominated by sympathizers to the ancient Greek aesthetic, calling yourself Rex Mundi is like introducing yourself as Taskmaster to a slave. It wasn't a name, it was a title, and it was diminishing to anyone who bought into it."

"So why did they fall for it?"

"I don't think they *fell* for it per se. I think to an extent, most of Asha was in agreement with him from the beginning. As you say, they only heard what they wanted to hear, and he was happy to say it to them. Earth began sending more and more ships, but they were cut off from communications. We began intercepting them farther out. We placed asteroid grids in their deceleration lines, and because we could communicate faster because they were so far away from their High Command, it was easier for us to respond to their more powerful forces in a set place. After a team of Druvidian scientists developed a form of instantaneous communication called the Whisper Node, we mounted a counter-attack on Eros and Mars to slow their advance. We had a set of spies planted to subvert their attempts to develop their own Whisper Nodes. Earth hammered at our forces, but we whittled away at their defenses, and we minimized our casualties, but their ranks seemed endless. Eventually, they would have overpowered us, even though it seemed like we were gaining ground."

"How do you know?"

"Because one of our spies informed us of a plan of counter-attack. The Whisper Nodes allowed us to communicate directly with spies we had planted on Earth. Espionage became our greatest weapon."

"Which explains why the Archons now are so viscerally afraid of 'espions' from Earth."

"Makes sense, they had sent a set of monitor drones within the Set system that communicated info from warships that had folded in past Asha in an attempt to catch us in a pincer. Mundi knew this info, but would not give me the resources to defend."

"Why the reluctance? What's the point in hoarding resources to build a city that will be destroyed if you don't use them?"

"Because he was setting me up to take the fall. So in the center of Eurydice, I had construction units erect a stage with the debris from fallen Earth warships and frigates, and I divulged the intel on the attack to the public. I convinced them that we could win the war, but it would take a decisive attack, something more resolute than the cakewalking and pandering we had engaged in because of fear. I told them that the very stage I stood on was evidence that we could win."

"So what happened?"

"A plan had already been in the works to send a team of saboteurs and spies to earth on an FTL ship disguised to look like a near-light ship they had sent to Asha before the war to confuse them long enough to stop them from countering the attack."

"Wait, there was only one ship sent before they developed the faster-than-light ship you came on, so the only ship you could mimic was..."

"The Paracelsus. Above all else, that is why they detained you, and undoubtedly treated you poorly."

"But they didn't seem to want to hurt us."

"Denali, I'm sure, knew of the more sensitive details of the Defiance, even though I'm sure his men were underclassified. He would have known that more likely than not, you were authentic, but I'm sure he knew something was off its axis."

"Would he know our connection?"

Highly unlikely. He would have known about the Paracelsus, and the Mjolnir being disguised as it, and the appearance of it in Ashan orbit would have been exceedingly disturbing to him, but that would have been the end of it. Most ties to Earth had been destroyed or inveigled into severe classification levels."

"Wait, if you've been locked in here for hundreds of years, how do you know about Denali? How did Paeryl and his men know about the Paracelsus when everything seems to have been obfuscated into oblivion?"

"I am an interactive neural processor. I'm tied into the units outside, the monitors, and the fly-eyes. Plus, there is a discrete comm-sat comb installed here that has absorbed transmissions to and from Eurydice and Druvidia since we first came here. What's wrong?"

"What do you mean?"

"Your heat signature is elevated."

"I just want to know why. Why?"

"Because here, even though things weren't exactly stellar, I could see the Uni for what it really was. It was a canker—a festering sarcoma draining Earth and humanity of any pride or dignity that happened to emerge from the hardships it created. And as the eminence of their attack shrouded us, and as our defenses were left crippled and inadequate, all I could think of was Genivere Lim."

"Why her?"

"Because all through the rest of my Novitiateship, through Laureateship, all the way through the Arcology, I never beat her. Not once. She was always one step ahead. But it wouldn't have been so bad if she had just been better, smarter, or stronger. She wasn't, and she wasn't appreciative. She just held her nose in the air, as if she deserved everything she had. Like she was entitled to it. Like the day she didn't get anything she sought after, someone else must have screwed up. I realized that was, always had been, and always would be the Uni's modus operandi, and I couldn't just sit and watch as they dozed us over—and I most certainly wasn't gonna take the goddamned blame for it. So I personally changed the programming in the Mjolnir, sent the spies and saboteurs on a ship to Mars, destroyed the fold-relay units that could have conveyed warning of an approaching ship, and I did it. The one thing I knew would put the Uni back in its place."

Cyrus was silent for a long while. Darius was about to speak but waited. Cyrus looked down at his own hands, shook his head solemnly, and then looked up at the image of his son. "This is my doing. I brought this upon the Uni."

"My actions were my own," Darius responded.

"Yes, but that notion, and everything else, all of your reasoning came from me—from these lips to your ears. I'm sorry, Dari. I...I don't know what else to say."

"Then don't say anything. It is true you molded me into the man I am, but no mere words, ideas, or indoctrination could have given me what I felt here when I pressed the button to launch that ship with my own hand."

"Well, if there is nothing to say, at least there must be something I can do."

"That is exactly why I left the Xerxes system here. Something Uncle Xander found in the Bereshit Scar triggered all of this. It is too dangerous for the Apostates to venture so deeply into the darkness, but not for you."

Cyrus nodded and stood. He didn't know what he would be looking for, or even if he would know what it was if he found it, but even if he had to walk there alone, he would look anyway. It was the least he could do to quell the storm that was building in his own heart from the moment he discovered his son, his own flesh and blood, had consigned the entire Earth to its ghastly fate.

• • • • •

"What do you think of these people?" Uzziah asked. He sat next to Tanner just outside the large iris built into the wall of what Milliken said was a crater. Milliken and the others were milling around inside, canvassing the equipment and rooms they were allowed into. Uzziah and Tanner sat on a mound of packed dirt, their shoes forgotten behind the iris.

"I mean that's what you do right, observe people and their habits?" Uzziah scratched at his beard, irritated by the day cycle's exertion as he and Tanner basked in the light that streamed through two peaks at the far edge of Milliken's crater.

Tanner noticed the denizens of this crater had positioned their strangely open civilization in the wide wedge of light that stretched across the impression in the earth. "They love sun...and their freedom. And they are disturbingly agoraphilic."

The people went about their menial tasks, but even though none approached them, few went for very long without casting long, uncomfortable looks in their direction.

"But why do they all congregate here? Where are their homes? Don't they have better things to do than to mob up here?"

"Look closely for a moment."

Uzziah watched them for a long moment. Some sat, some were standing. Men and women moved around in what looked like chaos, but the movements had a hive-like stability. There was a large round tablet in the center of the crater that they all seemed to avoid. Two of the older men had stood there while Uzziah and Tanner were observing and had addressed different parts of the milling crowd. The areas of the crowd they had spoken to had stopped what they were doing and had given the older men their undivided attention until the two men had finished speaking.

As Uzziah watched, an individual woman caught his eye. She was reading to four small children. It was her animation and intensity that drew his eye to her. She held the book steady in her hand, but the rest of her body moved expressively, with an odd grace that only came with self-assurance. She stood erect, her stance sure as she pantomimed some notion that made the children jiggle with laughter. Then a man passed by them, watching his own feet as he walked. There was another man standing next to some unrecognizable effects, talking to a rather tall, particularly skinny woman. Her movements were less direct than the storyteller, but she too stood with her head raised, shoulders back, and as she acknowledged the man who had stood about a meter away, awaiting attention, she excused herself with a motion that was zephyrical—as if the wind alone had carried her away.

Uzziah let his eyes pass over the crowd to the opposite edge of the clearing. The distance was great, but his eyes had been laser corrected to military specs, and he could make out forms that must have been a circle of women suckling their children, except most of the children seemed relatively advanced in age. Those younger and older in the group seemed to be at the wide end of the wedge of light, while the rigors of the group seemed to take place in the more shaded area at the tip of the wedge. And then he realized what looked like human bric-a-brac was only chaos to one who looked upon the scene darkly. There was reason within the throng. These people did indeed have better things to do at home, and they did them here because this was their home. "Oh."

"Yeah. It's like a longhouse community. Only no need for shelter because it never rains and there are no predators."

"Wouldn't they burn or dry out or something?" As soon as he asked, Uzziah noticed that not one of them moved for very long without drinking from small wineskin-like pouches they all seemed to carry. Some took small breaks from their work to dip their pouches in thin channels that ran between them.

"They drink constantly, but other than the children feeding off their mothers, I haven't seen anyone eat."

"And in the entire time we've been here, I haven't seen anyone urinate, defecate, or even excuse themselves to any secluded area. Extremely odd when you look at it. In a holostream, you would never notice, but here, after an hour or so of watching a couple hundred people, it's a little off-setting."

"Yeah, no kidding."

"There's something else that's been tipping me off the level a little."

"What's that?"

"Your name."

"Excuse me?"

"I don't like rolling with anyone I can't call by his given name; call it an idiosyncrasy."

"The whole UCF thing tip you off?"

"I noticed it the moment I got to your name on the roster. Your dossier and your demeanor only verified it."

"Something wrong with my demeanor?"

"Not at all. It's been a pleasure and an honor—at least since you removed the chip from your shoulder..."

"Well, I'd say you knocked that well clear for me." Uzziah chuckled.

"...it's just that, Azariah and Uzziah, depending on what you're talking about, could be interchangeable, and the Hebrew name of the Babylonian Abednego is a little too convenient for a Jew born in the Fringe."

"Okay, I thought I was supposed to be the highly dubious spy. Now you're scaring me."

"That's what I do. I observe people's habits, and I make connections. Besides, your dossier said you were a resident of Haifa, but after the Uprising of 2455, citizenship was only granted to Fringe refugees that had fled the war because Israel considered them exiles rather than expatriates. Most who fled went to the Caucasus. When the Uni was formed, and they quelled the uprising, the surge of Fringers trying to get back into the Unified zones was barred, but Israel felt a need to honor some level of Law of Return and allowed exclusionary status to the families that could prove prior citizenship. Your dossier listed a tour in Karachay-Cherkessia, which was a Fringe state until 2485. The conflict there was classified until 2492 when the whole Prometheus scandal exposed the Uni's activity in the Caucasus. Thing is, they would only have sent someone who could blend in, someone who had an excuse, and a valid one, to know Karachay, Circassian, and Abaza—all listed on your dossier—with no discernable accent. Admittedly, you could have been sabra, but your response when I brought it up pretty well galvanized the notion that you were not."

"Damn, you really do have me on your gram. Just curious as to why you singled your focus on me."

Tanner smiled, "Don't flatter yourself. You're not special. Just wasn't as quick of a read as everyone else." Tanner reclined a little and gave Uzziah a brisk pat on the back. "But I'm glad you are who you are because I don't know if we'd be here to talk about it if you weren't."

Uzziah allowed a smile to spread across his face, "You know, you're right, not one of them has piss or shit in like two hours."

"Not even excused themselves to some lav space or possible latrine—which doesn't seem their style given their openness with everything else. And I was hoping one would so I could follow him because now my adrenalin levels have normalized, I realize I need to go in a fierce way." Tanner stood with poise but definitely more clumsily than Uzziah was used to seeing of him.

"Azariah is my real Hebrew name, but my given name, at birth, is Bozkurt Asena. My mother's first husband was one of the first killed in the Uprising, and my mother fled with her family to a refuge that was run by a group of Karaites in Karachay-Cherkessia. There she met my father, a Turkic proselyte who ran the refuge. He gave me my Turkic name. He named me Bozkurt because even though it had some negative connotations in the past, he wanted me to live my life so that what happened to my mother and the rest of my family would not happen to anyone within my arm's reach again. He wanted me to live up to the original meaning of the name."

Tanner nodded revealing a smile. "So you're the Grey Wolf," he continued to smile, "It fits."

• • • • •

Cyrus seemed as if he was melding into the contour of the barren valley floor. His statuesque form gave an impression of quiescent but unforgiving introspection silhouetted against the unmoving stream of light that passed between the two peaks standing in vigilant defiance. The sun squeezed its clementine rays slowly into a cuneiform swath that enshrouded Cyrus with an aura of quiet self-accusation.

Uzziah could not tell whether it was Cyrus's stature, the eerie light, or both that made the mild quivering of his hands apparent.

Uzziah walked quietly behind him, shuffling his feet across the brushed dirt to signal his approach before he placed his hand on Cyrus's shoulder. Cyrus looked up from his hands at Uzziah as he sat next to him, and in Cyrus's face he saw an expression that could only have been fomented by the lingering touch of death. He had seen it before, and he knew it was never an easy jaundice to shake.

"You do it with your hands?" Uzziah asked.

"Yeah."

"You know, if it's easy to get over, something's off the level."

"Yeah."

Time passed in a procession. It was as if the universe itself had answered the tolling of the bell, dragging behind it a somber humility, stretching the quiet between them until it broke. "You know, the first time I had to was from a hundred meters away. It was a guy about to throw a plasma grenade. He fell back into the building, and the whole place burst into flames in the explosion. After it was over, I had to keep telling myself I had to. That if I hadn't, he would have immolated my whole team. But for a long time, I kept telling myself maybe there was another way. To this day, I wish I had done it with my hands. I don't think it would have been an easier pill to swallow, but at least I would know."

Another exaggerated still fell between them. It felt as if not even the air moved between them. Cyrus gasped, taking in the unmoving calm, "It's not so much the one I caused. It's the one I couldn't stop. I can still feel it in me slowly growing inside. I killed a man. I watched the life seep from his body. But it wasn't enough."

Whether it was from the exertion of the day cycle or the weight of hands leaden with guilt, the weariness in Cyrus's eyes brought Uzziah's own fatigue crashing to the surface. "It never is, my friend. It never is." He let his hand rest on Cyrus's shoulder in hopes that it could somehow dispel at least a hint of the dread that coalesced between them, but he knew, all too well, that particular brand of dread only left when it damn well pleased, and once it found a home, it usually nested in pretty good.

Cyrus stopped Uzziah before he could turn to leave. "I need to talk to all of you later."

"About what was in the vault?"

Cyrus nodded.

"Just say the word."

Cyrus extended his hand. His shoulder protested, and it took effort, but he hid the strain as best he could. "Thank you," he said as their hands clasped. Uzziah nodded and left. As he turned his back to the sun, he sensed that Cyrus was hiding something. Not because he was trying to dupe any of them, but because whatever it was, they would find out in due time, and on their own terms. And if that was a luxury they could not afford, and Cyrus knew it, Uzziah also knew Cyrus would lay it out before he ever asked for anyone's help.

• • • • •

Cyrus found Paeryl talking with some of the Apostates just outside the entrance to the barracks. The men and women seemed to revere Paeryl as if he was a counselor and mentor in addition to a strategic leader. As Cyrus approached, some of the men stared a little too long for comfort, but that was becoming commonplace. Paeryl greeted as Cyrus approached, and then dismissed his audience. Cyrus had a more pressing question, but as the men and women walked away wordlessly, his curiosity got the best of him. "Paeryl, why is it none of the others will speak to us?"

"Because they have been ordered not to."

"By whom?"

"By me."

"Why is that?"

"Because being courteous is good and right, but being tricked is not sunny. If you are what we believe you to be, it will not stay like this."

"If you ordered everyone else not to talk, why do you?"

"As I said, to be courteous. Speech with someone is necessary. That level of communication may as well come from me. I have utmost faith in my ability to see through trickery, and if you deceive me, as sure as Set gives us life, I will hunt you down and kill you." He smiled and patted Cyrus on the back as if he had just offered him a cocktail. Paeryl laughed to himself heartily, "Not even the Chthonic Miasma will save you from my retribution. Do not allow my jocularity to misguide you. If you bring harm to my self or my people, there will not exist a crag or cranny that can shelter you from my wrath. Be sunny on that fact for sure."

He gave Cyrus another brisk pat on the back that rattled his aching shoulder. Paeryl smiled widely as his words still hang in the air, which to Cyrus, was more disturbing than any scowl or grimace.

But Cyrus appreciated all this. As oddly as it had been presented, everything had been laid out on the table—except for one thing.

"I have something else to ask of you, so I'll just get right to it. I need to borrow one of your levs to check out something in the Miasma—something that pertains to my son and my best friend. I assume because of the Eos, going into the Miasma would be too dangerous for you, especially since the trip will be about fifteen hours each way in a midspeed lev. So, I need you to teach us how to pilot whatever lev we can borrow."

"What are you looking for?"

"I'm not sure, but whatever caused the war six hundred years ago also killed my best friend, indirectly caused my son a life of exile, and lies somewhere in the Bereshit Scar."

"Well, you can have your lev, and I will train you myself, but keep in mind, too much dalliance and what rations we *do* have will run out, and Set, merciful as he is to those that have received the Eos, can be most savage to the uninitiated."

"If you don't mind, I would like to have my colleagues examine your Eos—under your supervision of course."

"Not a problem. But if you wish to accept the Eos, you must be initiated in the Cave."

"My men and I will observe any of your customs within our ability while we are in your hospitality." Cyrus bowed his head slightly, and Paeryl put his hand on his shoulder.

"That is most excellent to hear. You shall have your training, your reconnaissance, and the use of any lev of your choosing. Just be sure to let me know as soon as we are winning again."

Cyrus did not fully understand Paeryl's words, but even through his strange, histrionic manner, his inflection was clear. The Chthonic Miasma, the cold dark shadow that shambled across the planet, would soon overwhelm the crater that they called home. Their respite from this generation-long darkness had been taken by the Archons, and it would not be long before those same assailants descended on this place. The walls were closing in on them from both sides, and the only possible recourse lay in finding what had twisted the universe so far off its intended course. Cyrus was sure some clue rested somewhere within the crater created by the comet that had changed the fate of this planet itself, but he had his doubts as to whether or not that clue would shed a deeper understanding on his and Paeryl's situation. But these people had helped him at a point where he himself was not sure of what could have saved him. So he owed it to them and to Dari to find out whatever he could to help.

nineteen

—You okay, Dari? You've been acting strange for the last few days now.

—Yeah...

—Is it because mom's been gone?

—Nah, it's not that. I'm used to her work trips now. It's just...I don't know what to get you for your birthday. Tomorrow's August already, your birthday's only four days away, and I wanted to get you something stellar cuz it's gonna be the last one we have together for a while. But I don't know what to get you.

—That's it? You shouldn't worry about that Dari. I already have everything I need.

—I still wanna do something.

—Well, you know, just having you and mom here and maybe doing something as a family would be nice.

—Is mommy gonna be here?

—Well, she doesn't know yet. We'll see.

—Were you born at the same podcenter as me?

—No, they closed the place I was born. I was born when they still held extra-uterine births in hospitals.

—Do you know what time they opened your pod?

—17:38, August 4th, 2462.

—Ha, so you really were born at night.

—But not last night.

—I like it when you say that, even though I'm usually in trouble when you do.

—Do me a favor, Dari.

—Okay.

—Don't worry so much about what to do for my birthday. The best thing you could do for me is take care of your mom while I'm gone.

—Okay, Dada. But...

—But?

—I still don't want you to go.

—I know. Most of me doesn't want to go either, but part of me knows that I need *to go. It's nice knowing that, somehow, what I do is gonna be important. That's why they asked me instead of someone else.*

—I know you're good at what you do, but why you? Why not someone else's dad?

—Well, sometimes we have to do things that hurt now, so that the pain for us or others can be fixed later. We have to just take the pain we can handle, so we can stop the pain we might not get up from. As much as I complain about how things go in the Uni, if I didn't go to help colonize a new world when they asked, I would have to shut my mouth from then on out—and I'm not really prepared to do that.

—I guess I see your point, but I still don't like it.

—Well, one day, you'll have to make a decision that hurts someone to help someone else, and you'll understand that like and dislike really don't factor in.

—Maybe. I just hope, when that day comes, you're around to help me through it.

—Me too, Dari. Me too.

•　•　•　•　•

"You all know I wouldn't bring you here if I didn't have to, but I have something I need to do for myself and for my son; it might be dangerous, and I am going to need help."

Tanner held his hand above his head. "I'm in."

"You don't even know what it is."

"Nor do I need to."

Cyrus nodded and continued, "I need two more of you to go along. Obviously, it will be best if Davidson and Torvald stayed here to continue their research, but the nature of the venture might require some of your skills and knowledge Milliken." Milliken gave a nod that communicated both approval and acceptance.

"Which leaves Toutopolus, Jang, and Uzziah; honestly, I would prefer Uzziah comes along..."

"Just in case the monkeys bust through the vent," Uzziah interjected with a sense of levity that seemed a little forced and yet still sincere.

"I'd rather think of it as contingency, but yes."

Uzziah, Milliken, and Tanner all nodded in quiet approval.

"We will have to borrow a lev from the Apostates, preferably one of the smaller, faster ones, and we need to see if they have any geological surveying equipment." Cyrus paused as if he had something to say but was searching for the appropriate words.

"So what is it that has gotten you off your kilter?" Jang asked, standing to talk for no discernable reason, "You didn't seem *this* shaken inside that monkey shit prison."

"It's a little complicated," Cyrus looked up, his eyes quivering with emotion, but still wide with determination, "I've just been charged to look for information in the dark side of the planet. I'm not sure exactly what I'm looking for, but it lies somewhere within the Bereshit Scar. Paeryl's men can't go because it is too far into the darkness."

"So what did you see in that room that brought all this about?" Uzziah asked.

"Well, like I said, it's complicated," Cyrus seemed contemplative for a moment, and then turned halfway back to the iris, "As a matter-of-fact, it might be easier for me to just show you." He then turned and entered the code again. The iris opened, and Cyrus motioned for the scientists to enter the strange room behind him.

• • • • •

Uzziah set the grav-lev down at the edge of the enormous depression in the surface of the planet. They had cut the lights about three kilometers from the two-hundred-kilometer-wide indentation and then had set down behind a protrusion alongside the rim. Milliken had borrowed a surveying datadeck from one of Paeryl's technology specialists. The deck had been found in one of the levs they had 'apportioned,' what they called their frequent thefts from the Ashan cities and bases.

They had arrived at The Bereshit Scar, the impact crater that had been created by the comet—fancifully coined the Bereshit Egg by its discoverer—that had knocked Asha on its side and had provided the planet with its ocean, setting up the conditions that allowed life to exist on an otherwise barren volcanic rock. Uzziah ran a ten-K scan of the area, found it clear of any activity, and then proceeded with their descent into the hole. The lev they had borrowed from Paeryl had also been used for environmental surveys, and Milliken and Cyrus had selected it from Paeryl's garage as it provided both valuable sensors and a quicker lev drive.

They turned on the lights so Milliken could observe the walls of the cavern as they descended. He watched the walls and then returned to his holomonitor every few seconds to check the readings the craft's sensors gathered as they moved down the rim. He murmured almost unintelligibly as he scampered between the windshield and his monitor. "There is a large vein of quartz. There was unmolested volcanic activity here. There's shale. There is some marbling near the bottom." Then, something in the monitor image hovering in front of the control deck degenerated Milliken's murmuring into a considerably less scientific, "Wait a second. What the hell…"

Cyrus and Tanner immediately moved to either side of Milliken's chair, which he now, in stark contrast to his earlier scuttling, seemed fastened to. Uzziah stopped their descent. He looked over the holoscanner and zoomed out the image to check for any threat he might have overlooked.

"What?" Cyrus demanded. The magnitude and scale of the crater were overwhelming, and it limited Cyrus's patience for Milliken's silence.

"As far as I can tell, the vein in front of us goes around the entire rim of the crater. And in two different striations."

"Okay, so assuming I wasn't trained in geological surveying, explain to me what just knocked you on your cred stick."

"Gold. Each vein is about 650 kilometers long and about four hundred meters thick, and, according to these readings, is full of gold deposits."

"So what does that mean to us?" even as Tanner asked it, Cyrus remembered the cables of the orbital station when they first arrived.

Milliken shook his head. "Gold is a very dense metal usually found in flakes because it doesn't react to anything easily. Because of this, if you compressed all the pure gold ever mined on Earth—even including the last six hundred years that we missed traveling here—it would all fit in a room about the size of Paeryl's garage. This vein alone, however, even if these readings are wrong by 30%, should contain more pure gold than we could fit inside seven of those garages—that's a *lower* end estimate. And if that's not enough to get your core running, they've been mining this crater constantly from the very beginning."

"Oh," was all Tanner could muster as Milliken nodded to Uzziah and they continued down the side of the large bowl.

Then, Uzziah killed the lights and stopped the craft abruptly. "I got a blip," he informed as he cycled through the range increments of the hologram to reveal two crafts that appeared to be about the size of the assault lev that had pursued them through Eurydice. As Uzziah shifted the focus of the hologram and zoomed in on the vehicle, they could all see that it clearly was an assault lev, but something about it was very strange. The guns on the top had been removed, and the turret there had been fitted with two large, unwieldy looking tubes. The tubes had cables and piping that ran from them to the sides of the turret. Uzziah engaged the lights and began moving again. "Whatever reason they are here, that reason has not presented itself for a while." He tracked the hologram down the side of the crater to the bottom of the assault lev, which not only rested on the ground but had been moored in by dust and dirt. He then scrolled up on the hologram and focused on the tubes that had replaced the cannon and autoguns.

"What were they thinking?" Uzziah allowed escape under his breath.

"Are those what I think they are?" Milliken asked, recognizing what he had only seen in a videogame.

"Extraplanetary lasers," Uzziah's confirmation hung over everyone's head like an edged pendulum.

"Were they mining the gold with it?" Cyrus intoned as they moved closer to the tanks.

"Highly doubtful. Asteroids were mined with ship-to-ship lasers before the Uni, but trying to mine gold with an S-to-S laser would be like shaving your beard with a lawn razor."

"So what were they using them for?" Tanner asked, trying to take in as much as he could in the swath the lights of the lev cut through the gelatin of moonless darkness around them.

"Maybe this," Uzziah added as the craft began to swing to its left. For a moment they looked at the hologram, expecting it to shrink and pan, but they quickly realized the holographic imager, in this case, was not necessary.

As the lev rotated on its z-axis, the world before them panned right in the ultra-white beams of light until they revealed a tunnel opening, cut in a large, precise square about eighteen meters wide.

Uzziah pantomimed a set of commands over his holomonitor. A diagram and some figures that only he could see spread over the screen. Before anyone could ask about the readings, the craft was already moving forward. "Nothing jumpin' inside and it's plenty wide for a good K," he increased speed as the lev dipped forward slightly to match the decline of the causeway.

They moved at a relatively high rate of speed down the smooth-honed tunnel, but the kilometer seemed to take much longer to traverse than it should have. "There's an opening about another two K down." Uzziah was focused on his instruments and piloting, and his delivery was matter-of-fact. They sped along for another long minute, and then, Uzziah suddenly slowed the craft to a crawl. "You getting readings for any kind of volcanic activity?" Bewilderment was clear in his voice.

"No, shouldn't be. Most of the rock around us was formed by

cooling magma, not actual volcanoes, and as far as I can tell, that all stopped millions of years ago. Why?"

"Because according to my temperature readings, it's getting warmer—considerably warmer," Uzziah added.

"What do you mean warmer?" The bewilderment spread to Cyrus.

"I mean, the surface is an insane forty degrees below. Around us now is just around zero, and thermal scans show it only gets warmer ahead." Uzziah's words came out in a scoff.

"I don't see anything dangerous ahead," Milliken assured.

The craft began to move again, slower than before, and after another grueling minute passed, Uzziah slowed again. "There's an opening up ahead. A few blips, but nothing is moving."

They passed into a large cubic chamber about a hundred meters wide. There were various vehicles abandoned there, some were obviously designed for mining, and others were cargo lorries or earthmovers. As they passed through, Uzziah panned the lights across the chamber. There were three laboratory levs lining each wall. Evidently, something had been studied here relatively extensively, and yet the vehicles had all been abandoned. They looked like they had not been operated or moved in years, but they did not look as if they had sat motionless for centuries. There was not much wind or sand to erode away their features, but the mixture of humid salt-air would have taken its toll on the metals and alloys that these vehicles were built from. They might not have been used recently, but whatever they were used for was ongoing, which was probably why they had been left here rather than moved to a place where their presence would not arouse suspicion—even if whoever left them assumed no one would be crazy enough to stumble upon them.

They passed through the chamber into another perfectly square corridor, this one level. Then, as they passed slowly into the tunnel, they all saw the pinpoint of light hovering at the vanishing point of the artificially cut cavern. Uzziah stopped the ship instantly, prepared to reverse, and he double and triple checked his gram readings, zooming them out to their fullest extent.

"What is it?" Impatience and anxiety fueled Cyrus's question as he leaned forward and squinted.

"According to these readings...it's nothing at all, but thermals say it gets warmer for the next two K. What do you have Milliken?"

"Uhh," Milliken was focused on something on the holomonitor, gesturing over the flat image floating in front of him. "Uhh," he muttered again, settling on an image and moving closer to it to get a better look. "According to this, there's a very large...uh nothing...in front of us."

Everyone turned to Milliken except Uzziah, who stayed focused on his own controls and readings. Milliken expanded the floating monitor image and then waved his wrist so that the image turned to face the others. On the flat image was a three-dimensional rendering of the striations in the rock in front of them, they could see the hollow of the tunnel they were following leading to an enormous cavern, and inside the cavern, just as Milliken said, the image displayed nothing.

"What now chief?" Uzziah asked, still focused on his readings.

"Press on, but stay alert." Cyrus leaned forward to get a good look but looked over his shoulder to see exactly how far away the envirosuits and assault rifles they had brought with them were.

They moved down the hallway and the point of light grew. It became a square of blue light, stretching out just in front of the vanishing point. The sliver of light slowly began to keystone toward them until it became clear that whatever *nothing* existed in the cave in front of them gave off a good deal of light. The contrast between the palpable darkness of the tunnel and the blue-white glow spotted and blurred their vision. And then, as they rapidly approached the entrance to the cavern the headlights were no longer necessary, and their vision became clear.

Milliken looked up from his holomonitor. "Mother of all things great and small..."

The cavern did not appear to be a cavern at all. Before them lay the impossible, bathed in a white and ultraviolet light that could only come from a filtered yellow sun. Their pupils widened, thirsty for the light that whispered 'home' to their skin. They marveled at the sublime vision before them; a wall that must have stretched out for kilometers on either side and rose at least a hundred meters toward a sky that should not have existed. On either side of the cavern, there was an immense cataract of water flowing in calculated streams into a moat that was deep enough to hide the splashback from the bottom.

As Cyrus's vision adjusted, he could see the sky was not a sky at all, but an illusion created by stonework stretching across the ceiling of the cavern at least a half-kilometer away.

"There's an energy source ahead." Uzziah tried to stop the awe of their discovery from distracting him from the mission.

"How far?" Cyrus asked, leaning to see as much of the structure as possible. There was something that looked like a hole in a protruding section of the wall directly across them.

"You're not gonna believe this," Uzziah shook his head, "Hell, I don't."

"Disbelief seems to be a recurring theme these days." Tanner craned his neck beneath the slant of the windshield.

"If these readings are correct, which they must be because there's no reason for this particular sensor to even be *on* now, the power source is about 110 *kilometers* away. On top of that, the temperature is about twenty-five degrees in here, and it's consistent for the next three K in any direction."

As they moved closer, the distance from the wall became more difficult to gauge as light seemed to dance not just around, but inside the brickwork. As they approached, Cyrus realized that his initial estimate of one hundred meters high had been inadequate; the wall was clearly at least *two* hundred meters high, and as they reached the side, they realized the hole was as honed as the corridor they had traversed to get here. What had appeared to be an aberrant opening was a worked arch, and the protrusion was a wide gateway as smooth as glass. The brilliance of the light, the humidity in the air, and the marbling in the rock of the archway played a cruel trick on the eyes at a distance. But now, standing before the sheer monstrosity of the gateway, the depth of its strangeness was utterly unavoidable.

"What is this?" Tanner muttered to himself, looking up at the arch as they stopped in front of it, its sides stretching out forty-five meters in either direction.

"Whatever it is," Milliken answered unexpectedly, "it's made of one solid block of marble. And I don't mean the stuff they form out of asteroids with coring ships. As far as I can tell, Mother Nature herself made this whole block at once, and someone or something carved it."

"What about the walls?" Cyrus turned to Milliken to see a look of awe illuminated by a light they had never expected to see again.

"Quartz. Pure, untreated quartz. It seems to have been cut directly from the ground."

"Isn't all natural quartz cut from the ground?" Uzziah asked, rattled.

"Yeah, except the stuff made in labs or cored from asteroids and space rock. But that stuff, from asteroid or Earth proper, is usually *taken* to where it needs to go. There's no seam here between this stuff and the ground beneath it. This stuff was cut right out of the rock it was found in."

"What the hell can do that? Those S-to-S lasers?" Cyrus wasn't agitated, but his blood seemed to have lost the ability to warm his body, and gooseflesh spread across his skin as an anxious tremolo wracked his voice.

"Nothing I know of could do this. Nothing that could do this was even in speculation when we left. And even if something had been invented that could cut this much rock with this level of precision, it would still take more than six hundred years just to clear out the excess."

And then they fell silent.

All the wonder of the ominous underground waterfall, the perfect sunlight emanating from some unseen source, and the sheer walls cut directly from the stone they stood on, could not have prepared them for what lay on the other side of the gate.

There was a cluster of buildings set out in a pattern that immediately arrested the eye; the height and spacing of the buildings pulled the eye to what must have been the center of the city, where in the distance, a blinding ball of light that the mind would only believe was Sol itself, hovered and spread its light through the vaulted, crystalline ceiling. The play of light across the polished blue stone spread impressionistic clouds over the dome as far as the eye could see.

"Are the buildings made from..."

"Yes," Milliken answered before Tanner could finish his question. His readings showed that not all of the buildings were made from single crystals, but a great many of them, too many to keep the mind from boggling, were.

"The ave..." Cyrus didn't need to complete his sentence. The ave, which led through the lattice of perfectly sculpted buildings, shimmered beneath them in the light. It sparkled and shone as if some magical light projected from beneath it.

"Fused quartz," Milliken reported looking back and forth between the ave and the monitor floating in front of him. "Made from a vein of quartz similar to the one outside. It seems to be full of gold deposits as well."

"So this ave was cut from the ground too?" The magnitude was still overwhelming, but Cyrus's body was adjusting to the shock.

"No, this stuff seems to have been placed here, but this much fused quartz would have required an immense amount of energy and an incredibly accurate machine to not ruin the city around it, which most definitely was here when they fused it."

Cyrus looked to Uzziah, "Any threats on the gram?"

"Not so far. My readings are clearer now we are past the waterfall, but the whole place seems to be…dead, at least for the next four or five K."

"Okay, so anyone against seeing what's at the center of this place?" Cyrus didn't need to explain why he chose the center. It was clear, even before Uzziah began to raise the ship above the buildings, that something about this place drew you to its heart.

Everyone nodded, and as the craft cleared the level of the highest buildings they could see, Uzziah checked the holographic imager for blips, and then pulled the craft into full throttle.

As they passed over the buildings, they could see the layout formed a spiraling latticework reminiscent of a sunflower. The organization of the city compelled the eye to the center, and as they sped over the buildings, the pattern seemed to undulate beneath them. It was as if the city itself was alive—its breathing as anxious as their own. And after too many minutes of travel, Uzziah slowed the craft, quelling the hurried gasps of the city beneath them as their eyes were led to a solitary building resting alone on a mound. It seemed as if the other buildings lowered their heads in reverence to it; as if here, beneath the light of the artificial sun shining brightly above it, it was the only part of the city that really mattered. Four lions, each half the size of the central building, lay guarding respective corners. They were not rampant or vicious, but they still carried a look of vigilance accented by the play of light throughout their expertly carved, crystalline manes.

Uzziah set the lev down outside the squarish building and, after a short debate over whether or not to put on the two envirosuits they had brought with them, they double, triple, and quadruple checked their readings and then left the ship without them. Uzziah carried an assault rifle at his side, and Milliken slung one over his shoulder so he could bring along a portable datadeck that linked to the surveying deck inside the lev.

"Wait," Tanner motioned for them to stop moving as they moved to the center of the building even more magnificently rendered from the rock than the city outside. Tanner's voice was airy, less sure than normal, "I know what this is. But why here?" He looked around and, more to himself than anyone else, said, "*Bet ha-mikdash.*" He then stood there as if the words themselves had frozen him.

Uzziah looked around, and whatever had arrested Tanner took hold of him as well. He clutched at the sleeve of his shirt and pulled on it until the seam ripped apart at the shoulder. He repeated the action with his other hand and then looked to Milliken who looked like he was attacking the datadeck with his stylus. "Please tell me who could have possibly built this," Uzziah asked, more moved than anyone had ever seen him.

Milliken seemed as if he had not heard him, but he stopped pecking at the deck and looked up. "I have no idea who could have built it, but whoever did, did it a long time ago."

"Six hundred years ago?" Cyrus was trying to put too many things in perspective at once.

"Try six hundred *thousand*. This building was made the same way as the rest of the city,. cut straight from the rock. It seems *all* of these buildings were cut at the same time, and it seems, according to the radiometric scans, this fused quartz has not been worked for six hundred thousand years. The working of the aves and the carving of the buildings had to have happened concurrently, at least on a geological timeframe. And give or take even a hundred thousand years, no human could have done this."

"You sure of this?" Uzziah asked, his face flushed and his eyes quivering.

"As stupid as it sounds, I still said it, and I take my craft very seriously." Milliken looked indignant.

"It's the Third Temple." Again it sounded like Tanner was speaking to himself. He gathered himself, and then, without looking back at the others, he walked into the next room.

• • • • •

They emerged behind Tanner into an expansive foyer with shimmering quartz walls that stretched out about twenty-five meters on each side. Ahead of them were two pillars that stood at the head of protruding walls leading to another chamber at the center of the complex. Light filtered in through slits in the ceiling and played through the quartz, giving the walls life that made them look like they were not cut from stone but from the hide of some mythical beast. The scientists moved slowly across the pearlescent floor, which must have also been some sort of fused quartz, but was of a different luster and hue than the quartz that formed the aves of the city. Tanner led them into the hallway ahead and then suddenly stopped as if some wall of force prevented him from ascending the stairs at the end. It looked as if his very breath had been siphoned from his body when he took another step toward the center and was forced to lean against the wall for support. The others rushed up behind him, initially afraid that something had happened to him, but even as they rushed over to assist him, they understood.

The stairs led through to a square room about fifteen meters wide. Light streamed through a skylight in the center of the room and bathed the raised platform beneath it in a mystifying light. A ramp across from them led up to the platform where rays of blue and gold danced through the evanescent mist that filled the room from some unseen place, giving the room a fresh, airy smell.

Tanner steeled himself and walked to the top of the stairs where a sense of urgency sobered him back to awareness. "Wait!" he exclaimed, pushing himself away from the wall. He ran across the edge of the ramp to another set of stairs that led into a hallway. The others began to run after him, but he yelled back, "Don't follow me!"

When Tanner reached the stairs, he ascended quickly but stepped cautiously into the hall as if he believed his next step might cause the floor to collapse beneath him. And then he disappeared into the shadows separating the two rooms.

Uzziah moved to the edge of the ramp, waited, and then turned to face the others. He took Milliken's assault rifle and moved back to the hallway. "These have no place here."

By the time Uzziah returned, Milliken was fidgety with angst. "Is he okay?" spilled from Milliken's tensed vocal chords.

Before Cyrus could calm him, Tanner emerged with a look of defeat on his face, as if his own soul had been revealed to him inside that room, and it had been found wanting. "It's not there," he breathed between gasps. "There were settings for two of them. But why two?" he said more to himself than everyone else. "And it's...they...are not there."

"I think we should be leaving. This is bad." Uzziah said as he moved to help Tanner.

"You see something? Hear an alarm?" Milliken's anxiety had taken full hold of him now.

"No, nothing at all. And that's exactly what bothers me. This is too important. If there are sensors here, whoever is monitoring them *wants* to catch us."

• • • • •

As they sped between the waterfalls into the first corridor, Cyrus frantically pulled one of the envirosuits over himself.

"What the heck are you doing?" Milliken looked as if he was so rattled he would either fall over or burst.

"Trying to figure out the best way out of this. As a matter-of-fact, we should probably all put these on."

"We planning on going back on foot?" Uzziah asked, trying to add some levity to his own apprehension.

"No, but we might be doing just that if we don't put these on. We need to stop in the first chamber up ahead." Cyrus zipped up the front of the suit and started looking over the controls of the ship. "Milliken, that last tunnel out of here is straight, right?"

"Yeah, more or less," Milliken answered, slipping leg into an envirosuit.

"Good, because that may be the only thing that gives us the time we need."

The suit was stifling. The composites that formed the mask of the suit were designed to repel water, but breath still managed to clog Cyrus's already cloudy vision. Running blind was a special psychological torture. The transparent fascia of the suit not only made his beard itch, but it also made him feel like he was about to collide with some unseen wall. As he neared the mouth of the passageway, the HUD temperature reading counted downward like a stopwatch—without this suit, he would surely be frostbitten by now.

Cyrus could hear Tanner keeping pace behind him through the suit's sensors. Cyrus would have expected Tanner to be more comfortable running in the dark, but he had been rattled and silent since they left the strange temple at the center of the even stranger underground city. Cyrus tried his best not to focus on what might be next. If Uzziah was right, fighters were descending to kill them this very moment, and if they died, the significance of the strange underground metropolis would quite possibly remain hidden for another six hundred years.

For the third time in fewer days, Cyrus was legitimately afraid for his life. Less than a month ago, he was fighting grown, highly educated men off with sticks in sterile corridors and playing war games on a jury-rigged deck network. He and his colleagues had manufactured a sense of trepidation wherever possible. Now, the melees, skirmishes, stratagems, and above all else, the trepidation, were anything but manufactured. The blood, sweat, and angst were all very real, and oddly, as his lungs burned and he wondered how soon the danger would come, he felt completely and inexorably alive.

Light flooded the corridor just as Cyrus brushed his shoulder against the wall of the hallway to make sure it was still there. The flash of light caused Cyrus's pupils to dilate, and he strained as the surveying craft they had come in flew overhead at an alarming speed. The wash

223

from the flyover pushed him along, and in the brief light, Cyrus saw the end of the tunnel was only a few meters away. The surveying craft spread light across the two grounded assault levs outside as it swooped upward. The envirosuit had a low-light imager, but it required the use of a forehead-mounted light that Cyrus was reluctant to risk using, so he had to rely on his spatial memory as his pupils contracted again, making his already blurred vision even fuzzier. He picked up his pace as he reached the assault levs, praying that the large levs had not been left there because they were out of commission.

As Cyrus reached the assault lev, his prayer was answered. The lev door wasn't coded, passkey-triggered, or even locked, but he had to fumble around in the darkness to find the handle. He looked up to see the lights of their original craft disappear over the rim of the crater, and he could hear Tanner opening the other lev. As the door to his lev opened, Cyrus saw four shooting stars in the sky moving together and then outward. Two of the points of light shrank in size, but two grew. As Cyrus stepped inside the lev, he hoped that Milliken and Uzziah had the same luck.

When they had stopped inside the large chamber, Uzziah had spun the craft to face the entrance and had opened the door for Milliken. Uzziah had his doubts about the whole plan, but he went along with it because he could not think of a better one. He had dropped Milliken in the chamber to look for another unit that would start, and he had then flown to drop Tanner and Cyrus off half K from the end of the tunnel. Uzziah had quickly scanned the crater outside to make sure their unknown attackers were not already upon them, and then he had flown backward at a dangerous speed while trying to set the autopilot at the same time. By the time Uzziah had returned to the chamber, Milliken had started and readied a small mining craft about the same size as the ship they had come in. The ship Milliken chose was perfect. The onboard systems included surveying equipment as well as an articulate holographic imager. As articulate as it was, it could not make out individual humans if it moved faster than cruising speed; which meant, if this was the most advanced their imaging technology had become since this vessel was created, Cyrus's plan might actually work.

Uzziah piloted the craft without lights, using the imager at its lowest setting so as not to give away their presence too soon. Milliken powered up the mining lasers mounted on the four corners of the front of the craft, but Uzziah was too focused on flying with limited resources to pay much attention to Milliken's treatise on how the lasers worked. He did gather two things from Milliken's rambling though; these were not as strong as extraplanetary lasers, nor were they military grade, which meant they had to be fired within three hundred meters to be effective. That was too close to be up against trained pilots in gunships, but that was the hand he had been dealt, and folding would not do at this table.

To his dismay, this craft was not as fast as Paeryl's, and as their original lev disappeared at the end of the tunnel, Uzziah had a sinking feeling that this Fringe-fuck was not going to go as pleasantly as the last.

The washed out colors on the visor imager were disorienting, and it took Cyrus longer than he would have liked to find the power switch. He powered up the computers, but he kept the internal lights off. As soon as the holomonitor appeared, he was presented with a prompt preceded by a record of previous logins. It was apparent that someone had powered up this vehicle at least once every ten gyres. Most likely someone had been refurbishing the vehicles during that time because the holograms still worked, and a standard hologram unit had an average lifespan of about ten years. He was sure he could hear the assault vehicle next to him power up, so he canceled the prompt and powered up the jury-rigged mining lasers.

His holographic imager came into view, zoomed out to its fullest range, and to his dismay, showed two fighters spreading away from each other as they descended on them. The controls of the lasers were somewhat odd, and as they were set up to cut through rock that could not maneuver evasively, included a rudimentary, and unfortunately completely manual, targeting system. As Cyrus moved the sticks that controlled the turret, the hologram twisted in the air in front of him. He pressed the button to open the door, and then another that sent the assault lev rising into the air as he fired. The lasers streamed out from the top of the tank, and the assault lev shuddered from the power drain. The two white beams stretched into the sky like fiery lines drawn by some celestial being. They stretched on either side of one of the fighters, which dipped to its right into a spin, but a combination of Cyrus's adjustments and nervous twitches crossed the beams in an awkward pattern, slicing in an angle through the middle of the ship as if it was a hot sweetbar. Evidently, the lock-on warning systems of this craft were also still intact and operational because even as he leaned forward to get a better look at the vivisected ship plummeting from the air in the hologram, a shrill beeping and a pulsating red light alerted him to what was coming next. Cyrus dove out of the door of the tank, falling farther than he had expected to, but the padding in the suit and the lower gravity made the collision with the ground less traumatic than he expected. His shoulder burned from the shock of the impact, but he was beginning to get used to the pain.

Tanner had left the door of his lev open, and he began lifting from the ground as soon as Cyrus reached the door. Just as Cyrus jumped in, an explosion rocked the ground beneath them, temporarily lighting the immediate area. The blast of the explosion moved Cyrus's lev toward him as he pulled himself into Tanner's. As Tanner moved away, Cyrus saw the outside light up again as his tank caught fire, settled slowly to the ground, and then was hit by another missile.

Cyrus sat in the laser control seat and aimed in the hologram again. This time, he activated the left laser first, hoping to catch the fighter that had obliterated the other tank with the first shot. He missed, and the fighter evaded. Cyrus moved his left hand, carving a fiery swath in the sky as the fighter dipped and spun. This pilot could only have been used to dodging weaker planetary lasers. The war had been half a millennium before, but in simulators, he must have trained on being fired upon by an extraplanetary laser. The warships Cyrus had seen in the holocasts were usually equipped with several laser batteries with autolocking systems as well as trained gunners. No, using this type of weapon against fighters would be like using an assault rifle to kill a mouse; but the mouse, no matter how much he trained, would have difficulty adjusting once the bullets grazed his hide—especially when his friend was just obliterated. So as the ship dipped to the right of the hologram, Cyrus fired the right laser and pulled it toward the left stream as if he was bringing his hands together to swat a fly.

But the ship dipped downward and dropped beneath the two streams as they crossed, firing a missile as it fell. Tanner moved the lev into the air, but the motion of the modified assault craft was jittery. Tanner was not used to moving such a large vehicle, and his evasion did not move them out of the path of the missile. The missile exploded against the side of the lev and forced it to dip left, throwing Cyrus from his seat.

Tanner was strapped in, but the blast dimmed the controls for a moment, and his command inputs would not register. When the hologram faded back into clear view, Cyrus saw the fighter leveling off as Milliken and Uzziah's craft sped above the lumbering assault lev. Cyrus dove back into his chair to fire the right laser, but he missed again, sending a bright colored stream through the sky wide left. Cyrus knew his next shot would be his last chance because he was sure this assault lev could not take another blast like the first one.

A sharp twinge seized Uzziah's insides as he flew out of the cave entrance. The burning husk of the assault lev worried him, but the hologram gave him a clearer view of the outside, and he could see the other assault lev rising toward a fighter that was evading and dipping toward them. Cyrus's plan included diverting their attackers' attention, and most likely he had survived the diversion, but there was no time for Uzziah to worry. He opened up the throttle and sped over the rising tank toward the fighter. Using these outmoded, underpowered mining vehicles to fend off fighters was virtually suicide, and judging from the way the tank beneath him shuddered on the hologram, it had already been hit at least once. Neither evasion nor a dogfight was much of an option here. The only chance for survival was to catch the fighter in a Fringe-stampede and hope this dumpy mining lev could get inside the arming range of the fighter's missiles before it fired again.

Luckily, the fighter's sights must have been trained on the tank because it was slow to react to Uzziah's approach. Unfortunately, the fighter had reacted by slowing its descent, and the ship Uzziah was piloting, even at full throttle, was too slow to close the distance as the fighter leveled to fire.

And then two thick white lines spread out in front of him like the fluorescent landing guides of a lunar spaceport. For a moment, Uzziah was confused until he remembered the ship-to-ship lasers mounted on the assault lev beneath him. He continued his course toward the fighter, planning to roll left if the lasers did not move, but as he closed on the fighter, the lasers stayed the same distance in front of him. The fighter dipped to its left, but because it had slowed to fire, it was unable to maneuver completely out of the path of the lasers. One of the blue-white streaks passed through the fighter, illuminating the side of the craft as it shaved off an appendage.

Uzziah charged the coring lasers mounted on the outside of his own lev. Milliken had told him the lasers would have at least a ten-second lag before firing. "Grab on to something!" Uzziah yelled back to Milliken, who was rummaging through the mining equipment in the rear of the craft. Milliken only managed to get to a seat in the center of the craft before gravity changed direction. As Uzziah passed over the fighter, the line carved in the sky by the extraplanetary lasers disappeared. The piece that had been excised must have been a stabilizer of some sort because the clipped fighter recovered, albeit slowly. But Uzziah assumed the fighter was still just as deadly. Uzziah pulled the mining craft into a loop. The craft had obviously not been designed for that type of maneuver because the gravity drive and the thrusters seemed clumsy and out of sync. Even though Uzziah came out of the loop in the orientation he had planned, his descent still felt like trying to teach a turkey to dance. The contents of the ship were mostly tamped to the floor or the walls, but something hard, metal, and thankfully small hit Uzziah in the back of the head. He could hear Milliken yammering behind him, but Uzziah dared not look to check his condition. And then, as Uzziah closed the distance between his craft and top of the fighter, it fired its thrusters and began to move through Uzziah's path of travel.

But whoever was firing the assault lev lasers was on top of his game. The white lines stretched out again, this time to the right of Uzziah's craft, but directly in front of the fighter. The fighter's thrusters died immediately, stopping it directly in Uzziah's path of descent just as the coring lasers came on. The lasers formed four blue lines from each corner of the windshield, squeezed together at a point in the center of Uzziah's view, and then spread back out again in less than a second. The coring lasers left a blue X etched in Uzziah's vision as the fighter beneath him fell in five distinct pieces. Milliken was moaning in the back of the lev, and Uzziah turned to see him tossed face-down across the arms of one of the seats as the mining craft leveled. Uzziah checked the hologram and then spoke the command to radio Cyrus's envirosuit. "The credits ain't rolling yet. The fighters that chased Paeryl's lev are coming back. Is everyone over there okay?"

"Still breathing at least," came back over the transmitter.

"We should retreat back to the cave. If they lock their missiles, we won't stand a chance," Uzziah reported.

Milliken chimed into the radio stream, "The size and makeup of the cave should interfere with their long-range scanners just like it did ours."

Uzziah turned the mining craft and dove back toward the floor of the crater. "I have an idea. You pull in behind me," he reported to Tanner and Cyrus.

At the bottom of the crater, Uzziah flew into mouth of the cave and then slowed and spun the lev to face the entrance as Tanner pulled in the assault lev and turned in front of him.

Tanner waited about two hundred meters inside the mouth of the cave. Cyrus powered the lasers and prepared for their attackers to give chase. He trusted Milliken's assessment of how many meters of rock the lasers on the assault lev could cut through in a second, but he could not stop himself from going through the numbers in his head himself.

Tanner should have been afraid, should have been chilled to the center of his body, but he wasn't. He was ablaze, enraged by the confusion that was now building in him like an Artesian fount. He should have been overjoyed to see what they had seen in the cave, but everything about the strange city was catastrophically wrong, and he couldn't shake the feeling that everything he had ever believed, ever, was horribly and irrepressibly wrong as well. The idea alone reduced him to an automaton who followed instructions without complaint or digression, even in the face of impending demise.

Tanner killed the throttle and set the assault lev to hover. The tank rattled and shuddered disturbingly in protest, but it didn't matter to him now. He just waited, trying his best to focus and quell the conflagration of doubt that threatened to tear him inside out.

And then the mouth of the cave exploded in front of them. Flames splashed against the windshield, rocking the lumbering assault lev. The visor of the suit compensated for the high contrast between the flames and the darkness of the cave, but Tanner's eyes still ached as his pupils were squeezed to pinpoints.

As the flames died, Tanner expected a fighter to be sitting in front of him, but the smoldering assault lev was the only thing visible in either the windshield or the hologram.

Tanner's system of beliefs had been undermined, but his martial instincts died hard. As far as he could tell, a dogfight was not much different than a fistfight. The missile strike had been the dogfight equivalent of a blind technique—a wild attack directed at something the fighter could not see. It was not a good indicator of inexperience, but it was a definite indicator of a certain amount of desperation.

And that desperation might be enough to get them out of this jetwashed expedition alive. For a moment, the fire within Tanner dulled—the anger did not go away completely, but he could sense it may not stay forever.

And then the lev shook again, and the cave mouth was illumined by the massive lasers on the roof of the assault lev. The rock above them glowed a dismal orange and then gave way to the bolts of energy that bore through it. Cyrus counted one one-thousand, two one-thousand over the radio, and then moved the lasers in an arc. Tanner, despite his distress, was eager to see if their counterattack succeeded. Then, the wall of the cave shook around them, and Tanner saw the still-sputtering booster of one of the fighters plummet to the ground outside the cave. As it hit the ground, a confetti of shredded fighter showered the crater floor.

Even through his disillusionment, Tanner almost cheered, but his brief levity was squashed by the realization that the vibration had not stopped, and it was getting louder.

"Get the hell out! Go! Go! Go!" Milliken's voice eclipsed the rumbling, but it took a cascading rock smashing against the windshield to whelm Tanner's foot to the throttle. The lev moved, and Tanner saw Uzziah and Milliken's lev in the imager so close it looked like the two ships were connected. Then, the image wavered as the tank was bombarded by falling rocks.

And then the mining lev was on top of them, a slab of stone was on top of it, and they were all literally squeezed out of the mouth of the cave to the sound of metal and stone grinding. Another explosion spread around them as Cyrus and Tanner's assault lev bounced across the floor of the crater.

The assault lev slid, smacked against the other burning tank, and then spun to its left as Tanner fought to resist the momentum. The lev collided with something jutting from the ground and tipped to the right, but the z-drive kicked in, and Tanner lifted the lev from the ground before it could roll. It shuddered and shimmied as it rose from the crater floor but quickly accelerated up toward the crater's rim.

On the hologram, Cyrus saw Uzziah and Milliken's mining craft following close behind their assault lev, and the fourth fighter was right behind them. Cyrus spun the ship-to-ship lasers in an attempt to aim at their pursuer, but the turret was jittery, and he noticed on the gram, the left laser was off its mount and facing the opposite direction. The sheer awkwardness of their egress must have caused the second missile to miss. Uzziah killed the boosters, rolled to the right, and used the momentum to follow the assault lev. Uzziah put his foot back to the throttle, pitched up the nose of the mining craft, and against everything he had ever learned about fighter-to-fighter engagement, flew directly between the wobbling tank and the fighter that was moving behind them.

Cyrus yelled "Shit!" through the radio link, and Uzziah saw that the massive laser was mangled and twisted beyond usefulness. But it didn't matter, the fighter was staying beneath the assault lev, outside the arc of the lasers, and it was slowing down.

"He's dropping back to fire again!" Uzziah yelled, not sure what he expected anyone to do. And then, he felt the air pressure inside the mining lev shift as the door opened behind him. He turned to see Milliken carrying a hand-held coring laser in one hand while tying something around his waist with the other. Before Uzziah could ask what he was doing, Milliken yelled, "Fuck this guy!" and jumped out the door.

He was tired of being tossed around. He was tired of all the running, running, and more running. But most of all, he was tired of being scared. Adrenalin had numbed his face to stone for the second time in two days, and he had been knocked around by missiles and collapsing caves one too many times. So when he leaped from the mining lev, counting to himself as he activated the coring laser, the thought of, *What the bloody hell am I doing?* never crossed his mind.

Milliken fell downward, and even though he could not see the ground coming up to meet him, it still felt like either the diminished gravity of the planet or the heightened gravity of his choice had slowed time to a more manageable speed. The rigging strap caught him just beneath the lev. The wind pushed him back behind the doorway toward the fighter that was chasing them as the distance between them and the fighter slowly increased.

...but it was still close enough. Milliken closed his eyes to steady his head and then opened them again. He lifted the vibrating hand laser up past the edge of the mining lev and dropped it.

The air caught the laser, and it spun as it fell toward the fighter. The fighter didn't dodge because it didn't need to. The laser fell harmlessly beneath it—harmlessly, until it activated. A thin blue line of light shot out and then spun like an antiquated saw blade beneath the pursuing fighter. Sparks flew, and flames spurted from under the fighter, and it pitched, dipped, and then fell. But as it fell from view, a piece of it flew toward them. And then, Milliken realized it wasn't a piece of the fighter, it was a missile, and it wasn't aimed at them.

Cyrus watched the fighter fall off the hologram, but another shaft-like blip rose into view.

Cyrus yelled, "Incoming!" but the explosion eclipsed his warning. The assault lev dipped right, and the entire world spun around him. When it stopped, Cyrus was on the ceiling of the assault lev. He looked up to see if Tanner was okay, but his body was slumped awkwardly against the strap of the seat that was now attached to the ceiling. The back corner of the lev was twisted impossibly, and there was a rip in the back wall that defied understanding. As his cheeks began to tickle, and warmth began to rush back into his face, Cyrus realized through the rip he could see the nose lights of the mining lev as it moved beneath them.

Cyrus rushed to the controls to level the craft. Thankfully, Tanner was mumbling incoherently. Cyrus slid across the roof of the lev as it slowly turned to its side. The lev drive wheezed and sputtered, and then, just before the holomonitor dissolved and the control panel spewed sparks over him, Cyrus saw the altitude indicator running down too fast to read.

Cyrus jumped down to the side of the craft, stepping across odd panels and compartments. He stepped over to the door and hit the emergency release. The door separated with a pop and flew off into oblivion, and Cyrus again had trouble interpreting what he saw. As he looked down, he could see the doorway of the mining lev with a spotlight from the inside streaming toward him. Milliken was standing inside the lev, perpendicular to the doorway, with something tied to his waist. He motioned for Cyrus to come toward him, but Cyrus shook his head, "I have to get Tanner," he said over the radio.

It took some wrenching to get Tanner's harness to release, but when it did, Tanner fell right onto Cyrus's shoulder, and he carried him to the doorway. Tanner seemed to be unconscious now, and Cyrus wondered how he would get him to the mining lev, but when he reached the opening, Milliken was standing on the outside of his lev, now only a few centimeters from the doorway, and Cyrus dropped Tanner gingerly into Milliken's grasp.

Milliken sat against the seat in the center of the craft. Cyrus wondered how hard it would be to match the descent of the assault lev while flying beneath this close and sideways. And then, there was a thump against the now-bottom of the assault lev that knocked Cyrus from his feet. "We got a problem!" Uzziah yelled through the radio.

Cyrus noticed the laser's hologram was still active, even though the controls of the craft were dark, and it showed a fighter, most likely the same fighter, firing lasers into the sideways mining craft beneath his own sideways assault lev. Cyrus could only see a sliver of spotlight through the doorway now as sparks danced across the doorway hole in the now-floor. "You better get over here fast!" the radio reported as Cyrus hopped to his feet. Cyrus moved to leave but then returned to the laser controls. He saw the holographic ground rushing up at the single blob representing both levs as he grabbed the left shoulder harness, pulled it as far as it would go, and wrapped it around the control stick for the left laser. He yanked the tightening strap, and then, without bothering to think about the distance, dove toward the spotlight as the broken laser fired and tore through the center of the assault lev itself. Cyrus twisted his body in the air and fell through the door. The wind caught him as he fell, and he felt his stomach leap into his throat. Then, miraculously, he was inside the mining lev. He bounced off something hard but padded, and as the lev compartment spun around his airborne body, he was dumped painfully onto his shoulders.

Uzziah was sweating inside his envirosuit, and it made the air he was breathing thick and humid. When the fighter had rose up behind them again, Uzziah's resolve snapped, even before it fired its lasers.

And then, Cyrus fell into the mining lev, and the imager showed the S-to-S laser on the assault lev fire. The tank tipped and rolled slightly in the air above them, and the line of the laser spread through the blip of the assault lev and across the top of the pursuing fighter in the imager. The fighter's roof shaved off and flipped behind it, and then the fighter dipped, rocked shakily, and, just as it seemed like it would recover, half of the assault lev smashed into it. The fighter was knocked into a dizzying spin and spiraled into the ground as Uzziah cut the boosters and rolled back avoid hitting that same ground.

As Uzziah slowed, the rest of the assault lev came down in front of them. Uzziah's instincts told him to evade, but no one was belted in. He gritted his teeth and activated the coring lasers, skirting little more than two meters above ground. The assault lev hit the ground with the force of a titan. The mounted S-to-S laser, still firing, cut a swath in the ground dangerously close to them. Uzziah reacted, but he could not take his focus from the tank throwing dirt and rocks into the air as it appeared to roll toward them. Uzziah hit the throttle and pulled back on the controls, pitching the nose upward as he prayed his mining lasers would fire in time. The tank threw rent pieces into the air and, just as Uzziah was about to pass over it, bounced up off the ground. And as the coring lasers fired, Uzziah's training faltered, allowing innate human reaction to kick in. The maelstrom of debris was too much, so he muttered another silent prayer as he let go of the controls and closed his eyes.

There was a thump against the bottom of the mining lev, and when Uzziah's eyes opened, there was nothing but clear, starry sky before them. Milliken was checking Cyrus and Tanner as he removed their helmets. Uzziah removed his own helmet, and the cool, thin air of the cockpit soothed his anxious lungs. "How are they?" he gasped, unsure of what answer to expect.

Milliken took his helmet off and breathed an airy sigh, "They are out, but for all it's worth, I think they'll be okay."

"You?" Uzziah asked, trying to catch his breath.

"Me? I think it'll be a long while before I'm okay again." Milliken pressed the button to close the outside door, and Uzziah returned to the controls to correct their heading. And as Milliken put Tanner and Cyrus in more comfortable positions, they all sped toward the slowly expanding band of orange looming on the horizon.

twenty

—Dada, today during physical fitness, Scott Seal broke his arm.

—How'd he do that?

—He tied a jacket around his neck like a cape and said he was Power Stone and then jumped off the balcony.

—Well, that sounds like a boneheaded thing to do.

—Miss Hasabe said it's cuz children feel like they are indestructible.

—A lot of adults who have forgotten what it's like to have a sense of wonder and adventure say that about children.

—Yeah, I don't feel indestructible. It's just I can't imagine how bad breaking an arm or something would hurt.

—And now that Scott Seal knows what it feels like, I'm sure he won't do it again anytime soon.

—Do you ever feel indestructible, Dada?

—Never. Sometimes I feel entirely too vulnerable.

—That's strange cuz sometimes I think you might be.

—Well see, there's a trick to being indestructible. Something that should have killed you has to hit you for you to earn that label, and just because you keep going afterward, doesn't mean it doesn't hurt. How do you know that every time Dr. Mindbender's robots hit Power Stone with a mag-lev, or The Eviscerator blasts him with pulse lasers, that it doesn't hurt?

—I guess I don't.

—We just think Power Stone is great, and that he can't be killed because he gets back up.

—So maybe he isn't really indestructible after all.

—Exactly, and I bet he's the only man in the room that knows it. Bottom line is this—if you ever hit a man as hard as you can and he gets up like it didn't hurt, hit him again. And if anyone ever hits you so hard you're not sure you should have even gotten up, you do whatever it takes to make sure he never, ever hits you like that again.

• • • • •

Cyrus awoke soaked in sweat. The envirosuit was an excellent insulator, and in the frigid temperatures of the Miasma it kept the body warm, but that same insulation caused the body to marinate in the fumes of its own perspiration when the ambient air was closer to room temperature. He couldn't tell how long he had been out, or even what had knocked him out, but as Cyrus propped himself against the wall, he saw Tanner was groggy and already conscious. Cyrus's head pounded, only slightly out of sync with the whirring of the gravity drive and thrusters of the mining lev.

The sky was a milky yellow as if a film was stretched across it. A few stars could still be seen, but either the mining lev's speed or Cyrus's slowly shrinking pupils made it seem like the stars were fading from view by the moment. As his vision cleared, Cyrus could see a thin crescent of white low in the sky with an occasional glimmer beneath it. It must have been the J.L. Orbital Station.

And then Cyrus remembered the look on Tanner's face when they had approached the building that Tanner had called the Third Temple at the center of the strange city.

"Marcus, you okay?" Cyrus asked, his voice cracking under the strain of speech.

"Stellar." The sarcasm was disturbing coming from Tanner.

"What was that place back there?" Cyrus was unable to hold back his curiosity.

"As far as I can tell, that place was New Jerusalem; but it makes no sense." Tanner was more distraught than Cyrus had ever seen him.

"That place was carved directly from the rock it lay in. The entire city was like one gigantic statue. It's impossible to tell when those buildings were cut," Milliken chimed in. He sounded bewildered himself, but no more shaken than everyone else, "but the aves were made of fused quartz, which had to have been laid at the same time as, or after, the cutting. Those aves were fused approximately six hundred thousand years ago according to the data."

Milliken pulled his datadeck free of the clamps that held it beneath the base of the holographic imager.

"It's a good thing I tamped this thing down," he opened the deck and pulled up the map of the underground city. "My guess is somehow the early Ashans discovered that power source from the surface while they were scanning the area for gold deposits. Even though the entry cave looked smooth from the inside, you can see on this mapping it was pretty sloppy—not even close to the technical precision of the city itself." Milliken pressed the keys to link the deck to the holographic imager and then zoomed in on the hologram to give a clear view of how wavy the passage was. "This part was cut with the extraplanetary lasers. Evidently whoever found it was in a rush."

"It was likely Kalem. That city is probably what got him killed," Cyrus added.

"But why?" Uzziah asked.

"For the same reason they wanted to kill us."

"But *who* was trying to kill us?" Milliken asked without looking up from the hologram.

"The Echelon probably. *They* were started by that Rex Mundi character. *They* were the ones who gaffed us at the orbital when we got here. *They* were probably the ones that killed my friend." Cyrus was more animated now, but he appeared to be in pain.

"Why would they kill someone who could help them figure out what it all meant? You said he studied that sort of thing, right?" Milliken asked, looking up this time.

"Maybe they already knew what it was, or thought they did. Either way, Kalem's knowledge would be precisely what got him killed; which means we need to figure out what it is they think they know before they find us." Cyrus was nursing his shoulder, but it didn't seem to help.

"What was in the back room of the Temple?" Uzziah turned in his chair to face them.

"Nothing," Tanner answered, still distant.

"But you said, 'There were two of them.' Two of what?" Milliken turned to face him also.

"The Temple is supposed to house the Ark of the Covenant. There's supposed to only be one, and *that* was supposed to have been on Earth."

"How do you know there had been anything at all if the room was empty when you got there?" Milliken sounded indignant, but everyone knew he must have been feeling the same weariness they all shared— everyone except Tanner who was obviously more distraught.

"They were clumsy when they moved them. There were scratches on the floor. There were also depressions left in the floor where they stood before they were moved." Tanner's distance was haunting. He had always been the most composed of them all, his presence alone calming in the face of duress, but now his anxiety was unsettling.

"Depressions in the stone? How does something sit in one place and leave a depression?" Cyrus winced as his pulse pounded through his temples, squeezing his brain in a vice-grip.

"Could be from vibration." Milliken turned back to the hologram and shifted through the image. "As I said," he added, "according to this scan, those aves were made around six hundred thousand years ago. That's a long time for something to sit if it vibrates."

"How is that possible?" Uzziah asked.

"How is *any* of this possible?" Tanner belted. Cyrus stood and put his hand on Tanner's shoulder, but Tanner continued, unmoved. "How do you put a sun in a cave? How could all that exist before any of it was written down?"

"Well, maybe this isn't time to play devil's advocate, but that artificial sun seemed like some sort of cold fusion; a technology beyond our means but not beyond our understanding. And as far as writing things down go, things existing and *then* being written about is typically the logical progression." Cyrus tried to keep the sarcasm out of his words, but it must not have worked because Tanner scowled at him. Cyrus continued to grasp Tanner's shoulder to arrest his attention, maybe squeezing it a bit too hard. Cyrus waited until Tanner turned to look at him before he loosened his grip. "Remember, after the shock of it all, it's all still here." Cyrus pointed at Tanner's head. Cyrus began to speak louder as something welled up inside him, "All this time, you held me—us," he indicated everyone else in the lev, "together with your composure whether we shared the same beliefs as you or not." Cyrus's voice rose even louder. "And through all that, did you ever believe your Bible could stop bullets? Did you ever believe it could make the sun rise or stop it from setting? Did you ever believe it could bring back the dead?"

Cyrus's chest heaved as he waited for an answer.

"No," Tanner was still dejected.

Cyrus's cheeks and lips quivered with each impassioned word, "Then explain to me how what you believe *today,* even in the face of everything we've seen, is any different than what you believed *yesterday,* right here." Cyrus tapped Tanner hard over his heart. "So wallow in the shock if you must, but as soon as you're done, you let me know because we're gonna need every available mind to get to the bottom of this ocean of monkey shit, and I'll be goddamned if I'm gonna let you bow out before the rest of us do."

Cyrus stood breathing heavily. His fists were clenched, and sweat was running into his beard. Then, when he regained awareness of his surroundings, Cyrus retreated to the back of the mining lev and closed his eyes, hoping lassitude would again overwhelm his overzealous senses.

• • • • •

Cyrus shambled into the barracks and grabbed Paeryl, pulling him aside even as Paeryl bellowed, "Are we winning?" at the group as they entered. After Cyrus spoke to him, Paeryl immediately called another man, older looking than himself, and they both ushered Cyrus into a chamber they had previously not been allowed to enter.

As soon as the door slid shut behind them, the door to the lab area whooshed open and Davidson and Toutopolus stumbled over each other in childlike excitement. They brought a datadeck over to Tanner and Uzziah. "I think we've cracked the seal on this Eos thing," Davidson belted, almost out of breath.

"Where's Cyrus?" Toutopolus asked, a look of impending horror replacing his excitement.

"I think he's already made his decision." Tanner pointed to the forbidden door that was opening again. Two women brought indiscernible items to the doorway, and Paeryl beckoned them in.

"This cave is a sacred place. It contains the life-blood of our existence," the man Paeryl had addressed as the Hierophant of Cups delivered in a soft, monotonous voice that was a sobering contrast to Paeryl's bombast. "The cave lives with us, even outside these walls. It understands us better than we understand ourselves." The women who followed behind systematically handed Cyrus a folded cloth and a small box. They moved down a long corridor lit by dim, red lighting tubes. "You will present yourself to the Eos as you were presented to this existence, naked and wanting."

The procession stopped, and it took Cyrus a moment to realize they were waiting for him to remove his clothes. He was a little reluctant, but in the dim light, he saw Paeryl nod slowly, and then he thought of Darius. Whatever brought Darius to fratricide, however justified it may have been, and whatever brought about the death of Alexander, was not going to be uncovered easily, and whatever was in this cave that allowed these people and his son to survive in this environment, was paramount.

Cyrus removed his clothes, and the Hierophant collected them. "Alone and desperate you shall descend, but fulfilled you shall emerge. You shall present yourself to the waters, and your fate shall find you." The Hierophant shuffled a deck of cards methodically then handed Cyrus five cards, each covered in a sheath of plastic.

"Take these and find yourself."

Cyrus took the cards, and as he faced the pathway deeper into the cave, he felt another sharp pat on his back.

His chaperones retreated, and for the first time since he had been in that interrogation room, he felt utterly alone. Cyrus stood there for a moment. His belligerence had subsided, and now his stomach was tightening in on itself. He moved forward, shuffling his feet along the smooth, cool floor. The path was longer than he had expected, and he was sure he had walked for fifteen minutes when, finally, he reached the wide chamber. The dim red light cast an eerie hue and made the small pool in the center of the room look like blood. The room itself had an odd, barely perceptible scent of sweetness that resembled warm bread. Cyrus expected the cold of the room to send a chill over his body, but his gooseflesh must have been spawned from anxiety, as the chamber proved warmer than the passageway.

As he moved to the edge of the pool, the water itself shocked him. Not because it was frigid, but because the water was warmer than it should have been on its own accord. There must have been some sort of hot spring here that originated deep beneath the surface. Cyrus tested the floor of the pool with his feet and sat down, unsure how long he would have to sit or even what he was waiting for.

Inside the pool, Cyrus held the five cards in his right hand beneath the surface of the water as he had been instructed. He tried to clear his mind, but he could not stop thinking of Darius spending many hours each day chatting with a computer, a distorted effigy of his father his only company. Cyrus should have been there with him to help him through everything he had gone through. The Darius hologram seemed excited to see him, but what the Xerxes unit could not possibly know was that it had recorded and reproduced a pain in Darius's eyes that only Cyrus could know because he, and only he, had seen that same look and had shared that same pain as he boarded the shuttle to Eros before the waves and smiles of the spectators who had come to see the voyage off. And that is all they had been, spectators. Cyrus smiled and waved as best he could, but it was houndshit—a jetwashed attempt at portraying the image everyone had expected to see, feeble as the wills and minds that had made a mission that should have been exploratory necessary to human survival.

And the fury rushed into him again. Why did he get on that shuttle? Why didn't he turn around, spit in each of the faces of the flag-waving, cheering throng that urged him to walk away from the only thing he ever cared about for their own selfish survival...

...but they weren't the only ones that had been selfish, were they?

No, Cyrus didn't get on that shuttle for the good of the multitude that applauded as he left his own life behind; it wasn't for their livelihoods, the livelihoods of their children, or their children's children. He left because he—*he*—had to. And now, here he was, faltering under the weight of sheaves sown with his own hands. It was the fruit of his own pride. Pride that had demanded his son's penance—and what bitter fruit it was.

He didn't know how much time he had been there, but his vision began to fade sooner than he had expected. His blood seemed to chill even as his skin seemed to burn from the outside. Sweat formed thickly on his brow, feeling more like blood that perspiration, but he didn't bother to wipe it away. His eyes became heavy as if the bloody sweat tugged at his eyelids, pulling him deeper into the pool that seemed even bloodier as he sank deeper. And then, as his eyes closed, he was left with only the sound of his heartbeat thundering through his eardrums.

• • • • •

The landscape was immense. Cyrus was standing on a tuft of land that seemed to be rising. The horizon slowly bowed at the vanishing point as more and more nothingness crept into view.

And then he was running. The little girl was going to die. She was just on the other side of the horizon, and she only had moments to live. The perspective of the landscape shifted as he ran; he was descending the hill, but he could not feel the pull that gravity exerted on his body, nor could he feel the ground beneath his feet.

And then he was up higher, moving faster than he ever could have moved on his own volition. The sun sank below the horizon, and the sky became impossibly black. Dark tendrils of smoke billowed up where the sun had set as if the sun itself had crashed into the ground beyond the horizon, extinguishing itself in a grand conflagration.

The billows forming on the horizon grew, and even as dark as the starless, abysmal night was, they seemed darker. The billows filled the sky as he rode harder, and as they grew, the inchoate mass began to form more corporeal claws, teeth, eyes.

The young woman was there, full of ennui as before, seemingly oblivious to the abomination forming behind her.

Then the dark form reared back, bared its teeth, flexed its still forming haunches, and splitting the air with a roar that shook Cyrus's ribs, pounced on the hapless woman.

As the beast came down around her, the swirling cloud dissipated into a foul mist. The fog spread out toward Cyrus and wafted around him as he rode, threatening to consume him as well, but keeping its distance. The fog swirled and grumbled as if its hunger had not been satiated by the kill. A pressure began to build behind Cyrus's eyes, but he held it back and continued to move into the morass in abject refusal of the obvious truth.

And then he reached her, and he saw the truth had not been so obvious. The girl lay there in a perfect circle of blood. He could see her head, arms, and legs placed on the edge of the circle at five equidistant points. She was not dead, but she did not give the impression of life. The flame in her that burned within all living things had been reduced to embers, rendering her eyes glassy; her already affectionless gaze was now as vacuous as the starless night above them.

And there was a spear. At first it seemed like she had been impaled through the skull by it, but it sat there lodged in the earth, pinning a ring that pierced the girl's ear lobe.

Cyrus ran to the spear and grabbed the shaft, curious as to why the beast had left its prey here like this. He yanked at the spear, and it took more effort than Cyrus expected to pull it from the ground. A howling wind blew around him as the vapor stirred again. Then Cyrus realized it was not the wind, but the young girl screaming and pointing at the sky as she was freed from her strange shackle. And as the scream dug deep into his ears, curdling the fluid in his spine, he realized that the girl had not been the prey at all.

Cyrus looked up to see the mist coiling again, maw gaping, and horror transfixed him as he smelled the acrid breath of the beast and marveled at its size. He flipped the spear over in his hand to face the point upward, he let his knees bend beneath him, and as the ground pulled him in, and as the beast lunged at him with another, eager bellow, Cyrus caught his own weight, let out a cry of his own, and leaped spear-first into the leviathan's mouth.

twenty-one

—Dada, how come you don't wear the same fancy clothes some of the other dads do?

—I guess suits and ties aren't really my thing. Why do you ask?

—I dunno. Yesterday, when we went to pick up my Easter suit, she spent a lot of time looking through the grown-up clothes. Maybe you should put on a suit for mommy one day. I think she would like it.

—You know, I don't think any of my suits even fit anymore.

—Why do people like suits so much? They are itchy to me, and you gotta walk around like you're scared of everything so you don't get dirty—all prissy like Genivere—that part's complete bunkus.

—Well, maybe that's part of it for me too. Do you remember the story of the peacock and the puhuy?

—Ha, of course. Puhuy is such a funny word.

—Okay, so what happens?

—The birds all have their feathers in a bunch because the bird god—what was his name?

—Chaac.

—Yeah, well he says they need to elect a new king. The peacock feels like he should be king because he can sing so well, but he is ashamed to nominate himself because his feathers are all pasty and ratty. So he goes to the puhuy, who is all meek and quiet and never comes out of his nest but has a beautiful set of feathers. The peacock asks to borrow the puhuy's feathers until the election is over. The puhuy doesn't really want to cuz the peacock is kind of a jerk, but he does anyways.

—Go on.

—So the election day comes, and the peacock shows up with his new fancy feathers and sings and all the other birds are all wowed out. So the election goes down and they make the peacock the king. And the peacock is all happy, but the puhuy is so ashamed that he's all naked that he doesn't even go to the election. So the peacock just keeps the puhuy's feathers cuz he likes them so much and doesn't keep his promise. The puhuy never says anything, he just hides.

—So what happens?

—One day, Chaac is visiting the birds and sees the puhuy all by himself. He asks him what happened to his feathers, and the puhuy tells him the whole story. So Chaac goes to the peacock and lets him keep the feathers but makes him sound like a dying duck when he tries to sing.

—And what happens to the puhuy?

—Nothing I guess, but he doesn't get his feathers back. I guess in a way, he kinda gets punished too.

—Why?

—I dunno. I never really understood that part.

—Well, I have an idea. I think it's because the puhuy just let the other birds slap him around and didn't do anything about it.

—Shouldn't the god protect him more then?

—Well maybe, but what would their life have been like then? You want me and your mom to follow you around at school and make sure no one ever bothers you?

—Eww, no.

—Why not?

—Cuz then I'd look like a big sissy.

—Exactly. You see, from what I've seen, sitting in your own little corner and keeping your mouth shut is one thing; letting people walk all over you is something else. Bottom line, meek is as it is, but if you don't ever stand up for yourself, all you'll ever inherit is misery.

—Okay, but what does that have to do with wearing a suit?

—Well, look at the peacock. All he did to get elected was impress the other birds. No one even questioned where his feathers came from.

—Well, isn't being impressive important too?

—Sure, if something about you that helps you do your job is impressive. The point is, the peacock looked fancy and sang well, but deep down, he was still a turkey. Way I see it, if a man can't do his job in his underwear, he can't really do his job.

—So you don't wear suits cuz they make you look like you can't do your job?

—No, whether I wear a suit or not, I'm gonna do my best to do what I say I can do. I don't wear suits cuz they are uncomfortable, and I don't want to walk around acting like a sugar-coated sissy because I'm afraid to get dirty. If the suit makes the man, he isn't much of a man to begin with.

—Maybe Dada, but they do make you look stellar. Maybe sometimes that's enough, at least for mommy.

—Maybe you're right Dari, but sometimes with your mother it's hard to tell.

—Could be, but is there really anything wrong with looking stellar?

—I guess not, if you actually are stellar.

—*Well, I think you are Dada, so maybe you should wear a suit more often.*
—*Maybe one of these days the suit I don't mind wearing will find me, Dari, and then everyone will be happy.*
—*I think whenever that does happen, Dada, you'll look pretty stellar in it.*

• • • • •

Cyrus stepped into the vault in the white linen robe that they gave him before he entered the cave. He appeared weary and somewhat ill. The pallid light of the room set an odd sheen to his brown skin, but as he moved closer, it became clear that the odd, greenish-sienna hue was not due to any light in the room, but to the color of the skin itself. Tanner made space for Cyrus to sit on the chair, and Cyrus let his legs give, plopping into the chair like a bag of dirty laundry. "You look ill." Milliken moved toward Cyrus to get a closer look.

"It's the Eos. I felt like I was dying. For a while I passed out, and I was sure I *was* dead. When I finally awoke, I was surprised that I felt relieved." Cyrus exhaled, but his breath was not as exasperated as Milliken would have expected. "How long was I in there?"

"About fifty-five hours. Paeryl said that was shorter than most." Tanner leaned over to get a closer look at Cyrus's face and eyes. The green tint in Cyrus's skin and in his irises made him look as if there was a soft light following his every move from above.

Darius moved to the center of the room. "Dada, how does the sun feel to you now?"

"Honestly, it's hard to place. When I left the cave, they had me stand outside and walk. At first, I felt like I was going to vomit, and then, it felt like...I dunno...like coming home after a long, painful trip—only it never subsided."

"My namesake never talked about how it felt, so I don't know."

"Leaving the sun feels so dull now. Like a tomb. Honestly, it's not much different than the way I felt every day before we left Earth—at least the way I felt when Dari was not around."

Davidson stepped into the room behind Darius's image. "The info that we found before you blindly infected yourself shows that this Eos is harmless, depending on how you look at it."

Toutopolus rolled his chair over from the holomonitor. "Well it's a form of parasitic bacteria, like rickettsia, the kind that caused typhus. It is speculated that human mitochondria was originally an organism similar to the rickettsia."

"Observing this Eos most certainly supports that idea. It tricks the cells in the body into absorbing it. Once there, it begins to photosynthesize and works along with the mitochondria. It contains its own DNA and transfers itself to offspring through female gametes just like mitochondria."

"The downside is, if you're caught outside of the appropriate spectrum of light, it will go into its chemosynthetic phase and begin to breakdown the organelles of your cells."

"How long does that take?" Cyrus asked, a bit worried, but comforted by the fact that the majority of the humans in this compound had already made the same choice.

"As far as we can tell, about five to six days before the infection is irreversible."

"Why would it need a host? It has all the sunlight it needs here."

"For protection. Firstly, it goes dormant in moist, dark areas, which is why it's near the freshwater tributary here. Secondly, its DNA doesn't mix up like ours when it replicates. There's very little differentiation between generations—again like the mitochondria. It's how we can trace humans to one common ancestor called the Mitochondrial Eve. Problem is, when something doesn't differentiate its DNA, it's easy to wipe out with one drastic environmental change. Humans can adapt to survive a variety of environmental changes, and our bodies protect our cells with the tenacity of a juggernaut. Also, the Eos's nominal environmental temperature, when it is active, is about thirty-six to thirty-eight degrees. What better environment could it choose?"

Milliken stepped up, holding his datadeck the same as when Cyrus last saw him. "There's another concern that Torvald, Toutopolus, and I have been puzzling over. I didn't get the time to ask about the coal before we left for the Scar, but it did strike me as odd."

"What is odd about it?" Cyrus asked.

"Coal comes from decayed, heated, and compressed plant matter. On earth, it comes from swamps that decayed eons ago. Coal forms over a long time through a geologic process that slowly removes moisture, hydrogen, and hydroxyl groups from the vein."

"So let me guess, it took about six hundred thousand years to form?" Cyrus posited, the fog in his mind dissipating by the moment.

"Actually no. This stuff is anthracite—the best kind of coal. Most anthracite on Earth was formed in the Carboniferous period, which seems to be about the time it was formed here. That's the confusing part. That city was hundreds of thousands of years old, but this coal began to form about three hundred *million* years ago."

The clarity returning to Cyrus's mind was overshadowed by the impossibility of Milliken's words. "Which would mean..."

"There would have to have been a substantial amount of vegetation here hundreds of millions of years ago." Torvald finished Cyrus's conjecture.

Milliken continued with his treatise, "It also takes about ten to thirty meters of peat, which forms when swamps decompose and die, to make a one-meter thick vein of coal. Here we have about a four-meter thick vein, and it seems to stretch beneath the surface for more than three K."

"What does all this mean?" Cyrus could not help grabbing his head. It seemed the trip to Asha was a never-ending stream of shocking surprises.

"That the Eos was not the first form of life here, not by a laser-shot, and Davidson and I are pretty sure the Bereshit Scar didn't *create* favorable conditions on the planet, it *ruined* conditions that were more favorable." Milliken sat with his deck on the chair next to Cyrus.

"So there were life forms here hundreds of millions of years ago?"

"Well, don't get your head bent just yet. It gets better. You see this complex?" Milliken indicated the structure around them with his hands. "The steel in here is alloyed through a process I am not familiar with. My guess is, it was also somehow sealed against decay before the Ashans found it," Milliken continued.

"My son and the Apostates?"

"No, I mean the *Ashans*. Any of them. The generators, the outlets, the sync connectors, the fly-eyes, all of them were installed well after this place was built. Darius here says some of the things had to be refurbished, but this place had to have been set up at least five years before *he* came here. At some point, even by the Archons forgot about it."

Toutopolus now could not hold back his wonder over his own excitable puzzle piece. "Something has been bugging me too. The lion statues in the underground city had manes. But we are reasonably sure maned lions didn't appear on Earth until about 320 thousand years ago at the earliest. So if that city is as old as the scans say, why do the lions have manes?"

Tanner seemed exasperated. "Too many questions. Not enough answers. How do we find the truth?"

Cyrus began to laugh, and his laughter, more boisterous than most present had ever heard erupt from his lungs, startled them. Even the face and eyes of the Darius hologram mimicked everyone's surprise.

"What's so funny?" Milliken asked with a hint of indignant disapproval.

"What's so funny?" Cyrus said, still chuckling to himself. He stood abruptly, looking around the room. "Isn't it obvious? Look at us. We sit here, grown men, preeminent scientists of Earth, crying, as if our own world was not a distortion of reality. We came here looking for a reprieve; our loved ones were lost, but when the sting wore off, we remained in mourning. The adornments we chose fell apart at the seams and crumbled to dust—and again we cried, this time because we were naked and cold. We thought our truth was taken from us."

He paused for a moment and looked around, but laughter had left him. As he opened his mouth to speak again, the quivering in the corners of his eyes demanded pause, but he continued anyway, "What I realized on the trip back from the Scar is that we were wrong to be offended by our nakedness—the clothes do not make the man. Clothes are constructs, machinations. They are cheap gimmicks. Without them, we can be whatever we need to be. And yet, we sit here in this sterilized room, limbs flailing hopelessly at the ether as we plummet into the abyss, pissed to be damned because we have had the houndshit we used to clothe our world violently stripped from us. All the while, the only point we need to realize is that when the illusions are all burned away, however violently, that we are left with nothing *but* the truth."

A long tacit arrested the room, but Milliken, obviously flustered and unappeased by Cyrus's diatribe, thrust his back into the chair. "Well, what truth do we have that we do not make for ourselves?"

Cyrus faced Milliken. "We don't need to *make* the truth. We *are* the truth. We cry because our world has been stripped from us, but we should rejoice."

Tanner flustered, asked, "Why?"

"Because we've been given the chance to put the pieces together in the places they *want* to be—the places we never should have let them break away from."

"So then, what do you propose? Philosophical edification provides comfort, but it will not provide sunlight. And these people, as well as us when the stolen food runs out, will die without it," Torvald added, now somewhat flustered himself.

Cyrus was distant, his voice still airy and calm, "I think we need more raw data before we can decide anything. As you said, there are more questions than answers. Knowing how little we know is edifying, but will provide neither sunlight nor a viable stratagem. So we gather information, and we train. Those guys that chased us out of the Scar must have had their interests piqued."

"Then why don't we talk less and research more, and you can stop pontificating and go do some pushups," Milliken snapped then immersed himself in his datadeck.

twenty-two

—*Dada, did you and grandpa ever talk like this?*

—*Well, yeah and no. Your grandfather was a very quiet man. He didn't talk as much as me, and every word he said carried weight, so you listened because he wasn't big on repeating himself.*

—*Did you call him Dada too?*

—*No. I normally called him Dad or Pa. He seemed to prefer Pa.*

—*What was his name?*

—*David. David Moriah Chamberlain.*

—*Was he an astrophysicist too?*

—*No, your granddad actually worked for a living.*

—*What did he do?*

—*He calibrated and repaired the factory bots that built lev drives. Evidently, he was very good at it because he was a perfectionist.*

—*Was he more of a perfectionist than you, Dada?*

—*Oh yeah. He was scary. He made me make copies of all my deckwork so if I had any more than three mistakes, he would delete it and make me start the whole thing over again.*

—*Ouch.*

—*Yes, ouch. One night, he deleted my deckwork five times before I realized as far as my work was concerned, that man may as well have been a machine.*

—*I bet you hated that.*

—*At first, I hated it more than anything in the world, but as I got older, I could see what he was doing.*

—*What was that?*

—*He was determined to make me a better man than him whether I liked it or not. When I was tapped for Laureateship, he didn't say much. He only said that it would be even harder from there on out, but I could see it in his eyes. In his mind, I was beginning to do the things he wanted and had never been given the chance, and it swelled him up with pride.*

—*He never got jealous because you were better.*

—*No, never. How could he? He and your grandma were the main reasons I did* succeed. When I matriculated into the Arcology, I told your grandpa how much I appreciated him, and that I didn't know what I could do to repay him. He told me the best thing I could do to repay him was to do the same for my own child. That was also the first day he ever told me directly that he was proud of me. You know, that night, when I was by myself, I cried.

—Were you sad?

—No. It was the happiest day I can remember, because that day, even though I always knew it in the back of my mind, I knew I was good enough because David Chamberlain saw me as fit to carry his standard.

—Standard like rules to live by, or like the things you have to capture in Conquest of Ages?

—Ha, I think both, Dari.

—Do you think you lived up to his standard, Dada?

—Well, I am proud of you, and I think one day, you'll do a fine job of carrying the standard yourself, so I guess, yeah, I think I might have done okay.

—Gee Dada, I didn't really understand it when you said it, but I think maybe now I understand what made you cry that night. But it's okay Dada. I kinda like it.

• • • • •

Cyrus felt the now common tingle in his skin subside as he stepped into the room the Apostates called the Forum. Cyrus ran through how much time had passed since he first stepped through that circular doorway. If the notion of day cycles was distorted inside Eurydice, it was blasted into oblivion here. The Apostates counted from evensong to evensong, their daily vigil of meeting with the elders in the thinning shard of sunlight. The elders would fellowship and discuss issues while the children played or slept in the shadows of the crater. They still kept track of the hours and lumped them into chunks of twenty-four, but the moniker of 'day cycle' seemed more and more ludicrous as the sun, stuck in a never-ending sunset, demanded more and more of Cyrus's attention as his body adjusted to the Eos. "So what's our situation look like?" he asked, still thirsty for real light.

"Same as it did yesterday, like balls on a beta hound," Milliken scoffed as he synced his datadeck with the Xerxes system. After the patch cleared, he loaded the data of the underground city they had discovered day cycles before. A twenty-five square meter hologram of the strange city expanded in the center of the room and rose up from the floor.

Davidson, still queasy after emerging from Plato's Cave two day cycles before, propped himself up as best he could to see the image spread across the floor. Tanner, just overcoming his own grogginess from emerging before Davidson had entered, stood to get a better view. Jang was confined to the sunlight, under the care of the two women that had now ushered all of them except Uzziah into Plato's Cave. Toutopolus had been in the Cave for the last thirty or so hours, and probably would be there for another thirty more.

The door to the kilns and labs opened, and the image of Darius emerged from the hall beyond. Milliken leaned over to Cyrus. "Why does he do that? It freaks me out," Milliken asked.

"Well, if he learned from my son, I doubt half-assing the image of being real is a part of his program."

"Half-assed or not, it's still freaky," Milliken whispered as Darius approached, hands clasped behind his back, looking at the image of the city as if it wasn't being digitally transmitted directly into his—its—data grid. Milliken furtively shook his head. Darius looked up from the image of the cave, winked at him, and then craned his neck closer to the hologram. "Were these buildings ever inhabited?" Darius asked with an inquisitive yet serious look on his face.

Milliken moved his stylus across his datadeck, and the image zoomed in on a set of buildings. The buildings were angular, mostly square, with crenelated roofs. Some of the larger buildings had what looked like miniature versions of the smaller buildings on their roofs. "It's hard to tell from this scan. There wasn't enough time to gather acute details. However, from the lack of accumulation of dust, it was either hermetically sealed before they excavated it, or there was an extensive excavation of dust after they cracked it open. It would have required an enormous effort, even with the most advanced equipment, to extract a half-million years of dust. Given the obvious desire to keep whatever this is as quiet as possible, my guess is it was sealed. That's why they used the extraplanetary lasers."

"I doubt the pilots of those fighters even knew what they were protecting," Uzziah chimed in to get a closer look himself.

"How can you be sure of that?" Davidson asked.

"Because I would not have told them if I was their C.O." Uzziah moved closer to the image of the building in front of him. "These look familiar. I've seen buildings like these before."

"Ancient Mesopotamia," Tanner said with assurance, but with a perplexed look on his face. "They look Babylonian, but something is also very different about them."

"Other than the lack of monolithic slabs of limestone, massive veins of quartz, and laser bits between the Tigris and Euphrates on Earth?" Milliken asked facetiously.

"It's not just that. The organization is very different. It's as if it was designed by an architect trying to *mimic* Babylonian architecture, but without the need for practical placement. Irrigation, religion, and defense dictated where and how things were built in Mesopotamia. Those things don't seem to figure into the design here."

It sounded as if Milliken had giggled to himself, but when everyone turned to face him, he looked more serious than excited. "Speaking of design, look at what I noticed yesterday." Milliken maneuvered his stylus across the deck, and the image rotated until the roofs of the buildings faced Cyrus and Tanner. The image mirrored itself between them and zoomed out along the z-axis of the city at a speed that made both Davidson and Tanner reel. As it zoomed, it looked as if the buildings were swirling into some massive drain. Tanner closed his eyes and reclaimed his seat on the chair as his head lolled back against the headrest. When the city stopped falling, Cyrus could see the arrangements of the buildings formed a distinct pattern. Cyrus had assumed the moiré pattern he had seen when they had first passed over the city was a trick of light from the artificial sun interacting with the quartz coupled with their high rate of speed. Those factors alone could have made the buildings appear to undulate as they had passed over them. Now, however, looking at the entire breadth of the city from an impossible vantage point, it was clear the rhythmic pulse of the buildings was due just as much to the layout as it was to a trick of light and speed.

"It looks like one of those circles they used to find in the cornfields at the turn of the millennium," Davidson mumbled. The pattern looked like two swirls that interlocked in the center, each swirl forming half of a stepped aster that spread out in the eight cardinal directions. If the lines of the pattern they formed had actually been lines and not a trick of the eye played by the varying distances between the buildings and the roads and the colors of the buildings themselves, it would have made the aster look as if one half was drawn with a solid, unbroken line, and the negative space left behind formed the other half.

"The Hunab Ku," Darius said as he looked on, rubbing his beard.

"What?" Uzziah asked, not sure what the hologram had just said.

"The Hunab Ku is an ancient Mayan symbol. It is related to the Mayan calendar, but I don't remember how." Tanner didn't even open his eyes as Darius explained.

"How could you know that?" Milliken asked Darius.

"Balam Castenago, one of the engineers on the J.L. Orbital, used it as a logo for his engineering company. He was of Quiché descent. He called his company Xmucane Development. It was called 'the Hunab Ku' for Ashan trademark registration purposes."

Milliken opened his mouth as if to speak, but then said nothing. Tanner, with his eyes still closed, spoke the idea that must have frustrated Milliken to silence, "But the city looks untouched, right? At least untouched before the Ashans got there. So if no one lived there and it was zipped up like a vapor-lock for hundreds of thousands of years, who in the hell built it, and for what?"

"That's what's been scraping my brain for the last week. We can't even build something like this now, not even if we combined Ashan and Earth technology, well old Earth technology." Milliken shook his head as if he were trying to shake out the frustration. "No matter how you try to carve it, the timeframe always breaks a chunk off."

"Hmm," Torvald grunted as he looked up from the holomonitor connected to the Xerxes. He had kept silent until now but seemed completely engaged. "Look at the building shapes, Davidson's maned lions, Tanner's Temple, Cyrus's yellow sun. All these things are distinctly familiar to us, and yet would be completely foreign to anyone who existed on Asha today, six hundred years ago, or on Earth *or* Asha six hundred *thousand* years ago."

"So what are you saying?" Uzziah stood up rolling his shoulders back. To Cyrus, he looked unnerved, but it would have been barely perceptible to someone who had not trained with him.

"I'm saying the explication is more likely to be found in things familiar to *us* rather than in the unfamiliar. My guess is that city has more to do with *Earth* than Asha. Especially with the things Davidson and I uncovered in that cave."

• • • • •

Whether it was his body adjusting to the Eos, the resurgence of his own faith, or the fact that he was again in command of a dojo, Tanner was filled with new vigor as he barked the names of moves at his exponentially larger class.

The Apostates formed four lines of four and tried their best to follow the commands as Sifu Tanner gave them. Cyrus, Torvald, Davidson, Jang, and Toutopolus helped those who had trouble, while Uzziah, still nauseous from his emergence from the Cave, sat on the side basking in a sliver a light, trying feebly to look healthier than he felt.

The men and women Paeryl referred to as his van were remarkably limber and agile. There was a young student called Six because of a scar on his chest that resembled the Roman numerals. Six was extremely agile, and he learned techniques faster than anyone Tanner had ever seen. It helped that the Apostates had a fighting art of their own. It was young compared to the time-honored arts of Earth, but their art was practical, and years of necessity had honed it to precision; what it lacked in diversity, it made up for with its freshness.

Maybe it was their seemingly inexhaustible energy or the daily threat posed by the masters of Eurydice and Druvidia, but the Apostates absorbed Tanner's teachings like cheesecloth.

Each session began with calisthenics and then moved to techniques, but the second half always included the Apostates sharing their art, what Paeryl referred to as Crossing the Kheires and the others called The Hundred Hands. At first, the Apostates had only shared the concepts behind their moves, but after they became more comfortable with each other's styles, they began to spend the latter half of the class sparring. It was a chore at first. The Hundred Hands style had been given an accurate nomination. Each move chained to the next. The Apostates didn't seem to need to breathe between moves, and eventually, Tanner and the others found they didn't need to either. The Apostates would spin their smaller lighter bodies over and under attacks, moving their momentum into punch after kick in a stream that didn't seem to end until someone grabbed or kicked them. And Six was the fastest and strongest of the Apostates. He could easily take on any five Apostates, or any three scientists excluding Tanner or Uzziah—Tanner made up for what he lacked in comparable speed with wisdom, and Uzziah made up for both with sheer force and tolerance of pain. Yet on any given day, both Tanner and Uzziah would opt for some solution other than a real fight with Six if it meant someone would not walk away—because they could not guarantee it would not be them on the gurney.

Perhaps it was the difference in gravity on the Paracelsus, or the seemingly never-ending supply of energy afforded them by the Eos, but practice seemed to last longer than it ever could have on the ship, and it seemed to be more intense. The Apostates had an advantage initially due to their familiarity with their photosynthesizing metabolisms, but it wasn't long before Cyrus and his 'van' found that the advantages the Apostates had in speed and endurance could be balanced by the scientists' sheer temerity and strength.

They took time to fill their wineskins in the aqueduct and then paired up for sparring. Six walked over to Cyrus and spoke, "Sifu

Tanner holds the ensign jack, but you seem to be the vanguard." He puffed out his chest, causing the V and I etched in the flesh over his heart to expand slightly.

"I'm a student of the art just like everyone else," Cyrus said, looking around.

Six smiled as if he found Cyrus's answer amusing. "Are you aware I hold the Amphiphoreus?"

"Don't even know what that is," Cyrus was growing tired of humoring him, and he made it obvious he was searching the compound for something else to give his attention.

"It is the award given to the Hundred Hands sparring champion. Every gyre there is a tourney. I have held the Amphiphoreus for forty gyres," Six added, his chest still inflated as he smiled. With that grin, Cyrus recognized him as the man who had ogled him when they had fled Eurydice. Then, behind the smiling Six, he saw Jang, cupping the hand of Paeryl's daughter, Loli, in his own, demonstrating the correct way to form a tiger's claw by slowly, gently moving each individual finger into place. She smiled as she began to understand the technique. She was more focused on her hand than Jang, but Jang seemed to be more focused on her eyes and pursed lips.

"Excuse me," Cyrus said to Six without looking away from the scene across the pitch. Six nodded, a little dejected, and moved toward Tanner.

Jang traced the tip of his finger down Loli's forearm, demonstrating the proper way to hold her wrist. Even halfway across the pitch, Cyrus could see the gooseflesh forming on her upper arm.

"Sifu said he needs your assistance," Cyrus said before he had fully reached them. It wasn't completely a lie. Tanner *had* asked Cyrus to find someone to help him retrieve the weapons he requested from the forge.

Jang greeted Cyrus, hand over fist, bowed slightly, and then left, saying goodbye to Loli after the formalities.

When Jang was outside of earshot, Cyrus spoke, "He's a bit of a flirt, but he is highly respectable."

Loli held out her tiger claw, waving her dark hair to the side as she admired the claw next to her other hand. "Oh," she said through her smile. She was beautiful. The greenish tint made the lighter complexion of her skin glow in the orange light. The Eos must have absorbed most of the rays before they stimulated production of melanin. That made her paler than Cyrus was normally attracted to, but the glow made it hard to look away from her. She looked younger than what she must have been, but there was an odd understanding in her eyes. Then the understanding gave way to concern as she relaxed her fingers. "Oh," she said again, this time more warily. "Perhaps he is not aware I am already betrothed."

It took Cyrus longer than it should have to internalize what she had said. Their version of Commonspeak, as familiar as it was, was often elusive. Then, as realization crept in, he uttered his own, "Oh."

● ● ● ● ●

Uzziah stood at the front of the room as Aerik Twelve discussed the armament of the Ashan forces. He looked older than many of the others but did not look as old as Paeryl. There was something weary about his stature even though it looked like his bushy brown hair was only beginning to grey. A few of the elder Apostates called him The Hanged Man, but most referred to him as simply Aerik. He was currently holding two submachine pistols high enough for everyone to see. They looked more like staple guns from Earth, as they had finger guards beneath the barrel linking to the bottom of the handle.

"These are your standard issue automatic hand projectors. They fire standard hand slugs at rate of five every second." He set one of the auto pistols on the table while continuing to hold the other. "They have an active recoil compensation system that increases weight in the front of the hand projector as the slug is ejected. Their versatility and light weight have made them the main side weapon of the Eurydician Municipals, who are most always armed with sub-lethal disintegrating rounds."

He placed the two auto pistols on the table and lifted what looked like one of the assault rifles they had used in Eurydice. "This amazing piece of artillery is the Eurydice Acer IV. It has active recoil compensation, fires a long bore slug at more than twelve slugs per second, and has a capacity for 108 slugs."

Aerik set the rifle down on the table, and Uzziah picked it up to look it over. "We will familiarize you with techniques on using each of these as this is the artillery most available to us."

"What are those weapons behind you?" Milliken asked, referring to the holographic images floating behind Aerik

"Those are weapons you may encounter that it would behoove you to identify before they are used. For example, this little thing here." He moved his hand, and the image of a small silver device that looked like a chicken egg moved forward from the menagerie of weaponry behind him. "This seemingly harmless little device can block the sun on your whole sortie. He moved his hand again, and the egg began to vibrate as a low-pitched oscillation filled the room from hidden speakers. "The Valois Squib is a beautiful device indeed. It generates a small EM field that can attach to even poorly conductive metals, and thanks to an antimatter core, it can penetrate any—hearken to this—*any* surface. And because it has a small sound signature and rarely generates secondary explosions, it is the weapon of choice of the Echelon."

Torvald raised his hand to get Aerik's attention. "The Echelon?"

"You mind if I take this one?" Uzziah intercepted as Aerik opened his mouth. Aerik dipped his head deeply in more a bow than a nod, and Uzziah continued, "The Echelon are Ashan special forces. Similar to the team I was a member of on Earth." There was a silence in the air. No one gasped, but their faces looked like they were about to. Uzziah himself expected everyone to already know, but apparently Tanner and Cyrus were as stalwart as he had given them credit for. Everyone knew he was a military pilot, but none of them seemed to suspect anything else. Uzziah continued despite the silence, "Most of Asha considers them to be a myth, but Paeryl is certain they are the ones who captured Avalon and attacked us at the Scar. These are weapons Aerik and Paeryl have seen them use or were found by recon Darius Prime hacked from the Eurydician database."

"How is it the Ashans aren't sure they exist?" Toutopolus looked deeply confused.

Aerik leaned forward to answer the question, "Because, as far as we can glean, they operate out of orbital stations in the Miasma and out of Druvidia or Eurydice when they are azoic. We are certain they relocate just before each exodus, but there must be a secret waypoint in between each migration to avoid crossing exodus traffic and facilitation crews; however, until now, we have been unable to locate it."

There was a buzz among those assembled as Milliken raised his hand. "What is that gun there?" he asked, indicating a gun that looked like a shotgun from a futuristic holocast.

A wide smile spread across Aerik's face. "This amazing piece of hardware," he gestured, and the weapon moved forward, "is the Druvidian Entropic Quantum Rifle. Referred to as the DEQ rifle or the Spellcaster. This weapon is only rumored to exist. The recon was gathered through the comm-sat link here in the base, but we are not sure if it is a prototype or in limited production." He paused for a moment to gather his excitement. "When the slide here is pulled back, this weapon absorbs free energy in the surroundings. When the slide is pushed forward, it holds its charge. When the trigger is pulled, it fires compressed subatomic particles at virtually light speed. In theory, at full charge, it packs enough punch to stop an assault lev at full speed. It can be fired in a vacuum, and it has a duty cycle of ten thousand discharges."

"Why is it called the Spellcaster?" Milliken asked.

Aerik moved his hand, and an odd mist formed in the room. It must have been a rudimentary hologram because the mist was highly pixilated, but it shifted and formed like real mist. Aerik waved his hand again, and the slide slid back on the gun. There was a medium pitch whirr, and the mist swirled around the DEQ rifle much like mist around some arcane magician's hands. One final gesture moved the slide forward. The whirring stopped, and then the trigger slid back. There was a muffled thump that, despite its low volume, shook the room as the holoprojector simulated a dent in the wall.

Aerik was still smiling as Torvald raised his hand. "How is it you know so much about it if it's not supposed to exist?"

Aerik laughed, "Because it was developed to counter our attacks. And according to the Archons, *we* don't exist either." He smiled again and indicated the real firearms on the table as he waved to disengage the holographic display.

"So when do I get one?" Milliken asked, smiling to Toutopolus as he said it.

Aerik's smile faded somewhat. "When you learn to survive long enough against an Echelon Officer's escort to take it from his cold, dead hand." The seriousness in his voice sobered Milliken. "Not even Six has been that lucky, nor is he obtuse enough to try."

There was a tense quiet, and then Aerik's smile returned as quickly as it went. "Now, Azariah of Pentacles," Aerik indicated Uzziah as he referred to him by his Eos name, "and myself will acclimatize you to the use of the weaponry we *do* have in our cache."

twenty-three

—*Dada, I'm confused.*

—*What's wrong Dari?*

—*Today in class, Terry kept taking Sergio's stylus, and Sergio finally got tired of him and hit him in the mouth with his deck case.*

—*Did he get hurt?*

—*I think Sergio might have knocked out one of his baby teeth, but he didn't have to go to the med-lev or anything.*

—*What's confusing about that? Sounds like Terry finally got what he deserved.*

—*Well Miss Hasabe flipped her queue counter and starts yelling at Sergio in front of everybody, telling him all this stuff about violence never solving anything. But then, later in social studies, she goes off about how great the Unification War was for the world, and how they should civilize the rest of the Fringe states so we can live in peace. Thing I don't get is, Sergio just busted up Terry's mouthpiece with a plastic case, but in the War the Uni killed people—a lot of people. Terry's teeth are gonna grow back, but you can't grow back a whole dude. It makes no sense. Why is one okay and the other not?*

—*Most people neither have nor really want a clear understanding of what violence really is. They treat it like it is the root of all evil, when in reality it is neutral—a means to an end. It's the* ends *that make the difference.*

—*So you're saying the ends justify the means?*

—*No, Dari, I'm saying the means, in the case of violence, are irrelevant. It's the ultimate end that tells the real story. For example, everyone at school knows that Gallagher boy is a menace. I'm sure even he knows, and for whatever reason, no one does anything about him. They may as well teach him that his actions don't have consequences. He continues the same monkey business day-in and day-out until someone gets tired of him and talks to the monkey in a language he understands.*

—*Getting his face bust open.*

—*Exactly. And it wasn't the means that Sergio used that was the problem. It was the fact that no one put Terry in check before those particular means were necessary. They should have ended it well before that.*

—*Maybe so, but Miss Hasabe says violence is never the answer.*

—*And yet she condones the Uni War. She only railed Sergio and condones the War because she enjoys the ends the War created, while the ends of Sergio's actions meant she has to clean up Terry's blood and teeth and talk to parents in her conference hour. If she didn't want to see violence, she should have set the axis straight before it came to it. Violence is as necessary to life as anything else. When you clean your teeth in the morning, it's violent to the bacteria. Without some level of violence, we wouldn't have food to eat. Without some level of violence, we couldn't create this sterilized world that allows Miss Hasabe to stand in front of a classroom and pretend it doesn't exist.*

—*So you think violence is okay?*

—*I think violence is a tool, and just like any other tool, it has its uses and its misuses. And any man who wields it irresponsibly, who doesn't understand the nature of the tool itself, will eventually smash his own hand into oblivion.*

—*So, you think Sergio did the right thing?*

—*I think Sergio did what he felt he had to. I think Sergio's dad needs to lay in Sergio's ear for a bit. But most importantly, I think if Miss Hasabe wants to continue believing violence only exists outside her classroom, she needs to put a stopple on Terry before he aggravates people to the point where they feel it's necessary. Bottom line, you can't eat a sweetbar twice. You gotta handle a problem either at the beginning or handle it at the end.*

—*Well, I don't think Terry's gonna be aggravating anyone for a while.*

—*I hope you're right, but somehow I think as soon as his mouth heals, and as long as people like Miss Hasabe make excuses for him, he'll be in someone else's face, pissing someone else off, acting like consequences don't exist. You see, people like to believe violence is a disorder or an aberration. They think it only happens when diplomacy fails. But the thing they never tell you is that when courtesy goes down the lavpool, diplomacy goes with it. You see, violence is what happens when the dealer says all bets are off, but the gamblers won't leave the table. It's what happens when people have nothing left to say, but something, either the problem or one of the people, forces them to keep talking. Sometimes people don't get the point until someone gets hurt.*

—*I don't like hurting people, Dada.*

—*As well you shouldn't. Hurting another person is a terrible thing, but sometimes terrible things are necessary to keep the world turning. If you ever have to put your hands on another man or bring harm to his home, you stop yourself and ask if this is really necessary, and if you don't have an answer, you keep your hands to yourself because fighting is sometimes necessary, but it should only happen because you have to not because you want to.*

—*Miss Hasabe said there's never a good reason to fight, not even if someone else hits you.*

—Well, she's both right and wrong. There never is a good reason to fight, but sometimes you're left with nothing but shitty choices, and acting like a turd isn't a turd won't turn it into a sweetbar.
—Eww. Even if it did, I wouldn't eat it.
—Nor should you Dari. Nor should you.

• • • • •

Time began to stretch as it progressed. On the Paracelsus and under the Eurydice dome, the day cycles seemed shorter. The rotation of day and night in both was a clumsy artifice, but it had been enough to dupe the mind into a regimented schedule. Here, Cyrus found himself awake for hours on end, in greater need of the orange sun's embrace than rest. At first, he thought it was sheer belligerence that kept him going—the need to avenge the death of his best friend, to absolve the wrath of his son, and to find a respite for these strange men and women who had accepted him and his friends without expectations.

Or perhaps their expectation was subtle. They treated him the same as they would have treated anyone else. There had been no hoopla, no fanfare, and yet, when they looked at him, they looked at him as if his mere existence meant hope. He didn't realize it until he had come here, but it was the same way Darius looked at him. He had wanted more than anything to get the same look from Feralynn, and it was in search of that look that he had signed the papers sending him here. And now, the light from the orange sun swelling his muscles, he knew that he had taken for granted the dearest thing he had ever known.

The inside of the compound now seemed damp. Outside of the rays of the sun, there seemed to be a moisture that clung to his skin. He wasn't sweating, but it did feel like he had become more sensitive to changes in humidity. Jang was working with Milliken's datadeck, while the image of Darius was pretending to type at the holomonitor. It was funny to Cyrus how irritated Milliken could get by the persistence of the illusion of his son, but the illusion's antics comforted Cyrus. If he had created something like that himself, discounting certain differences in character and idiosyncrasy, he would have had his own image act in the same manner. There was no such thing as a halfway fake, and if an illusion were to be created at all, it should be maintained with the utmost effort.

Jang was enthralled by his own work, and Cyrus had to tap him to get his attention. Jang looked up slowly as Cyrus spoke, "You spend the least time outside of anyone else."

262

Jang's bangs had suffused his entire face now, but when he was working at a computer, it was like the hair was transparent to him. He brushed it aside as he looked up from the deck. "Outside is good, but there are no computers out there, and there is work to be done."

"Commendable, but I don't want you to futz around in here until you get sick."

"Trust me, I won't stay in here too long because I don't want the ladies to miss me too much." He smiled a facetious smile and began moving the stylus furiously across the deck again.

"Perhaps they are in need of some attention *now*," Cyrus said, smiling a little himself. Jang set his deck on a chair. He blew his hair from his face, and his own expression changed to match the seriousness in Cyrus's that the jest in his voice had not revealed.

"Sure, sure," Jang said standing, "I think I could use a little sun anyways." He stood and walked toward the iris.

"Just let anyone who asks know I'm in here," Cyrus yelled behind him.

Jang nodded and raised his hand over his head in acknowledgment as he left.

"You seem tense, Dada," Darius said standing from the holomonitor, "would you like me to lock the door?"

"Yeah," Cyrus said, sitting where Jang had sat. Then he realized the awkwardness of the question.

"How could you know to ask that?"

"Whenever your real son had that expression, he always issued the door-lock command. I just figured you might have the same inclination."

"I have a question, but I don't know how to ask it." Cyrus reclined in the chair, but his shoulders were still stiff.

"The only way I know is to open your mouth and speak," Darius smiled and Cyrus, with a little difficulty, also smiled at the statement that could just have easily come out of his own mouth.

"Did Darius," he paused for a moment and then reselected his words, speaking more deliberately, "did you," he paused again as the hologram waited anxiously, "talk about me much?" Cyrus breathed a sigh as if he were expelling air that had grown stagnant in his lungs.

"You were mostly all I talked about. Thoughts came freely because I was talking *to* you. I enjoyed our conversations before you left more than you know."

Cyrus looked at the floor. His feet were still covered with the sand that had seeped into his shoes while he was training. "You know, I enjoyed them too."

"I always thought you did. Even though most of the time you were getting in my ear about this thing or that. I was always into something."

"You had a knack for turning the most innocuous situation into a complete Fringe-riot."

"You always knew the right thing to say though. Even when you didn't know what to say."

"I'm sorry." The words seemed to snap off Cyrus's lips before Darius could finish his sentence.

"For?" Darius looked perplexed. It was a little exaggerated, but it made sense.

"For leaving you. For putting you through this." Cyrus sat up in the chair, sliding to the edge as he indicated the room with a wide gesture, "It's me who put you here. No one else." Cyrus's voice had raised to a volume that startled even him, but Darius seemed unaffected and, if it were at all possible, compassionate.

"You know, coming into this room day after day I realized something. I realized I didn't become the Knight of Swords after any particular battle; I became the Sword Scourge the day you stepped onto the shuttle to Eros. And that led me to another realization—the realization that the second worse day of a person's life is the day they realize their parents are irrevocably human."

Cyrus could feel his eyes shaking, but he steeled himself. It may have been a construct of the complex nanocomputer system humming lightly to itself on the other side of the room, but at this moment, as far as he was concerned, Darius's eyes spoke truth to him—the figure before him was his son, and he needed Cyrus to be strong as much as Cyrus himself needed it. "If that's the second worse day, what day could be worse than that?"

"The day that person refuses to get over it," the inflection and the facial expression matched perfectly. "As you said time and time-squared times, I made my own choices, and just as you said, *that* and that alone made the difference. I still had nightmares, but they were brief. And even on the nights when they proved an insurmountable foe, the mirror never took up arms against me."

"Not once?"

"Never. When I looked in the mirror, I saw the only man in the universe who could judge me."

Cyrus nodded in understanding, "Yourself."

"No," the contradiction came like an airlock tocsin. "*You*. War is war.

It's what happens when the gauntlet is thrown, when all bets have been called off, when courtesy has failed beyond redemption, and when acting like a lavpool isn't a lavpool doesn't make it pudding. Humans fighting humans on an interplanetary scale is an abomination, but so is bartering your beliefs for comfort. Something was amiss here on this planet—something still is—and I knew we could win. So I made the call Rex Mundi didn't have the stomach for."

"But look what happened. Instead, it was for naught. They tried to kill you. They ran you out of town. I wish I had taught you to be wiser."

"And since when has Doctor Cyrus Tiberius Chamberlain considered selfish wise? Self-preservation, yes, but not once have I seen you run from a problem because you might get hurt." Those words hit hardest of all. Darius may not have known any better, and certainly not his effigy, but Cyrus knew he had run from the only thing that had ever really mattered, and it burned the lining of his stomach. Darius took notice of Cyrus's expression but continued. "Besides, the only way to stop whatever dominoes had been set to fall was for me to stay alive—for me to pass on the message to the only person I knew could maybe get at whatever is at the bottom of this hound's pit."

Cyrus looked at Darius. There were parts of the hologram that seemed artificial—not for lack of articulation on the part of the imager—every pixel had been color-matched, every line anti-aliased. The minutest of details were rendered to perfect clarity, but the clarity was too perfect. Reality was hazy and indistinct—it had rough edges and was all-too-often ruddy—and yet, in the midst of the awkward exactness of the overall image, Darius's eyes boasted a veracity that convinced Cyrus of the sincerity of the simulacrum's words.

"You know there was one thing I did run from. One problem I never knew how to solve." Cyrus said, diverting his eyes from the eyes of the image.

"I know," the answer caught Cyrus off-guard—the matter-of-fact inflection as perfect as if it had come out of a real mouth. "Mom." That word shook the chair around Cyrus, generating gravity waves that pulled him back into the seat despite the tension in his shoulders.

"I just couldn't tell what she wanted from me."

Darius laughed and looked down at the floor. The image paused for a moment, exhaled in way that seemed ostentatious as it transmitted through the sound imager, and then he met Cyrus's eyes again with the same substance as before. "All she wanted was you to be hers like you had promised, but you refused to belong to anyone."

"Not anyone."

Darius paused and then nodded his understanding. "Fair enough."

Cyrus clasped his hands in his lap as he sat forward in the chair again. "So where do we go from here?"

"Well, my suggestion is you go back outside, train some more, and send Jang back in here so we can find a way to crack the Echelon satellite system."

Cyrus stood, moved to leave, and then stopped. He met Darius's eyes again. "Thank *you.*"

Darius himself stood and smiled. "No, thank you."

Cyrus realized the words had a strange inflection. They were spoken in Darius's voice, but they rose and fell differently. As if someone else had spoken through him. "For what?" Cyrus asked, thrown off by the strange delivery.

"For allowing me to come as close as I possibly could to feeling emotion. I thank you both." The image bowed theatrically, and as he stood, Cyrus swore he could see a glimmer on his cheek. Then Cyrus turned, the iris opened, and he left, hoping the guileless Ashan sun would clear away the glimmer on his own cheek.

• • • • •

Cyrus rushed into the Forum sweaty, metal staff in hand. He noticed the sweat seemed to evaporate instantly as the iris closed behind him. "Toutopolus said you found something," he said to Jang and Darius.

Milliken was already inside, his broadsword still in hand, intently moving his stylus with his right hand over his datadeck as he, Jang, and Darius observed some hologram Cyrus could not see. Cyrus moved over to them quickly so he could view it himself. "What is this?" he asked as he stood next to the Darius image and let one end of his staff rest against the floor.

"It is what it looks like." Milliken's answer could have been perceived as snide, but tension often had that effect on his voice.

"But where?" Cyrus asked, looking down on the gold-topped white pyramid that spread across the floor at their feet, each corner marked by an obelisk several meters from the vertex, also white with a gilded pyramid at the top.

"Eight degrees and thirteen minutes north of the equator," Milliken added without looking up from the datadeck. "The prime meridian runs bang through the center of it. The position of the pyramid is so precise, I found an error in our calculations, which were only off by four ten-thousandths of a second."

266

"How did you..." before Cyrus could finish his question Jang was already answering him.

"Darius and I were working on a shadow-sync with the Ashan satellite system. On a test run, we found an odd microwave power signal that led us to this thing," Jang informed.

"The Ashans built this?" Cyrus asked, pivoting his staff around the point where hologram of the pyramid touched the floor.

"I don't think so, but I'm working on that now. The satellite is being difficult, and Jang's algorithm keeps unsyncing," Milliken snapped, dropping his sword with a clang.

"Well, would you rather get caught and taken back to that hound's cage we escaped from, or worse?" Jang snapped back.

"Either way, it's a pain in my ass," Milliken snapped again, furiously moving the stylus on his deck.

"Wait," Cyrus stopped his staff in mid-pivot. "This thing was sending out a microwave signal?"

"No, it was *receiving* one," Darius turned and answered. "We think the top of the pyramid is the rectenna, and the base shape somehow helps diffuse or channel the energy."

"The edge of the Miasma also rests inside the obelisks on the south side of the pyramid."

A sudden impulse moved Cyrus to the holomonitor next to the main Xerxes unit, "Hmm," he said more to himself as he rested the staff against the computer, sat in the chair, and began tapping frantically at the keypad. Darius walked over to the holomonitor and looked over Cyrus's shoulder, eliciting a grimace from Milliken. "Asha's precessional period is 16,392 Earth years. About 9,920 years have passed in the current period, which means in the next 6,472 years, the Miasma's edge should rest here." Cyrus emphatically hit a key, and the light that was cast over the image of the pyramid shifted. There was no other clear difference until Cyrus pressed another key, and a fluorescent red line spread through the image, tracing a path directly through one of the vertices of the pyramid, across its center, and through the opposite vertex.

"What does it mean?" Jang asked, ruffling his coat.

"It means that this thing was most likely built 9,920 years ago, or some multiple of 16,392 years ago, well, that and plus 9,920 years."

"Thirty-six!" Milliken belted jubilantly, the tension now gone from his voice.

"What?" everyone, including Darius, said in unison.

"Thirty-six precessional periods. The gold on the top, according to these readings, was laid approximately six hundred thousand and thirty-two years ago."

"Which matches the dating of the underground city," Darius added again.

There was a cold quiet in the room. It was a silence that caused the vibrations generated by the holoprojectors to thicken the air. "I don't know about you guys, but this shit is scary as hell to me," Milliken said, wiping his brow despite the chill.

"The microwave signal. Where is it coming from?" Cyrus asked.

"The source is shadowed, even on the restricted band, but we've run across five similarly shadowed signals, and they have all been what we think are Echelon bases or orbitals," Darius added.

"We need to get Paeryl and Tanner in here, stat," Cyrus said, standing from the seat and retrieving his staff.

"I think Paeryl's holding a special evensong. He said not to disturb him." Jang scratched at his forehead as Cyrus passed.

"I don't care if he's giving birth. He needs to see this. And we need Tanner's brain. I'll get Paeryl. You get Tanner." Cyrus took his staff and left through the lab entrance.

Cyrus walked out of the compound with his staff and began scanning the crater for Paeryl.

"I see you came prepared," he heard to his right as the iris closed behind him. He turned to find a polished spear tip glinting with orange light at his right eye.

"I don't have time for games," Cyrus said stepping away, but the spear tip followed him. He felt the anger filling his joints and expanding his muscles. The weapon pointed at him was across the line. He stepped aside and knocked the spearhead down with his staff. There was a crowd forming around them, but Cyrus barely saw it. Cyrus could only see the tip of the spear and the eyes of Six, who, if he didn't stand down his weapon, would soon become Cyrus's adversary.

Cyrus held the spear down with his staff, but the other end of the spear came around again and pointed at his eye. "Step off or step into the round. I don't have time for games." Cyrus snapped, the fury in his voice unmistakable, yet Six's eyes seemed relaxed. He was either overconfident, unable to discern Cyrus's rancor from his grace, or he didn't care.

"I thought you would never ask," he smiled and stayed his weapon, but it did nothing to abate the incense swirling around in Cyrus's head. Cyrus stayed calm as the spectators began to form around them because he knew once he stepped into the round, rage would be of no use to him against this man.

Whether Six knew it or not, there was more at stake than a ceramic cup. These people, as relaxed and demure as they seemed in their little crater, were warriors. Inside this hole they called home, they were afforded some pause, but to the Eurydicians, they were outcasts, true apostates. They were animals trapped in a constricting corner, and they fought as such. It was no mistake that Paeryl had become their de facto leader. He was loud, he was melodramatic, but he also possessed a command over the spirit oft neglected by those with less naturally salient power.

Which meant for Cyrus to accomplish his already sketchy plan, he needed to win this fight.

The problem was Six was fast—too fast—and he was stronger than the other Ashans. His attacks were sharp, and his defense seemed impregnable, but he was cocky and aloof—which meant his precision in battle did not necessarily translate well in armistice. When the fight was over, he was uncouth and brazen just like any other Apostate, but unlike the others, when the swords were on the ground, he was also sloppy.

Six attacked first, as Cyrus had expected, but he had not expected the attack to come with such force. Cyrus could see how sharp the tip of Six's dual-ended spear was as their weapons clashed. Cyrus rebounded from blocking the attack and swung a counterattack, but Six had already brought his own weapon into the path of Cyrus's swing and had moved the opposite spearhead around. Cyrus side-stepped, ducked under the attack, and moved his staff toward Six's midsection. Six planted the tip of his spear into the ground and hopped over Cyrus's attack, using the leverage to lift his body as he spun over Cyrus's staff and swung his legs at Cyrus's head. Cyrus ducked under Six's airborne body to a gasp of the crowd. As Cyrus passed beneath Six, he brought the back end of his staff into the bottom of Six's spear. The spear dislodged from the ground, and Six lost his leverage, but he managed to get his feet beneath him and thrust his spear toward Cyrus. Cyrus moved and parried, but the other end of the spear came around in a blinding flurry of stabs. Cyrus was amazed at the speed, but he managed to wheel his staff in front of him and block as he backpedaled away from the assault.

Then, Six spun the opposite end of the spear toward the outside of Cyrus's leg. Cyrus had anticipated the attack, but it was still too fast for him to dodge completely. He stepped his left foot over the attack and stopped it with the bottom of his right shoe. He brought his right leg around, swiveling his body and, clasping the shaft of the spear between his legs, he spun his own staff around at Six's head. Six ducked just as Cyrus had expected. The crowd gasped again as Cyrus spun his staff behind his back and then thrust it out at Six's ribs, forcing him to let go of his spear as he hopped clear of the attack.

Cyrus followed the lunge with a sweep of his staff, but Six, with the poise of a feral cat, flipped backward over Cyrus's attack, and in mid-air, grabbed his own spear with both hands, wrenching Cyrus from the ground with the momentum from the flip. Cyrus had seen the whole move play out and still could do nothing to maintain his footing as the momentum of his swing shifted his weight just before Six's unorthodox attack. Cyrus breathed out as he fell, avoiding the shock of his lungs contracting, but his head still smacked against the ground. A dark static spread from the inside of his vision outward as the impact passed through his head, but Cyrus instinctively rolled backward to avoid any attack that may have followed. The momentum of the roll, however, wrenched his own staff from his hands. Expecting to use the staff as leverage to get to his feet, Cyrus did not quite get his legs beneath him, and, as the dark haze over his vision faded, it revealed Six, standing on Cyrus's staff, lunging the spear point toward his chest.

But Cyrus continued to roll onto his shoulders, kicking the spear attack skyward with the flat of his left foot. He flipped his hands behind his head and hopped from his shoulders onto his feet beneath Six's spear. The ease of the kip-up convinced him that his own cartwheel over his staff could work. As his body moved forward, he let his legs move over his head as he grabbed the staff with both hands and snatched it from beneath Six's feet. Six side-stepped as the staff came from beneath him and, as Cyrus came to his feet and whipped his staff around, Six was no longer where he had been standing, and the spear was coming around at Cyrus's leg again.

This time Cyrus was able to jump over the attack, and as he rose, he pulled his staff around to his side. He had expected Six to parry, but Six moved toward the attack. He lifted his spear over Cyrus's staff. Six then spun toward Cyrus and knocked the staff from his hands, sending it spinning into the crowd. Before Cyrus could react, there was a foot in his ribs. Cyrus heaved, managing to absorb the shock without losing his breath, but stumbled backward. He pedaled his feet behind him to gain footing, but he saw Six's spear closer than it should have been— and he realized the spear was airborne. Cyrus pedaled faster, but there was a sudden flash in Cyrus's consciousness as if his mind was trying to spare him the horror of his own impalement. When the flash cleared, he was falling, and all he could see was the irrationally short shaft of the spear glinting in the sunlight as something caught underfoot and sent him to the ground.

And then he realized it was the spear stuck in the ground behind him that had taken his legs from under him. He had not been impaled. His senses had not censored his injury. It had been the glint of light, reflected just perfectly into his own eyes that had blinded him. His coccyx hit the ground hard, sending a peal of pain up his spine as he looked up the shaft of the spear to see Six barreling toward him.

Six should have known he was vulnerable to attack, and yet he was still charging. He must have been gambling on his own ability and speed to counter any attack Cyrus would have thrown in the nanoseconds it took to cross the two meters between them.

So Cyrus didn't attack.

Cyrus cowered, threw his hands up, and planted his foot as if to scurry. And then, just as Six was almost on top of him, Cyrus sat up, grabbed the middle of Six's spear with both hands and twisted it. Cyrus scooped the blade from the dry earth and sent a shower of dirt and dust directly at Six's face as the blade came up in the wake of the silt. The blade moved up through the skin next to the scar on Six's chest just over his heart. Six reeled from the attack, and Cyrus spun the other end of the spear around while planting his heel into the outside of Six's knee—not hard enough to dislocate it, but hard enough to send him to the ground. Six bounced when he hit the ground. He tried to get his hands up, but by the time his body settled, the spear tip was already at his neck.

Six sat there, wordless and huffing, as the dust around them cleared. There was something in his eyes Cyrus could not place. It was not hatred or disdain, but it wasn't reverence or congratulation either. But it didn't matter. The din of the crowd told Cyrus he had won, whether Six's eyes admitted it or not. Cyrus set the spear down and climbed wearily to his own feet, while Six sat there with his blank stare of refusal. Cyrus walked over and extended his hand, but Six huffed again with blood trickling from the fresh, superficial wound on his chest. When Cyrus did not withdraw his hand, Six slapped it away and stood abruptly. Cyrus dropped back, throwing his hands up into a defensive stance. From the corner of his eye, he saw Tanner and Uzziah surge forward slightly from the crowd, but Six was already pushing his way through the mob on the opposite side. As Six disappeared, the crowd moved toward Cyrus with looks and cheers of wonder, all recounting their favorite parts of the contest. Someone mentioned that if the scar did not heal, they would now have to call him Seven, and there were several snickers from the crowd, but they all seemed more focused on Cyrus than Six—which was more than Cyrus could bear. He had not come to this compound to usurp a position in Paeryl's van or to abdicate the Apostate's champion. But their champion had called him to the round, he had thrown down the gauntlet, and if Cyrus was going to ask these men and women to risk their lives for him, he could not pick up that gauntlet and hand it back.

But Six had crossed the line, and Cyrus had to put him back on the side where he belonged. In a real fight, Cyrus was certain he had little chance to win, but if Six's childish pursuit reared itself again, now Six too would wonder about the outcome. And *that* was all Cyrus needed.

Cyrus moved outside of the congratulating crowd to find Loli. He found her in one of the darker corners of the crater dipping her wineskin for water. "I don't mean to bring it to you like this, but your people are straightforward." Cyrus was respectful, but his words were firm. "Let your betrothed know that I only extend my hand to a man once to have it slapped away. If you have any love for him in your heart, tell him that if he comes at me sideways again, I will set his six down to zero."

Loli laughed at Cyrus's comment, and it took him aback. "Why would he challenge you again? He saw what he wanted to see."

"Why would he challenge me in the first place? He tried to kill me."

"If you are not in the crematorium now, either he wasn't trying to, or he couldn't. My betrothed has many idiosyncrasies, but imprecision in battle is not one of them."

"Fair enough. Just seems like he's had a breach in his keel about me since I came here. I just want to make sure it's over."

Loli laughed again, "How can something that never existed come to an end? Six issued an open challenge *because* he believed you were what he wanted you to be, not the other way around."

"Maybe that's the way youth expresses admiration."

"Youth? He's always been like that—for the 180 gyres we've been betrothed, and the 109 before. Since he first set foot in Avalon, he has let his emotions carry him beyond the Miasma in that way, and kept them to himself in the other. It's as if diplomacy was erased from his mind the day he watched his parents die."

Cyrus looked both dumfounded and apologetic.

"You didn't know? My father went on an acquisition to Druvidia. He sent Aerik and the rest of the van back to get the grav-lev. What my father didn't know was the reason why the silent alarm had been so easy to circumvent was it had already been triggered by mistake by a man who worked in the building during the day. The maintenance man had brought his family to the building for evensong and to watch the dome darkening. When the Echelon saw the van leaving, they assumed everyone on their scan was an Apostate, and they leveled the building. My father managed to get to the basement and cover before the top floors collapsed. After the dust cleared, he found Six pinned under a support beam. He was bleeding heavily from his chest. The Druvidian scouring crew came to search for the bodies, but Aerik and Tessla were able to rescue Six and my dad. They were, however, too late to stop Six from finding the remains of his parents in the rubble. They brought him back here because they felt guilty but mostly because the Eos could save him better than Druvidian medicine. His wound healed, but it left the scar on his chest. Afterward, he refused to tell anyone his name. I think it was because it reminded him of his life before. We don't bring children here without their parents; the ones that have come here due to misfortune or duress never really get over it. He never told us his Ashan name, so we just called him Six. It was still a reminder of his past, but he seemed to glom to it."

"Why not his drawn name?" Cyrus sensed another awkward moment even as the words left his mouth, but he had to know.

"Oh," Loli smiled again, but this time she seemed taken somewhat aback herself, "we would never evoke *that* card."

Cyrus felt the swelling in his chest subside. He didn't realize the fight had uplifted him to such a high degree until he felt the pride receding as the pall of his own ignorance overshadowed him. He could see Loli, normally unaffected, was visibly uncomfortable, but he had to know.

"Which card?"

Loli hung her head a bit. It was less shame than it was the weight of something much greater than Cyrus could see. "My betrothed is the only Apostate since the exile that has drawn the Death card.

And then, without thinking about it, it hit him; 180 gyres was close to fifty years on Earth. When Darius told him the Eos extended life, he didn't tell him how much it extended it. Humility washed over him, forcing out the shame of his own ignorance. "I sincerely want to apologize for bringing this to you like this," they weren't the best words, but they were all he had.

"Not necessary. How could you know?" Loli smiled again, this time naturally.

Cyrus wanted to say something else, but he simply nodded and took his leave.

When Cyrus returned to the Forum, he found a thin, silver, double-handled vase sitting in the center of the floor. At first, he did not noticed it, but it did not take long for him to realize what it was. It was the Amphiphoreus—the spoils of the Hundred Hands champion. Cyrus did not know how to feel about this quiet concession, but it was a quiet concession indeed; and most importantly, it meant that despite all his harrumphing, Six had gotten the message.

• • • • •

Tanner sat working a small piece of limestone with a knife. There were other pieces of limestone in two different colors laid about him as he worked. He looked up briefly as Cyrus approached and then went back to his work.

"What are you building?" Cyrus asked.

Tanner worked diligently at the piece of rock in his hand. "I promised Fenrir I would teach him to play chess, so I'm making a chess set."

"I know you're a purist and all, but Jang and Darius could probably throw a hologram together in the time it took you to ask them." As the words leaving his mouth resonated in the air, Cyrus saw the folly in them.

Tanner pored over his carving as he spoke, and it was hard to hear his voice over the scraping, "Have you noticed how melancholy the inside of the compound feels now? And how no matter what burden has nested in your head, the sun always brings some sense of levity. At first, I thought I imagined it, but look at these people. They live in conditions we would have called squalid—conditions we might have experienced our first year, but we would have long since overcome by now. And yet, they don't just accept it, they relish it. I sit here, carving this bishop out of the earth they live on, and I can't help see exactly how far east of Eden we have gone."

Everything about Tanner had always been corporeal. He was a man born three thousand years too late, and the fervor that guided his hands in the carving of the stylus-tip head of the chess piece was his defiance of the sterile, automated world that imposed itself on him.

Cyrus sat next to Tanner and picked up the spare knife sitting next to the pile of rocks. "Well, I may as well help."

Tanner set his knife down and picked up one of the larger, browner stones. "I could use a king," he said as he handed over the rock.

Cyrus took it from him wordlessly and began carving himself.

• • • • •

Jang and Toutopolus worked with Doree of Sevens and Thendyr of Wands to configure a stand-alone gravity drive to the Xerxes unit so that Darius could control all the parameters needed for training in the practice room. If everything went as he expected, they would be able to set the room to mimic anything from three Gs to the gravity of Earth or even a zero G environment. That was specifically why Tanner had requested it. He had facilitated some zero-G training on Eros, and he wanted to institute some here just as a precaution. He and Cyrus had also set a regimen for increasing the gravity to closer to Earth specs for endurance and agility drills because training in Earth's gravity on the Paracelsus had made a difference in the escape.

For such simple people, Doree and Thendyr internalized Jang's requests very quickly and rarely had to have anything, even the more complicated ideas, explained to them more than twice. When Jang *did* have to explain something again, it was usually because of the language barrier. Many of the ideas from Earth didn't translate well in the Apostate's dialect and vice-versa, but the barrier never held up for long. And now, as Jang worked to calibrate the Xerxes unit to the specs Cyrus had set, the barrier didn't seem to matter at all. Everything was foreign to everyone, and it was exhilarating having to figure out some way around new problem every day—especially with Doree's help. Fenrir and Aerik spent most of the time in the forge building materials Tanner and Uzziah requested. And Thendyr spent a lot of time learning planetary physics from Cyrus, so that gave Jang and Doree a great deal of time alone. Jang had initially thought it impossible to want to spend this much time around one individual woman, but until now, he had barely noticed. It was when Doree was not there, or when there was no tedious task like trying to phreak the Echelon comm-sat, that Jang would feel the drain of being away from sunlight that Cyrus had warned him about, and it was hard to convince himself that it was not largely due to the absence of Doree rather than his new biological augmentation.

Jang moved to connect the cable leading to the control unit that would remotely control the gravity drive, and he noticed a strange discoloration at the back of the Xerxes unit precisely where the neural processor was housed. He froze in place, horrified, thinking backward through his movements for the last hour, trying to figure out what he could have done to burn out the unit. Then, when the Darius avatar appeared behind him to peer over his shoulder, he realized that the unit was still functioning, and that it was not a burn mark at all. The back of the unit housing had been caved in slightly, and what he saw now was a large cluster of cracks in the paint.

"What is that?" the Darius avatar asked.

"I'm not sure," Jang said, plugging in the cable and looking closer at the aberration. "It looks like someone kicked it, but the dent is too subtle, and the cracks are much too uniform."

"Well, unless you or my father kicked it, I don't know who would have. No other human has set foot in this room for hundreds of Earth years."

And then it hit him. Although it eluded him why this type of damage would be here. "This looks like the kind of damage Cyrus warned Thendyr a faulty gravity drive could cause, only on a much smaller scale," Jang stood perplexed. "I'm not sure what it is. It could be nothing, but if it does mean something, maybe your father will have an idea."

Jang found Cyrus and showed him the cracks as he helped put the Xerxes unit in place. "Do you have any idea what might have done this?"

"None at all," Cyrus said, looking closer, "but it looks like someone put a miniature gravity drive inside this thing. Maybe that's why it's so heavy." Cyrus joked, but he could see Jang was still confused.

Finally, Jang shrugged it off. "Maybe it's nothing, but it is strange. I suppose it could have happened when the original Apostates stole it. Who knows?"

Cyrus laughed. "Indeed. Who knows anything anymore?"

twenty-four

—*Dada, I can't find my stylus.*

—*Your datadeck stylus?*

—*Yeah, and I have a composition due tomorrow.*

—*Didn't I just buy you a new pack?*

—*Yeah, but none of those have been print-synced and verified yet.*

—*Where did you look?*

—*I looked in my rucksack, the deck compartment, and in my desk, but I can't find it anywhere.*

—*Weren't you in your mother's office earlier? Did you look in there?*

—*Why would it be in there?*

—*Because it's not in any of the places it should be. You know every person who every lost something couldn't find it for the exact same reason.*

—*What's that?*

—*Because they only looked in the places it wasn't. The reason you can't find it is you keep looking in the places you expect to find it, but if it was in any of those places, it wouldn't be lost. People get hung up on where they think things should be all the time, even people who you would expect to know better like scientists, historians, and anthropologists. It's a human weakness. But what should we do with our weaknesses?*

—*Turn them into our strengths.*

—*Exactly. People like Michael Faraday, the guy who solved the electromagnetivity equations, Richard Feynman who came up with sum over histories, Albert Einstein and his relativity, Jurg Klugmann who discovered gravity wave generation, all those guys looked in places the other eggheads refused to look.*

—*So if I can't find something like my stylus, the first places I should look are the places I've been that don't seem like places it should be?*

—*I'm sure if you do, things will turn up missing less often.*

—*You do say the only reason I don't lose my head is it's always in the same place.*

—*Ha, true. Maybe half the battle is just keeping an open mind and realizing your own fallibility.*

—*And the other half of the battle?*

—Taping everything of value to your head so you can't lose it.

• • • • •

When the blast horn sounded to alert the compound of an approaching friendly vehicle, no one expected the vehicle that returned to be followed by another large black vehicle with Six standing atop it, his arms folded, basking in in a triumphant pose in the waning the rays of Set.

Everyone stopped as they rode in, and Paeryl watched the procession with a look of distress on his face that Cyrus had not imagined possible from such an imperturbable man. It was the look of a predator that had just caught the scent of a furtive scavenger creeping through the tall grass, bent on devouring the predator's brood.

As Six pulled in through the iris, Paeryl walked toward the compound with a determined gait. Cyrus moved behind Paeryl along with Cyndyl, Paeryl's betrothed, who also looked distraught. The other scientists followed behind.

Once inside, Paeryl's courtesy, his most prized characteristic, overshadowed his distress. "Have you misplaced your senses?"

The triumph melted from Six's face as he jumped down from the vehicle. He must have expected a hero's welcome, but Paeryl's rage seemed to pour from his eyes, his calm shattered by some deep aversion to the spoils of Six's venture.

Six opened his mouth to speak, but Paeryl's bellow quelled anything that might have come from his mouth, "This is an Echelon vehicle. You are *inviting* them to descend upon this place as they descended upon Avalon."

"Thendyr disabled the tracer. They've already been spoofed. They think this thing went down in the Miasma."

"You attack the Echelon without orders. You challenge our guest openly—the father of our Patriarch no less—and now you openly defy me with an unsanctioned excursion into the Miasma. You have stepped well outside of the sunlight, young one. You are becoming a liability."

Six started to reply but stopped short and hung his head. Cyrus could see what happened. Six was satisfied that Cyrus was what everyone expected of the father of the Man of Swords, but in the discovery of that fact, his pride had been more deeply scarred than he had gambled, and he had gone out of his way—way out of his way, risking not only his own life, but the lives of Paeryl's most prized warriors as well—to salvage the dignity he thought he lost.

But it had been unnecessary. If Cyrus was in danger of taking anyone's place, it was Paeryl's, not Six's. Paeryl himself knew that but was too wise to fear it; it was absolutely implausible in Cyrus's mind, and he would never accept such a position, de facto or otherwise. Paeryl was as good a judge of character as he professed to be, insofar as Cyrus could tell, and Paeryl had so far given him carte blanche because he knew Cyrus's ambitions, however self-centered, would never supersede the Apostates' best interests.

However, Six's latest apportion had crossed that line. And however wise he was, Paeryl's love and protection of his charges was now overwhelming his better judgment—a judgment that, under less stress, would have allowed him to see that berating Six in front of elders and Cyrus's van would only stoke whatever fire had already consumed Six's self-esteem. The same weakened self-esteem that moved him to barrel headlong into a mission that, as jetwashed as it seemed on the surface, had borne obvious, although dangerous, fruit. Even as Fenrir and Thendyr emerged from the black fighter with supply crates, Cyrus found himself at Six's defense, "Perhaps this is a good thing..."

Before Cyrus could finish, Jang spoke, "This lev will help Darius and I finally crack some of the ciphers in the Echelon network. I can use their own protocols to manufacture completely indelible spoofs against their safeguards and countermeasures." Jang was literally shaking with excitement like a kid on a cred spree. And then Aerik, who had emerged from the forge upon their entrance, pried open a supply case marked 'Artillery,' and became giddy himself as he withdrew what looked like a case of at least thirty Valois Squibs.

Chandra opened her crate, revealing a stack of black body suits. There was another box inside labeled 'Subvocalizing Units' that sent Aerik and Doree into unintelligible jubilance.

Although Paeryl's admonishment had already taken its toll on Six, he seemed to absorb the thrill of Jang, Doree, and Aerik—but it had not been enough. Six met Cyrus's eyes as he turned to walk outside of the garage and he nodded, acknowledging the attempt Cyrus had made to absolve him. It seemed as if everything Loli said about him was true, and Cyrus found comfort in the fact that even in the midst of the maelstrom that must have been raging through his skull, Six still found the presence of mind accept the responsibility—and that meant, no matter how much of his dignity he thought had been lost, somewhere, inside his wayward soul, Six still had dignity in spades.

• • • • •

At the eighteenth hour, all the elders were sitting before the slowly receding sliver of light. They had met on the information that Cyrus, Milliken, Tanner, and Jang had relayed to them on the existence of the pyramid, which, as far as Jang and Darius could discern from collected data, appeared to be the Echelon base that housed the two Arks from the strange temple in the underground city. Milliken had suggested calling the city Zion, but Tanner had starkly opposed that moniker, suggesting Mu instead.

They discussed the usage of the items Six had procured in his apportion, and at Jang's behest, also discussed the safety of phreaking the Echelon network. At the end of it all, they had—given Cyrus's growing reputation—conceded to every stipulation the scientists had given them except one—that Cyrus's van would take on the burden alone. The elders offered all their resources, with blessings from Cyndyl and Paeryl alike, and those blessings were confirmed by the nods from all the Ashan warriors who would carry out that offer.

· · · · ·

Cyrus sat talking to Tanner when he noticed Six get up from his place next to the water duct and walk over to Paeryl. When Six moved to leave his discussion with Paeryl, Cyrus intercepted him.

"I can't take this," Cyrus said, unveiling the Amphiphoreus from his pack.

Six looked down at it with a slight sense of regret in his eyes, but when he met Cyrus's eyes again, he was smiling.

"You already did," was his only reply. He pat Cyrus on his back and took his hand, shaking it awkwardly, but it was awkward only because Six was not used to the gesture. He then walked away.

Cyrus watched Six as he passed into the shadow next to the mound Jang and Doree were perched on and stopped. Six turned back to Cyrus. "Trust my words, next gyre, I will get it back the right way." He smiled and walked to where Loli was waiting. She took his arm and they retreated to their own shaded corner of the compound. Loli was right. Six wanted to believe Cyrus deserved the card he had drawn, even at the expense of his own pride. And although it had not graced Six's plate in quite some time, defeat, for the proud, was indeed the toughest cut to swallow.

· · · · ·

The Forum seemed dimmer with so many people inside. Cyrus, Paeryl, Uzziah, and Darius presided over the gathering. It had taken the Apostates, who had never ventured inside the vault, almost an hour to process the existence of the Knight of Swords inside the room that had been closed to them for hundreds of years. The matriarchs stood at the front of the mass prepared to scrutinize any idea that put their people in immediate danger. Cyndyl, in particular, had opposed most of the weapons and martial supplies that were being amassed in clear sight of the children, but she could see the sun setting, and she had listened openly to the stories of the Echelon's ever more foreboding presence in the wastelands. Even with her great reluctance, she saw the possible necessity, and whatever reservations she had she only communicated to Paeryl and Loli.

Paeryl himself had a great deal of difficulty with the Darius holoprojection. He stood and stared at the image of the Sword Knight as if he were watching the ghost of an old friend.

Six had to be at least four-hundred-gyres-old from what Loli had told him, which meant the Eos had extended the life of a man who appeared to be in his twenties to about 110 years. Which would mean that Paeryl, if he was born with the Eos, would have been at the least, three to four-hundred-years-old himself.

While Darius addressed the group, Cyrus suddenly understood, and he moved over to Paeryl. "You knew him?" Cyrus whispered.

"He was my teacher," was all Paeryl said. He then patted Cyrus on the back and moved back to his wife and daughter.

When Darius finished, Cyrus took the floor. The vault was silent. It seemed like even the machines stopped whirring and humming. "Before I speak, I have a question to ask. There is no information from Earth at all that we can access?"

There was a quiet din among the Apostates, and then Aerik spoke, "Perhaps there is some hidden codex deep within the bowels of the Praetoriate, but everything from Earth was either hidden or destroyed. According to the image of the Sword Knight, there were a few things he managed to salvage, but they were mostly things of personal value."

"What is the chance that we could get into this Praetoriate codex?" Cyrus asked.

"We might have a better chance of going back to Earth itself than apportioning anything within the Praetoriate. And even if we managed to get inside, there is a clear chance that we find nothing at all," Aerik spoke matter-of-factly, but the grumbles from the other Apostates validated him.

"Why the interest in information from Earth?" Cyndyl asked, sidling closer to Paeryl.

"Because my van has uncovered things on this planet that are undeniable links to early Earth, and as astute as every member of my van is, we all believe very strongly in research. But without information to research, we are in the Miasma just the same as anyone else. These links are links the Echelon has gone to great lengths to hide. They may even be the *reason* why the Echelon allowed all this information to be destroyed. I need everyone to think of anything that might be a source of information from Earth. There is a device we need to apportion from one of the Echelon bases in the Miasma. We will need at least two teams, and my van is not large enough by itself. Unfortunately, we need one of the teams to create a distraction while my van goes for the apportion. The sortie will be very dangerous. It will not only garner the attention of the Echelon, but it will bring us into direct contact with Ashan forces within the Miasma. I would not ask you to risk your lives on a whim. This may be the link that Darius, your Knight of Swords, left this vault here for us, and he needs—*I* need—your help."

"What sort of distraction will you need?" Thendyr asked, fumbling with one of the holomonitors.

"I'm not sure yet, but it needs to be big because what they are hiding in that base got my son exiled and my best friend killed. They have protected it for five hundred years, and they will not let it go easily."

Cyrus looked over the faces of the Apostates who seemed much less disturbed than him by his request. He walked to the iris and left everyone inside the vault to parlay while he went to mull over his thoughts. Paeryl confirmed that the degrees of separation between him and Darius were fewer than Cyrus thought, but he could not tell just yet if that closeness, at this place in time, was a consolation or a curse.

Cyrus sat on the mound looking out at the peaks cradling the orange sun. The idea was ridiculous, but he was sure the sliver of light strained by the promontories was considerably smaller than it had been yesterday.

"Having second thoughts?" It took Cyrus a moment to realize Jang was behind him. He sat on the mound next to Cyrus and looked across the valley. The Apostates went on about their duties as usual, and as usual, they paid no mind to the scientists perched on their thinking spot. Doree of Sevens was the only Apostate who averted her attention from her weaving to wave happily at the two. Jang smiled and returned the wave, and Cyrus nodded.

"She seems to have taken a liking to you," Cyrus said, still transfixed on the retreating wedge of light.

"Must be the lab coat I guess." He ruffled the collar of his coat and ran his hand through his now shoulder-length hair.

"You *are* looking pretty stellar since you got it washed."

Jang preened himself more blatantly, but then, as if his original thought had come careening back into his brain with the force of a meteor, his expression became starker. Cyrus saw the change and responded, "You know," he paused as if the words were stuck in his diaphragm, too heavy to be moved with speed, "Villichez died when we escaped." Cyrus looked back toward the edge of the crater. "I went back to get him, but I couldn't stop it."

Jang waited for Cyrus to meet his eyes. He began to speak, seemed to lose the words, and then gather himself, "The tough thing about artificial intelligence is that a computer can't mimic consciousness. It can mimic a human being's behavior but not his thought process." Cyrus seemed distracted. Jang paused for a moment as he saw the gloss that was forming over Cyrus's eyes. "The avatar program is based on Villichez's and Winberg's work on human consciousness." Jang almost winced when he spoke Villichez's name, but he kept going. "They set up a complex set of paradigms to mimic human behavior. It was my job to program the processor to move through the algorithms so fast that physical, emotional, and cognitive responses could be mimicked without making the user aware. We worked tirelessly to create side-algorithms that mimicked 'human' responses when the system got hung up. People worried about trying to defeat the halting principle, but Winberg came up with a way to avoid it altogether."

The orange light seemed to turn Cyrus's eyes blood-red as he turned to face Jang again. Cyrus's lips shifted under the shallow curls of his beard, and Jang realized he was rambling. "The short version is, if the avatar is modified the way I think it is, if we run some subroutines to get the Xerxes to access the Agamemnon database, we could get Darius to help us put the pieces together in ways that we never could without him because stubborn and closed-minded are algorithms we had to fake. They aren't inherent in the programing and therefore won't restrict him like they do us. I think this might be the only way to save these people before the Echelon comes to see us." Doree, finished with her weaving, looked over at them as she placed the cloth in her bin, and Jang smiled. "And honestly, I'm starting to like it here."

The crimson tint seemed to wane from Cyrus's eyes. He nodded, and Jang nodded back. Jang then hopped off the mound and moved toward Doree, trailing his lab coat behind him like a cape. As he secured his coat by the lapels, Jang turned back to Cyrus and brushed his hair to the side. "You did save us all that day—more than once." He then turned and walked out of the shade and into Doree's embrace.

Before Doree and Jang could retreat to the shadows, Cyrus called out, "Notify the elders. I think you may have found our distraction." Jang stopped, not sure that his idea had even been a plan, but Cyrus continued, his spirit lifting as he spoke, "We train for one Dhekad, then we mobilize. Get to work on phreaking the comm-sat system, stat. I need to contact our friend Denali."

• • • • •

Torus Balfour Denali stood addressing two Hexads and four Pentangles at the conference table. He had begun by speaking on the recent rash of Apostate attacks and on how a high alert had been issued from the Prolocutor himself. He knew that the Echelon would be called in to handle any large-scale offensive, but he could not mention them in this meeting because the existence of the Echelon was classified to anyone with less than six vertices.

The Apostates had become so bold as to attack Echelon units directly over the last Dhekads, and it seemed that another attack was imminent. Denali also briefed them on what they learned of the escape that had taken place on the Advent. Apparently, they were completely mistaken, and the men who escaped actually *were* a team of scientists from Earth. He kept his men in the dark because, even though they had not experienced much combat, the fact that they had been utterly defeated by eight scientists who had little, if any, military training, would have sent their already waffling morale through the baseboards.

He spoke of the Apostates' tactics and how his advisors thought the Apostates might find a way to attack Druvidia, which Denali believed was nonsense because he was privy to information that was classified to even higher vertices—the Apostates were all infected by a disease that meant extended lack of sunlight would be deadly to them. So, the information passed down to him through this highly dubious Prolocutor was either deliberate misinformation or evidence that even the great and elusive Echelon had no idea what was coming down the cable.

Denali had just regained the ability to speak without pain a Dhekad ago. Most of the damage from Cyrus's unorthodox attack had healed, but his voice still crackled after long speeches as his vocal cords had grown weak in the day cycles he was not allowed to speak. He stood to point out a possible location of the Apostates' base of operation on a hologram above the conference table, but he was stopped as the door slid open.

"Torus Denali, there's a holo-sat transmission for you. It is has a six-vertex caption." Denali looked at the others in the room and did not need to speak. The Pentangles all stood simultaneously, dipped their heads slightly as they crisply placed their hands over their hearts, and then lifted their heads just as sharply before they walked through the door. Denali nodded at the Quadrad that had delivered the message, and he too left the room.

Denali sat, and a hologram appeared on the table in front of him that made his blood stop in his veins. On the table in front of him stood Dr. Cyrus Tiberius Chamberlain, the eminent astrophysicist from Earth who staged an escape by setting a room on fire and hanging from a dais by his very own neck.

"How are you gentlemen?" he said. The greenish tint in his skin, indicative of the disease that afflicted the Apostates, was clear even in the grainy holo-sat signal.

"What do you want?" Denali asked, reclining in his chair. The Hexads seemed as flustered as Denali, who felt this very transmission, despite what Cyrus had to say, was insulting.

"Forgive me for being rude. How is your neck?" Denali grumbled and inadvertently brushed his hand across his throat, but before he could respond, Cyrus continued, "I have been assured that your men cannot trace this holostream, but as I do not have time to tarry, I will be brief." Chamberlain folded his arms in the image and focused on Denali.

"Get to your druthers Chamberlain so I can tend my business."

"For starters, that name is no longer welcome to you. You and your monkey-boys can relate to me as the Knight of Wands." The image of a knight on a horse wielding a flaming staff appeared, obscuring Cyrus. The knight reared back on the horse as he spun the flaming staff over his head in a glowing blur. "I am the father of the Knight of Swords and the vanguard of the Children of Set."

"Spare me the soliloquy, you..."

"Continue to test patience, and I will continue to test your ears. I have but one demand—return to me the body of my murdered colleague from your necropolis."

"And if I don't?"

"I will set something on fire..." The knight on the horse appeared again and pointed his flaming staff at Denali. "...and I guarantee it will be something you will miss."

The knight waved his staff and flames erupted around him on the table until his image was obscured. Cyrus's voice persisted through the room. "Bring Dr. Villichez to the J.L. Orbital at precisely the fourth hour of the twelfth DC Ketomuriox, or I shall test more than your tolerance for oration."

Denali yelled that no one made demands of him, but the feebleness of his retort became clear as the flame on the table faded into nothingness.

"What should we do?" Hexad Thule asked, obviously trying to help Denali regain the dignity his outburst had drained.

Denali breathed heavily to himself as he massaged his throat again. "We will do as he asks," he almost stopped there, but the need to reassert himself overwhelmed his tongue, "and we will wait for him to make a mistake."

twenty-five

—Dada, you ever wish you had another child?

—Well, the Uni prohibits it in population controlled areas.

—I don't mean another one like a second. I mean like instead of me.

—No Dari, why would I wish something like that?

—I dunno. Sometimes it seems like I give you and mommy such a hard time. And sometimes mommy seems sad. Like sometimes she doesn't have anyone to talk to like you and me talk. Maybe if I had been a girl...

—No Dari, I definitely do not want another child. Both your mother and I love you very much and would never trade you for anything.

—I dunno, Dada. I want to be good. I mean I never really want to be bad, but it's hard sometimes. Like school is so frustrating, and I try to deal, but before I know it, I'm getting yelled at again.

—I think that's a part of life, Dari. We all have our roles. I have to let you try and figure things out on your own, but when you do make bad choices, your mom and I have to be there to reset your kilter. If it didn't work that way, no one would ever grow.

—So you're saying that me being a clownfish sometimes helps you grow too.

—Exactly. There are things you come up with that I never could imagine, and sometimes it's good stuff, sometimes it's absolute bunkus, but it's always challenging. It's stepping up to the challenge that makes us grow, whether we want to or not. But I would never wish you were something that you were not. I only want you to be the best you you can be. But sometimes, even though you may not realize it, I do understand you, and I sympathize, but we all need someone to get our butts on the lev sometimes.

—You never need anyone to get your butt on the lev.

—I think your mother would beg to differ, but I do have someone who gets me on the lev even when I don't want to.

—Who's that? Mommy?

—You.

—But how Dada? I never make you do anything.

—Believe me. Because of you, I have done many more things I should have done but wouldn't have.

—Well, hopefully, there will come a day where you won't have to.

—I hope not. I like doing those things. You make me a better man. From now until the end of days, for you, I would walk to Hell in a propylene undersuit, walk right up to the devil, slap him in his face, and then stand there and wait for his reaction.

—Ha. That's funny Dada, but I hope it never comes to that.

—Even if it did, Dari, I wouldn't regret one nanosecond.

$$\bullet \quad \bullet \quad \bullet \quad \bullet \quad \bullet$$

There was a ringing in Cyrus's ears that no amount of yawning could remedy. At first, he thought it was the field created by the z-drive on the lev, but these gravity wave levs didn't create the same fields as the ones on Earth, and even his sensitive ears should not have been able to pick it up. This was something else—something from within. The more he thought about it, the more he understood. All the dire situations he had experienced here on Asha had all been brought to him. Some of those situations might have had more diplomatic solutions, but each of them had, in some way, been constructed by others. But today he was initiating contact. He was bringing *his* fight to *their* lobby, but these were not just Flying Monkeys. It wouldn't just be reservists ordered to hold their fire. There would be highly trained, methodical jobbers who had given up their own society for the power that training and method afforded them—and they would kill to maintain that power.

Men were going to die today, and they would die from Cyrus's own initiative. The need to turn around and order the whole thing off arrested him, but he shrugged it off. The deaths would be hard to stomach, as they should be, but one thing the escape had taught him is that it would be a much easier supplement to swallow if the men that died were not his own. Whatever was going on here was bigger than any of them. It was bigger than the Echelon, the Ashans, and—perish the thought—even his son. If the Ashan pyramid and the underground city were truly built by some civilization more than a half-million years ago, it could even be larger than all of humanity. And if a handful of megalomaniacal men, for their own sordid purposes, sought to inveigle an idea that affected all of humanity at the expense of human life, those men needed to die. It was a grim truth to embrace, but it was truth nonetheless. If things went as planned, that truth would not have to be realized. But Cyrus did not have to live an Eos-life to know that the best-laid plans of mice and men often went worse than awry when lives were on the betting table. He tried to push all this to the back of his mind, but it settled in like a mag-lock bolt. But soon enough, the gooseflesh, the jitters, and the lip-biting would give way to survival instincts, martial training, and field tactics, and at the end of it all, they would be successful, or success would no longer be an issue. That ephemeral comfort was enough to keep him looking toward the darkening sky reaching out to him from the end of the thinning atmosphere. He just prayed everyone else had found the same pause.

Jang could see all the ships moving on various partitions of the holomonitor from his deck. There were three individual holoscreens around him. It was like Conquest on Galvacet, and the idea, as nerve-wracking as it should have been, exhilarated Jang to the point where his fingers quivered with excitement.

And then, the last of the eight ships was in place. There was no need for silence in their current position, but he needed to get used to it, so he subvocalized anyway, "The chicken's in the breadpan peckin' out dough." Only Jang, who got the phrasing from an ancient music sphere, had any idea what that originally meant. Even if his countermeasures did not spoof the Echelon's broadband scanner, no one on Asha would know the line meant that everyone was in place, and now was the time to commence their individual orders. He found himself oddly comfortable in this space that was barely large enough to house him with all the decks and monitoring equipment. But nestled inside the secret compartment in Cyrus's ship was the best place he could be to communicate with everyone. Using the Echelon's own communications system would be easier at the source, and it would generate less notice from anyone who happened to see the bandwidth he was using. Somehow, knowing that made sitting in a compartment the size of a lav stall much more palatable, even though it made his toes numb. Then Jang forgot about his toes, and his own anticipation began to rise as they approached the Orbital on the holomonitor

Cyndyl watched the ground beneath them pass by in waves. She had seen the interiors of the cities a few times, and each time she was overwhelmed by the ominous sprawls of buildings and the grav-levs moving in long lines that wove between them like lasers. All the sights, the artificially lit aves, the monstrous domes that robbed the cities' denizens of the glory of the sun, were, to her, abominations. Born in the sunlight of Avalon, she could barely believe the stories she heard of human fetuses reared in metal amniotic sacs, of people passing their entire lives without ever feeling the unfiltered rays of the sun, and of the innumerable dead, logged and filed in droves in the stagnant necropolis, waiting without dignity to be recycled into nutrients for the artificial soil of the common fields. The very thought of it, as Ashan dunes rose and fell beneath them, filled her throat with a slight twinge of bile.

Cyndyl had never been sent to apportion a bier ship before. There was something slightly dubious about the nature of their mission, but to her, as they sped on their course to intercept the ship carrying the body of a man the Knight of Wands called Doctor Villichez, this mission was payment of overdue respects to the dead. And as the target blip appeared on the holographic imager, Cyndyl gave the command to activate Taewook of Cup's signal scrambler. In a few moments, they would spare the body of Knight of Wands's colleague from an unnatural fate, and they would set the plan in motion that would save the Knight of Wands himself.

Cyrus spun the craft around and backed it into the docking moor. When he did finally leave this Orbital, it would most likely be in a hurry, and having to rotate the lev on its z would only be a waste of time—time they might not have. As the ship rested against the moor, Cyrus heard Jang's voice mimicked by the network computer, "Setting the spoofs now. I'll be in the entire system in ten minutes."

Cyrus thought about telling Jang not to rush. He did not realize that the subvocalizing unit picked up even unintentional signals until Jang responded, "This is like trying to get into a whore's pants. All you need is the right assets."

"Cut the chatter, monkey boys," came through Cyrus's earwig in Uzziah's voice as Cyrus stepped out of the ship to face four armed Eurydician soldiers in vacuum gear.

"Welcome back, beta-hound," one of them said over the speaker in his suit, and even through the distortion of the face shield, Cyrus recognized the last voice he had heard on his first trip to the Orbital.

Cyrus was a little surprised by the familiar voice that made the blood vessels in the back of his head throb in remembrance. What he also did not expect, after they had searched him and he had been led— with more respect this time—into the hallway adjacent to the docking bay, was Dr. Winberg, dressed in full Eurydician regalia. He wore a pendant of a hexagon on his chest above a nameplate and a number, which must have been chosen by him, 24601—the prisoner that had somehow become a hero.

"I trust your landing this time was much more...pleasant." Winberg's lips formed his trademark smirk as he offered his gloved hand to Cyrus.

Cyrus shook his hand reservedly, hoping his reservations would be perceived as confusion rather than distrust, especially since he did not know which emotion held the most sway over his reaction.

Cyrus knew the bier ship would not arrive for another half-hour, but they could not have known he knew, and he was interested to see how they would stall him. Two men walked before them and two men behind, but they seemed to defer to Winberg. They led Cyrus to an observation deck overlooking the sun. The windows of the deck were tinted to protect against the direct light from Set, but even through the tint, the rays of sun on his face felt like a long missed lover's touch. As they approached the glass, Winberg waved his hand, and their escorts stopped behind the line where the tiled floor ended and carpet began.

Winberg pantomimed a gesture, the men took three more steps back, and then Winberg led Cyrus to the edge of the glass. "Beautiful isn't it?"

Tanner watched the others as they all passed through darkness across the barren, featureless plain. The chill of the Miasma pierced to the marrow. It wasn't just cold, it was something more sinister—and he was all too acquainted with it. It was the same desolation he felt in the awkward years before Laureateship, when he had rebelled against his ailing mother before he had begun practicing kung fu, and before he had accepted Jesus Christ as his Lord and savior. Part of it was the Eos. Being separated from the light with no reprieve in sight made him shiver, but deep down, he knew his anxiety was only the tip of the laser bit before him.

As Jang announced the approach of the Echelon ship they were tracking, he had expected at least a little chest-beating and sword-biting, but everyone was solemn as if they processed in a funeral, and their austerity was calming. They were walking into the laser-mesh of a grove-harvester. They were well-trained and had seen some combat, but only Uzziah had seen anything like what was about to actualize before them. Tanner himself had been in some rough spots—especially before the Arcology—but even he was unprepared for what the Miasma held for them.

He breathed in and then out again, focusing his *qi* and steeling himself. As cold breath expelled from his lungs, he noticed the others did the same. Paeryl stood at the windshield of the lev, stalwart in the face of the darkness that had completely consumed them more than an hour before. There was something about Paeryl that reminded Tanner of Cyrus. Apart from bombastic delivery, he had never seen Paeryl be anything but calm, and yet there was something in his eyes, something about the way the corners of them creased when he smiled, that indicated to Tanner that Paeryl was truly not to be crossed—that was how he had gained the deference of the hearty Apostates, even the high-strung Six. Perhaps he too had a bear shirt in his closet.

Paeryl's shoulders were tensed, his form statuesque, but if he did possess a bear shirt, he had not yet put it on. That was an excellent sign. If Paeryl could keep it together, everyone would. But Tanner had a deep suspicion, one that no lev drive could stop from sinking, that before this day ended, they might all need a bear shirt of their own.

"You picked a hell of a day to come up here and rouse the rabble," Winberg said, keeping his face toward the glass. He cast his oily smile at Cyrus as he turned his head, but there was an odd sincerity to it Cyrus had not noticed before.

"What makes you say that?" Cyrus asked, trying to keep the puzzlement from expressing itself on his face: Winberg was stalling, but for what? Cyrus ran all the modes of ambush he could think of in his head as a check against his own plan of attack, but he was left with only bewilderment—it seemed as if his plan so far could cover any anticipated ave-blocks, but he couldn't help feeling like he missed something.

"We are anticipating a rash of stellar flares today, and they tend to wreak havoc on low-level communication devices," Winberg added, scratching his chest with his right hand. Cyrus watched Winberg's hand without averting his eyes to it, and he noticed him slip a few fingers inside his shirt as he scratched. Cyrus began to tense, but he rolled his shoulders back to try to hide his reaction.

"You fanned up quite a stench with your theatrics Mr. Knight of Wands." Winberg smiled again, a little more uncomfortably this time, but he continued to look at the starscape beyond the edge of the planet. Before Cyrus could respond, Winberg continued, "They figured out what really happened shortly after you escaped," his tone and inflection were different now, as if he was having a different conversation. "However, they were intrigued as to how you organized the escape with the Apostates—especially after they discovered the Knight of Swords was your son."

Cyrus looked directly at Winberg, making no attempt to hide his gaze this time. "How did you rise in the ranks so quickly?"

"Actually," he paused to smile at Cyrus, and it was the awkwardly honest smile again, "my acceptance and promotion was primarily due to *your* antics on the Advent. After they found the truth and combed the Paracelsus, they found everything that *I* told them on the Advent to be true. They kept me around as a control of sorts, but they were forced to promote me to Hexad because I knew too much." He began scratching again as he turned back to the stars, but this time, his fingertips crossed beneath his lapel much more forcefully.

"So why would they send you to meet me here?" Cyrus said. Winberg was up to something, but the sincerity in his eyes led Cyrus to believe that his trickery was not targeted at him. Winberg was several types of abhorrent to Cyrus, but bald-faced lies and dubiety did not seem in keeping with his repertoire.

"Because the increasing attacks of your new friends and your direct challenge on the Torus himself have cast suspicion upon *me*." The smile came again, but he continued to face the window and scratched his chest. "I don't blame you for that. I've seen enough of you to know that, though our approaches are different, we are more alike than either of us would be comfortable admitting." He coughed and patted his chest firmly—in the exact spot he had been scratching. "They were going to close the louvers on you and the others and release the hounds. I convinced them it would not work. It didn't save you, but it bought you time. Now I need you to return the favor." He cleared his throat and rubbed his chest again, but spoke before Cyrus could answer, "The bier ship should be at the space lift in five minutes." His tone was completely different.

"Tell your men to stay away from it and me when the ship arrives to avoid any trouble," Cyrus's voice resonated off the window.

"Are you threatening us Dr. Chamberlain?" he asked in the same haughty tone that came between chest rubs.

"You know me well enough to know I don't bluff." Cyrus met Winberg's gaze again. Something was going on, but for once, it did not seem like Winberg was his enemy, so Cyrus played along.

Winberg scratched his chest again beneath the lapel and turned to the orange glow of Set. He waited a beat before speaking, and when he did speak, it was mumbled and guttural, but Cyrus heard it anyway, "In about thirty minutes, all hell is going to break lose. When it does,

I need a favor from you." He coughed again, and then looked back at Cyrus. Winberg's tone was full of hubris again, "Mark me when I speak, cross the Torus again, and you and your monkey friends are finished, complete."

Hexad Scoffield Trageue monitored the eardot that had been secretly placed into Hexad Winberg's vertex badge. Eardots were normally active devices used to communicate on the earwig network, but they could be rendered passive and used for surveillance when anyone with higher vertex clearance entered the individual code. Torus Denali had wanted the Hexad monitored continuously throughout this entire operation involving the capture of the Knight of Wands. Trageue himself had a vertex added to his badge just for this six-vertex sensitive mission, and it would stay, pending the outcome. But the earwig network was not cooperating. There had been a rash of stellar flares for the last two day cycles, but today had been the worst by far. He was monitoring and recording The Knight of Wands and Hexad Winberg as he simultaneously watched the approach of the bier ship from Eurydice on a holomonitor. The signal from the tracking satellite had a much stranger signal, but the eardot, especially so close to the window of the Orbital, was fritzing sporadically, cutting out half of what the Hexad was saying. And then, just after Hexad Winberg warned the Knight of Wands that he would be, "...finished, complete," what must have been the largest electromagnetic surge in the last three day cycles caused the bier ship to momentarily disappear from the holoscan and faded the Hexad's voice into nonexistence under a bevy of static.

The Eurydician vacuum suit was stifling. Not only did it seem bulky, but it covered most of Fenrir's skin. He could feel the perspiration building beneath it even as he pulled it on, and now the vapors that filled the space between his body and the suit immersed him in a colloidal mixture of his own excretions—an unwelcome sensation the Eos normally eliminated. Steeping in his own fluids was an unnerving thought, but so was not arriving on time. What made things even more unnerving is that he and Chandra of Swords were carrying more Valois Squibs than he had seen in all 165 gyres of his life. He recessed the assault rifle into the hermetic enclosure on the right sleeve of his suit and pushed his morbid cargo into the lift on the lev-gurney as the other four in his van, concealed in their own vac suits, followed in behind him. As the door closed behind them, and they took their positions on the four corners of the gurney, Fenrir could not help wondering when he would feel the warmth of the sun on his skin again.

It had taken two and a half hours to reach the Orbital, and the ride to the top had been unnerving. It was a special torture to see the sun this close yet still be unable to feel the deep caress of its rays. To Chandra, it seemed harder to breathe even though the suit had an air filter for hospitable atmospheric conditions and only switched to hermetic mode when those conditions became inhospitable. Even some conditions inhospitable to normal humans would afford a certain level of survivability to Apostates, and yet, it still felt as if the suit itself made the simple act of breathing a conscious chore.

When they had reached the half-way mark, Taewook of Cups's earwigged to them, "The Devil's in the house of the rising sun," which, however cryptic in original meaning, meant the fly-eyes in the lift had been spoofed and that it was time to set the Valois Squibs and the ubiquity charge that would set them all off simultaneously.

Chandra worked quickly with Fenrir, setting the Valois in the corners and roof of the lift as Aerik had instructed them. She seemed at ease, but these harmless looking silver devices made her uncomfortable—especially since she once saw an Echelon soldier's arm and a chunk of his torso vaporized by one that Six had caught and tossed back at him during the attack on Avalon. She had been a young girl then—only seventy-three gyres in life—but she remembered it as clearly as if it happened only a few moments ago. The event itself had saved her life and the lives of her father and mother, and yet the thing that stuck most in her mind was the quiet yet absolute destruction that had paved the ave of their escape. Even as she placed the Valois, she could not help thinking the same thought that crossed her mind on occasional sleep cycles. And even here, as the benevolent face of Set rose above the edge of the horizon, she saw herself, not the Echelon soldier, maimed beyond hope, body collapsing into a pile of its own bowels as blood spurted in a stream from a heart that lay exposed in the cavity created by the device she now held in her hand.

But the thought brought efficiency and focus to her placements and ensured she followed her training to the mark. She placed the last Squib and stood, almost ashamed of herself, as she hoped the destruction these devices brought would, for the rest of their gyres on Asha, leave a macabre image, in every lurid hue, etched in the minds of those who sought to destroy her and her clan so many gyres hence.

Cyrus watched on the holomonitor that appeared in the center of the meeting room as the crew of the bier ship and their cargo came to a comfortable stop inside the Orbital. Here, next to Winberg, Cyrus's heart began to whip itself into a mounting frenzy as the looming promise he had made only moments earlier began to solidify in his mind.

Torus Denali watched as Hexad Winberg and this trumped up dexter, the self-styled Knight of Wands, met the crew of the bier ship with their macabre cargo. Either these menacing Apostates had some semblance of honor, or this was a dupe. Either way, the vermin snare was set, and this time, Dr. Chamberlain, or the Knight of Wands, or whatever he wanted to call himself, was walking right into it. The bier floated to the center of the room and hovered as Chamberlain walked over to inspect the body. He leaned over the bier to open the bag near the head and lowered his face to get a clearer look.

That was when Denali ordered his men to spring the trap.

Cyrus leaned forward to inspect the contents of the body bag, trying to look as if he did not already know what was there. As soon as he leaned over, two doors that led to a hallway on either side of the chamber opened, and Denali's men flooded in from both sides. But not one of the eight men who flooded into the room expected Cyrus to stand up with a gun.

Pentangle Dezmon Djarre rushed into the room expecting an easy overwhelm and capture. The target was supposed to be surrounded, surprised, and weaponless, but when Dezmon rounded the corner behind the rest of his phalanx, he saw the mark was infact surrounded, but he was not surprised, and he was not weaponless. After that, the louvers allowing light from outside closed, and the lights of the hall all shut down, and for a moment, Djarre saw nothing at all.

In the second it took his goggles to adjust to darkvision, reality as Pentangle Djarre understood it was drastically altered. The corpse that had been delivered by the bier crew leaped from lev-gurney firing two automatic handguns. The corpse kicked the gurney, flipping it, and deftly looped his arms into the straps that had held the body bag. He turned to face the opposite hall using the gurney as a shield. Others in the phalanx had been quicker to fire their weapons, but Djarre saw that now, even they were being cut down by the bier crew itself. As one of the bier crew turned toward him, Djarre dove backward, and shells sparked off the floor around him. The filters that transferred sound into his helmet muffled the sound, but even the diminished noise of the hail of bullets was too much.

Without looking up, Djarre began crawling away from the maelstrom that tore into the floor behind him. He had dropped his gun in his dive, but there was one just in front of him. He turned to see the bier shielding the Knight of Wands and the animated corpse as they retreated to the opposite side of the hall, and the four members of the spurious bier crew back-pedaled into one of the lifts.

As Six retreated, using the gurney as a rucksack, he could feel the pull of it trying to right itself. Six angled behind Cyrus to shield him from the shower of projectiles. There was a strange whirring sound as the projectiles seemed to strike everywhere except the back of the gurney. Six fired in the direction he was moving, and two of the men who came in through that door went down. He could feel the wind from the projectiles that whizzed past him, apparently curved around the bier by the grav-drive that was still engaged. Cyrus fired the gun Six had given him and grabbed the officer next to him by the throat. He dragged the officer toward the men, using him as a shield. As they advanced, the men at the door hesitated, unwilling to take a shot at Cyrus and his hostage. Instead, the two men left standing moved into cover inside the hallway and focused their aim on Six.

Six was in the middle of his next step when he hopped and twisted in the air, allowing the gurney to pull him up and back as it righted itself parallel to the ground. The first of the barrage of projectiles slammed into the edge of the bier. Most of the rounds were pushed into the floor as the gurney turned and leveled off with Six on his back. The bier moved toward the doorway with Six on top headfirst. For a moment, his heart seemed to have forgotten to beat as he was sure the next barrage would find its mark in his flesh. But he had time to raise his hands above his head and look forward with the world turned upside down as he prepared to fire.

Cyrus had snatched Winberg by his neck with his left hand and was forcing him toward the gunfire, keeping him in the firing line between himself and the two men Six had not taken out. Out of the corner of his eye, Cyrus saw Six spin and fall as if he had been hit. Cyrus fired and caught one of the men in his arm, knocking him against the wall. Then, suddenly, Six was parallel to the floor, his back still against the bier, firing his guns toward the hallway as the bier carried him toward the entrance. Cyrus had distracted the men long enough for Six's volley to find their intended targets. The men fell, and Six fanned his arms at the edges of the doorway as the bier passed through it. There was a pop where the door controls should have been, and Cyrus knew what would happen next. Cyrus kicked Winberg in the back, and he fell into the sparking entranceway, arms flailing as the doors began closing. Cyrus turned on his own heels, firing his weapon to make sure anyone on the other side of the room kept his head down. Cyrus back-pedaled and barreled into Winberg, forcing him to the ground. Cyrus continued his suppression fire as he saw the last of the bier crew step into the lift, but one persistent solider in a pile of bodies managed to squeeze off a volley as the doors to the lift slammed shut.

Pentangle Djarre had steadied the assault rifle handle on the floor and the barrel on the shoulder of Pentangle Thames's bleeding body. Just as the bulkhead doors to the lift had closed, he had held the rifle as steady as he could with his off-hand, and he had squeezed the trigger, hoping the recoil would not send the gun back into his face.

As the doors to the lift closed, Fenrir stood in the opening and fired off a final volley of suppression fire. He turned to make sure Chandra and the others were okay, but before his head could turn back inside the visor, he found himself off-balance, and as he moved his legs to regain his footing, he found the ground was further away than he had expected. Sharp spikes of pain pierced through his lower ribs and back, and he almost forgot the vac-suits were made of Comptex. Then, as the side of the lift came to meet his head in this awkward position, the ability of his clothing to resist gunfire became irrelevant. His head snapped back as his shoulder collided with the wall. His body stopped abruptly, and he felt the entire universe tilt on one axis. It felt as if his entire consciousness kept moving even after his body stopped, and then, as his vision filled with a perfunctory gray fog, it didn't feel like anything at all.

Winberg slid across the ground on his chest, sheltering his face from the carpet. Spittle erupted from his mouth as he gasped for air. He was snatched to his knees by his collar. The firefight seemed to be less advantageous than Denali had planned, and all sorts of panicked chatter filled Winberg's earwig as Cyrus forced him down the hallway using him as a shield.

Once again, Dr. Chamberlain was full of surprises. Even being dragged along as a hostage, Winberg could not help but admire the man. He was brash and insubordinate, but he was cut from a much sterner ore than any of the men Winberg had come across in his short tenure in the Eurydician military. He wondered what was left in Dr. Chamberlain's bag of tricks as Cyrus ushered him around a corner to face another phalanx, and it became apparent Dr. Chamberlain was not the only member of this team with tricks.

The bald green man kicked the floating bier around the corner as soon as they rounded it. He then ran behind the bier toward the five closely packed men before they could spread out. Winberg was yanked to the side by his collar as two men fired, and Chamberlain ducked behind him. As they fired, the bald man dropped and slid beneath the bier as it moved into them. Their bullets trailed across the floor and ricocheted off the top of the bier and around the sides. The man sliding under the bier extended one arm and fired at the ankles of the two men, sweeping their legs from under them. Suddenly, the bier flipped upright, and the bald man hopped off his shoulders behind it. As he landed, he fired the guns in both his hands, but Denali's men were quick and dodged behind the flipping bier. The bald man fired at the flipping bier, and it sparked as the bullets tore into the top. He must have hit something vital because the bier landed on the two men who had fallen to the floor and a third who was sheltering himself from the impact. Then, as the bald man's guns clicked ineffectually, the two at the rear of the phalanx moved to either side of the pile. But the bald man was already running across the metal slab that now rested its full weight on the three men. He yelled, "Go! Now!"

Cyrus pushed Winberg along the wall by pressing the barrel of his gun into the back of his skull. Winberg saw the bald man dive from the bier and grab a man to his left by his collar. The bald man then stretched his body out and whipped his legs around to catch the other soldier in the face. He landed behind the man he had grabbed and brought his elbow forcefully down on the soldier's collarbone. Winberg was pushed even more forcefully from behind and could only make out the muzzle flashes as the bald man fired the gaffed soldiers assault rifle into the soldier who stumbled from under the bier.

Heinrick Euston had requested a transfer to the J.L. Orbital after the fiasco in the Eurydice Gamma base. He understood that the men they had been overwhelmed by were not even real espions. They were merely a group of scientists. Scientists. Not trained Earth soldiers.

They had been nothing more than a bunch of poindexters on a badly timed colonization mission. And they had somehow coordinated an attack with no obvious way of communicating, and with no weapons, had taken out two battalions in less than twenty minutes.

It was embarrassing. Especially since the dexter they called Milliken had separated Euston's shoulder and broken a bone in his forearm in the process. They had given him a medal for his supposed valor, and one for being injured in combat, but those medals had been so much of an insult to him that he had merely left them in his storage cubby to collect dust. His injuries had afforded him priority, though, when he requested to be reassigned to the J.L., which was the safest duty on Asha, and along with the transfer had come a promotion to Pentangle. However, one of the punty scientists that had somehow helped the Torus sort the whole mess out was promoted to Hexad, all the way to Hexad, just because he knew too much. The sunfried manpunter didn't even have any combat training.

...which was probably why he was being dragged down the hall by his neck. But Euston had his own problems. A bald, green madman was single-handedly carving up his crew. Even as Euston reeled from the awkward kick that caught him in his jaw and sent him stumbling, he saw Genly Washburn go down beneath the sparking and sputtering lev-gurney he was trying to climb from under. Euston caught himself with his right foot, regained his balance, and was faced with a decision— turn and help the pathetic, feist-hound of a Hexad, or take aim at the bald lunatic. Euston realized it was not much of a decision at all. He had only spent the last twenty-three Dhekads with the men of his phalanx, but even if he had spent twenty-three *gyres* with the Hexad, the Hexad would never truly be a part of his crew.

Euston lifted his gun as the Hexad was shuffled away. Anno Moony collapsed, his head twisted like a mistreated doll, and Euston looked up to see an auto-pistol, slide in the open, empty position, filling his field of vision. He felt his head snap back, and before his mind could fully register what had happened, he felt the back of his head smack hard against something as his consciousness seemed to leave his body on the wave of air that escaped his lungs.

Cyrus could see the Paracelsus through the window of the hallway. There was a jetway leading to it from the main body of the Orbital. Mooring spires held it against a backing plate, and it was aimed toward the planet as it had already been prepared for descent by the Ashans to be studied planetside. But he couldn't go now because there would be too many soldiers in the way, and he still had his promise to fulfill.

"I have good news and bad news," Jang's voice reported over the earwig. "The bad news is an Echelon ship is docking as we speak. The good news is there's a stellar access point ahead, two doors to your right."

Winberg made a good shield, but moving with him was slow as he was neither light nor agile. Cyrus forced him around another corner and saw the door Jang had mentioned. He ushered Winberg forward, keeping his collar twisted in his left hand so he could not scream for help. Perhaps if Cyrus loosened his grip and allowed him to breathe they would make better progress, but as Cyrus reached the second door, more footsteps than Cyrus could count came from down the hall. Cyrus stopped, keeping Winberg between himself and the hall as at least four men on each side formed a fan in front of him.

"Make another move, and your precious officer gets finished!" Cyrus yelled, cranking on Winberg's collar even more.

"You have three seconds, or we finish you both!" one of the men yelled back, which was not the response Cyrus was looking for.

And then gunfire came from elsewhere in the hall, putting at least three of the men on the ground. Cyrus fired off a volley of his own and yanked Winberg backward through the door that Jang offered to open through the earwig.

Cyrus fell and pushed himself clear of the opening, and he pulled Winberg down with him as gunfire rang out in every direction. The door was lit up in a cascade of sparks as it closed, and they both fell in a confused heap. Then, suddenly, Winberg was standing with newfound agility, his own sidearm rising to Cyrus's face as Cyrus stood and raised his weapon. For a moment they held each other in their sights as a concerto of gunfire and screams played in the hall. There were retreating footfalls and a banging on the door.

Finally, Cyrus spoke, "You don't have the heart."

"Perhaps not, but I do have the ambition, and shooting you will add another vertex to my badge." There was that smirk again, but his hand was shaky. He had probably never held a gun in his life unless it was to attach it to his belt, and that was probably only in the few month cycles since he had been adopted into this mockery of a military. Jang should have spoofed the fly-eyes in this room by now, but as Winberg spoke, Cyrus subvoced to leave them on for just a moment.

If you don't sell it, they won't buy it. That is what Winberg had told him after he had made his request. Standing here face-to-face with the man that he was gaining more respect for with each passing moment, Cyrus found it much harder to follow through with his promise.

And then, Winberg swung his gun into Cyrus's wrist and sidestepped. Cyrus fired off a round but missed as the butt of Winberg's gun buried into his wrist. Cyrus's hand went numb, and his pistol fell to the floor, but Cyrus did not let the shock get the best of him. Winberg had startled him, but before Winberg could raise his gun again, Cyrus moved his leg up in a crescent and kicked the back of Winberg's wrist. Winberg's gun flew against the wall, and he stumbled. Cyrus moved toward him, but he realized Winberg had not stumbled at all. Winberg turned, pulled a hold-out pistol from behind his back, made a full rotation, and then fired.

The gun went off, but Cyrus did not wait to see if he had been shot. He lunged, grabbing the gun, and as Winberg went to fire again, the trigger stopped against the safety catch that was engaged by Cyrus's finger. Cyrus brought his elbow across Winberg's face, spreading a splatter of blood from his right nostril to the left corner of his mouth. Cyrus snatched the gun from Winberg's hands as he fell back against the wall. The banging on the door increased, and Cyrus heard a cranking sound that meant the Archons were trying to manually open the door. Winberg slumped to the floor and Cyrus flipped the gun in his hand. He disengaged the safety, but as his vision adjusted, he saw Winberg, still slumped against the wall, with his original gun in his hand—and he was raising it.

Pentangle Thurgood Sturgess had pulled the trigger on the speed-driver to rotate the bolt that manually opened the door. Control in Eurydice was belting frantically in the earwig for him to get the door open, but he could not make the tool go any faster. The bald man wearing the strange green make-up of the Apostates had retreated back down the hall, drawing the full attention of an entire phalanx of men. Sturgess and two other Pentangles had been left to deal with the hostage situation. The door had only raised half a hand-length above the ground when the indiscernible screaming rising to a crescendo from Command was drowned out by a gunshot on the other side of the door. Pentangle Carlsbad dropped to the floor as another shot rang out. He yelled that he could not see anything even as the door continued to rise and the earwig chatter became scoffs of disbelief claiming the fly-eyes had failed. Then there were two more shots.

When the door was open high enough, Carlsbad scrambled inside and radioed that the Hexad was down. When Sturgess had finally crawled inside himself, he saw the strange Hexad from Earth slumped against the wall. The Hexad held a smoking gun limply in his hand, and his upper chest was covered in blood.

...but it didn't make any sense.

The only reason they had orders to shoot them both was the Hexad had been ordered to wear a dual layer Synthlar vest before even coming up to the Orbital. Synthlar was much heavier than Comptex, but neither the weapons on the Hexad's person nor that in the possession of his attacker could have penetrated it—and there was no way his attacker would have known that.

Then, Hexad Winberg lolled his mouth open, and it became obvious where the blood had come from as a rivulet of blood and a tooth oozed from his mouth and dribbled in a thick globule onto his chest, darkening the stain that had already begun to lighten as it seeped through the weave of his uniform. The Hexad feebly lifted his hand and pointed above his head. There was a panel there that led to a vent. It was set firmly in place, but there seemed, upon closer inspection, to be ruptures in the metal where the screws should have been.

"Disengage the laser grids," Cyrus subvoced, moving through the vent as quickly as he could.

"They are coming in behind you," Jang's voice reported over the earwig. The laser grid that impeded Cyrus's progress through the vent disappeared, and he was immersed in complete darkness. The lenses on his eyes adjusted, and as he moved forward, he realized that what had just happened bothered him more than he could have imagined.

They won't believe me unless you shoot me, Winberg told him inside the observation hall, *and if you don't sell it, they won't buy it*. Cyrus hadn't expected the pompous professor to put up such a fight, but for some reason, whatever comfort Winberg enjoyed in being in charge, even on this horribly mixed up wasteland of a planet, was impetus enough for him to put up a fight like an uberhound on the fritz. He made Cyrus shoot him, even when Cyrus had second thoughts about it. Cyrus tried to shake off the image of Winberg's body launched backward by two bullets to the chest at point-blank range. At that range, chunks of flesh should have flown from the wound, and exit wounds should have splattered the wall behind him as he lurched away with each shot—but they hadn't. He asked Cyrus to shoot him but didn't let Cyrus know he was wearing a vest. Even in an admirable gesture, he still left enough doubt in Cyrus's mind to make guilt an issue. But that was Winberg's gift, wasn't it? Manipulating people. It wasn't much different than the gift Cyrus himself seemed to have—only Cyrus did not use it for self-service. Or did he? At that very moment, he was scrambling through an airway like a vent-monkey, hurrying away from the echoes that pursued him—and for what? Was it really for the Apostates? Was it really to find out what link this place had to human history? Or did he only want to know what was happening on this miserable rock so he could, at least in his own mind, absolve his son of that monstrous deed? Was it all just so he himself did not have to feel like he had failed as a father?

The thought weighed heavily, but when Jang radioed he was reactivating the laser grids to trap Cyrus's pursuers, Cyrus realized that whatever guilt he had in shooting Winberg, and whatever self-serving notions might have brought him to this point, didn't matter because Jang, Paeryl, Tanner, and even Six believed in him. Darius believed in him. Villichez, although Cyrus realized it all too late, had believed in him. Men and women put their livelihoods on the line because somehow, to them, even to the notorious Dr. Windbag, the scourge of the Los Angeles Arcology, Cyrus represented a means to an end. And whatever those ends were, whether he felt he deserved the attention or not, he felt compelled, in defiance of his own shortcomings, to oblige them. Cyrus set the timed smoke charge that Aerik had given him and used the miniature speed-drive to grab the backsides of the bolts that held the vent cover in place. As the vent cover fell, Cyrus dropped into the hallway, which Jang assured him was empty.

Cyrus hoped that whatever ends Winberg sought, that he had helped facilitate them for no other reason than Winberg trusted him. And if his five-year-long enemy could trust him with his own life, what man or woman couldn't? The idea, as burdensome as it could have been, dispelled any guilt that could have settled in Cyrus's mind.

twenty-six

—How was school today Dari?

—It was kinda interesting today, Dada.

—Another side-track on astrophysics today?

—Nah, but it still made me think about you.

—Was it about grumpy old monsters that erase their kids' deckwork when they make more than three mistakes and get in trouble with their wives for treating their children like grown men?

—Ha. Nah Dada, nothing like that. Miss Hasabe talked about great leaders. You know, like George Washington, President Truman from World War Two, Martin Luther King, and that Alphonse Johnston guy from the Uni War. You know, a bunch of people that everybody loves. But then Sergio brought up guys like Napoleon, Hitler, and Stalin, then some guy named Yosef Purse he said was in the Near East Fringe War—a bunch of guys his dad told him about. He said they were mean guys, but they were good at beating other countries, and the people they ruled over loved them, and he said even though they did some bad stuff, good things came out of what they did.

—What did Miss Hasabe say?

—She seemed like she got kinda bent, then she just said those guys were all monsters and were not what she was talking about, and she just kept going, but Sergio wouldn't let it go. He said he was sure George Washington was a monster to the British, Truman in World War Two was a monster to the Japanese, and the Uni must have been monsters to the Fringers that wanted automousy.

—Autonomy.

—Yeah, that's it. Well, Miss Hasabe got so fritzed up she almost sent Sergio to the Disciplinarian. She said the Uni represented justice and safety, but what Sergio said made me think. I mean, you're like the leader of this family, and you care about justice and safety, but sometimes you seem like a monster to me, but then later I understand and get over it. But sometimes, I think even you might make mistakes. I'm not saying you aren't a good leader and Dada, but I guess even good leaders make mistakes sometimes. It's just that when you do, you can just apologize, cuz your mistakes don't make people dead.

—I think you do have a point there, Dari. You know what I think? I think the worst monsters we have to fight aren't people at all but misplaced ideas. Monsters that don't have bodies are the hardest to fight because even the best of us can help create them ourselves without even knowing it. Leaders like Martin Luther King, Jr. and Yosef Purse at the beginning of the Fringe War fight the hardest battles against oppression and human selfishness. But the problem is, sometimes it's hard for even the strongest of us to fight monsters. Hercules and Perseus were both half-gods, and I'm sure the Hydra and Medusa didn't think they were too stellar when they showed up in their houses to get rowdy. A man named Friedrich Nietzsche said, "He who fights monsters must see to it that he does not become a monster in the process. And when you stare long into the abyss, the abyss stares back into you." I think Nietzsche had it wrong though. I don't think you can truly fight evil unless evil itself sees you as such. If those you see as evil can abide by you in any way, then why should they listen to you? Your true enemies should hate you—even if you don't hate them. And sometimes that makes you look like a monster.

—What about the abyss part? The abyss is like Hell, right?

—Worse than Hell. The abyss is nothing. Oblivion. Complete separation from everything. If you focus on that which would devour your very soul, it will tell you something about yourself, and sometimes, you may not want to hear it.

—So maybe the heroes in history are the ones we agree with, and the monsters are the ones we don't because you can't really be those guys without being a little monstrous. And the only thing that can tell us is our own soul.

—And unfortunately, whether it's deckwork getting erased or people losing their lives, when the abyss stares you in the face and checks the level of your keel, the only comfort you will have is whether or not, at the end of the day, you can leave your monstrosity in the abyss where it belongs.

• • • • •

When his pupils finally expanded enough to allow in light, it felt as if the light would laser-cut two holes in the back of Euston's head. It was as if his entire head had been put in a pincer lock while he was unconscious—and the alarms did not help. Moony, Capshaw, and Scalia lay before him. Capshaw was moaning, but the others seemed completely insensate. Euston stood and steadied himself against the wall to let his body adjust. He felt the stiffness in his elbows and knees washed away with impulse. This had happened one too many sunfried times, and he would be damned to the wastes if he let that houndspawn get away with it again.

Most of the soldiers here with the same vertices only knew the

306

Knight of Wands as another wastebaked leader of the Apostates, who claimed, impossibly, to be the father of the Sword Scourge. But Euston knew how he had gotten to Asha, and if this man had organized an ill-laid escape from a military installation, albeit lower vertex security, without even talking to most of the punting headgamers in his crew, then it would be a safe assumption that he didn't select the Orbital as a meeting place for the beautiful starscape. Euston knew where he had come from, and given the fact that his ship had completed launch preparation this very day cycle, he knew where he was most likely going.

Uzziah moved in closer to the black vehicle Jang had placed on their course marker. The holographic imagers showed it closer than it looked in the shrouding darkness of the Miasma. Without warning, a light flashed on the ship they were following, and a yellowing flame danced around the back of the ship and briefly lit up the craft to reveal the large gun that was firing at them. Bluish and orange sparks played across the windshield of their lev in sync with the flickering muzzle flash on the enemy craft. The astrapi shield that surrounded them caused any material below a certain mass and beyond a certain velocity to disintegrate before impact and kept the gunfire from penetrating the stolen Echelon craft.

Two more fighters appeared on the imager, closing in from the opposite side of the craft they were pursuing. According to Jang, those two crafts, piloted by Apostates, were visible on their imagers but invisible to the Echelon. It was an unorthodox approach, but it would maybe buy them enough time for their plan to work. No doubt, the Echelon ship had already sent word that it was under attack, and it needed to be taken out before more fighters could scramble. The two ships rolled and spread out in the imager as the gunfire buffeted the shield and Uzziah continued to close the distance.

When the Ace of Wands, who was piloting one of the fighters, gave the signal, Uzziah activated what Jang called his special sauce—a modification that was achieved by removing the heat limiter on the thrusters. This allowed them to achieve a massive burst of speed for a brief moment. It was only good for about three uses, as it irrevocably damaged the thrusters themselves, but as it launched Uzziah up and over the speeding Echelon craft, he hoped he would not need it a second time.

Mottled and sweat dripping from the ends, Cyrus could not keep his hair off his brow and hold the Agamemnon unit at the same time. By this point, it seemed his nerves could not be rattled any more, and yet he could not shake the feeling that the luck he had experienced up until now had been used up. He stood in the main hall of the Paracelsus contemplating his next move. What the Agamemnon unit lacked in volume it made up for in density, and it was pulling his arm into the floor. Cyrus was tempted to radio Jang to lower the gravity settings on the ship, but that would have been too complicated a process just to appease laziness. Besides, the sooner he got out of here, the sooner he could set this thing down.

But he couldn't leave. Tanner hadn't had his z-axis properly set since they found the underground city. Just getting this unit back to the Xerxes and retrieving the Ark would not guarantee Tanner's mindset would improve. Cyrus knew parts of Tanner's past were sordid, and that his faith kept him from degeneration into whatever dark reaches his soul had passed through. Tanner was a grown man, and was responsible for his own sanity, but Tanner was the dearest friend he had left, and if his dear friend's grip on sanity was not strong enough to stand fast without help, what good would all the information on Asha or Earth do for Cyrus? He could not stand to lose another person close to him.

So he set the Agamemnon unit down in the hallway and headed toward the living quarters. If Tanner's Bible was the hoist that had pulled him from the troubled depths of his soul before, perhaps it could provide the same ballast on this barren rock.

"We can't blow the charges until you get back to the ship," Jang's voice was calm, but was of little help. He must have noticed Cyrus's locator moving in the wrong direction.

"I don't think I'm coming back to the rendezvous point," Cyrus said, moving into a run.

"Just to let you know, the Echelon is going to be beating at the jetwalk any minute now. That bulkhead isn't going to hold them much longer."

"What the hell am I doing?"

"I don't know, and now I'm a little worried because I was hoping you could tell me," Jang's reply startled Cyrus as he was not aware that he had said it aloud. It had probably been under his breath, but the nerve signals had been enough to send the subvocal communication across the network.

"Just leave without me," Cyrus added, speeding around the corner to Tanner's room.

"And exactly how do you plan to get planetside?"

"I'll take this thing."

"Not sure exactly what you mean by that, but it doesn't sound like a good idea."

"What about this entire idea has been good?"

The Echelon fighter that Six had acquired had proven indispensable. Jang, Doree, and Aerik had been able to recalibrate the electromagnetic countermeasures to interfere with the frequencies of the astrapi shield so that, with precision flying, a burst from two fighters on either side of the craft would render the shield sporadic for ten seconds—enough time for an auto-cannon at point-blank range to turn the nose of the craft into a sieve.

As Toutopolus fired the auto-cannon, the composite windshield of the craft shattered in tiny rivulets, and the Echelon fighter dipped violently. The nose of the craft dug into the ground and bounced, and one of the men fell through the windshield, but he was caught by someone inside. Toutopolus fired another burst of auto-cannon fire into the front of the ship as it slowed to recover, but only sporadic bullets hit the craft as the partially restored shield flickered randomly in and out. The earwigs Toutopolus had in each ear were synced to the cannon, allowing them to cancel the overbearing report of the mounted gun, but it was still difficult to hear. Milliken tapped Toutopolus on the shoulder and then, when he continued firing, shook his shoulders vigorously to get his attention.

Toutopolus stopped, and Milliken subvoced through the earwig, "Stop this ship. Now!" The command, filtered by the earwig network, was calm, but Milliken's face was not.

Toutopolus had no idea why Milliken had asked Uzziah to stop the ship. As the fighter behind careened toward them, Toutopolus saw the Echelon soldier inside rear his arm back to throw the silver egg, and it made even less sense. And then, the most confusing thing of all happened—just before the nose of the Echelon fighter smashed into the flatdeck of their own craft, Milliken took a running leap through the windshield firing his weapon and screaming as if he had lost whatever tenuous link to reality that remained.

When Milliken leaped through the windshield of the craft, he expected to be knocked right back onto the flatdeck. The other half of him expected to be dead by the time he landed. Both halves agreed, however, that this was the single stupidest thing he had done to date, but he couldn't just sit there and wait to be disintegrated. He squeezed the trigger of the assault rifle as he cleared the broken, tooth-like shards of windshield. The muzzle flash caused some of the obscured figures inside to recoil, but the one rearing back to throw the silver egg fell in their midst as tiny, dim sparks danced across his chest.

Milliken landed on his butt on the console of the ship and slid knee-first into the face of the pilot. The pilot slumped over the controls, raising the nose of the ship behind Milliken, which dumped him deeper into the craft as the figures inside surrounded him. He continued to fire the assault rifle into the mass of men, but something was odd. Even though at this range there was a high chance the bullets would penetrate the Comptex or, at the least, cause serious internal damage, Milliken's presence did not seem to gain the undivided attention he expected.

And then he realized what had their attention—the armed and now lost Squib.

In his moment of hesitation, someone smacked the rifle from his hand. Milliken stepped into a defensive stance, but the ominous reality of the position in which he had placed himself became lucid. He was standing in the midst of trained killers, whom he had just single-handedly put in mortal danger. And he was alone. But he would be damned to the lowest coward's cage in hell if he would let any one of these men, killers or not, take him without him taking some of them with him.

Jang watched as the 'C' blip stopped in a room in the living quarters of the Paracelsus. He moved his eyes down to the corner of the holomonitor where the eight other miscellaneous blips hovered around the bulkhead blocking the hall leading from the airlock to the jetway. They had been there for an uncomfortably long time, and pretty soon Cyrus's path of egress would be swarming with them. He saw the 'S' next to his own compartment on the screen, but his heart still jumped into his throat when something banged against the compartment door.

"We're running out of daylight!" Six's muffled voice was loud enough to penetrate the wall of the compartment as it echoed in the earwig.

"Cyrus went back for something. He said we should leave him," Jang was still subvocalizing, even though at this point it was not necessary.

"We're not leaving without him! If we're going to ride your Earth ship down, we had better get moving."

"I hate to add chatter, but it takes three *trained* pilots to land that ship, and it takes five minutes to power up the re-entry systems," Uzziah's voice interjected from the network.

Jang set the self-destruct sequence on the explosives Fenrir and Aerik had set up inside the compartment, typed a sequence into his datadeck, and pressed the button that opened the panel. Six was pulling him out of the compartment as soon as the door slid open.

"Old boy is going to get us killed," Six said as Jang landed on his feet.

"Luckily he has as much of a knack for getting out of these situations as he has getting into them."

When they rounded the corner, they could see the glow from the laser-bit as it completed a ragged square in the bulkhead. Inside the jetway, they heard the loud thump of the excised piece of bulkhead hitting the ground. Six stopped and turned to face the men pursuing them, but Jang grabbed him by his collar. "There's a better way," Jang said. "Voice Command:" he reported through the microphone, not bothering to subvocalize. "Drop bulkhead BF-49."

As he and Six cleared the opposite side of the jetway he belted, "Confirmed," his calm disturbed by the echoing footfalls of the Echelon. There was a metal slam behind them as the pressure change seemed to give them a push forward.

"We need to get to the command center," Jang subvocalized. "Cyrus, I hope you have something magnificent planned to get us out of this debacle," the system added involuntarily.

Cyrus rounded the corner empty-handed. It was not fully articulated, but after the Echelon broke through the initial bulkhead, and Six and Jang moved to the bridge, there was now only one way out of this—which meant Tanner's Bible could stay in his room for now. Jang's last words rang through Cyrus's head as bile rose into his throat. He was endangering people on a whim, and it sent cold stilettos through his veins.

And then, something, magnificent or not, did come to him. "Jang, are you tapped into the Paracelsus base system?"

"We need the Agamemnon to cross reference the functions, and I'm already reconnecting it through comm-sat, but I'm gonna need no less than four to five minutes to drop this thing without burning up."

"Don't worry. I'll buy us the time. When you get it back online, I need you to do three things: close all the external vents from the waste processing center except the one that leads into the jetway, then, get yourself and Six bolted in, and when I give you the word, cut the gravity."

"Okay, so what are you planning to do in the meantime?"

Cyrus arrived at his room just as Jang's words came over the earwig, and he found his staff leaning against the wall exactly where he had left it. "I'm going to be a good host and meet the Echelon at the door."

Toutopolus, without bothering to subvoc, screamed, "We have a problem back here!" as the Echelon fighter recoiled from the collision and rose into the air. Toutopolus craned his neck, debating whether or not to fire at the Echelon fighter with Milliken in it.

And then his question was answered for him.

A tiny glint, like a new point of starlight in the Miasmic sky, streaked over the edge of the black craft and fell toward him. Instantly he knew what it was, and he didn't need to see the bluish aster, as the egg moved slow enough to penetrate the electromagnetic membrane that protected the ship, to dive from the seat of the auto-cannon.

Toutopolus hit the flatdeck hard, and when he looked up, he saw the auto-cannon cut clean through to the bottom section where the ammo belt fed into the gun. Part of the gyroscopic base was gone as well as the seat—the fucking seat he had been sitting in. The rest was disintegrated, cleanly wiped from reality itself, just as the top half of his own body would have been if he had not looked up at the moment he did.

And the idea alone, knowing he did not want empirical knowledge of whether or not having his molecules turned to radiation would hurt, seemed to lift him from the flatdeck by itself. He stood, removed his sidearm from his belt, and with clear, calm inflection, subvoced Uzziah to take him up to the Echelon fighter.

Milliken dove for the soldier that kicked the Squib out of the windshield, dipping his shoulder as he smashed him into a weapon rack. The ship was still climbing slowly, but the incline caused Milliken to slide away as his footing faltered. An unseen kick missed Milliken and hit the soldier he had tackled, crumpling him. Milliken steadied himself against a bar on the wall, but it came loose, and he realized it was a weapon. He took another step back and planted his butt against the wall to regain his balance, but his legs were clipped from under him. His butt slid down the wall, and his tailbone hit the floor, sending a shock down from glutes to his toes.

Something hit him in his chest, sending mucous from his nostrils as the air in his lungs evacuated. Then, in a flicker of light, he saw something moving toward his face that could have only been someone's boot. And as he moved his head, he realized he still had the gun in his hand. It felt like a shotgun because his hand was on the pump. As the kick missed his head and slammed against the wall, Milliken cocked the shotgun. He brought the butt of the gun into the back of the kicker's knee, and then brought the barrel across to the inside of his other knee. The man collapsed over Milliken as something hit Milliken's left temple. Milliken still managed to catch the falling man's crotch with the muzzle of the shotgun and pull the trigger, not bothering to shelter himself from the inevitable spray.

Yet there wasn't any. There was only the loud peal of thunder as the darkness in front of him receding into an array of flickering orange lights. Something hit him hard, and his own body was bounced off the wall behind him as if he was shot himself. He felt knees and shins collide against him as his body rolled across the floor of the fighter.

When he finally stopped rolling, he was in a pile of writhing bodies, and he was unarmed. He felt his brain rolling around in his head, but the darkness and instability of the room itself made his own vertigo seem more stable. He spun his legs beneath him, crossed and extended them, but as he stood, he was caught in the chest with another kick. This time, thicker fluid than mucous erupted from his nose, and a metallic twinge filled his nostrils. He stumbled backward up the incline toward the front of the still climbing fighter. The wind buffeted his back as he steadied himself, and despite the howling of the air rushing in through the destroyed windshield, he heard the pilot moan. The soldier in front of him emerged from the darkness into the soft blue glow of the holomonitor. The man was drawing a dull-colored knife from his belt as he moved over someone on the ground. Milliken lifted his leg and thrust it backward into the pilot's seat, knocking the pilot's dazed body forward. The pilot's weight was more than Milliken had anticipated, and it knocked him off balance, but as the pilot flopped across the controls, the ship dipped back toward the planet, and the soldier with the knife stumbled toward Milliken. Milliken launched himself forward and drove his forearm into the man's face, snapping the man's head back violently and dropping him.

But another kick came out of the darkness and hit Milliken in his stomach, knocking him to the side across the controls. The ship dipped a little more, but Milliken caught himself against the wall with his foot and launched his body at the man who kicked him.

But the man was fast and ducked under Milliken's punch, parried his elbow, and then twisted Milliken into a choke hold. Milliken managed to slide his left hand between the man's forearm and his own throat, but he could not stop the man from securing his grip. Milliken flailed his legs and hit the pilot in the face. The pilot's body collapsed to the floor, and the ship tilted back in the opposite direction. Milliken saw the stars outside eclipsed by another black blob, but he couldn't tell if it was the other fighter, a building, or the ground—and then the man yanked him around. Milliken felt for something vital around the man's waist to grab but only found round, cold metal. He grabbed it, but it loosed from the man's body and provided no leverage.

Another figure emerged from the darkness with a knife screaming something about painting the floor with bowels, but Milliken's head was pounding, and the sound of "We're coming!" across the earwig overwhelmed his hearing. The man trying to choke him leaned to pull Milliken off his feet, but Milliken bent his legs and dropped his weight. When the man steadied himself to yank again, Milliken planted his feet beneath a body on the floor and allowed himself to fall. An arm or a leg must have tripped the man choking him because they both fell forward, barreling toward the man with the knife as Milliken let out a fury-filled scream. The man with the knife lifted it and lunged, catching Milliken across his hipbone. The pain sent cracks of agony through Milliken's body, but it abated his scream.

Milliken's battle cry was not an emotive reaction, however, but a calculated and acute distraction used to conceal the activation beeps of the Valois Squib in his hand. And though the pain and warmth from the stab wound and the man gaining leverage and tightening his hold behind him were both disillusioning, the fact that the man who had stabbed him now had an active explosive device magnetically stuck to his gun gave Milliken the poise he needed to lift both his legs, fold his knees to his chest, and kick out with all the strength left in his body. The man, evidently unaware of the Squib in his belt, tried to resist, but when Milliken connected, the strength in his legs, after months of training in Earth's gravity, sent the man reeling backward into the wall.

Milliken lifted his arm to shelter himself from the bright flash as the ear-splitting whine pierced the air in the room. He felt the man behind him press into his body as they hit the wall. His grip loosened, but as Milliken tried to step away toward two more men emerging from the flickering shadows, the wound in his hip protested, and he found himself stumbling into a stronger chokehold, without his hand to protect his neck.

Septangle Fennon Thurber was about to reactivate the laser-bit when the bulkhead began to slide upward on its own. He placed the bit on his belt, raised his sidearm, and took a low defensive stance. Halber and Ori dropped to the ground on either side of him to cover the jetway from beneath the rising bulkhead.

As the bulkhead rose, it revealed an empty jetway. The visor on Fennon's mask revealed a pathway that seemed innocuous other than a strangely low oxygen count. Octad Dunhill moved forward, observed the jetway, and then pointed to five of the seven men under his charge. With two fingers, he waved them forward to the airlock door on the opposite side of the jetway.

They made their way across the floor until a metallic thud shook the entire jetway. They turned and saw the bulkhead shut behind them, separating them from the Octad and two others as chatter began spreading over their earwigs. Gherig carried the other laser-bit, and in only a matter of minutes, they could cut through the bulkhead. But as the airlock door before them slid open, Fennon wondered if they may actually have the minutes they needed. He took two forced breaths to trump himself up and barked through his microphone, "Sharpen your elbows!" as they all focused on the rising bulkhead that slowly revealed a solitary man wearing a gas mask and holding a wooden staff. Even through the mask, they could see it was the Knight of Wands—the man that had roused so much trouble that he had flushed them out of hiding.

"Set down your weapon!" Fennon yelled, his mask amplifying his words through speakers mounted on it.

"Come and take it from me," the man said, holding out his staff.

They all raised their guns, training a bead on this man who was either completely off his day-counter, or knew something they did not.

"We will count to five, and then will we open fire," Fennon bellowed through his speakers.

"Might I suggest..." the man began saying, but Fennon interrupted him with a resounding, "One!"

"...that while you count to five..."

"Two!"

"...you check your methane reading."

This man's calm in the face of their phalanx was unnerving. They were protected with Comptex battle suits, lightweight, bulletproof, and certified against chemical and biological agents as well as radiation. As far as they knew, there were at least two malfies inside the ship but no more than four or five. What could he possibly think could save him? So Fennon subvocalized the command to switch his mask to atmospheric analysis so he could at least see what the father of the Sword Scourge had in his medicine bag.

And then he saw; the methane count in the air was well beyond safe levels. Fennon expected the Knight of Wands to give them some sort of demands, or to tell them to stand down as he retreated into the ship, but he didn't. He merely took an emphatic step forward and dropped into a fighting stance as the airlock door closed behind him.

Ori's grip tightened around his weapon. "Punt five, I'm going to burn him rightforth!"

"No!" Fennon yelled, dropping his own gun in an exaggerated motion as he tried to secretly slide his left hand behind his back. "If we cast slugs in here, it might blow. That's what he's gambling on."

"You going to stand here in the poot gas all day, old man?" Fennon asked, slowly moving his hand further behind his back.

"No. I only need three...more...minutes." The gas mask shifted on his face as his eyes squinted behind the visor, and Fennon was sure he was smiling at them. Fennon drew the hold-out knife from behind his back and took a step forward, but the jetway shook beneath them, and the stars outside the window jiggled as if the entire universe was being rattled. And then the Knight of Wands, that deranged lunatic, rushed toward the five of them with no visible weapon except a wooden staff.

As Cyrus's feet moved him toward the five armed guards, he could not help wondering how his life had gone so wrong that this seemed like a good idea. But the charges set in the space elevator detached three of the tether cables, and the centripetal force of the planet itself sent the J.L. Orbital wrenching against the remaining cable. As the cable caught, a wave rolled through the jetway floor and seemed to propel Cyrus forward. The guard who was the leader of the black-clad, bug-eyed men drew a combat knife from his back—most likely some kind of resonating blade. Cyrus slid the staff up through his left hand and swung the left end of it forward. Even in their Comptex suits, these men were fast—just as Cyrus had expected. The jetway lurched beneath him as the man to Cyrus's left caught the staff.

Cyrus planted his feet and threw his legs forward as the leader brought his knife around, aiming at Cyrus's ribs. "Invert the G-drive now!" Cyrus subvoced.

The man who grabbed the staff wrenched at it, but it was too late. The gravity waves around them flatlined, and the kinetic energy that Cyrus had built before the inversion sent his legs into the man with the knife and the man next to him with concussive force. Something scraped against one of his ribs, and as Cyrus extended his legs, he saw the knife that had cut him spin across the jetway trailing hovering droplets of blood. The two men flew backward, bowled into the man directly behind them, and knocked another off balance. The man who grabbed the staff had stiffened his body to pull at the staff, and now, thanks to his own tension, was rising off the ground. Cyrus held on to the staff with his left hand, planted his right hand on the edge of the jetway, and let the slight resistance from his kick send him back toward the wall like a feather. As the man tried to reorient himself, Cyrus pushed off the wall and brought his legs toward his chest. The man tried to block, and Cyrus forced the staff into his visor. His head snapped back, and as Cyrus's feet connected with his arms, he spun into a flip.

The largest lurch yet rocked the jetway. Cyrus pulled his feet underneath him and used the momentum of the wavering jetway to launch himself at the soldier who had been twisted. The soldier was pulling his feet to the floor as he activated magnetic clamps on his boots.

Cyrus pulled the staff back into his right hand and snapped it around as the man's rubberized boots stuck to the jetway. The man lifted his knife to advance on Cyrus, but must not have expected Cyrus or Cyrus's staff to be right in his face. Cyrus brought the staff across the man's throat, twisted his own body over the staff as it stopped on the man's neck, and pulled against it as if he were trying to stop himself using the man's chin for leverage. The motion stripped the man's mask from his face, and as Cyrus's momentum slowed, he twisted again in the air, carrying the man's mask with him. Cyrus flung it from the end of the staff at a man next to the bulkhead who was trying to activate his boots.

There was a wet heat building in Cyrus's midsection now, but he had to keep going. Cyrus moved his feet to the ground and bounded again. The Orbital must have broken loose from its tethers because the lurching had stopped completely. He stretched out and reared the staff back to swing again, but he stopped abruptly. The man whose mask he had snatched off was holding his ankle. The man gagged as the thickening methane assaulted his lungs, but using his magnetic boots as an anchor, he yanked Cyrus's ankle back.

Cyrus twisted the staff as the man swung him, and he planted the staff against the wall as he smashed into it side-first. The staff slowed the collision, but his shoulder, even though the Eos had healed it, took a wallop.

Cyrus leaned against the wall and threw his free foot at the unmasked man. The man dodged, but Cyrus brought the end of the staff back into the man's knuckle. He wailed as his hand released Cyrus's ankle, and Cyrus quickly pulled his knees to his chest and placed his legs between his body and the wall. The three men against the bulkhead had activated their clamps, and there was a bluish line of fiery light from the laser-bit spreading from the floor on the bulkhead behind him. Cyrus was running out of ave, and three minutes was a lot longer than he had anticipated.

He launched himself toward the three as they reached for weapons. The two on either side of the leader drew knives, but the leader, who dropped his knife, reached for something else. Cyrus held the staff out with both hands, hoping one of them would grab the end of it, but they would not fall for the same trick twice. The two men stepped to either side, their magnetic clamps mechanically activating and deactivating with the natural motion of their ankles. The leader turned as he moved, pulling a strange shotgun from behind his back as Cyrus collided with the bulkhead.

Something slashed across his back, sending a bolt of pain through his entire left side, but Cyrus kept moving. He drove the staff downward across the switch on the man's boot to his right and quickly snapped the staff up under the man's chin. The boots disengaged, and the man flipped as Cyrus heard a familiar, yet hard to place, whine. The gas that filled the room, invisible before now, swirled and caused the lights in front of his face to bloat and tweak.

The Spellcaster. Its nickname made complete sense now as the whine began to rise in pitch. But Cyrus knew if he let his fear of the weapon get the best of him, it would all be over. There was only one way back home, and it did not include that gun pointed at his head. Plus, if what Aerik said was accurate, at this range, it would hurt both of them just as much.

So Cyrus took his chances, brought his elbow up beneath the barrel of the gun, and as the leader resisted, he used the leverage to bring his foot down across the side of the leader's boot, deactivating the magnet. Cyrus pushed against the bulkhead with his other foot and dropped his staff. Cyrus simultaneously reached for the leader's gun hand with his right, while grabbing a strap on another man's shoulder with his left. Cyrus's palm hit the leader's hand and he squeezed. There was a low oscillating whirr and then a sudden thump that expanded the air and spun Cyrus like a turbine blade. There was a snap, like a plant being snatched up by its roots, and the jetway spun around him like a malfunctioning hologram. Cyrus's legs collided with something with enough force to send a shockwave of pain up to the base of his skull. Cyrus had to focus to hold back the spasms in his esophagus as bile filled his throat. His head pounded, and when his vision cleared, he saw the man to his left slumped awkwardly against the wall of the jetway, feet still pinned to the floor, and another man vomiting blood in the corner as he clutched at his chest. Cyrus now held the Spellcaster in his own hand and was holding a floating slug thrower by a strap that had globules of blood floating behind it.

"We are set to go," resounded over the ringing in his ears as Cyrus regained his equilibrium and looked to see who was left. Cyrus turned slowly and saw the unmasked man gagging in the thickening methane, but there were at least two men still active on the jetway.

Cyrus pulled the slide back on the Spellcaster, and he heard a muffled thump, but before the gun began to whine he was blindsided. The leader had reactivated his boots, and Cyrus didn't seen him until his own body twisted and smashed into the bulkhead. The metal of the bulkhead felt like it caved in slightly, and for a moment, Cyrus thought he imagined it. He then realized the fissure in the door was nearly complete and had caved in under the force.

The leader had somehow retrieved his knife, and the other man brandished his pistol like a cudgel, and they both advanced on Cyrus from either flank. The burning on both sides of his body, despite the chill in the jetway, made clear what would happen if he spent any more time there. He was sure he had been stabbed, and even if he made it out of this passage, he might not make it back planetside. But he was damned if he was going to lay down arms here for these Fringe monkeys. Cyrus grit his teeth, and as he heard the crescendo of the Spellcaster, and he felt the vibrations in his hand, he turned his back to the two advancing men and told Jang to open the airlock.

Jang and Six could not believe the macabre scene playing before them on the holomonitor. Cyrus's instincts in zero-G were good, but they were no match for these trained men with mag-clamps. He fought valiantly, never failing to catch his opponents off-guard, but they had hurt Cyrus almost as much as he had hurt them, and now, there were two of them left, and three more about to break through the bulkhead. And it didn't help that Cyrus's blood was trailing around the hall like Uni Day streamers. Worse yet, Cyrus was on the wrong side of the jetway.

When Cyrus sent the order to open the airlock, Jang didn't know what to think. There was no way Cyrus could get to the door in time enough to stop the Echelon, and even if he could, if they set that laser-bit on the airlock door, they could forget about using the Paracelsus as anything except a glorified mausoleum.

But as much as he feared the outcome, Jang gave the command to open the door anyway, and when he did, he was even more shocked when he realized what was coming. "On my mark, fire the boosters," Jang said to Six calmly, an awkward delivery given his facial expression.

With his back to the men advancing on him, Cyrus raised the automatic pistol in his right hand and the Spellcaster in his left. Then, he tucked his knees to his chest and fired the Spellcaster against the bulkhead.

The loud clap should have been deafening, but he heard the airlock open as he flew straight back like he was launched from a slug cannon. Cyrus smashed into the leader, knocking him backward and spinning him off his mag-clamps. Cyrus's right elbow collided with the mask of the other soldier as he passed, and then his right hand was firing wildly, sending bullets tearing through the thick gas in the jetway. Several of the rounds hit the bulkhead, sparking and igniting the noxious air in the jetway as the flash from the muzzle simultaneously ignited the air around him.

"Now!" Jang yelled as he pressed the button to close the airlock. In the time it took for the word to travel from his mouth to Six's ear, they watched on the holomonitor as Cyrus flew through the threshold of the ship with a ball of flame washing mercilessly from the conflagrated jetway after him. And then it billowed around him, filling the airlock chamber.

Jang fought back the swelling behind his eyes as he watched the flames engulf Cyrus. The airlock door slammed shut, the Paracelsus tore away from its mooring, and the J.L. Orbital spun away from them into a deeper orbit, emptying the bodies from the jetway into atmosphere too thin for them to survive.

Watching all this in the holographic imager, Jang barely noticed the flames in the holomonitor twisting and spinning in a turbulent but awkward swirl as they funneled into the gun between Cyrus's hands.

When Six got to him, Cyrus was still shivering on the floor in a swelling pool of his own blood. Both hands were locked around the Spellcaster and covered in a sheath of ice crystals. The gun was also covered in flakes of ice and was still whining its aria. Six checked Cyrus frantically. The ends of his hair were singed, and the tips of his beard hairs had been grayed, but there were no signs of burns on his skin. "Are you okay?" Six asked without subvocalizing. There was no sound at first, and it worried him, but then there was a slight crackle over the whining of the Spellcaster as Cyrus's thumb stood erect from the encasement of ice.

"I'm full of joy," came over the network in Cyrus's voice, obviously manufactured by the computer, "but I'll be better when you get my black and green ass home."

When the flatdeck moved up to the front of the Echelon lev, Toutopolus felt as if the floor dropped from beneath him. Milliken looked dazed but had snapped to full awareness as a figure drove a knife into his gut. He kicked the man with the knife away from him, and there was a blinding flash. That was when Toutopolus shielded his face and jumped through the windshield of the craft. He stumbled across the console, and across something that felt like a body, and when his pupils finally dilated, he found himself next to a man holding Milliken in a chokehold. The man's own eyes must have been still adjusting to the flash, because as Toutopolus raised his gun to the man's head, the man seemed to pay him no mind. The interior of the ship was dark, and even the flashing orange of the emergency lighting was flickering to a halt, but Toutopolus could still make out the shape of the man's head as he fired.

Before he could turn to fire at the other figures, someone grabbed his gun arm and twisted it. Toutopolus heard a resounding snap, like someone throwing a towel against the wall, and as a blistering cold shot from his elbow to his shoulder, he found himself yanked toward the gaping hole that was excised from the side of the fighter by the Valois. He leaned away from his unseen attacker's grasp to yank his arm loose, but the pressure in his arm, as the man countered and pressed against the inside of his shoulder blade, sent a wave of pain through his body that weakened every muscle he was aware of. As Toutopolous's momentum carried him toward the hole in the wall, he wondered, even amidst the pain that made consciousness seem like background noise, what falling from so high would feel like. Then something stubborn caught underfoot, and Toutopolus saw the stars of the night sky spreading out before him. The Miasmic air entering through the hole felt much colder than the air he had left on the flatdeck.

Milliken found himself on the floor in the twitching grasp of a body in the last of its death throes. The back of his own head was covered in muck he did not want to contemplate, and something rocklike, probably the knee of a spasmodic leg, fluttered painfully against the small of his back. And then, as his vision adjusted to the slowing of the metronomic orange light, Milliken heard a pop that sounded like someone opening a champagne bottle in another room.

But there was no other room. And as he saw Toutopolus's body, his arm bent in a place it should not have bent, hurled toward the opening that had been left by the Valois blast, he pushed himself off the twitching body beneath him and extended both legs into the outside of the knee of the soldier hurling Toutopolus toward the hole. There was another snap, like the final snap just before timber collapsed under its own weight, and the man did just the same as the timber, slowly collapsing on his own knee, which was now folded in the wrong direction. As the man tumbled over, Milliken found a knife beneath him, and as the man hit the floor, Milliken brought the knife down onto his torso, digging through Comptex and breastbone alike. A fount of blood issued from the man's writhing body and subsided as his lung collapsed. Milliken stood, snatching the knife from the man's body, but Toutopolus, who must have been dizzy and shaken by the damage to his arm, stumbled out of the hole on his own accord.

Uzziah had managed to keep the craft level with the front end of the damaged fighter resting on the back of it, but the other fighter was losing power rapidly, and Uzziah could not hold both of them steady for long. Aerik moved quickly toward the flatdeck as he saw Stavros of Five stumble out of a hole in the side of the fighter and Paulice of Swords catch him by his ankle. "Devil's in the house of the rising sun," filled his earwig, which meant two things; the Knight of Swords's computer had secured the codes for the docking doors that led beneath the pyramid. It also meant that scrambled Echelon fighters, which had made it possible for Taewook to steal the codes, had used those codes to open the doors and were now speeding toward them.

And then, as Paulice pulled Stavros's limp body back into the craft, one of the figures rose up into a sitting position from the dark mass of bodies, and a sparkle of light glimmered across the muzzle of a gun in his hand—and it was pointed at Paulice.

Aerik instinctively raised his rifle and fired, but the bullets dissolved on the still functioning astrapi shield of his own fighter. He screamed both in frustration and in hope that the sound waves would penetrate the barrier his bullets could not.

Milliken thought he heard something over the sputtering of the damaged craft and the howling of the wind. He wasn't sure, but he flipped the knife in his hand and instinctively dropped as bullets rang out around the hole in the wall. Milliken heard Toutopolus groan and saw him fall to the floor at the edge of his vision. Milliken loosed the knife in his hand, and it flew with an accuracy that surprised even him., but it only thudded handle-first against the soldier's face. The soldier fell backward from his sitting position, but caught himself. Milliken snatched Toutopolus's gun from the floor, and as the soldier sat up, he fired, snapping the soldier's head back violently as something unseen in the darkness splattered against the opposite wall.

Milliken stood, tucking the handgun into the belt of his suit, and he hoisted the moaning Toutopolus onto his shoulder. Toutopolus was going into shock and would need attention that he could only get on the other fighter, assuming they could make it there. Milliken saw Aerik standing at the end of the flatdeck, one foot on the nose of the wrecked fighter, extending his hand. The ship shuddered as Milliken shuffled toward the front. It was not as hard to carry Toutopolus as it would have been on Earth, but moving through the unstable fighter littered with bodies and a grown man on his shoulder drew sweat from his brow. As he stepped onto the console, which was now showering sparks in intermittent bursts, Milliken heard another indecipherable yell, but this time, his foot slipped, and in the instinctive struggle to hold Toutopolus and not lose his balance, he was unable to move.

Toutopolus's whole body was cold except his arm, which was now completely consumed by hot, stinging needles and was dangling helplessly in the air. As he tried to steady himself, someone yelled, and he looked up. It was hard for him to breathe in this position. The Eos stopped it from mattering normally, but in the thick of the Miasma, the lack of oxygen, in addition to the pain, distorted the reality around him into an impressionistic blur. As he raised his head, he saw one man blurred into two, rearing his arm back to throw another Squib.

Unsure if the tips of his fingers, even on his good arm, would even be able to feel the metal of the pistol, Toutopolus snatched the gun from Milliken's belt expecting it to drop to the floor. But his hand obeyed the commands from his brain, and the gun fired a burst, sending the figure to the floor.

But only one of the double images fell, and Toutopolus realized, as the endorphins now rushing through his body afforded his vision a moment of clarity, that they had not been a double image at all, and the other, very real image, was training Milliken's assault rifle on them.

Milliken felt his body shake as Toutopolus fired the gun from his belt at something behind them. Aerik urgently reached out his hand, but then collapsed back onto the flatdeck as a fan of blood sprayed out of the back of his leg with the sound of gunfire. Milliken reached for Aerik's hand, but when it fell back through the astrapi shield, Milliken's own footing faltered again. But this time, as Toutopolus muttered a more disturbing "Uhh," Milliken lunged with the leg he still had beneath him, and dove through the astrapi toward the flatdeck.

Toutopolus cursed his vision for becoming clear just long enough for him to have front-row seats at his own death. But then, suddenly, just as the muzzle aimed at him spat flames, he found the macabre image receding. And as the darkening fighter moved outside his vision, he swore he could see the actual bullet just before it sparked out of existence against the astrapi no more than two centimeters in front of his left eye.

Toutopolus, Milliken, and Aerik plummeted to the flatdeck as a barrage of blue sparks showered around them. And then, as a Cyclopean jolt of pain ripped through his body when he attempted to steady himself with his shattered arm, Toutopolus saw a bright flash in his darkening vision as the dropped Squib exploded, splitting the fighter they had fallen from in half as it spiraled away into the darkness of the Miasma. And then his vision faded, and he himself spiraled away, flailing into his own personal Miasmic gloom.

Six bandaged Cyrus's wounds and propped him up in one of the passenger seats on the bridge. Cyrus's wounds were superficial, and he would be fine so long as he sat still, which was likely going to be difficult in the next few minutes, but Six made sure he was securely buckled in the five-point harness on the chair. Cyrus was groggy, which was probably less due to loss of blood and more due to the blast shock of being too close to not one, but two Spellcaster discharges, but he was not so bleary he couldn't function. Above all else, he seemed tired. His body was still adjusting to the Eos, and this was the longest time he had been out of the sun. Six had set him as close to the windshield as he could, and perhaps the sunlight would help him regain his wits.

Jang patched the earwig network into the hailing system of the bridge. "Sensors say we're starting to heat up, what do I do about that?" Jang yelled at the holomonitor, no longer bothering to subvocalize.

"When you hit the atmospheric threshold, the HUD pipe should pop up on the windshield," Uzziah's voice came back filtered but quick enough to sound preoccupied.

The ship began to vibrate around them, but the compensators did their job to keep the floor and consoles steady. The vibrations became more and more apparent, and the temperature gauge on the holomonitor was rising at a rate that made it unreadable. Jang was sure something was wrong. If this wasn't the atmospheric barrier, what was?

And then, the dark rings of the re-entry pipe appeared on the screen, and a warning about reentry calmly filled the comm system. A jolt too violent for the compensators to adjust sent a ripple throughout the ship. Jang felt his seat leave his body and then rise suddenly back into his tailbone. The surface of Asha in the windshield began to spin with an obvious wobble. The rings of the pipe began to rotate in sync with the planet's surface. Jang grabbed the controls and tried to manually adjust to the pipe. The ship began to slow its spin, but in correcting the spin, Jang overcompensated, and the ship veered too much to the right.

"Whatever you do, make sure you don't go out of the pipe or lose your x-axis," Uzziah's words were more like a condemnation than a warning. Just as the words entered Jang's ears, the pipe moved to the edge of the windshield, and the side of the Paracelsus collided with the inside of the imaginary pipe with enough force to send another unmitigated shockwave through the bridge.

And then the ship began to spin again, and this time, the x-axis lost stability, and the entire visible surface of Asha smeared in the windshield. Then they saw space, and then the fierce orange Set, and then Asha again mixed in a blur. The gravity drive kept Jang in his seat, but the image through the windshield made him dizzy.

"What in Miasmic death are you doing?" Six yelled as Jang closed his eyes to keep his head from reeling.

"Stop whining and hit the thruster kill!" Jang could have reduced thrust himself, but in his daze, his feet could not find the proper pedal.

"Which one is that?" Six yelled back.

"The bright red one flashing under the warning light!" Jang's ankles were numb, and his feet were unsure. The whirr from the thrusters died down, and the litany of warning beacons dropped two alarms from their chorus. Jang threw his body over the controller and wrenched at it. The spinning slowed steadily, and the view from the windshield settled with half a starscape on the left and the Ashan plain on the right. Dark bands on the HUD display sped from right to left across the Ashan backdrop and registered fluorescent yellow and green against the desolate black of space.

The vibration became too much for the balancing systems to adjust, and the metal rims around the windshield began to glow until they spawned wispy flames.

"Our situation is not improving!" Six belted at Jang.

"You're coming in sideways!" Uzziah's voice spread over the intercom.

Jang sat up firmly in his chair, threw his hair from his face, and gripped the control wheel again. "Will everyone shut the hell up and let me fly!"

The nose was pitched more toward space than Asha, and as Jang tried to correct to the right, he feared another bout of overcorrection. He whipped the stick to the left—the direction the ship wanted to spin in. The ship spun 270 degrees and settled back into the pipe, spinning at a more manageable rate.

Uzziah's voice came back over the loudspeakers, "Good, you're back straight. As long as the ship is still in good shape, the three of you should be able to guide it back to the original LZ." His filtered voice was calm, but it still had the hurried sound of preoccupation.

Jang looked over his shoulder. Six was there, but Cyrus was gone. "You think *two* of us can do it with a ship that's on fire?" Jang asked, not bothering to subvoc.

"The fire will go away as soon as you get out of the buffer zone," Uzziah reported.

Jang was so calm in his delivery, for a moment it sounded like he was still subvocalizing, "Will the fire *inside* the ship go away too?"

"What do you mean *inside* the ship?" Uzziah belted.

"Well, I looked to see if I could find Cyrus by his locator, and I noticed one of the zones in the holomonitor is on fire alert. I cancelled the halon system because Cyrus's blip is in that section."

"There's no way the fire should have breached the hull. That hull can take a meteor hit, or maybe two, before it loses its integrity."

"I'm just giving the news, not the editorial," Jang said, again matter-of-factly as he struggled to keep the ship inside the pipe. The Paracelsus had electromagnetic and gravity compensators that made adjustments smooth, but this flying hotel was still too large for his tastes. As smooth as the corrections were, the overall process was like trying to guide a levitating brick through an elephant's bowel tract.

Six threw off his harness and grabbed a fire extinguisher. "I am going to see what's keeping old boy."

"Great," Jang mumbled to himself, unaware he was subvocalizing, "I get to crash-land a burning, three-man brick all by myself."

Septangle Mueller Kanto sat monitoring the lev traffic control gram but was baffled. One of their ships had disappeared from the imager. It could have been destroyed, but by what? There had not been anything else on the radar since the ship radioed it was being attacked by another ship that had never actually appeared on the gram. The stellar flares had bungholed the communications on the J.L., and it was possible the flares could have been interfering with the systems on their base, but it seemed unlikely because the comm-sat they were receiving their signal from was geosynchronized over the dark side of the planet.

But nonetheless, the ship had disappeared, and Septangle Kanto was barking orders at the Hexads beneath him to get his system back up and running again. They had scrambled two other light attack fighters to assist the distress call, but suddenly, the ship was back on the gram and was sending in the coded entry signal. The command to open the bay doors was issued, but before the doors even opened all the way there was a hail of missile fire and the controls went dead. He himself could feel the familiar tingle of electromagnetic pulse that raised the hair on his neck. He had instinctively dived away from the window, but as he stood, he saw the entrance to the hangar bay consumed in flames. It was hard to keep breath inside his body as he felt for the communicator controls on his badge. "Plan Theta! Plan Theta!" he yelled, not bothering to subvocalize as he issued the command to evacuate the most coveted secret of the Shadow Prolocutor.

Cyrus stumbled from Tanner's room holding his side. The ship shook periodically as he walked, rattling his wounds painfully against his clothes and bandages. He had gotten up because the holomonitor reported that the living quarters were on fire. And he, Jang, and Six had been through too much nonsense to leave the item that had stalled his escape to burn. He knew the living area was on fire, but standing there, watching it spreading through the hallway around him, he was perplexed at how the fire could have started *inside* the Paracelsus. The ship was designed to handle the stresses atmospheric reentry exerted, and someone would have to screw up much worse than they had to have generated this much internal damage.

Cyrus tucked Tanner's Bible under his left arm away from the cut in his side. It sent a burning sensation through the wound in his back, but it was much better than the pain he expected to come from pressing the hard-bound volume against his ribs. Each step sent ripples of anguish through his side, and his body's involuntary reactions stiffened his walk. He steadied himself against the wall, staying away from the side of the hall that was burning. It was amazing how hot it was even at this distance. How the fire could have started here continued to perplex him until he rounded the corner and the answer became abundantly clear.

Before him stood Six with a gun to his head, held hostage by one of the Eurydice regulars with a face Cyrus vaguely recognized. Whoever this monkey wrench was, he was not nearly as bright as he was ballsy—setting the fire had lured Cyrus back here, but the only reason the halon system had not engaged automatically was because either Jang had deactivated it, or the Shipmate had not rebooted. If that system had engaged, this man would have found himself locked between bulkheads and gasping for oxygen-deprived air. But sometimes balls were enough.

"You're going to set the locator beacon on this refuse heap to all frequencies, or we're *all* going to die right here," the soldier demanded.

As flames spread from the floor up to the ceiling, Cyrus wondered why the designers of the ship had not used more flame resistant materials. Then a wisp of smoke arrested his throat. It was not a toxic smoke, but it was enough to tweak his lungs into a spasm. A cough escaped his throat, and the band of the subvocalizing unit constricted painfully against his Adam's apple, conveniently reminding him of its existence.

He was careful not to mouth the words as he subvocalized, "I need you to kill the internal grav-drive."

"Under these circumstances?" came back. Jang's reluctance was unnerving, but Cyrus knew he would at least check his holomonitor.

There was a shimmy in the ship. "Nothing to say, dexter? Give the order now, or I finish him, complete!" The soldier's face contorted as spittle erupted with his threat.

"Do it now," Cyrus subvocalized, sure his lips had moved this time. He took a short step forward, but before he could put his foot down, Six was already in motion.

Six moved his head from the path of the gun and reached across his own body, twisting the soldier's wrist along with the gun until the barrel pointed at the soldier's own chest. Cyrus ignored the pain in his side and lunged forward. Six moved to adjust his grip, but the soldier moved faster than either of them had expected, revealing a small hold-out pistol from behind his back. The ship shimmied again, and they were all airborne when the gun fired.

Uzziah marveled at the scale of the hangar beneath the pyramid as he saw the lines etched into the wall in shapes and forms that were hard to discern at this speed. He no longer needed to watch the smaller square in the holomonitor that showed the reentry trajectory of the Paracelsus, but he left it on anyways. He took a moment to press the record button on the holographic imager as he noticed shimmering lines of light dancing here and there behind the mysterious lines carved into the rock. The Echelon was firing small ordnance at them from the ground, but their fighter was moving too fast, and the shield protected them. Paeryl quietly manned the weapons systems from the seat next to Uzziah as the two small Apostate fighters returned and synchronized their attacks as they sped ahead the apportioned Echelon craft. According to Jang's scans, the pyramid had four bay doors on each side that led to a large chamber beneath it, which was flanked on each side by smaller hangars. Even knowing the layout, it wasn't until the door leading to the central room opened that he realized the ominous room they had just sped through was one of the smaller rooms.

The sheer scale of the central hangar boggled the mind into vertigo. "What in the Miasma is this?" Uzziah heard Paeryl murmur as they passed the massive transport-type ships inside the central hangar that seemed to be in the final stages of construction. The transports were of relatively contemporary Earth design, but they were much larger than any Earth endeavor could have created. The Sagarmatha Mobile Fortress was halfway constructed by the Uni before the Uni had reassigned the funds to this ill-fated mission to Asha. That monstrous ship would have been at least a quarter smaller than one of the five titanic constructs before them. And then, the words Uzziah's rapidly beating heart had been waiting for came over the earwig, "Fire on the mountain, run boys run."

Paeryl fired off two more incendiaries and two pulse missiles as their escort fighters fanned out and slowed as Uzziah activated Jang's overboosters.

Six heard the command to disengage the gravity through his earwig and was surprised that he knew the Knight of Wands well enough to have expected it. What he did not anticipate, even as he brought his right elbow up and back into the chest of whoever had gorgejacked him, was the gravitational shift to relieve the leverage he had exerted on his assailant's gun hand enough for the assailant to draw a small slug caster from behind his back.

Cyrus had lunged forward, and the loss of gravity caused him to twist as he flew across the hallway. Six felt an emptiness spread across his stomach, and he realized the gravity dampers had not been inverted, they had been turned off, and Cyrus, he, and the soldier were all falling. Then the gunshot obscured his thought. Cyrus's body snapped backward, and his legs flipped upward at different rates, forming an odd scissor as the shot set him spiraling backward against the burning wall. The Comptex should have protected him, but its integrity was compromised by the damage he had taken in the jetway.

Rage built up in Six like kiln. He turned to face the man who had put the gun to his head, but the elbow Six had delivered as the freefall began separated them by half a meter. Six's turn shifted his weight away from the man as he snatched away the inverted gun, but the man was now pulling his other gun around to aim at Six. Six used the momentum of his spin to bring his legs around, and he planted both feet into the man's chest. The gun fired and Six felt the whip of wind as the slug coursed past his cheek.

The man's body rolled as it floated away and Six twisted, planted his feet against the wall, and launched himself toward the opposite, burning wall as another shot ricocheted behind him. Six flipped the gun into the proper position in his left hand and returned fire, but the ship shimmied again. The ship's velocity or angle must have changed because the burning wall lurched toward them as Six fired. He missed dramatically and braced himself as the fiery wall smacked into him, jarring the gun from his grasp. The gun flipped away to the opposite wall, but Six ignored it because the barrel of the gun in his attacker's hand was now just a half meter away—and it was pointed at his left eye.

Taeryn of Four took her obligations very seriously. As the lieutenant of Paeryl's van, and the drawer of the Justice card, she had developed a reputation for being exacting and callous in battle. So when the glimmer ship emerged from the bay doors beneath the pyramid, she descended on its holo-imager signature like a fritzed-out uberhound

330

on an abusive master. Flying the mining ship that Cyrus and his van had appropriated from the Miasma was like trying to pilot a lev gurney by standing on it, but the mining lasers equipped on the front were a weapon the Echelon neither would expect nor could defend against. Even as the glimmer ship powered up its glimmer drive, which would have rendered it virtually untraceable under the Miasmic sky, Taeryn, unseen to them thanks to black paint and Jang's spoofing program, activated the four mining lasers on the face of her craft.

She had practiced this technique numerous times, and here, above the disappearing fighter obliviously coursing into her firing path, her practice paid off. The bright flash of the lasers illuminated the cockpit as she pulled back on the controls and shaved the back end, including the glimmer drive, from the fleeing Echelon stealth craft. She smiled at the imager as a hologram of the severed rear end of the ship flew over the apportioned Echelon craft that sped from the doors of the pyramid escorted by two light fighters.

The blast hit Cyrus like an unsuspected kick. When his body snapped backward, it felt as if his brain shifted in his head. He couldn't tell if he closed his eyes, but he knew he could not see or feel a thing as his body spun through the air until it collided hard against the wall. He was surprised when he did not bounce, and the wall pressed against him as if he had hit the ground instead. Then, as a tongue of flame licked at his ear, vision flooded back into him, and he realized he was still carrying Tanner's Bible.

It felt as if gravity was pressing him against the wall, so he used it, and he pushed himself away from the flames on all fours. The flames were unimaginably hot, but they did not seem to affect him in the Comptex. Even though his right shoulder throbbed as if it was on fire itself, the bullet had not penetrated the Comptex. He worried his bandages could catch flame, but they were evidently too saturated with blood.

And then, Cyrus noticed Six was incredibly still, and he knew something was wrong. Cyrus reached up and grabbed the doorframe, realizing gravity had little effect on his orientation. He ignored the excruciating pain that came as he tensed his arm, and he snatched himself forward with all the strength he could muster.

If Euston could finish the bald-headed manpunter in front of him, he might stand a chance. The pressure the wall exerted on his left shoulder kept his pistol steady, but then, just as he steadied the gun at the Apostate's face, the pressure shifted away from his arm. The bald man moved, and his motion was so quick Euston was not sure what had happened. Suddenly, Euston's arm was hit from underneath, and he fired into the ceiling. Then the bald man's body moved away from the wall revealing the Knight of Wands flying through the flames. Euston tried to bring the gun back down, but it was too late. Something collided with his chest, forcing the air from his lungs as the burning wall retreated from him.

As Six moved toward the opposite wall, he saw Cyrus speed past him and collide with the Eurydician soldier. The wall had stopped pressing against him, and Six's apparent weightlessness sent him all the way to the other wall. Cyrus's attack sent the man back-first in the same direction as Six. The Eurydician moved faster than Six, and as he passed, Six tapped the switch to open the door to the room beside them. The man passed into the room, and Six dove away, but as he moved back toward the burning wall, Cyrus yelled, "Look out!"

Six turned to see the man hanging from the door frame by his right hand and lifting the gun toward them with his left. Then suddenly, there was a snag at Six's shoulder, and as the gun discharged, Six found himself outside the path of the bullet, heading toward the bulkhead warning line, and he heard Cyrus yell, "Activate the halon system, now!"

The mining lev piloted by Taeryn pulled up in front of the stolen Echelon fighter as both crafts closed the distance on the ship that fled from the pyramid. The fleeing ship looked like it was sitting still as Tanner reached for the submachine gun stowed on the wall next to him. The two short swords he brought along, meticulously forged by Fenrir, caught his eye, and he remembered why he brought them—the mesh weave of Comptex could stop a round-tipped bullet, but did very little to stop the linear slice of a blade. He stood, forgoing the gun for the two swords, while Aerik, his own leg bandaged, began attending to Milliken and Toutopolus's wounds.

Taeryn's lev sped ahead, momentarily disappearing in the darkness and then reappearing, illuminated by a bright blue glow. There were sparks of electricity across the back of the fleeing Echelon craft as a largish chunk of misshapen metal flew free from its rear and through the astrapi shield. Tanner cringed as Taeryn fired, afraid the precious cargo inside would be damaged. But his fears were quickly allayed as Taeryn's precision and poise had been honed in the training simulator that Jang, Uzziah, Paeryl, and Darius had developed–she was Paeryl's lieutenant for a good reason.

The lights on the front of their fighter came on, illuminating writhing figures inside the craft. The light caught a glimmer of gilded angel's wings as Tanner pulled the swords from their sheaths. The grips felt oddly warm in his hand, but he realized the warmth was not coming from without, but within. He could feel it swelling throughout his body. It was a familiar, although estranged, feeling, but this time, as the fury he had tried to hide from most his life filled him once again, he welcomed it.

These heathens had held this relic for far too long, but he was determined that at the end of this exchange, whether breath still filled his body or not, they would not hold it for one minute longer. Uzziah retracted the windshield of their fighter, and as they collided with the rear of the stealth craft, Tanner, to Paeryl's loud protesting, vaulted over the console and through the fissure in the rear of the other vehicle.

Cyrus had snatched Six with him toward the bulkhead. Unable to focus in the smoke, Cyrus had yelled the command to Jang. As they floated toward the bulkhead line, the ship shuddered. The wall came to meet them again, and the closing bulkhead seemed to retreat as red caution lights and an alert siren filled the hall. Six and Cyrus fell against the wall again, harder this time, with Cyrus on his back and Six on top of him. The cut on Cyrus's back scraped against the wall and he could feel what must have been the flaps of the wound separating as the bandage slipped. His whole body tensed and a haze washed over his eyes. But even through the haze, as Six used the pressure of the wall to stand against it, Cyrus saw the crazed Flying Monkey prop himself against the door frame and dive toward them as he lifted the gun again.

Six felt Cyrus's body stiffen beneath him as he mumbled something that came across the earwig as gibberish. At first, Six assumed it was the pain of falling on his wounded back, but as Cyrus started to point at something behind Six's back, he knew it could be only one thing. So despite the fact the pain alone might knock Cyrus out, he grabbed Cyrus's collar and dove toward the closing bulkhead as the cold gas spread around them. Then, another vibration sped through the ship, and the hold the wall had on them was gone. Cyrus mumbled again, but this time, Six glanced over his shoulder to see the pistol only a half-meter away from the back of his head.

As soon as Tanner's feet hit the corrugated steel floor, it was as if time itself slowed down for everyone except him. Before he pulled his feet beneath him, he had already cut two men who were reaching for either guns or grenades.

When he landed, two more men were moving toward him from either side of the Ark, and Tanner lunged toward the Ark, stabbing on either side. One soldier dodged, but Tanner moved too fast for the other. Something hit Tanner from behind, but as soon as it touched him, he was spinning away from it, finishing off the man he had stabbed. An assault rifle swung at his head, but he was already under it, continuing his spin, and he brought the sword underhanded into the attacker's hamstring. Tanner followed through between the man's legs and dragged the blade back through his sciatic, spraying out blood with force. As Tanner stood, he saw someone on the other side of the Ark taking aim. Tanner let the sword from his left hand fly. It impaled the man and slumped him against the wall. Tanner spun again, bringing the other sword across the back of the wrist of another soldier reaching for his sidearm. The man's body reeled away involuntarily, and Tanner moved into him, bringing the sword up and across the man's neck just before kicking him away from the Ark.

Tanner was now at the front of the craft by himself as the remaining soldiers in the ship drew their weapons. One turned to fire to keep anyone else from advancing through the fissure. Tanner dodged to the side as the pilot, now up from his chair, tried to stab him in the back. Tanner kicked backward and spun, bringing his sword around in a backhand across the pilot's eyes. The sword jostled in his hand as it passed through nose cartilage, but Tanner held on. He dove toward the man impaled with the sword, who was still feebly trying to pull the blade out when a gunshot rocked the metal chamber. Tanner expected to be thrown back by the force of a bullet, but he kept moving anyway. There was another deafening shot as Tanner snatched his sword from the man's belly with his free hand and dug the freed blade into the ribs of another soldier. Tanner saw the man who had fired into the other fighter was now gone, and the one taking aim at him was now collapsing to the ground. Tanner slashed the sword across the ribs of the last soldier he had stabbed as he tried to remove the blade. Tanner kicked him toward the back of the ship, and as the soldier hit the edge of the fissure, the front of his head exploded with another gunshot.

The body stumbled a bit and then slid down the edge of the fissure, revealing Uzziah and Paeryl both with the barrels of their assault rifles trailing smoke. Tanner finally felt the steaming gore that covered his hands, his thighs, and the right side of his head and torso. He could barely hear the bellow of, "Tanner, are we winning?" over the pounding of his own heart. Standing there, the blood of others dripping from his hands once again, he wasn't sure of the answer until he lifted his head and saw the gilded cherubim shimmering in the light streaming through the fissure.

Cyrus tried again to yell, "Look out!" but as Six dragged his body through the pressurized air of the ship, the pull of his collar against his throat only allowed a garbled mumble the earwig network could not translate. Six turned, but he was holding Cyrus, and he had too much momentum pulling them through the closing bulkhead. As weightlessness returned and halon gas spread around them, there was nothing Six could do as the Eurydician soldier, with better leverage on his leap, advanced on them with his slug pistol.

The man's finger tensed around the trigger, but he was too close, and Cyrus, already curled into the fetal position after full freefall returned, extended both legs into the man's midsection. Cyrus sent the man back into the halon-filled hall as the gun fired into the bulkhead that closed between them.

The ship felt like it was falling apart. The controls were vibrating, and half the stabilizing systems had overloaded. The thruster controls kept speeding up and slowing down the ship, and even if Jang had issued the voice command to reactivate the gravity stabilizer, it wouldn't have worked because the systems that routed energy to them had malfunctioned. It took every bit of strength in Jang's arms, and some leverage on the part of his legs, to keep the ship inside the pipe, and having to activate and deactivate systems to save Cyrus and Six was not helping. Now, a glimpse at the holomonitor revealed the man who had waylaid them flailing his arms and gasping for air, consumed in thick gas that robbed the hallway air of oxygen as the ventilation system shut off the airflow to that part of the ship. Then, as the black rings on the HUD disappeared, the dimly lit sky gave way to the brilliant wasteland of Asha. As the ship slowed, Jang watched on the holomonitor as Cyrus and Six settled on the floor of the hall beyond the bulkhead. They shakily regained their footing and began shambling back toward the bridge. The ship continued to shudder, but it moved smoothly as Jang leveled the x-axis and cruised toward the sunside crater they had designated as their rendezvous point. Jang had just received word that "Johnny received his fiddle of gold," from Paeryl, which meant that he and Uzziah had retrieved the package, and so long as the spoofing system held up, Cyndyl should be waiting for the Paracelsus at the rendezvous point.

They might be able to power up the vehicles stored in the garage bay of the Paracelsus to make their escape, but this flying disaster was not going anywhere after it landed in that crater—assuming it made it there at all. Besides, Jang had expected to reenter with a ship with a much smaller footprint, and the programs that he had phreaked into the Echelon network would not be able to hide a ship this large for long. So as Cyrus and Six, both battered and limping, entered the bridge, Jang just shook his head. Six was carrying the Agamemnon unit, and Cyrus was carrying a large, hardbound corporeal book.

"What the hell was that all about?" Jang snapped, the crater growing in the windshield in front of him.

"It was for Marcus," Cyrus said dazedly, and then, after he buckled the harness over both himself and the book, he closed his eyes and passed out.

twenty-seven

—What's wrong Dari? Why the stink-face?

—I'm mad at Sergio.

—I thought you and Sergio were best friends.

—We are. That's what's so frustrating. Best friends are supposed to be like brothers, right? But Sergio's being a total trash monkey right now.

—Well, I know you're upset, but you need to dock your epithets.

—I'm sorry Dada, but I'm heated up. He and Terry have been palin' around a lot lately. And Terry just got a HoloStation Prime. He invites Sergio over. Sergio has gone like a couple times now, and he always talks to the others about how much fun he has, but I never get invited. He doesn't even talk to me about it. He acts like it's never even happened. But today, I find out from Scott Seal that he goes sometimes too, and that the reason why Sergio's acting so hinkey is Terry says he doesn't want me to come over. But then today, Sergio comes to me and asks why I went behind his back to talk to Terry because Terry told him he can't come over anymore because of something I said, which is complete bunkus.

—So you're mad because the whole thing's turned into a preteen holodrama?

—I'm mad because Sergio's first thought is that I'm flying sideways. He should know better.

—Hmm. You know, this reminds me of a story. Did I ever tell you the story of the Whowie?

—Whowie? What kind of name is that?

—Well, it's an Australian Aboriginal myth, so I would assume it would be something that meant something to them. Either way, the Whowie was one of the most fearsome beasts among the animals. It was six meters long and looked like a Komodo dragon with six legs.

—That's big, but why was it so scary?

—Because the only things alive then were animals. Only in this story, I think the animals represent people. Anyways, the Whowie ate anything that crossed his path, and the animals were forced to band together because they were afraid. One day, the animals devised a plan to destroy the Whowie, and they all got together when he was sleeping and set a big fire in front of his cave.

337

—*Wouldn't the smoke fill up the cave, Dada?*

—*That was exactly why they did it. The Whowie was a burly creature, but after he breathed enough smoke, he would die like anything else. So the Whowie thrashed about in the cave for days, choking on smoke and roasting in the heat, but he wouldn't die. The animals kept feeding the fire until the Whowie could not bear it anymore and rushed through the flames. When he emerged charred, blind, and weak on the other side, the animals pounced on him and tore him apart. Afterward, they tried to decide what to do to set up a sort of government, but no one could agree because everyone was selfish. And some came up with dumb ideas just so they could be heard and then were stubborn and indignant when no one would hear them out. Eventually, because of sneakiness on the parts of the some of the animals, an all-out war broke out. The lyrebird suggested that there had been enough violence already and that they should try to figure out what problems they were having so that an entire group of animals did not wind up like the unreasonable Whowie. Eventually, the birds and the land animals separated into two groups, but as they fought, the sun tried to hide from all the bloodshed and horror. It became darker and darker until the bat showed up. He was the strongest fighter and the only animal that could fight effectively in the dark. But the bat was sneaky, and because he liked the attention, he would go help the birds, then, just before they won, help the land animals. Eventually, it came to the point where none of the animals could speak the same language anymore, and the bloodshed and death became too much for even them to bear. They finally held a council to find a solution, and the bat used his boomerang to separate the night from the day, and he chased the sun out of his hiding place with it. In the end, there was peace again, and the night animals and day animals had their own place, so it did not seem so crowded, but they had been too separated by the language barrier and could no longer be the same unified group they had been against the Whowie.*

—*So the sneaky bat, who had been a big problem in the war, saved everyone in the end?*

—*Precisely, but he played the ends against the middle before that, and for what?*

—*Because he wanted the attention?*

—*Yes, and because he didn't think he could get it by being nice. In the end, he was wrong, but it took a Fringe-riot for him to get it.*

—*So you think Terry is like the bat, or like the Whowie?*

—*I think Terry is like Terry. But I think the Aborigines had that myth so we could see several things. Selfishness ultimately drives us apart, and sometimes, having a common foe is what makes it easier for us to stay together. I think people get bored easily, and when real problems don't exist, sometimes we make them up, and those are by far the hardest to overcome.*

—*So what you're saying is this entire argument could be bunkus.*

338

—Exactly. And you need to examine what's more important, your friendship or your feelings because sometimes, bunkus conflicts are easier to fight over than the real problems.

—So, I should try to be more like the lyrebird and not fall for the bat's tricks.

—Yes, because if they had listened to the lyrebird, the sun would never have left them.

—But the animals were hardheaded like you say I am sometimes.

—Well, you and I aren't the only hardheaded people on the planet, and sometimes, the hardheaded have to lose their sun to appreciate its warmth.

—So I should squash my bug with Sergio and just move on before I futz around and lose the warmth of his friendship.

—That sounds like a plan to me.

• • • • •

Villichez's rites were brief but poignant. All of Cyrus's van was present, along with Paeryl and Cyndyl, but the other Apostates had requested, having not known the soul while it was living, to be absolved from communing with the dead. Paeryl explained on the way to the crematorium that the Apostates believed the soul and the body were independent of each other, and that the body provided an anchor in this world. When the body no longer possessed the energy to maintain the link, they believed the soul was released, free to roam the ether until another body required its enervation to spring to life and beguiled it into its grasp. When consciousness faltered, and the body did not require constant attention, the soul was sometimes free to wander, but in the waking hours, to the uninitiated, it was trapped. Only strong souls could rise from their material masters at will, and when they were finally freed, only strong souls remained constitute, while other, less tempered souls became dissociated wisps in the spiritual morass. They believed that the thoughts of those who were close to the soul while it had inhabited the body could help it stay constitute while it awaited a new host.

Cyrus thought it an odd and yet resounding ideal, and he held vigil next to Villichez in the crematorium until his knees ached. He did not utter any words, but the weight of his thoughts resonated through the cave lit only by the ignition torches and the pyre itself. Before they had laid Villichez on the funeral bier, Cyrus's mind had flooded with questions, but as he sat before the stone chamber carved from the ground itself, his mind was clear. Though many questions still remained unanswered, when he finally stood, and he and Paeryl lit the pyre, he felt by the last hour of the day cycle, whether they be to his liking or not, that the answers, indeed, would come.

Cyrus sat next to Toutopolus while he waited for Paeryl to finish his business with the other elders.

"How do you feel?" Cyrus said, resting his hand on Toutopolus's shoulder.

"Like I got my ass kicked," Toutopolus said without enough sarcasm to elicit comfort.

"I heard the other guy won't be in the counterattack." Cyrus smiled, but Toutopolus just cradled his shattered arm and grunted.

"This sort of injury never heals right, even with bone fusion, but Taeryn says the Eos will help it heal if I stay here in the sun."

Cyrus looked around. There were two others in the most intense key of light in the crater. Aerik's leg was set in a metal brace, and he lay out in the tangerine rays of Set. He looked as if he were relaxing by a pool at some posh resort rather than convalescing from a battle wound. They had removed the shell from his leg, and after only one day, it already shown signs of healing. The other was Fenrir. He had suffered a concussion in the battle and had been given some Eurydician medication subcutaneously. Afterward, they had laid him here in the sun. His breathing seemed regular, but he had not yet awakened, but no one, not even his betrothed and his children, seemed distraught.

Cyrus marveled at the comfort the Eos and the sun afforded these people. It made life simpler and less distorted. Cyrus considered what Tanner said about being east of Eden, and he too could feel the fissure. It was though humans had grown so attached to the wiles of technology that they had divorced themselves from the natural ebb and flow of the universe for fear of adversity, and yet in all their dodging, all they ever seemed to create was more adversity. So if these people, who knew their small corner of the universe in a way Cyrus had never known anything, could have indelible faith that their methods would bring one of their own out of a coma, then it would take little effort to expect, even in the face of his own apprehensions, that Toutopolus should recover the full use of his arm.

"You did well back there. From what I hear, no one would have made it if it weren't for you and Milliken." Cyrus met Toutopolus's eyes. "I trust these people and their methods. You will be fine. Just bear with it and do as they say." Toutopolus nodded as Paeryl approached, but he still seemed melancholy. Once he began to feel himself healing, he would be fine.

"It appears we are winning," Paeryl said, the usual levity in his voice. "There were a few foibles, but things seem to be in order, yes? You retrieved your information unit?"

Cyrus nodded. "Dr. Jang is installing it now per Aerik's instructions."

"Aerik wanted to help directly, but I fear he must stay in the light. Wounds like theses only heal properly under the supervision of Set," Paeryl paused to turn his own face to the rays of the sun, "We placed your other relic, this Ark, in the storage chamber next to the forge. My van says it has an odd background count, and it oscillates at a frequency lower than any of our equipment can effectively monitor. It also has some sort of electromagnetic assist when it is moved."

"We will have to study it in more detail once we are done with our reconnaissance. I actually came to invite you and your council to our dialectic."

Paeryl smiled and patted Cyrus on his back. "Inside that vault lies your history," he made a broad gesture with his hands indicating the sky, "out here lies my people's future." He turned back to Cyrus, and for the first time, Cyrus saw a furrow of concern in his brow. "Perhaps, in that vault, you will find exactly how those two are betrothed, and how we can stave off the impending scourge."

Cyrus never communicated his concern that his actions would elicit unwanted attention from the Echelon, but Paeryl was a wise man. Cyrus assumed that in his wisdom, Paeryl supported his efforts because he knew the Echelon was coming for them anyway, and either the Echelon or the sun would set on them eventually. But until now, Paeryl's faith and his reliance on Cyrus's cunning and ingenuity had not seemed like a cry for help. Paeryl was a good man and an even better leader, but Cyrus could see, as the creases in the corners of his eyes spread their asters along the side of his face, that Paeryl was out of answers, and it pained him to the core.

Cyrus extended his right arm, took Paeryl's hand into his own, and held it firmly. He needed words to say, but none that came to mind were worthy. Paeryl met his eyes, and without words, he accepted Cyrus's unspoken promise.

● ● ● ● ●

"So what are missing here? Any ideas on the connections between the city, the Hunab Ku, the microwave pyramid, and this place?" Cyrus paced the floor. At this point, it was clear that Mundi, or whoever was behind this plot, had most likely disconnected Asha from the collected history of Earth purposefully. It seemed like Cyrus's plan had to work, but if it didn't, he would have trouble accepting the fact that he had risked the lives, the health, and most certainly the solace the Apostates enjoyed in this crater for a snipe hunt.

Darius looked to the floor, a hollow gaze in his eyes, as if he were in deep thought, "Well, the pyramids, or at least this one on Asha, have both an inherent function and symbolic relevance in their design, correct?"

"Yeah," Jang answered, unsure if the others knew the rhetorical questions the avatar posed were an algorithm within the complex-conditional parser used to mimic the ability of humans to form false conclusions—an ability that was at once responsible for the greatest achievements and worst atrocities of human existence—but an ability which no computer could sincerely possess, and therefore, the question, as rhetorical as it may have been, still required answering for the dialectic to continue.

Darius was still distant, seemingly enthralled by his thoughts as he spoke, "So perhaps the designs of all the structures are as symbolic as they are functional."

There was an awkward pause, and then Cyrus spoke up, "That makes sense."

Darius rubbed his beard. He walked over to the holomonitor and accessed it, eliciting a grumble from Milliken. A holographic blueprint of the complex they were in appeared in the center of the floor and rotated. "This is the layout of *this* facility," Darius turned and pointed to the three-dimensional map as it rotated in the center of the floor before them.

Tanner moved forward, his mouth half open in stunned recognition. "Oh my," he said as the image rotated and revealed ten circles—three circles to the right, four in the center, and three on the left—all interlinked with passageways. "The Tree of Life," Tanner said to himself.

"We are here," Darius said as he walked toward the image and pointed to the only circle that could be called the center, "and Plato's Cave is here," he added pointing to the last circular room in the middle row of four that rested the furthest from the others.

"What about the Hunab Ku?" Tanner asked, still in awe. Darius returned to the holomonitor, and the image of the complex retreated and settled in a top-down view in front of them, resembling a drawing. As Darius pretended to type, a miniaturized diagram of the city appeared next to the ten linked circles and then rotated and zoomed to resemble a drawing of the Mayan symbol.

Darius turned and clasped his hands behind his back. "Although the Hunab Ku was theorized as part of the head of the Mayan pantheon, it is only listed in antiquity as the symbol on an Aztec ritual cloak with a reference to spider water. There are theories that the idea of a creator god was conflated by Christian missionaries in contact with those cultures."

"Which doesn't necessarily mean that there isn't a valid shared idea that led to the confusion," Cyrus added.

Torvald could not hold his own confusion any longer. "Maybe, but what is the significance of this Tree of Life?"

Darius turned and indicated Tanner, allowing him to answer, which Jang knew he would do. The avatar only filled in the blanks that the user did not have, or corrected the user when he was unequivocally wrong. It was a magnificently designed program, but it was still just that, and its unwillingness to be fallible was its worst flaw.

"It's a Kabbalistic symbol representing the flow of energy throughout all aspects of the universe. Each circle, called a sephiroth, represents an aspect of existence. The topmost sephiroth, where Plato's Cave is, represents the unknowable godhead. As a term, the Tree of Life relates to the tree in the Garden of Eden that Adam and Eve were separated from when they ate from the Tree of Knowledge of Good and Evil." Tanner still seemed bewildered, as if the pieces that were beginning to come together made *less* sense.

"What about the Hunab Ku?" Davidson asked, looking between Darius and Tanner. This time, also as Jang expected, Darius stepped forward to give the explanation, "According to Mayan mythology, conflated or not, the father of the gods created the world and destroyed it three times. The first world was inhabited by a race of dwarves, the second by a defiant race of beings called the Dzolob, and the last was created for the Maya themselves, or rather humanity as we know it. The general notion is that the symbol represents an idea of oneness, a blending of opposing forces in the universe to find harmony very similar to the *yin* and *yang* of the Taoists. Its name also implies that same oneness brings one closer to the godhead, as Tanner put it earlier."

"So we have three symbols that represent the harmony of energy within the universe," Cyrus stated.

"Well, wouldn't the pyramid be a symbol of death or the afterlife?" Milliken presented.

"Well, there was never any conclusive evidence that the primary function of Giza pyramids was to serve as tombs," Darius chimed in, exactly as he should. As unnerving as the situation before them all was, Jang's chest swelled with a warm pride as he watched the marriage of his own programming and the ingenuity of Cyrus's son play out before them.

"Besides," Torvald added, "haven't we already established that at least the pyramid here is designed to collect the ambient energy of the universe? Seems like an accurate enough analogy for me."

"Okay, so we have three different symbols of universal symbiosis, but what does it mean?" Davidson asked, as equally perplexed by Tanner.

"Creation," Cyrus said, "Let's assume the Hunab Ku symbol does represent the creator god of the Mayans, and the Tree of Life relates to the Biblical creation..." Cyrus paused to gather his thoughts, but Davidson interrupted.

"But weren't the pyramids related to Osiris, the god of the afterlife?"

Darius interjected again, "Actually the association with Osiris is due to references to The Book of the Dead on the walls of the Great Pyramid and is reinforced by the somewhat dubious assumption that they were tombs. However, there have been theories throughout history that the pyramids were related to the sun god Ra or the sky god Horus. But even the connection with Osiris would be valid because Osiris not only received the dead but also decided which beings would enter the world."

"There's also a more concrete relationship," Cyrus stepped forward, "This particular pyramid collects the energy from the CMB. The CMB is the microwave residue left over from the Big Bang and would, therefore, relate the pyramid symbol even more directly to the creation of the universe."

The scientists all nodded except Tanner, who seemed to be struggling with something elusive in his own mind. After a moment, he lifted his hand and spoke, "We're missing one other connection—the societies from which each of these civilizations originates. The Tree of Life is a Kabbalistic symbol, but pieces of the Garden of Eden story can be traced back to the ancient Babylonians. The Babylonians, Mayans, and Ancient Egyptians all have one thing in common; they all possessed technology and a level of civilization that seemed to come from out of nowhere. They all have civilizations they can trace their origins to: the Babylonians, earlier Mesopotamians, the Maya, the Olmecs, and the Egyptians, the nomadic tribes of the Nile delta, but each of these civilizations either gained their knowledge directly from the previous culture, as is the case with the Maya and the Olmecs, or there is little direct correlation between these civilizations' predecessors and the aspects that make the cultures noteworthy."

"What does that mean?" Milliken seemed lost.

"I'll give you an example. We can trace Commonspeak back to American and British English, and those languages we can trace back to the Germanic tribes and various French, Roman, Spanish, and Greek influences. We can even trace the Roman writing backward and see its logical progression. There are stratifications in how the Egyptians built tombs, but if you go on the assumption that the pyramids are *not* tombs, that distinction is loose at best. It's like a group of people show up with a language no one has ever heard of, that isn't related to any other language on the planet. Basically, with the Maya, the Egyptians, and the Babylonians, despite their differences, you have civilizations that suddenly developed complex knowledge of the stars and the sky that Western civilization did not quite master until the nineteenth century at the earliest."

"Well, what does *that* mean then?" Milliken was visibly frustrated.

"Well, if a student doesn't know anything in class and then suddenly aces a take-home deck exam, what do you assume?" Tanner asked.

Davidson and Milliken both answered in unison, "Someone told him the answers."

Tanner continued, "Exactly, but we know the Mayans learned from the Olmecs, but where did the Olmecs learn it? There is very little record of anything pertaining to where they came from or where they went. Why did all these civilizations develop complex calendars? They had a need to know the seasons but not to the extent that they did. The Mayan calendar has three-thousand-year periods. The pyramids suggest time periods ten thousand years apart. But there is no record of them building up to the knowledge. It's like they showed up to the examination and suddenly had all the answers without ever registering for the class."

"So are you suggesting there was some sort of *teacher* that gave these civilizations a cheat sheet?" Davidson challenged.

Cyrus chimed in with the retort, "Given the age of the links we found here on Asha, is it so hard to believe? The presence of these things here, if our assessment of their connection is correct, implies that either advanced humans or some other race of beings created these edifices and then taught these Earth civilizations their trade secrets. Ockham's razor cuts deeply on this one."

"But what's the real connection between all three cultures? Even if the kid cheats on his exam, he has to get the answers from somewhere."

"Atlantis," Darius answered. It seemed so much like an unfounded logical leap that it even took Jang off-guard. After the verbal expressions of doubt and disapproval subsided, Darius continued. "The most likely connection is Atlantis. Plato wrote about it in two works as if it was an actual place. It exists on more than one ancient map in some capacity. And if it did exist, it should be fairly obvious how time itself could obfuscate its existence."

"How is that?" Torvald asked.

"The destruction of the Library of Alexandria, the burning of indigenous South American relics, artifacts, and tomes by zealous Catholics, the destruction of the first and second temple in Israel, the uncountable wars, conquests, and religious inquisitions throughout human history have all undoubtedly ruined vast amounts of ancient knowledge. Look at how easy it was here. Even if the pyramid and the city here were uncovered tomorrow, the majority of the Ashan populace would have no inkling to their relevance. So to say that something cannot exist because we know nothing about it is like taking Schrödinger's cat literally—sure some of you may see the philosophical relevance, but would any of you volunteer to take the cat's place, even if guaranteed no one would ever open the box?"

The avatar's conjecture amazed Jang beyond words, but he searched his mind for explanations. The real Darius, in his numerous days before he modified the prompting engine, must have used such an analogy.

"So let's look at this conjecture indirectly. If we assume Atlantis *must* exist, then where would it have been? Where did it go?" Cyrus mediated.

There was a short pause until Milliken spoke up, "There are large landmasses that we know precious little about due to them being covered by miles of ice."

"Greenland and Antarctica," Darius added.

"If beings that provided Milliken's cheat sheet did exist, wouldn't they most likely spread whatever knowledge they did at approximately the same time?" Torvald chimed in.

"There are theories that the sphinx is around ten thousand years old—possibly the pyramids as well. There is also some evidence that Olmec civilization thrived around that time," Darius was pacing between the scientists and the images of the city and the complex that still floated in the center of the circular room.

"There are Sumerian and Judaic myths that claim advanced knowledge was given to humans by a god or offspring of divine beings and humans, but I'm not sure about the South Americans," Tanner added.

"Viracocha," Darius added, "was a civilizer that taught men to not act like beasts, and a form of him exists in many South and Middle American myths. He was pale-skinned and wore glistening fish scales, which was what enabled Pizarro and Cortez to so efficiently molest the people of Middle America."

"Noah was also pale-skinned, and his father was disturbed, but he took counsel with Enoch, his grandfather, who was enlightened and told the father not to worry. In Sumerian myth, Utnapishtim, who is analogous to Noah, received knowledge from Ea, the god of water who sympathized with the humans," Tanner added.

Darius looked enthusiastic now. "Viracocha also means 'one that came from the water.'"

"In Greek mythology, Poseidon, who if I recall correctly was the patron deity of Atlantis, had his country destroyed because of a dispute with Zeus and Athena," Tanner shot back. They were rolling now. "There is also Oannes, a Babylonian god credited with giving knowledge to mankind, and who also had the body of a fish."

"There is also debate as to Plato's dating of the existence of Atlantis. He says it existed about nine thousand years before his writing in the *Timeus*, but historians find that date hard to accept," Darius continued.

"But that date fits right into these calculations," Milliken joined in on the round.

"The royalty of Atlantis was populated with Poseidon's children, Ea took a human wife, and there is also the story of the Nephilim—the children of the fallen angels that gave forbidden knowledge to man and took wives of human women. The Nephilim were supposed to have been pale-skinned in a region that did not necessarily lend itself to pale skin. "Except the Aryans," Darius was visibly excited and Jang was again disturbed by the display of emotion.

"So we're dealing with some sort of civilizer, or race of civilizers, who were somehow displaced from their original base of operation and, potentially, brought their knowledge to various regions on Earth when they moved. But, they also commingled with the civilizations they visited and then disappeared suddenly." Davidson finally spoke up. "All these various myths seem to correlate. They even seem to agree on timeframe—a timeframe we originally overlooked as ridiculous."

"But a timeframe much less sublime given the empirical evidence on this planet," Cyrus indicated the images floating above the floor in their midst.

"So maybe the people of this Atlantis were displaced, but why would they all travel to different locations on Earth if they had stayed hidden for so long?" Milliken added, the look of understanding quickly leaving his face.

"What do you mean?" Torvald asked.

"I mean, we left Earth because we were somewhat displaced, but we didn't spend our energies sending emissaries and colonists to the four corners of the universe. We concentrated our efforts on the Set system, despite the existence of potentially inhabitable planets in other systems. If there was some sort of cataclysm, it would make these connections less likely, not more."

"We are missing one vital point, though," Tanner posited. "The city itself. Its design is a confluence of two ideas in that the Temple is at the center of the Hunab Ku. The buildings are also vaguely Babylonian. Sensibilities of Mesopotamia and the Quiché Mesoamerica are also undoubtedly interlinked there."

"What about an Egyptian link?" Cyrus asked.

"Perhaps one exists there as well," Darius added, "The lions guarding the temple. It has been oft-proposed that, given the dimensions and the perspective of the Sphinx, it originally had the head of a lion, and was recarved with a man's face at a much later date."

"Could we call that defacing?" Milliken looked for a laugh, but the weight of anxiety would not budge. He shrugged his shoulders at the awkward silence. "How do we account for Torvald's manes though?"

"Well, what if maned lions came along with the knowledge of how to build these buildings? What if the architects of these constructs on Asha also dabbled in genetics?" There was more grumbling, but Davidson continued, "Is it so hard to believe? How else would two disparate species 'have offspring?' If these alien gods truly did mate with the daughters of men, would it have to have happened in the traditional sense? Besides, isn't that what we do in pod centers? We toil away, separating the chaff from the genetic wheat. Each of these cultures, Mesopotamia, Egypt, and South America, were they not plagued with either blood cults, blood sacrifices of some sort, or obsession with the dead? And all this morbidity in the service of these so-called gods."

The grumbles became more affirming, and then Uzziah, who had been quiet and contemplative throughout most of the proceedings, finally spoke, "There's something else," he paused for a moment, looking not unlike the Darius hologram when it searched for information.

"The Temple is at the center of the giant spiral. Your eye is drawn to it by the design, even on the ground level. The artificial sun is directly above it. The Temple must hold some sort of significance that we are missing—at least some significance other than the obvious."

Then Uzziah answered with Tanner in unison, "The *Aish Tamid.*"

"The what?" Milliken asked, more puzzled than ever.

This time Uzziah answered alone, "It is the eternal flame that burned in the tabernacle in the Temple. In idea, it represents a living Torah—a flame that a person who has experienced Torah on a deeper level carries with him."

"Which can lead us back to Davidson's lions," Tanner added before Uzziah even finished. "In Egypt, lions were also connected with Ra or Horus because they guarded the rising and the setting of the sun as it passed from the underworld, through the world of the living, and then back again. This idea could also represent a guarding of a kind of esoteric knowledge."

"I don't get it though. We have Oannes, Viracocha, Poseidon, Ea, Osiris—all bearers of knowledge to different civilizations. But the Temple is distinctly Judaic, correct? It's not just Near Eastern. Where is the Judaic civilizer?" Everyone looked to Tanner then to Uzziah, and then back to Tanner again. Tanner began to look extremely uncomfortable until Darius spoke, "Azazel."

Tanner did not look as if the name surprised him, but his expression was of unmistakable discomfort. Darius continued, seemingly insensitive to Tanner's discomfort, "Azazel was the leader of the fallen angels after the original leader, Samyaza, gave in. Azazel had experienced a displacement of sorts. He had chosen to cohabitate with humans and to take wives of the daughters of men, but most importantly, he brought esoteric knowledge to the humans against the will of the godhead. He taught men to wage war, possibly against the gods themselves, and he and his progeny were punished."

"Let me guess," Milliken asked, the discomfort leaving his face, "with a flood."

"Yes, the godhead sought to eliminate the damage that Azazel had caused and had Azazel imprisoned by his nemesis in a place called Dudael," Darius added.

Cyrus could not hold his curiosity any longer and addressed Tanner directly, "What is so disconcerting about this information?"

Tanner paused for a moment, exhaled, and then spoke, "If Azazel is the equivalent to those others we mentioned, it would imply Noah was somehow the offspring of the fallen as Lamech had feared—that Noah himself, in some way, either literally or figuratively, was Nephilim," Tanner shuffled in his chair. "Which makes the Old Testament godhead, as Darius so tactfully put it, look more like the Demiurge of the Gnostics. Since knowledge seems to be at the root of the problem, both here on Asha and in the Old Testament..."

Cyrus crossed the room and rested his hand on Tanner's shoulder. Cyrus did not want him to continue any more than Tanner himself wanted to. Tanner had come to this planet just like the rest of them. Just like the rest of them, he was looking for answers. But unlike the rest of them, all the answers presented to him had tested what he understood of the world in a merciless kiln.

Milliken tried to work through his own confusion, seemingly oblivious to Tanner's internal struggle. "So if this Azazel guy is at odds with the godhead, that would make him Satan, no?"

"*HaSatan* is merely a title that means 'the Adversary,'" Darius corrected, "It implies conflict but not evil. The title is sometimes used to refer to the being Samael, who serves as the Judaic Angel of Death. Samael is also sometimes referred to as this Demiurge that Tanner mentioned, or as the head of the Sitra Achra, one of the Kabbalistic representations of chaos. Samael is sometimes represented as both good and evil—more a necessity to the universe than a representation of wickedness."

"So let's assume this Azazel did set all this up and was banished and had everything he helped build destroyed. What does that mean for us?" Davidson was intrigued.

"It would mean that the loveliest trick of the Devil was not to persuade us that he didn't exist, but rather to trick his opponent into siring and nurturing his children," even Cyrus was unamused at the revelation as he said it.

"Or at the least, instilling in us the knowledge that this Demiurge wanted to hide," Davidson's qualification settled Cyrus but did nothing for Tanner.

"Knowledge of what though?" Torvald asked, as oblivious to Tanner's struggling as Milliken.

"The Garden of Eden story says it is knowledge of Good and Evil, and of humanity's own 'nakedness,' or, more accurately, ignorance, that was hidden from us. Enoch says Azazel taught men to wage war and women to wear make-up—implications of base ideas, but also of self-respect. The Mayans say this being taught men to be less beastlike. The Greeks say men learned acculturation, while the Sumerians say Ea taught the secret of eternal life. They all imply that whatever knowledge was taught by these 'civilizers' made humanity closer to the gods than the gods were ultimately comfortable with." Darius's treatise settled the room. The implications the hologram used must have been from criticisms and annotations, but they were profound nonetheless.

Torvald was the first to speak, "This all makes sense in reference to myths and primitive peoples, advanced or not. But what could they stand to show us or the Ashans in this day and age?"

"Whatever the Ark, or the Arks in this case, are designed to facilitate mechanically," Tanner said, surprising Cyrus.

Cyrus nodded to Tanner, who returned the nod, and began to pace. "So what knowledge pertaining to modern humanity would Mundi see the relevance of as soon as the existence of the city was communicated to him?"

"Maybe the city was just an afterthought. The war could have been started because Mundi discovered the *gold deposits* in the scar. Think about it. The man who shows up to a troubled planet with a ship full of gold would surely be seen as a god among men."

"But how could he move enough gold to impress an entire planet, however destitute? The density alone would be too much," Milliken retorted.

Darius looked as if he were contemplating something and everyone stopped, to see what he had to say. "What about the five ships beneath the pyramid? Echelon records show the resources to build those ships were collected over the last hundred years."

Cyrus should have been used to the weight that seemed to pile onto his shoulders whenever he spent extended time in this room, but it seemed every nuance in the conversation made the air heavier. "But what's the point in setting up something of this scale if you don't live to see the end of it? Did Mundi even have any descendants?" Cyrus was perplexed, it all made sense, and yet it didn't.

"As far as I can tell, there's no conclusive proof Rex Mundi ever existed," Darius said.

"So why would..." a thought stymied Cyrus in mid-sentence. "Wait, you said they only made one of those star skimmers?"

"It was made and then put to dry-dock, but after that, there is no record of it. Although..." Darius looked as if he were trying to remember something again, "There are several records of inquiries from Mundi, and then suddenly, nothing."

And then it all came together like the doors of a mausoleum.

Cyrus looked to Tanner, but it seemed like Tanner was looking beyond him. "What was the Ark used for again, traditionally?"

"It was placed in the tabernacle, where the priests would communicate with God. They also placed the blood of the sacrificial lamb on the mercy seat, the place between the cherub wings."

Tanner seemed to be in contemplation himself, the lids of his eyes straining under the pressure the last few months had placed on his faith, and he seemed not to notice as Cyrus muttered "sacrificial lamb" to himself and then wandered through the door toward the storage room.

When they rounded the corner, Milliken and Tanner gasped as they saw Cyrus drag the blade of a knife across the palm of his hand. He looked over his shoulder, acknowledging them with a smirk that seemed as disturbed as it was confident—as if deep down he was hoping he was wrong.

"Maybe they dabbled in genetics," he said aloud to himself. He then turned, squeezed his fist over the mercy seat of the Ark, and then he froze in place as if he was a holo-image on the fritz. Tanner moved to touch him, but even as he approached, it felt like the static in the room held him back, and he found his feet refusing to move him within arm's reach.

No one said a word, and Tanner was not even sure he could speak if he tried. He tried to take a step back, but he realized he could not retreat either. He was stuck there, his arm outstretched toward Cyrus, unable to move.

And then he realized he could not feel the usual twinge from holding his muscles in place. He could not feel the floor against his feet, the dense air of the barracks against his skin, or the beating of his own heart. Dust particles no longer moved in the air, light no longer played across the gilded edges of the Ark. It was as if the physical world was frozen in time but somehow his mind still functioned.

He tried to blink and found he could not, but it didn't matter, the sensation of dryness in his eyes, of irritation from holding his arm out for too long, of anything for that matter, was non-existent. And when he tried to think of how much time had passed, he realized time no longer had meaning. It just didn't matter. Nothing mattered. Not time. Not the strange revelations that had been laid before him today. Nothing.

But something did matter. There was a connection around him that he had not noticed before, perhaps because there was only one time in his life he could remember feeling it—a time he had forgotten until this frozen moment reminded him. It was the indelible consciousness of every life around him. Of Milliken, Uzziah, Cyrus, even the Apostates outside the complex. Then, he realized it stretched farther than that. It stretched out to Eurydice, Druvidia, the J.L., even back to Earth. The sum total of all human consciousness somehow resided with him in this timeless brainspace. It should have seemed foreign to him, should have been a shock, but instead it was familiar and comforting because he understood that life, all life, began this way, or at least it should. He found his memory of it very clear. It was the same connection he had shared once before, although more acutely, with his mother, before he was born. It was there, in that timeless sanctuary, his soul, as it slowly melded to a growing body, had felt this connection with the rest of humanity. He wondered if those unfortunate enough to have been born in pods were afforded the same comfort of knowing, at least for a moment, that they were a part of something greater. And if the dread that whelmed his soul had any effect on his body in that eternal moment, he would have cried for every pod-born person ever for they were the true apostates.

As far as Cyrus could tell, his eyes were still open, but the world around him shrank into a pinpoint in the distance. Cyrus felt completely disconnected from his body. It was like dreaming, but at the same time drastically different. In a dream, you still had a concept of self, but here, self was the only thing that seemed *not* to exist. Instead, he was left with everything and everyone else. Then, as suddenly as it shrank, it expanded, and he was standing in a room that he could not see, but he somehow intuitively knew formed two pyramids that connected at the base and were inscribed in a sphere. He could not see the sides, the roof, or the floor because, in this place, sight did not exist. Eyes had no sway in this world.

He stood in the center of the concurrence of the axes of the pyramids, and at the vertex directly in front of him, impossibly, Cyrus could feel, standing in the center of his own sphere, exactly who he had expected to find—his best friend, Alexander Kalem.

part three

Some day, the piecing together
of dissociated knowledge will open up
such terrifying vistas of reality, that we
shall either go mad from the revelation
or flee from the deadly light into the
peace and safety of a new dark age.

H.P. LOVECRAFT

twenty-eight

—So what's this I hear about you getting into fights at the tram stop?

—It's bunkus, Dada. Don't worry about it.

—Why shouldn't I be worried about it? You're starting to get a reputation as some kind of hooligan, and it don't exactly rest on the axis with me.

—I know Dada. That was the whole point.

—I'm afraid I don't follow, and you need to explain it to me so I get it, or there's gonna be arrears to pay.

—It's all houndwash, Dada. A rumor to throw everyone off the ave.

—What ave?

—I don't wanna say.

—You don't have a choice, cuz I'm two steps off taking your HoloStation Prime and selling it to a more honest kid.

—I did it to help someone, and they asked me not to tell.

—What is it that's so important or bad you can't tell me?

—I promised I would not tell.

—Did you promise you would lose your HoloStation?

—You can take it if you want, but I think that's foul that you would sell it because you don't believe me.

—Dari, you haven't been the most copasetic student the last few months. You need to be straight-forward with me so I can believe you.

—Danny Silberman, the new guy from New York. His nose started bleeding at the tram stop and he ran off. I went to look for him and found him in the bushes by the recharge station. His nose was bleeding, and he tried to clean it up, but some of it got on his collar and he couldn't really hide it. I tried to help him, but at first he was like, 'Get away from me,' but after I wouldn't leave, he told me he had this disease that made his nose bleed and made him hard-of-hearing in his right ear, and sometimes it made him pee funny, and he said that was one of the things that convinced his family to leave where he used to live, and he was scared the jokes and stuff would follow him here if people found out.

—So how does this involve you?

—I told him I would help him. I told him to go running back to the tram stop

357

and cry and not talk to anybody. And then later, I came 'round and sat on the opposite side of the bench from him and looked bent. Then, before we got on the tram, I snuck and told him to complain about me being a repo-giver but refuse to tell people exactly what happened. I normally sit next to him on the tram and in most of our classes, but we sat on opposite sides of the tram and room and didn't talk to each other all day.

—All this so people would assume you fought?

—And evidently it worked. Nobody pulled me into the office, but I bet they comm-satted you and asked you to talk to me, didn't they?

—Yeah.

—Because you adults always take what you see and put it together to be what you want to believe. All someone has to do is set it out on a plate and ring a bell and you run to it like beta-hounds.

—You watch yourself, Dari.

—Well, it's true. It's the only reason why you're standing over me sideways right now threatening to take something away from me to get me to say what you expect me to.

—Dari, I'm sorry if I didn't believe you, but you haven't made it easy the last few months.

—Fair enough, but, I may be a lot of things, but I've never been a liar, and I've never been a stoolie, and if I have to catch a couple degrees of heat to help a friend, well then so be it.

—So this was all an elaborate rumor?

—I didn't really even expect it to work, but the beta...I mean Disciplinarian scarfed it up like sweetbars. It's amazing how willing people who call themselves authorities are to believe their own back-wash. Especially when all they had to do was open the nurse's file on the datadeck.

—I guess you do have a point. Sometimes when something stinks, it is a lot easier to jump to conclusions than it is to lift our own arms and smell ourselves.

—Well, maybe you guys should smell yourselves more often, cuz sometimes things stink more than you guys know.

—You do have a point, Dari.

—Well, thank you for saying so.

—Dari.

—Yeah Dada?

—I love you. And I'm sorry.

• • • • •

"**Surprised to see me?**" Alexander asked, looking exactly the way he had looked when Cyrus last saw him. It was not him, at least not his body, nor was it a projection. Cyrus could not see him so much as he could feel him, and his mind filled in the blanks.

"No," Cyrus had very little to say. The mélange that welled inside him forbade speech.

"You appear cross, *doostam*. Why such malice when greeting an old friend?" Evidently, this conduit, limited in its ability to convey basic senses, transmitted what other forms of communication could not.

Cyrus, to anyone else, would have delivered a snide retort, but here, his very soul bare before his best friend and now worst enemy, could only manage naked thoughts. "You were behind this from the beginning. You used my son. You turned him into a monster. Why?"

"What cuts most deeply is that you can't bring yourself to even see the answer," Kalem's words were melodramatic, but the Ark sent his emotions through as clearly as his speech. Kalem was not hurt, he was smug, content, and most disturbing of all, jubilant. "I did not need to supply your son with the capital that matured him into the Knight of Swords. You supplied all the raw materials for that. All it took was a push."

"But you lied to him. You lied to me. You said you would take care of him." Cyrus was not sure if it was the detachment from the physical world or his own resilience that kept him from crying, but he was sure, in this place, Kalem could tell he wanted to—but it did not matter.

"Once again, the pot gives his grand treatise on the blackness of the kettle. In your catalog of lies you have missed the greatest lie of all," his words came across as calm, but Cyrus could feel the laughter behind them. And intertwined with the laughter, there was something else. Something he had felt once before but had long forgotten. It was similar to what he felt for Darius, for Tanner, for Villichez, but there was a distinctly different flavor to it. It came from Alexander, and even though it was muddied with a scathing twinge of hatred, it was not directed toward Cyrus.

"Feralynn," was all Cyrus needed to say, the rest moved between them on its own.

"You took for granted what you had. What, even after you squandered it, even after you left it behind for selfish wanderlust, I could never have." And now the space between them was filled with anger, and it moved both ways.

"All this because you were spurned by my wife after I left?"

"Still, at the very precipice above it all, you fail to see. I didn't do this because of her. I did it because of *you*. Ruining her life was just one in a grand litany of sins."

"Numerous as they may have been, they were my sins. Mine! Not Darius's."

"Well, you know what they say about the father's sins."

And then a stream of laughter, as bitter as it was unexpected, streamed back at Kalem from Cyrus. "And now *you* are the blind man who heralds the kettle's retort."

"You twist and wheedle as you always have, but you cannot turn this conversation." Behind his words was a hint of something, almost like a scent, and one Cyrus knew all too well—fear.

The laughter from Cyrus morphed into a fire, caustic despite its lack of form, stoked by the ambient shroud of betrayal that hang over both of them. "The conversation turned when you found the vein of gold inside the Scar. You always loved to play the martyr. That's probably why Feralynn never took to you—because you could never bring your troubles directly to the man. But the martyr's robes, this day, are stained with the blood of his victims. Because a true martyr never sees the fruit of his labor; he doesn't hide away so he can collect his spoils. And therein lies the sordid truth. You didn't sacrifice my son for something as noble as the honor of my wife. You just used her as an excuse so your liver could drum up the bile and rancor you needed to pull this off. And at the end of the day, what does it amount to? Just more digits on a cred stick. You have always wanted to be Rex Mundi, the King of the World, but you were always too much of a coward. In the scenario where you play the hero, I pay for my sins, but you die in contentment five hundred years ago—and yet, here you stand, alive and spineless as ever, floating around some dark, distant star, waiting to reap the bloody crop you've sown."

"Well..."

"Enough!" the force of the word dispelled every emotion that moved between them. "I've heard all I can stomach. Perhaps I should have paid more affection to my wife. Perhaps I should have been less selfish. I could have been a better husband and father, but if any absolution for me exists, it will be in the utter destruction of your miserable plot."

"The seeds I have sown were in the wake of your plow," the words were shakier now, the laughter and hubris lingering in a past that could not exist here.

"Perhaps, but when you return to Earth, you will find your field fallow, and me standing there with salt in my hand. Your pathetic plan you'll find trampled beneath my boot, and finally, Darius, my son, shall have his earth and water. Make haste, little man. Do not keep me waiting."

And then they were no longer connected. The sphere folded into itself, and Cyrus, moored by some ethereal cable that had escaped his awareness previously, was snatched back into his lonely body, where, before his warped senses could reorient themselves, he collapsed to the floor.

When Cyrus regained his senses, Tanner was standing over him. "What happened?"

"My best friend. My brother. Kalem. He did this to me." Cyrus's pupils adjusted to reveal a look of bewilderment from Tanner and Milliken. "The Ark. It's a communication device, but it seems to link the users' consciousness without any kind of redshift or time lag. They must have reverse-engineered it to make the Whisper Node." Cyrus held his head as he stood. It didn't hurt, but it didn't feel stable either. Whatever using the Ark did to him had not quite subsided.

"Some strange stuff happened on this end too," Tanner added, checking Cyrus's eyes to make sure he was okay.

"So Mundi wasn't on the other side of that thing?" Milliken asked eagerly.

"Kalem *is* Mundi—always has been. This was all his doing. But it gave me an idea. We take the Apostates back to Earth. They can have their reprieve, and I can have my druthers."

"How will we get them there?" Tanner's perplexed look intensified.

"The ships under the pyramid." Cyrus stood now, arching his shoulders to send hollow pops down his re-aligning spine.

"But how will that stop Mundi?"

"Mundi plans to emerge as the savior to a starving Earth, bearing gifts of gold. But it is hard for people to starve if they don't need to eat."

The bewilderment in Tanner's face subsided like the shadow of a waning eclipse, "The Eos."

"What use is gold to a man that has learned to live off the light?"

"But how?" Milliken asked.

"How do we get the Apostates and the ships together?" Tanner added.

"That, given our current situation, may be easier than it seems."

Torvald saw Cyrus sitting by himself in a dark corner of the compound. Normally, when he wandered off by himself to contemplate, it seemed best to leave him to his thoughts. But today it seemed as if something was amiss, as if whatever kept him going was winding down. Torvald believed that when someone had something pressing on their mind, that once they could no longer take the pressure, they would speak up, but this seemed different. Belligerence kept Cyrus going as much as pomp kept Paeryl—they could be construed as negative qualities, but the fact that they used them to keep the wavering worlds around them on the level made them qualities to be admired, despite not being healthy prescriptions for everyone. Perhaps that was why, despite drastically disparate approaches, they had so much respect for each other. It was most assuredly why Torvald had respect for both of them, even though he may not have expressed it clearly. But here, Cyrus seemed as if whatever fire had burned within him was dwindling.

"Are you okay?" Torvald asked, kneeling next to Cyrus in the shadow of the promontories.

"I'll be fine," Cyrus said unenthusiastically, continuing to stare at the side of the crater.

Torvald stared at the orange aura over the summit. "You know that day Sifu ransacked us in the Paracelsus?"

Cyrus nodded wordlessly.

"You know what was going through my head when I ran into your room?"

Cyrus turned to face him.

"I didn't know what you would do. Hell, I didn't even know you that well. But something about you told me that if anyone could stop Sifu, it would be you."

Cyrus nodded again. He paused for a moment, and and then he let out a guttural sound. Torvald turned to look at him and words finally formed in Cyrus's mouth, "Can I ask you a question?"

"Anything."

"In Eurydice, when we escaped, you said you froze. What got you unfrozen?"

Torvald let out a light chuckle, "You know, I remembered something from my childhood, but the clearest thought that passed through my mind, and I'm almost ashamed of it now, was that you were in trouble, and if I didn't help you, I wasn't going to make it."

Tanner was walking over to them from the light corner of the crater carrying his Bible with a stern look on his face. "I came over here because my ears were burning." Then he smiled wider than he had smiled since the day cycles on the Paracelsus. "I heard the whole reason you had to land the Paracelsus at half-speed was because you went back for this."

Cyrus shrugged.

"I also heard you took on five Echelon soldiers single-handedly, and you set yourself on fire."

Cyrus shrugged again.

"Incredibly stupid," Tanner added with spite, eliciting a scowl from Cyrus, but arresting his attention, "but thank you." Tanner reached his hand forward to shake Cyrus's, but when Cyrus accepted his, Tanner yanked him from the ground and hugged him, patting him brusquely on the back. Cyrus felt something warm and wet against his ear, but when Tanner finally pulled away from him, there was no trace of it on his face.

"You seemed a little lost without it," Cyrus said matter-of-factly.

Tanner smiled again, wiping his face for certainty. "You know, losing it, may have kept me from hiding behind it. Maybe stepping from behind the duck blind will make it easier to find what I'm looking for. Especially since what I think I'm looking for is *me*."

Cyrus patted him on the back. Torvald looked to Tanner and spoke, "Don't you turn sacrilegious on me too. I think one heathen in our van is enough."

Even Cyrus smiled now.

Torvald did not smile, but inside he felt his mind at ease. This was still the same Cyrus. Whatever had stricken him in that storage room was fleeting—and that's what made Torvald run to that room that night cycle and what got him to fight through Ashan soldiers to get to Cyrus. The only thing that could lift Cyrus's spirits was the need of others to have theirs lifted. Cyrus, himself, may not have realized it, but it didn't matter.

Cyrus nodded, and, without turning, said more to himself than them, "How could Kalem do this?"

Tanner stopped for a moment and grabbed Cyrus by his shoulder until he raised his head. "You see this," he held up his Bible, "this helped me through a good part of my life. So did training. But coming from the Scar was the worst I've felt in a long time—maybe the worst ever. And you know what brought me out of it?"

Cyrus looked as if he might have known, but he did not feel like it was his place to say.

"You did. And it wasn't with sweetbars and houndshit. It was with the truth. The truth. All these years, I've been looking for it, never realizing it was always right in front of me. You were right. *We* are the truth—no more, no less. And as you say, the only reason it's so hard to find is because we always look for it where it isn't." Torvald could see some of the fire rekindling in Cyrus's eyes, but it wasn't enough for Tanner. "Remember, after the shock of it all, it's still *here*." He took his hand from Cyrus's shoulder and tapped him forcefully over his heart, "so how in Hell to come is what you believe *today* any different than what you believed yesterday in there?" He tapped him in his heart again with enough force to move his torso, his voice was louder now, and tiny droplets of spittle sprayed with each accent. "I understand betrayal hurts, but we ain't quite at the bottom of this barrel of monkey shit just yet, so hurt or not, we need you. And I'll be goddamned, you hear me, *goddamned* if I let you bow out before we do. So when you get yourself together, you come see us so we can finish this, complete."

The look on Tanner's face was unyielding, but Cyrus met his eyes. The strength of Cyrus's own gaze returned as his jaws clenched, raising his temples slightly with each contraction. They stood that way, face-to-face, for a moment that was as unfaltering as their opposing stares, and then Cyrus took a short step back, clasped his right fist in his open left hand, and bowed his head. Tanner met his bow, and then, as they met eyes once more, hugged him again and whispered something long-winded and sincere in his ear. Torvald wasn't quite sure he heard the words Tanner said to him, but he didn't need to because he felt them too. *You may have lost a son and a brother, but you have gained an entire family. Your legacy is in all of our hearts, and we, even through the Cimmerian fires of Hell itself, will never leave you.*

• • • • •

The EMD 423 was an amazing piece of technology. No matter how many times Septangle Dagobert Manitoba watched a target pass by unawares while he sat there in plain view, he had difficulty keeping his skin from crawling as he wondered if this one would see him. But they never did. Not even today when the Apostates stopped four times to scan the area both coming and going. He had orders to keep watch over the fallen Earth ship Paracelsus after the salvage crew's shift ended each DC, and each DC, glimmer mode activated even upon approach, Dagobert sat next to an outcropping of rocks, waiting for something he never expected to happen. But today he was surprised.

The skiff had shown up so close to shift-change that Dagobert initially thought it was a salvage crew returning to retrieve something. But there was no chatter on the radio frequencies he was monitoring, and the four Apostates who had emerged from the craft had spent under an hour inside the ruined husk of the outmoded spacecraft before emerging with several boxy pieces of equipment levied on conveyor lifts. They then moved quickly and efficiently back into their skiff. On the holomonitor zoom, Dagobert had easily identified them as Apostates from the sparseness of their clothing and the jaundiced tint to their skin.

They turned their skiff away from the sun and moved toward an outcrop of hills barely visible from this distance. Fortunately for Dagobert, he was able to move his craft in behind them, as with their backs to the sun, the twilight haze rendered his glimmer ship even more difficult to detect. Dagobert issued an alert call and began transmitting his telemetry to the Metatron network. He dropped back to ensure stealth, but he made sure to keep the skiff on his holo-imager.

They were most certainly leading him back to the base of operations that had eluded the Echelon for too long.

He would receive another vertex for this.

• • • • •

It took several evensongs to convince the elders to agree to Cyrus's plans. Several presentations on the ecologies and habitats of Earth were necessary to get them even to consider leaving their home, however inevitable an Echelon attack was. The prospect of losing the sun once each day cycle was abhorrent to them—more abhorrent than the potential of predators and diseases that would be alien to their bodies. After considering different regions, and after Cyrus and Milliken warned that the climates of the planet might be altered after the Advent, they decided on landing initially in the Fertile Crescent. While they deliberated, Torvald and Davidson prepared the soil processing lev from the Paracelsus to carry the Eos, while Toutopolus, his arm healing but still in a sling, worked with Darius to figure out optimum conditions for the Eos in the ship's hold. Jang used wiring schemes he phreaked from the Echelon network to plan how to most efficiently connect the suncasters to the ship they were planning to requisition from the pyramid, and he worked with Doree to facilitate the most effective way of transferring the Xerxes and Agamemnon units to the new ship that Tanner had already christened the *Sweet Chariot*. Tanner spent the time training Apostates and scientists alike with renewed vigor. His original liveliness had returned as if whatever demons that surfaced in Eurydice had been exorcised or, at the very least, relegated back to their respective cages in the depths of his consciousness. Cyrus himself felt something he had not felt before. For once, he was able to realize an end to all of this. He knew Kalem well enough to know that he would not leave this to this end. He anticipated Kalem would come back in some capacity or another, but he looked forward to it—any resolution to something that taxed the souls of so many would never quite be resolute until whoever was at the helm on either side met face-to-face; there would be no mate in this match unless it was king-on-king. And even though he knew that day would be a dark one, he looked forward to it, because though the light had been reintroduced to him in a way he could never have anticipated, darkness was now an inexorable part of his soul—and that darkness demanded its reprisal.

As the finishing touches were placed on each of the necessary requirements, and the elders finally conceded to all the terms, Paeryl pulled Cyrus aside one evensong. He was uncharacteristically quiet, but with the lower volume came a candor that was not indicative of him; he was a man who said what was on his mind as far as it pertained to the arid world around him, but he never spoke so much about himself—at least he hadn't before. "It seems for once there is no reason to ask." he said, patting Cyrus on the back.

"Yes, finally, I feel like we are winning." Cyrus returned the pat on the back.

"You have given me something I never imagined I could possess." Paeryl's eyes were fixed on Cyrus's, the creases at the corners of them and around his mouth shuddered, but the rest of his features seemed relaxed.

"What's that?" Cyrus met his gaze but was unsure of where the conversation was going.

"A solution. A goal. Something *to* win that might set all this to rest." He smiled, stilling the wrinkles of his face.

"Your people are lucky to have such a wise and compassionate leader."

"Yes. Yes, they are." Paeryl's lack of modesty seemed odd until he gripped Cyrus's shoulders with both hands and held them there, a lone tear streaking from his eye, and Cyrus realized he was not talking about himself.

"But I...I can't..."

Paeryl just nodded, strengthening the embrace. "You already have." He shook Cyrus's shoulders firmly and then turned to walk away. But before he walked into the light cast by the setting sun, he stopped and faced Cyrus again. "Our people need only one leader, and that leader is plenty strong. I have decided to stay here, to rescue any wayward souls that may wander into the wastes of Asha from the darkness of the Miasma. Just as you have done for us."

"But..."

Paeryl just raised his hand to stop Cyrus's rebuttal, and then he turned to take his betrothed's hand and stand in the fleeting rays of the orange sun.

twenty-nine

—Dada, why do I have to learn Farsi?

—Because it's part of your heritage. You are half Persian.

—I don't understand. The whole Uni uses Commonspeak. Why do I have to spend Saturdays in class learning something for no reason?

—Well, it's not for no reason. Your mother speaks Farsi. Uncle Xander speaks Farsi. Your grandmother and grandfather spoke it.

—Well, you and mommy only speak Commonspeak to each other.

—True, but I can understand basic things she says in Farsi. I learned in college as a courtesy to her and your grandparents. I'm just not comfortable speaking it.

—Do you ever feel jealous when Uncle Xander speaks Farsi to mommy?

—Not really. I trust your uncle. He's a little too, what's the word, bombastic to hide what he's saying about someone.

—You think when you leave, he and mommy might get together?

—Why would you think something like that Dari?

—Well, mom's really pretty, and sometimes she and Uncle Xander seem to get along better than you and her. Just sayin'. It's not that I want it, but why wouldn't any man want to be with mommy? And if you're not here, who's to stop them?

—Well, your mother will either play Penelope or she won't. But if she doesn't, I expect you to play Telemachus.

—I don't know what that means Dada. Who are Penelope and Telemachus?

—Penelope and Telemachus are characters in Homer's Odyssey. There's a holofilm version you and I should watch some day. But what it means is, if your mother wants someone else, Uncle Xander or otherwise, no amount of Farsi could stop it.

—Why would she want someone other than you, Dada?

—One of these days, Dari, you'll understand that your Dada is human, and he makes mistakes too.

—So if you make mistakes too, why are you so hard on me?

—Because I don't want you to make the same mistakes I did.

—Oh, that makes sense, but it's still hard to see the mistakes you make.

—Sometimes it's hard for me too until it's too late. But I can give you some

advice Dari. Try not to take anything good you have for granted because there may come a day when taking it for granted makes it not good any more.
—I'm not really sure what that means.
—Well Dari, I sincerely hope you never have to learn.

• • • • •

Cyrus walked over to Jang, who was holding hands with Doree and basking in the sun. Jang brushed his hair to the side and she giggled as Cyrus approached. Jang seem to notice the intent in Cyrus's face, and he himself began to look more serious before Cyrus even opened his mouth, "How soon could you, Doree, and Fenrir get the gravity drives off all but two levs in Paeryl's fleet?"

Jang seemed stymied by the question and only muttered, but Doree answered, "Perhaps twenty *hors* if we work nonstop, and if we have help."

Jang simply nodded.

"And how long would it take to bury them out there," Cyrus pointed to the path that led into the compound, "and then connect power lines to them and cover them in concrete?"

They were both stymied by the question and only managed to look at each other and murmur, which, as far as Cyrus was concerned, was an excellent sign. Jang was one of the sharpest human beings Cyrus ever knew, and Doree seemed to be his match. If the two of them had no idea what he was talking about from those two questions, then the likelihood that the Echelon would figure it out before it was too late was virtually nil—and those were odds Cyrus was willing to gamble on.

• • • • •

As Torus Denali stood at the helm of the command barge, he relished the warm anticipation that spread through his body. The thirty fighters that cruised before him across the Ashan plain, skimming the ground to avoid early visual detection, filled his mind with comfort knowing that justice, today, would be served—justice for this pride at the containment facility, justice for the men who died at the pyramid hangar, and justice for the men still stranded in deep orbit on the detached J.L. Orbital. For this DC would be the final DC of reckoning for those loathsome Apostates, and the prospect of watching their too long eluded demise first-hand almost broke his composure.

And it had been so simple. They had just been looking for the wrong things. In all their searches they had looked for constructs and shelters—some sign of civilized life in the barren wastes. But in a land where the meaning of predation had been all but lost, and the rains only occurred underground, there was no need for shelter, especially not for photosynthesizing savages who lived only to gorgejack and pillage.

And now, the Apostates' greatest heist would prove their downfall and Denali's glory. As his battalion cruised no more than fifteen meters from the ground, less than four kilometers away from the constant signal the Ark transmitted, Denali prepared to give the command for the fleet to rise to detection altitude to triumphantly blot out the Apostates' beloved sun as they approached.

But something wasn't right.

Denali squinted and leaned forward to get a better glimpse, and he saw the fighter on point flip in an almost comical motion and then careen into two fighters behind it. The three fighters caromed into a large fighter as the laws of reality seemed to distort. And then Denali saw the dust and rocks, along with debris from the spinning wreck before him, falling *upward* just before another fighter exploded, catching those around it in a chain reaction as the outermost fighters spread to either side to evade the chaos. And then he saw the rocks around his ship suddenly rise from the ground, and before he was tossed from his perch on the helm, he knew that, once and for all, he had been beaten. And as the world contorted around him, and the air inside the bridge began to scald, he realized, it was not as bad as he imagined.

thirty

—*Dada, do you think you could beat Uncle Xander in chess?*

—*Maybe. We've never played.*

—*Kinda strange that you guys are old friends and you never played.*

—*I don't think he wants to risk it.*

—*Why not?*

—*Because he doesn't like to lose.*

—*Last time I checked,* you *don't like to lose either Dada.*

—*Well, your Uncle is different. He has held a grudge against everyone who has ever beaten him.*

—*So you've never beaten him?*

—*Like I said, he avoids competition with me.*

—*He always beats me at chess.*

—*I always beat you at chess too.*

—*Yeah, but he's more like a machine. You're different every time.*

—*That's because I adjust to you. I take what I know about you, and I use it against you.*

—*Like what?*

—*Like the fact that you always try to think too far ahead, and because of that, sometimes, you miss things right in front of you.*

—*Yeah, I guess so.*

—*Your uncle is a lot like that too. If he did lose, it would be because I frustrated him into a loss.*

—*Yeah, you are kinda frustrating to play.*

—*Well, I'm glad to be of service.*

—*Ha. Well, one of these days, it would be interesting to see you go up against Uncle Xander, but you might have to let him win.*

—*You should know by now Dari, I never let anyone, and that means anyone, win. Anyone who ever beat me earned it.*

—*Well, maybe he would earn it.*

—*Maybe, Dari, but friendship is hard to come by, and pride comes and goes. I*

371

personally would never want to be in a situation where I let my pride ruin a friendship, and I would be hard-pressed to forgive a friend who did.

· · · · ·

They sat on the edge of the Miasma with Set barely visible on the horizon for four hours, absorbing the last rays of the orange sun they would ever feel before they began the march to their destination. The Ace of Wands and Taeryn had led the caravan there and had flown back to have their levs dismantled. Six was well outside the earwig network following a plan with no contingency; it would either succeed or fail epically, and Taewook of Cups did not want to risk any chance of his signal being phreaked. So Six led the bulk of the Apostate clan into the Miasma at a jog, dual-tipped spear in hand, toward the gilded tip of the pyramid that peaked just above the darkened horizon. He was not comfortable bringing the children and elders with him, but there was no other way. So he marched, at the point of his phalanx, and he hoped with every optimistic nerve in his body that this plan would go smoother than the last.

Several hours later, the Ace of Wands flew next to Taeryn, waiting for one of the Echelon levs to leave the pyramid so Jang could phreak the opening codes again. They were sure there would be countermeasures to keep the same attack from happening twice, but this time it wouldn't matter.

This time they were equipped with only three weapons each—one pulse missile, one mining laser taken from the craft they had stolen earlier, and one directional bomb that Fenrir, Aerik, and Davidson had made from the processed waste products brought back in the soil processing lev they were now using to carry the Eos. It made it hard to dodge the laser batteries now spread around the pyramid, but thanks to Taewook spoofing the imaging system, the Echelon could not use their computer to lock on to targets, and they had to fire the lasers manually. The controls of the crafts they now powered were familiar, but the ships themselves were sluggish and did not respond to commands as smoothly as the grav-levs of Asha. They had needed all the grav-drives to set the trap for the Echelon attack force, which according to the last earwig transmission, had worked beautifully. And as Taewook of Cups advised the Ace of Wands and Taeryn to get ready, the bay door to the pyramid opened just as they swooped down side-by-side, and they dropped their bombs when their HUDs gave them the mark. The Ace hoped that the rest of this plan would work as beautifully because all the lives that meant anything to him were at stake.

When Azariah, Paulice, and Cyrus had devised the plan, Cyrus said they would use a tactic the Echelon could not anticipate because they had no reason to have ever seen it. Six could not fathom what a small band of outcasts, resourceful as they may have been, could come up with that was outside of the Echelon's understanding. Cyrus's van assaulted the pyramid immediately after the fighter attack. Six had to wait for their mark to give his own command. The ten minutes Six had to wait after the bombing of the door seemed like an Eos-age. The anticipation filled Six with doubt as he could hear the calamity inside the hangar. But when Six blew his horn to signal the entire band of Apostates, some two hundred men, women, and children, to pour in through the smoke from the ruined blast door, he himself understood the power of a Fringe-rush.

• • • • •

Cyrus's van had entered the pyramid ahead of the Apostates and stormed the hangar to clear a path for Six and the others. They had cleared a thin swath through the guards in the hangar and had proceeded on to prep the ship they were going to apportion. Six marveled at the sheer size of the hangar but was floored as they reached the door that was blasted open on the opposite side, and he saw the larger holding area. Six could hear the whine of the lasers as the two fighters drew fire and cut down the foremost guards beyond the second bay door. By the time the Echelon soldiers inside had gathered themselves, the Apostate men, women, and children they had terrorized for more than half a century descended upon them in a swarm—it was a satisfying sight, but it was not pretty.

By the time the Apostates reached the furthest ship marked with Greek letters that spelled 'Grigori,' Cyrus and all the members of his van except Taewook had already powered it. The guards inside the hangar seemed to have been lower vertices, and by the time their commanders fully processed that their Torus had fallen to a trap and they were being counter-attacked, the Apostates had already filed into the gargantuan cargo hold of the apportioned ship, and it was passing through the smoldering bay doorway directly in front of it.

Six waited behind the others inside the massive ship as it pulled away from the pyramid. And as they skirted the ground, moving out of the hangar as Taeryn and the Ace of Wands met their ship outside the range of the Echelon lasers, Six wondered if he really would miss this miserable ball of errant rock and was surprised by his answer.

The Ashan desert became lighter as they sped further from the Miasma. Two Earth mag-levs retrieved from the Paracelsus cruised behind them, closing in slowly on the open cargo door so as not to alarm the Apostates being ushered into the barracks quarters. The soil processor carrying the Eos settled first, followed by the dozer carrying the supplies and suncasters that would keep them alive during the trip to Earth. Finally, Jang pulled in behind the other two levs in the dragon lorry they had stolen in their escape. Just as he settled the lev between the others, Uzziah asked where the Ace of Wands and Taeryn were over the earwig, but before Jang could answer, two Echelon fighters flew in behind them and positioned themselves to fire.

Fenrir and Chandra emerged from the crowd and fired their assault weapons, but the bullets only flashed against the astrapi shields on the Ashan fighters. The laser nodes on the front of them began to glow, and the Apostates still in the cargo area fell to the ground and covered their heads. There was the whine of a laser strike, and Jang had expected showers of sparks in the cargo bay, but the sparks only danced across the top of the closest fighter. There were two more bursts, a bright flash, and then the two fighters piloted by the Ace of Wands and Taeryn descended to take the place of the shattered Echelon fighters as their debris fell from the cargo bay. As Taeryn and the Ace of Wands pulled into the hold, Jang began to exit his own lev, but as he opened the door, there was a strange static in the air that raised the hairs on his arms, neck, and face. Instinctively, he checked the rear view on the holomonitor, and his worst fears were realized. A vaguely lev-shaped blur grew in the monitor as sparks flew from the base of the cargo bay. A green lev faded into view through the distorted image of sky and ground behind it.

A door opened in the burred nothing, and automatic weapon fire rang out, sending the Apostates to the floor again. Someone was hit, and Jang, without shutting his own lev off, realized Uzziah had not yet activated the grav-compensators on the main ship. Jang disengaged the compensation thrusters on the dragon lev, engaged the z-drive, and dove from the pilot's seat.

As Six held down the head of one child, he saw another child take a bullet in the arm, and he felt as if his own heart exploded in his chest. By the time he realized what he was doing, Six was already charging forward, spear in hand, dodging between levs. As he moved behind the dragon-shaped lev, it suddenly lifted up, and Taewook of Cups flew out of it. The lev moved away from both of them at an alarming speed. It collided with the now visible glimmer ship with a screeching crash, sending two soldiers to the floor and the others back into the ship as it slid toward the cargo bay door. The head of the dragon flew off as the lorry flipped and flew out of the bay to roll across the barren Ashan plain. The glimmer ship slid to the edge of the hold, screeching the whole way, but stopped just at the caution line before the door. The men stood to fire again, but Six was already between them, impaling one through his stomach and then bringing the other end of his spear up beneath the assault rifle of the other. Six twisted the spearhead inside the first and then snatched it out and around, flinging bits of entrails through the air as he brought it across the other's face. As they fell, Six turned to the door leading inside the glimmer ship, but there were already two assault rifles pointed at his chest.

Cyrus had to push two women and a child out of the way as he burst through the doorway to the cargo hold. As he ran across the large cargo bay, he could hear whimpering children and adults as they crawled and stumbled toward the main hold of the ship. A man's leg buckled, and he collapsed as Cyrus moved past him. The gunfire stopped, and Cyrus drew his sidearm as he ran toward Six, who was cutting through the two men who had initially opened fire. As Cyrus ran, he saw Six jump to his right, flipping his legs over his head in an aerial, and Cyrus instinctively dropped to the ground into a slide as rifle fire erupted again. The screaming and cries had died down now, and Cyrus assumed most of the Apostates had made it inside. Six rotated further away from the door as Cyrus slid to a halt. Cyrus balanced his right wrist over his left arm and fired two single shots at the doorway. One hit the side of the ship, but the second sent one of the gunmen back into the darkness of their craft. More gunfire came from the doorway as someone moved up to take the place of the fallen soldier. Cyrus rolled across the ground behind Taeryn's fighter as bullets hit the ground behind him and then tracked toward him, sparking across the edge of the lev. Then he heard a scream echo out of the glimmer ship through a pause in the gunfire and a clatter against the metal of the cargo bay floor. When he peeked around the edge of the fighter, Cyrus saw the tip of Six's spear stabbed through the wrist of the man who had replaced the fallen soldier. The spear pinned the man's arm to the inside of the glimmer ship door frame. Blood spurted from the wound, and the soldier next to him slipped, but he managed to reach his rifle around the edge and fire. Six's body buckled as his leg and wrists took hits. He grunted and stumbled. At that range, even if it did not manage to penetrate the Comptex, the rifle fire would have shattered bones and damaged vital tissues.

Six grabbed a panel to maintain his footing, but the panel fell away from the ship. He pressed the panel to the ground, halting his descent with it. As he propped himself up, he saw the fallen panel revealed a hose leading to the rear of the glimmer ship. A gunshot rang out from behind Cyrus, and then another, and the man who shot Six fell back into the ship.

Cyrus didn't look to see who was firing. He leaped from behind the lev and ran toward the glimmer ship, but another soldier stepped forward. Six tried to move, but his leg would not support his weight. Six grabbed the hose to steady himself, but as Cyrus ran toward him, he realized Six was not trying to gain leverage at all.

From what Cyrus heard, the glimmer ships needed an immense amount of power to create the illusion of invisibility. The domes of Eurydice and Druvidia that the glimmer ships mimicked used the light that they absorbed during their day cycles to power the interference waves they created during the night cycles. But these ships, tiny in comparison, would have needed to be able to play their tricks of light even in complete darkness, and that expenditure would have taxed their fusion cores to the limit—but they would still need to move, often while they were cloaked. So when Six snatched the hose away from the ship, steadied himself with the end of his spear, pulled his sidearm from his waist with his other hand, and jammed the barrel into the tube, Cyrus knew exactly what he was doing—and it horrified him.

Even through the explosion, Cyrus heard his own scream. And then the shockwave took him off his feet as a gust of hot wind washed over him. Six's body was consumed in flame, and he was thrown back into the cargo hold as the glimmer ship lifted off its side and rolled out of the bay. Cyrus hit the ground and slid as Six, spear still in-hand, flipped through the air as if he was in free fall again. Six hit the ground, his limbs flopping uncontrollably as his smoking body slid to a halt in a twisted, awkward position. An Echelon soldier hit the ground a few meters from Six with a Valois in his hand. The soldier rolled and then stopped face down. He lifted his head and the Squib, but before he could activate it, a volley of alternating gunshots knocked his body left, and then right, and finally back to the ground in a shower of blood.

Cyrus was already up and running to Six as the Squib clattered harmlessly on the metal floor. Six coughed and dark smoke issued from his mouth and nostrils as Cyrus approached. When Cyrus got to him, it seemed as if Six was smiling, but it was hard to tell because much of his upper lip had been burned away.

Six coughed again and tried to speak, but his voice was gravelly and came out with a wheeze. "Works better...with...a...Spellcaster," he breathed.

And the tears came before Cyrus could stop them. Cyrus sobbed and held Six tightly, his flesh smoldering under burned away holes in the Comptex. And then Six grabbed Cyrus's shoulder and pulled himself upward. One of Six's legs twisted awkwardly beneath him, but his grip, even in the last throes of death, was Herculean. Cyrus could smell bile and hydrocarbon fumes in Six's breath as he wheezed again, "A real...king...needs...an edged...weapon." He pulled his other arm around, but could only set the spear to rest on Cyrus's leg before his body finally released its last gram of strength.

Cyrus held Six in his arms, weeping as footsteps approached from behind. He could feel what must have been their hands on his shoulders, but it was hard to feel anything except the void that was left inside him. Everyone had been hinting at it since the escape. Tanner, the other scientists, the Apostates, Six, Paeryl, even Winberg—they all wanted something from Cyrus, and deep down, he knew it was always something he wanted them to want. It was what he had wanted from his wife, but she didn't know how to give it. It was what Kalem refused to give, and what had driven him to madness. And even though Cyrus had traveled across the ether for hundreds of light years in search of it, it all seemed worthless as the feeble heaves of Six's body, in desperate refusal to go easily, finally ceased in Cyrus's arms.

And then one of the hands on his shoulder pulled him firmly, and the earwig shattered his miserable solitude, "We ain't out of this hound pit yet."

thirty-one

—*Dada, after we all get to Asha, do you think we'll ever come back to Earth?*
—*It's hard to imagine what would have to happen to make us come back.*
—*Do you think we'll mess up Asha as bad as we messed up here?*
—*Well, that's part of the point of why we're going in the first place. Why do you think I make you erase your deck essays and start over sometimes?*
—*Because you're a homework despot?*
—*Despot? Who teaches you these words?*
—*You do, Dada.*
—*Fair enough. But no, it's not because I'm a megalomaniac. It's because sometimes the best way to correct your mistakes is to just wipe the slate clean and start all over again.*
—*So Asha is like a way for us to start over again?*
—*Yeah, kind of.*
—*Are you going to miss us Dada?*
—*Terribly.*
—*Uncle Xander says you're the best in the world at what you do, and that's why you have to go. I can understand that, but I feel kinda selfish.*
—*Why selfish Dari?*
—*Because I think you are the best at what you do to, but I don't want to share you with the rest of the world. Forgive my mouth, but I don't give a damn what the rest of the world wants from you—I want what I want.*
—*I understand that Dari, but whether I'm here, there, or in the world to come, you, and you alone, will always have that from me. No matter what I choose to, or not to, give to anyone else. Above all else, you remember that there is nothing in this world or the next that means more to me than you do. Not the Unified Department of Science, not my job, not even Uncle Xander or your mother. Maybe, I shouldn't be telling you that, but you are smart enough to see it already.*
—*If that's true, then why are you leaving me for them? For the damn Uni? For this Asha place?*
—*Believe me Dari, it's not for them. One day, probably not today, probably not tomorrow, but one day, you will understand that sometimes, even though*

he cares more about someone else than even himself, a man has to do what he knows he has to do, because if he's not right with himself, he can never be right with anyone else. And I would do anything, even leave you, if staying means I can't be what I said I would in your eyes.

—*So you're leaving for my own good? That's houndshit.*

—*Dari, I understand you're angry. I'm angry too. But we will see each other again, and by then, I'm sure, in your own way, you'll understand what I mean.*

—*What if I don't?*

—*Dari, you are too much like me not too. Maybe I need to leave so you can figure out how to not make my mistakes.*

—*Maybe you're running away.*

—*You could be right. But if I am, it's not you I'm running from, and there isn't a force in this world that can keep us apart for long.*

—*Well, if the world does take you away from me, one way or the other I will find a way to make it pay, and pay a lot.*

—*Look around you Dari. The world has already paid for its sins. The question is whether or not each of us has paid our due. Maybe my leaving is a form of penance.*

—*For what?*

—*Wrath, maybe. Maybe pride. Maybe for what I've done to your mother.*

—*So I have to pay for your sins too?*

—*Sometimes that's the deal, Dari. I don't like it, but regardless of what creed you subscribe to, sins have to be paid for, whether it be the father or the son. Honestly, if I leave, maybe our collected debt won't be so great.*

—*What if I mess up and increase the debt?*

—*Then I will go wherever I need to go to set the books straight.*

—*Even if it means coming back here?*

—*If it's within my power, yes.*

—*You know if it did happen, it wouldn't be on purpose right, Dada? I may not care about the rest of the world, but I would never hurt you because of something I wanted, even if you did it to me.*

—*You know, maybe you are a better man than me.*

—*I love you, Dada, more than anything.*

—*I love you too Dari—more than you know.*

· · · · ·

Tears filled Cyrus's eyes as he stepped into the bridge. This ship was designed, probably like most of the other ships in the Ashan fleet, to reach interstellar speed and fold through the continuum quickly and without a slingshot. It was a magnificent piece of technology, spawned by miraculous breakthroughs in astro- and quantum physics, and yet all of it would be useless if the five fighters, coursing toward them from the darkening sky, were allowed to have their way.

"Does this thing have enough power to engage the main drive in the atmosphere?" Cyrus asked, his nerves steeling even as the tears dried on his face. He noticed he was still carrying Six's bloodstained spear and that one of the heads had broken off in the explosion.

"It would create a vacuum because it's so hot," Jang reported, "but it would be possible."

"They have armed their missiles!" Uzziah bellowed.

"The grav-suppressors here are more efficient than ours, no?" Cyrus asked.

"They make the Paracelsus look like a cutty sark," Jang reported, managing to stay calmer than Uzziah.

"Then burn the main, full power, now!"

Paeryl stood with Cyndyl, Toobah, and the few Apostates that had stayed behind, and he watched the troubled ascent of the Chariot through scanning goggles. Once the cargo doors had finally closed, it pulled up toward the atmosphere only to confront another, larger formation of Echelon attack fighters. But then suddenly, there was a bright flash, and a bizarre still filled the air. There was a resounding clap, and the Chariot was gone. Two of the fighters that had rushed toward them spun erratically as Paeryl's eyes adjusted. The two ships plummeted for a moment before regaining their composure, but the other three fighters that had stood in the path of the Chariot were no longer visible. And then, from behind them, came a breeze the likes of which neither Asha nor Paeryl was accustomed to. It moved the hairs on the back of his neck and the graying hairs on his head, and it wavered his clothing as it rushed up toward the sky like children behind a procession. Paeryl smiled, knowing the breeze was not the only thing Cyrus had left behind, and the air was not the only thing he was taking with him. He reached over, took his betrothed's hand, and they walked further into wastes that had been most hospitable to them until now, to find a place where they could bask in the rays of their beloved Set, unmolested by the Archons that cowered from the light, to await anyone who could leave enough of themselves behind to embrace new life that only the light could provide.

The orange light of the Ashan sky gave way to a starscape in a flicker, and before the louvers came down fully, the stars on the edges of Cyrus's vision stretched out like the spindles of an aster. The stars before them seemed to bloat and swell, their light burning brighter and brighter until they felt as if they would bore holes into Cyrus's very consciousness. Even after the louver closed, and he retired from the bridge, the stars still seemed to be burning in front of him, their intensity overwhelming his mind's eye until it seemed his entire existence was full of light. Doree and Fenrir were already sending the others to facilitate the installation of the suncasters in the living quarters. They had already set up two in the infirmary, and Toutopolus, Torvald, and Davidson worked with the automated medical unit to administer aid to the men, women, and children that were wounded in the final battle. Loli made preparations in the crematorium to allow each of those who had passed in their final endeavor the chance to properly return what they had borrowed from the universe. Cyrus walked over, and before he could open his mouth to say what he did not know how to say, Loli embraced him.

"I'm sorry," was all he could manage before emotion built a swell in the corners of his eyes.

"Don't be sorry for him. This is what he wanted from the time he came here—to be given a chance to live up to his drawing and still win," even though they came out between sobs, her words were strangely soothing.

Cyrus pulled her closer, accepting the warmth of her body. "I meant for me and you." She did not reply. She only held him until she felt like she could finish what she needed to do, which was not long enough for either of them. Six had gotten what he wanted, had saved the entire sortie, but if there was victory in his death at all, at least for now, he was the only one with license to feel it.

But that was how it was, wasn't it? Cyrus had come to Asha and had sacrificed dearly because he could no longer live in a world that had forgotten how to. It did hurt, it chafed to the bone, but probably not that day, probably not tomorrow, but at some point, he would feel differently because that was what sacrifice meant. It meant not being afraid yesterday of what you might lose today because a man who is true to himself and those around him could not lose what was most important today so long as he set the world right for tomorrow. So at Six's cremation Cyrus would not weep or feel sorrow because these Apostates had lain meekly in the wastes of a planet long forgotten by its original inhabitants, and thanks to Six, and the sacrifices of all those on this ship, and all those who did not make it, the meek were now free to claim their inheritance.

www.ingramcontent.com/pod-product-compliance
Lightning Source LLC
Chambersburg PA
CBHW070203120726
47909CB00001B/232